F (RANCIS) SCOTT (KEY) Fr███████████████
Minnesota in 1896. He atte██ ⌂ P9-BJM-781 ee years
before joining the Army in 1█ ██, where he served as aide-
de-camp to General J. A. Ryan. In 1920 he married Zelda
Sayre; they had one daughter. He died in 1940. With the
publication in 1920 of his first novel, *This Side of Paradise*,
Fitzgerald gained immediately both popularity and critical
attention. Among his other well-known works are: *The
Great Gatsby* (1925), *All Sad Young Men* (short stories,
1926), and *Tender Is the Night* (1934). *The Crack-Up* was
originally published by New Directions in 1945.

THE CRACK-UP

F. SCOTT FITZGERALD

With other Uncollected Pieces, Note-Books and Unpublished Letters

Together with Letters to Fitzgerald from Gertrude Stein, Edith Wharton, T. S. Eliot, Thomas Wolfe and John Dos Passos

And Essays and Poems by Paul Rosenfeld, Glenway Wescott, John Dos Passos, John Peale Bishop and Edmund Wilson

Edited by 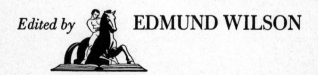 **EDMUND WILSON**

A New Directions Paperbook

Acknowledgments

Of the pieces by F. Scott Fitzgerald reprinted here, Echoes of the
Jazz Age *first appeared in* Scribner's Magazine; Ring *in* The New
Republic; Early Success *in* American Cavalcade; *and all the rest
in* Esquire. *The poem called* Lamp in the Window *and the in-
troductory verses by the editor were published first in* The New
Yorker. *The essay by Mr. Rosenfeld is reprinted from his book*
Men Seen. *The poem by Mr. Bishop, the essay by Mr. Wescott,
and part of the essay by Mr. Dos Passos originally appeared in*
The New Republic. *Acknowledgment is due* Cosmopolitan Magazine *for permission to include* My Lost City, *which was bought
but never published by it.*

*The editor is indebted to Mrs. Samuel Lanahan, Miss Peggy
Wood Weaver, Mr. Gerald Murphy and the late John Peale
Bishop for supplying him with letters from Fitzgerald; to Miss
Gertrude Stein, Mr. T. S. Eliot, Mr. John Dos Passos and the
literary executors of Thomas Wolfe and Edith Wharton for
permission to print letters written to Fitzgerald; and to Mr.
Harold Ober and Mr. Maxwell Perkins for help in collecting
Fitzgerald's articles.*

Library of Congress Catalog Card Number: 56-13361

(ISBN: 0-8112-0051-5)

First published as New Directions Paperbook No. 54 in 1956

Manufactured in the United States.
Published in Canada by McClelland & Stewart, Ltd.
New Directions Books are published for James Laughlin
by New Directions Publishing Corporation,
333 Sixth Avenue, New York 10014.

TWELFTH PRINTING

CONTENTS

DEDICATION

SCOTT, *your last fragments I arrange tonight,*
Assigning commas, setting accents right,
As once I punctuated, spelled and trimmed
When, passing in a Princeton spring—how dimmed
By this damned quarter-century and more!—
You left your Shadow Laurels *at my door.*
That was a drama webbed of dreams: the scene
A shimmering beglamored bluish-green
Soiled Paris wineshop; the sad hero one
Who loved applause but had his life alone;
Who fed on drink for weeks; forgot to eat,
"Worked feverishly," nourished on defeat
A lyric pride, and lent a lyric voice
To all the tongueless knavish tavern boys,
The liquor-ridden, the illiterate;
Got stabbed one midnight by a tavern-mate—
Betrayed, but self-betrayed by stealthy sins—
And faded to the sound of violins.

Tonight, in this dark long Atlantic gale,
I set in order such another tale,
While tons of wind that take the world for scope
Rock blackened waters where marauders grope
Our blue and bathed-in Massachusetts ocean;
The Cape shakes with the depth-bomb's dumbed concussion;
And guns can interrupt me in these rooms,
Where now I seek to breathe again the fumes
Of iridescent drinking-dens, retrace
The bright hotels, regain the eager pace
You tell of . . . . Scott, the bright hotels turn bleak;
The pace limps or stamps; the wines are weak;

The horns and violins come faint tonight.
A rim of darkness that devours light
Runs like the wall of flame that eats the land;
Blood, brain and labor pour into the sand;
And here, among our comrades of the trade,
Some buzz like husks, some stammer, much afraid,
Some mellowly give tongue and join the drag
Like hounds that bay the bounding anise-bag,
Some swallow darkness and sit hunched and dull,
The stunned beast's stupor in the monkey-skull.

I climbed, a quarter-century and more
Played out, the college steps, unlatched my door,
And, creature strange to college, found you there:
The pale skin, hard green eyes, and yellow hair—
Intently pinching out before a glass
Some pimples left by parties at the Nass;
Nor did you stop abashed, thus pocked and blotched,
But kept on peering while I stood and watched.
Tonight, from days more distant now, we find,
Than holidays in France were, left behind,
Than spring of graduation from the fall
That saw us grubbing below City Hall,
Through storm and darkness, Time's contrary stream,
There glides amazingly your mirror's beam—
To bring before me still, glazed mirror-wise,
The glitter of the hard and emerald eyes.
The cornea tough, the aqueous chamber cold,
Those glassy optic bulbs that globe and hold—
They pass their image on to what they mint,
To blue ice or light buds attune their tint,
And leave us, to turn over, iris-fired,
Not the great Ritz-sized diamond you desired
But jewels in a handful, lying loose:
Flawed amethysts; the moonstone's milky blues;
Chill blues of pale transparent tourmaline;
Opals of shifty yellow, chartreuse green,
Wherein a vein vermilion flees and flickers—
Tight phials of the spirit's light mixed liquors;

[8]

Some tinsel zircons, common turquoise; but
Two emeralds, green and lucid, one half-cut,
One cut consummately—both take their place
In Letters' most expensive Cartier case.

And there I have set them out for final show,
And come to the task's dead-end, and dread to know
Those eyes struck dark, dissolving in a wrecked
And darkened world, that gleam of intellect
That spilled into the spectrum of tune, taste,
Scent, color, living speech, is gone, is lost;
And we must dwell among the ragged stumps,
With owls digesting mice to dismal lumps
Of skin and gristle, monkeys scared by thunder,
Great buzzards that descend to grab the plunder.
And I, your scraps and sketches sifting yet,
Can never thus revive one sapphire jet,
However close I look, however late,
But only spell and point and punctuate.

EDMUND WILSON
February, 1942

Autobiographical Pieces

The following pieces have been selected from the articles written by F. Scott Fitzgerald between 1931 and 1937. They make an autobiographical sequence which vividly puts on record his state of mind and his point of view during the later years of his life. The dates given are the dates of their first publication, except in the case of My Lost City, *which here appears in print for the first time and which has been assigned to the month when it was received by Fitzgerald's literary agent, Mr. Harold Ober.*

ECHOES OF THE JAZZ AGE

November, 1931

IT is too soon to write about the Jazz Age with perspective, and without being suspected of premature arteriosclerosis. Many people still succumb to violent retching when they happen upon any of its characteristic words—words which have since yielded in vividness to the coinages of the underworld. It is as dead as were the Yellow Nineties in 1902. Yet the present writer already looks back to it with nostalgia. It bore him up, flattered him and gave him more money than he had dreamed of, simply for telling people that he felt as they did, that something had to be done with all the nervous energy stored up and unexpended in the War.

The ten-year period that, as if reluctant to die outmoded in its bed, leaped to a spectacular death in October, 1929, began about the time of the May Day riots in 1919. When the police rode down the demobilized country boys gaping at the orators in Madison Square, it was the sort of measure bound to alienate the more intelligent young men from the prevailing order. We didn't remember anything about the Bill of Rights until Mencken began plugging it, but we did know that such tyranny belonged in the jittery little countries of South Europe. If goose-livered business men had this effect on the government, then maybe we had gone to war for J. P. Morgan's loans after all. But, because we were tired of Great Causes, there was no more than a short outbreak of moral indignation, typified by Dos Passos' *Three Soldiers.*

Presently we began to have slices of the national cake and our idealism only flared up when the newspapers made melodrama out of such stories as Harding and the Ohio Gang or Sacco and Vanzetti. The events of 1919 left us cynical rather than revolutionary, in spite of the fact that now we are all rummaging around in our trunks wondering where in hell we left the liberty cap—"I know I *had* it"— and the moujik blouse. It was characteristic of the Jazz Age that it had no interest in politics at all.

It was an age of miracles, it was an age of art, it was an age of excess, and it was an age of satire. A Stuffed Shirt, squirming to blackmail in a lifelike way, sat upon the throne of the United States; a stylish young man hurried over to represent to us the throne of England. A world of girls yearned for the young Englishman; the old American groaned in his sleep as he waited to be poisoned by his wife, upon the advice of the female Rasputin who then made the ultimate decision in our national affairs. But such matters apart, we had things our way at last. With Americans ordering suits by the gross in London, the Bond Street tailors perforce agreed to moderate their cut to the American long-waisted figure and loose-fitting taste, something subtle passed to America, the style of man. During the Renaissance, Francis the First looked to Florence to trim his leg. Seventeenth-century England aped the court of France, and fifty years ago the German Guards officer bought his civilian clothes in London. Gentlemen's clothes—symbol of "the power that man must hold and that passes from race to race."

We were the most powerful nation. Who could tell us any longer what was fashionable and what was fun? Isolated during the European War, we had begun combing the unknown South and West for folkways and pastimes, and there were more ready to hand.

The first social revelation created a sensation out of all proportion to its novelty. As far back as 1915 the unchaperoned young people of the smaller cities had discovered the mobile privacy of that automobile given to young Bill at sixteen to make him "self-reliant." At first petting was a desperate adventure even under such favorable conditions, but presently confidences were exchanged and the old commandment broke down. As early as 1917 there were references to such sweet and casual dalliance in any number of the *Yale Record* or the *Princeton Tiger*.

But petting in its more audacious manifestations was confined to the wealthier classes—among other young people the old standard prevailed until after the War, and a kiss meant that a proposal was expected, as young officers in strange cities sometimes discovered to their dismay. Only in 1920 did the veil finally fall—the Jazz Age was in flower.

Scarcely had the staider citizens of the republic caught their breaths when the wildest of all generations, the generation which had been adolescent during the confusion of the War, brusquely shouldered my contemporaries out of the way and danced into the limelight. This was the generation whose girls dramatized themselves as flappers, the generation that corrupted its elders and eventually overreached itself less through lack of morals than through lack of taste. May one offer in exhibit the year 1922! That was the peak of the younger generation, for though the Jazz Age continued, it became less and less an affair of youth.

The sequel was like a children's party taken over by the elders, leaving the children puzzled and rather neglected and rather taken aback. By 1923 their elders, tired of watching the carnival with ill-concealed envy, had discovered that young liquor will take the place of young blood, and with a whoop the orgy began. The younger generation was starred no longer.

A whole race going hedonistic, deciding on pleasure. The precocious intimacies of the younger generation would have come about with or without prohibition—they were implicit in the attempt to adapt English customs to American conditions. (Our South, for example, is tropical and early maturing—it has never been part of the wisdom of France and Spain to let young girls go unchaperoned at sixteen and seventeen.) But the general decision to be amused that began with the cocktail parties of 1921 had more complicated origins.

The word jazz in its progress toward respectability has meant first sex, then dancing, then music. It is associated with a state of nervous stimulation, not unlike that of big cities behind the lines of a war. To many English the War still goes on because all the forces that menace them are still active—Wherefore eat, drink and be merry, for to-morrow we die. But different causes had now brought about a corresponding state in America—though there were entire classes (people over fifty, for example) who spent a whole decade denying its existence even when its puckish face peered into the family circle. Never did they dream that they had contributed to it. The honest citizens of every class, who believed in a strict public morality and were powerful enough to enforce the necessary legislation, did not know that they would necessarily be served by criminals and quacks, and do not really believe it to-day. Rich righteousness had always been able to buy honest and intelligent servants to free the slaves or the Cubans, so when this attempt collapsed our elders stood firm with all the stubbornness of people involved in a weak case, preserving their righteousness and losing their children. Silver-haired women and men with fine old faces, people who never did a consciously dishonest thing in their lives, still assure each other in the apartment hotels of New York and Boston and Washington that "there's a whole generation growing up that will never know the taste of liquor." Meanwhile their granddaughters pass the well-thumbed copy of *Lady Chatterley's Lover* around the boarding-school and, if they get about at all, know the taste of gin or corn at sixteen. But the generation who reached maturity between 1875 and 1895 continue to believe what they want to believe.

Even the intervening generations were incredulous. In 1920 Heywood Broun announced that all this hubbub was nonsense, that young men didn't kiss but told anyhow. But very shortly people over twenty-five came in for an intensive education. Let me trace some of the revelations vouchsafed them by reference to a dozen works written for various types of mentality during the decade. We begin with the suggestion that Don Juan leads an interesting life (*Jurgen,*

1919); then we learn that there's a lot of sex around if we only knew it (*Winesburg, Ohio,* 1920) that adolescents lead very amorous lives (*This Side of Paradise,* 1920), that there are a lot of neglected Anglo-Saxon words (*Ulysses,* 1921), that older people don't always resist sudden temptations (*Cytherea,* 1922), that girls are sometimes seduced without being ruined (*Flaming Youth,* 1922), that even rape often turns out well (*The Sheik,* 1922), that glamorous English ladies are often promiscuous (*The Green Hat,* 1924), that in fact they devote most of their time to it (*The Vortex,* 1926), that it's a damn good thing too (*Lady Chatterley's Lover,* 1928), and finally that there are abnormal variations (*The Well of Loneliness,* 1928, and *Sodom and Gomorrah,* 1929).

In my opinion the erotic element in these works, even *The Sheik* written for children in the key of *Peter Rabbit,* did not one particle of harm. Everything they described, and much more, was familiar in our contemporary life. The majority of the theses were honest and elucidating—their effect was to restore some dignity to the male as opposed to the he-man in American life. ("And what is a 'He-man'?" demanded Gertrude Stein one day. "Isn't it a large enough order to fill out to the dimensions of all that 'a man' has meant in the past? A '*He*-man'!") The married woman can now discover whether she is being cheated, or whether sex is just something to be endured, and her compensation should be to establish a tyranny of the spirit, as her mother may have hinted. Perhaps many women found that love was meant to be fun. Anyhow the objectors lost their tawdry little case, which is one reason why our literature is now the most living in the world.

Contrary to popular opinion, the movies of the Jazz Age had no effect upon its morals. The social attitude of the producers was timid, behind the times and banal—for example, no picture mirrored even faintly the younger generation until 1923, when magazines had already been started to celebrate it and it had long ceased to be news. There were a few feeble splutters and then Clara Bow in *Flaming Youth;* promptly the Hollywood hacks ran the theme into its cinematographic grave. Throughout the Jazz

Age the movies got no farther than Mrs. Jiggs, keeping up with its most blatant superficialities. This was no doubt due to the censorship as well as to innate conditions in the industry. In any case, the Jazz Age now raced along under its own power, served by great filling stations full of money.

The people over thirty, the people all the way up to fifty, had joined the dance. We graybeards (to tread down F. P. A.) remember the uproar when in 1912 grandmothers of forty tossed away their crutches and took lessons in the Tango and the Castle-Walk. A dozen years later a woman might pack the Green Hat with her other affairs as she set off for Europe or New York, but Savonarola was too busy flogging dead horses in Augean stables of his own creation to notice. Society, even in small cities, now dined in separate chambers, and the sober table learned about the gay table only from hearsay. There were very few people left at the sober table. One of its former glories, the less sought-after girls who had become resigned to sublimating a probable celibacy, came across Freud and Jung in seeking their intellectual recompense and came tearing back into the fray.

By 1926 the universal preoccupation with sex had become a nuisance. (I remember a perfectly mated, contented young mother asking my wife's advice about "having an affair right away," though she had no one especially in mind, "because don't you think it's sort of undignified when you get much over thirty?") For a while bootleg Negro records with their phallic euphemisms made everything suggestive, and simultaneously came a wave of erotic plays—young girls from finishing-schools packed the galleries to hear about the romance of being a Lesbian and George Jean Nathan protested. Then one young producer lost his head entirely, drank a beauty's alcoholic bath-water and went to the penitentiary. Somehow his pathetic attempt at romance belongs to the Jazz Age, while his contemporary in prison, Ruth Snyder, had to be hoisted into it by the tabloids— she was, as *The Daily News* hinted deliciously to gourmets, about "to cook, *and sizzle, AND FRY!*" in the electric chair.

The gay elements of society had divided into two main

[18]

streams, one flowing toward Palm Beach and Deauville, and the other, much smaller, toward the summer Riviera. One could get away with more on the summer Riviera, and whatever happened seemed to have something to do with art. From 1926 to 1929, the great years of the Cap d'Antibes, this corner of France was dominated by a group quite distinct from that American society which is dominated by Europeans. Pretty much of anything went at Antibes—by 1929, at the most gorgeous paradise for swimmers on the Mediterranean no one swam any more, save for a short hang-over dip at noon. There was a picturesque graduation of steep rocks over the sea and somebody's valet and an occasional English girl used to dive from them, but the Americans were content to discuss each other in the bar. This was indicative of something that was taking place in the homeland—Americans were getting soft. There were signs everywhere: we still won the Olympic games but with champions whose names had few vowels in them—teams composed, like the fighting Irish combination of Notre Dame, of fresh overseas blood. Once the French became really interested, the Davis Cup gravitated automatically to their intensity in competition. The vacant lots of the Middle-Western cities were built up now—except for a short period in school, we were not turning out to be an athletic people like the British, after all. The hare and the tortoise. Of course if we wanted to we could be in a minute; we still had all those reserves of ancestral vitality, but one day in 1926 we looked down and found we had flabby arms and a fat pot and couldn't say boop-boop-a-doop to a Sicilian. Shades of Van Bibber!—no utopian ideal, God knows. Even golf, once considered an effeminate game, had seemed very strenuous of late—an emasculated form appeared and proved just right.

By 1927 a wide-spread neurosis began to be evident, faintly signalled, like a nervous beating of the feet, by the popularity of cross-word puzzles. I remember a fellow expatriate opening a letter from a mutual friend of ours, urging him to come home and be revitalized by the hardy, bracing qualities of the native soil. It was a strong letter and it affected us both deeply, until we noticed that it was headed from a nerve sanitarium in Pennsylvania.

By this time contemporaries of mine had begun to disappear into the dark maw of violence. A classmate killed his wife and himself on Long Island, another tumbled "accidently" from a skyscraper in Philadelphia, another purposely from a skyscraper in New York. One was killed in a speak-easy in Chicago; another was beaten to death in a speak-easy in New York and crawled home to the Princeton Club to die; still another had his skull crushed by a maniac's axe in an insane asylum where he was confined. These are not catastrophes that I went out of my way to look for—these were my friends; moreover, these things happened not during the depression but during the boom.

In the spring of '27, something bright and alien flashed across the sky. A young Minnesotan who seemed to have had nothing to do with his generation did a heroic thing, and for a moment people set down their glasses in country clubs and speakeasies and thought of their old best dreams. Maybe there was a way out by flying, maybe our restless blood could find frontiers in the illimitable air. But by that time we were all pretty well committed; and the Jazz Age continued; we would all have one more.

Nevertheless, Americans were wandering ever more widely—friends seemed eternally bound for Russia, Persia, Abyssinia and Central Africa. And by 1928 Paris had grown suffocating. With each new shipment of Americans spewed up by the boom the quality fell off, until toward the end there was something sinister about the crazy boatloads. They were no longer the simple pa and ma and son and daughter, infinitely superior in their qualities of kindness and curiosity to the corresponding class in Europe, but fantastic neanderthals who believed something, something vague, that you remembered from a very cheap novel. I remember an Italian on a steamer who promenaded the deck in an American Reserve Officer's uniform picking quarrels in broken English with Americans who criticised their own institutions in the bar. I remember a fat Jewess, inlaid with diamonds, who sat behind us at the Russian ballet and said as the curtain rose, "Thad's luffly, dey ought to baint a bicture of it." This was low comedy, but it was evident that money and power were falling into the hands of people in comparison with whom the leader of a village Soviet would be a gold-mine of judgment and culture. There were citizens travelling in luxury in 1928 and 1929 who, in the distortion of their new condition, had the human value of Pekinese, bivalves, cretins, goats. I remember the Judge from some New York district who had taken his daughter to see the Bayeux Tapestries and made a scene in the papers advocating their segregation because one scene was immoral. But in those days life was like the race in *Alice in Wonderland,* there was a prize for every one.

The Jazz Age had had a wild youth and a heady middle age. There was the phase of the necking parties, the Leopold-Loeb murder (I remember the time my wife was arrested on Queensborough Bridge on the suspicion of being the "Bob-haired Bandit") and the John Held Clothes. In the second phase such phenomena as sex and murder became more mature, if much more conventional. Middle age must be served and pajamas came to the beach to save fat thighs and flabby calves from competition with the one-piece bathing-suit. Finally skirts came down and everything was concealed. Everybody was at scratch now. Let's go—

But it was not to be. Somebody had blundered and the most expensive orgy in history was over.

It ended two years ago,* because the utter confidence which was its essential prop received an enormous jolt, and it didn't take long for the flimsy structure to settle earthward. And after two years the Jazz Age seems as far away as the days before the War. It was borrowed time anyhow—the whole upper tenth of a nation living with the insouciance of grand ducs and the casualness of chorus girls. But moralizing is easy now and it was pleasant to be in one's twenties in such a certain and unworried time. Even when you were broke you didn't worry about money, because it was in such profusion around you. Toward the end one had a struggle to pay one's share; it was almost a favor to accept hospitality

* 1929

that required any travelling. Charm, notoriety, mere good manners, weighed more than money as a social asset. This was rather splendid, but things were getting thinner and thinner as the eternal necessary human values tried to spread over all that expansion. Writers were geniuses on the strength of one respectable book or play; just as during the War officers of four months' experience commanded hundreds of men, so there were now many little fish lording it over great big bowls. In the theatrical world extravagant productions were carried by a few second-rate stars, and so on up the scale into politics, where it was difficult to interest good men in positions of the highest importance and responsibility, importance and responsibility far exceeding that of business executives but which paid only five or six thousand a year.

Now once more the belt is tight and we summon the proper expression of horror as we look back at our wasted youth. Sometimes, though, there is a ghostly rumble among the drums, an asthmatic whisper in the trombones that swings me back into the early twenties when we drank wood alcohol and every day in every way grew better and better, and there was a first abortive shortening of the skirts, and girls all looked alike in sweater dresses, and people you didn't want to know said "Yes, we have no bananas," and it seemed only a question of a few years before the older people would step aside and let the world be run by those who saw things as they were—and it all seems rosy and romantic to us who were young then, because we will never feel quite so intensely about our surroundings any more.

MY LOST CITY

July, 1932

THERE was first the ferry boat moving softly from the Jersey shore at dawn—the moment crystalized into my first symbol of New York. Five years later when I was fifteen I went into the city from school to see Ina Claire in *The Quaker Girl* and Gertrude Bryan in *Little Boy Blue.* Confused by my hopeless and melancholy love for them both, I was unable to choose between them—so they blurred into one lovely entity, the girl. She was my second symbol of New York. The ferry boat stood for triumph, the girl for romance. In time I was to achieve some of both, but there was a third symbol that I have lost somewhere, and lost forever.

I found it on a dark April afternoon after five more years.

"Oh, Bunny," I yelled. *"Bunny!"*

He did not hear me—my taxi lost him, picked him up again half a block down the street. There were black spots of rain on the sidewalk and I saw him walking briskly through the crowd wearing a tan raincoat over his inevitable brown get-up; I noted with a shock that he was carrying a light cane.

"Bunny!" I called again, and stopped. I was still an undergraduate at Princeton while he had become a New Yorker. This was his afternoon walk, this hurry along with his stick through the gathering rain, and as I was not to meet him for an hour it seemed an intrusion to happen upon

[23]

him engrossed in his private life. But the taxi kept pace with him and as I continued to watch I was impressed: he was no longer the shy little scholar of Holder Court—he walked with confidence, wrapped in his thoughts and looking straight ahead, and it was obvious that his new background was entirely sufficient to him. I knew that he had an apartment where he lived with three other men, released now from all undergraduate taboos, but there was something else that was nourishing him and I got my first impression of that new thing—the Metropolitan spirit.

Up to this time I had seen only the New York that offered itself for inspection—I was Dick Whittington up from the country gaping at the trained bears, or a youth of the Midi dazzled by the boulevards of Paris. I had come only to stare at the show, though the designers of the Woolworth Building and the Chariot Race Sign, the producers of musical comedies and problem plays, could ask for no more appreciative spectator, for I took the style and glitter of New York even above its own valuation. But I had never accepted any of the practically anonymous invitations to debutante balls that turned up in an undergraduate's mail, perhaps because I felt that no actuality could live up to my conception of New York's splendor. Moreover, she to whom I fatuously referred as "my girl" was a Middle Westerner, a fact which kept the warm center of the world out there, so I thought of New York as essentially cynical and heartless—save for one night when she made luminous the Ritz Roof on a brief passage through.

Lately, however, I had definitely lost her and I wanted a man's world, and this sight of Bunny made me see New York as just that. A week before, Monsignor Fay had taken me to the Lafayette where there was spread before us a brilliant flag of food, called an *hors d'oeuvre*, and with it we drank claret that was as brave as Bunny's confident cane—but after all it was a restaurant and afterwards we would drive back over a bridge into the hinterland. The New York of undergraduate dissipation, of Bustanoby's, Shanley's, Jack's, had become a horror and though I returned to it, alas, through many an alcoholic mist, I felt each time a betrayal of a persistent idealism. My participance was prurient rather than licentious and scarcely one pleasant memory of it remains from those days; as Ernest Hemingway once remarked, the sole purpose of the cabaret is for unattached men to find complaisant women. All the rest is a wasting of time in bad air.

But that night, in Bunny's apartment, life was mellow and safe, a finer distillation of all that I had come to love at Princeton. The gentle playing of an oboe mingled with city noises from the street outside, which penetrated into the room with difficulty through great barricades of books; only the crisp tearing open of invitations by one man was a discordant note. I had found a third symbol of New York and I began wondering about the rent of such apartments and casting about for the appropriate friends to share one with me.

Fat chance—for the next two years I had as much control over my own destiny as a convict over the cut of his clothes. When I got back to New York in 1919 I was so entangled in life that a period of mellow monasticism in Washington Square was not to be dreamed of. The thing was to make enough money in the advertising business to rent a stuffy apartment for two in the Bronx. The girl concerned had never seen New York but she was wise enough to be rather reluctant. And in a haze of anxiety and unhappiness I passed the four most impressionable months of my life.

New York had all the iridescence of the beginning of the world. The returning troops marched up Fifth Avenue and girls were instinctively drawn East and North toward them —this was the greatest nation and there was gala in the air. As I hovered ghost-like in the Plaza Red Room of a Saturday afternoon, or went to lush and liquid garden parties in the East Sixties or tippled with Princetonians in the Biltmore Bar I was haunted always by my other life—my drab room in the Bronx, my square foot of the subway, my fixation upon the day's letter from Alabama—would it come and what would it say?—my shabby suits, my poverty, and love. While my friends were launching decently into life I had muscled my inadequate bark into midstream. The gilded youth circling around young Constance Bennett in the Club de Vingt, the classmates in the Yale-Princeton Club whooping up our first after-the-war reunion, the atmosphere of the millionaires' houses that I sometimes frequented—these things were empty for me, though I recognized them as impressive scenery and regretted that I was committed to other romance. The most hilarious luncheon table or the most moony cabaret—it was all the same; from them I returned eagerly to my home on Claremont Avenue—home because there might be a letter waiting outside the door. One by one my great dreams of New York became tainted. The remembered charm of Bunny's apartment faded with the rest when I interviewed a blowsy landlady in Greenwich Village. She told me I could bring girls to the room, and the idea filled me with dismay—why should I want to bring girls to my room?—I had a girl. I wandered through the town of 127th Street, resenting its vibrant life; or else I bought cheap theatre seats at Gray's drugstore and tried to lose myself for a few hours in my old passion for Broadway. I was a failure—mediocre at advertising work and unable to get started as a writer. Hating the city, I got roaring, weeping drunk on my last penny and went home. . . .

. . . Incalculable city. What ensued was only one of a thousand success stories of those gaudy days, but it plays a part in my own movie of New York. When I returned six months later the offices of editors and publishers were open to me, impresarios begged plays, the movies panted for screen material. To my bewilderment, I was adopted, not as a Middle Westerner, not even as a detached observer, but as the arch type of what New York wanted. This statement requires some account of the metropolis in 1920.

There was already the tall white city of today, already the feverish activity of the boom, but there was a general inarticulateness. As much as anyone the columnist F. P. A. guessed the pulse of the individual and the crowd, but shyly, as one watching from a window. Society and the native arts had not mingled—Ellen Mackay was not yet married to Irving Berlin. Many of Peter Arno's people would have been meaningless to the citizen of 1920, and save for F. P. A.'s column there was no forum for metropolitan urbanity.

Then, for just a moment, the "younger generation" idea became a fusion of many elements in New York life. People of fifty might pretend there was still a four hundred or Maxwell Bodenheim might pretend there was a Bohemia worth its paint and pencils—but the blending of the bright, gay, vigorous elements began then and for the first time there appeared a society a little livelier than the solid mahogany dinner parties of Emily Price Post. If this society produced the cocktail party, it also evolved Park Avenue wit and for the first time an educated European could envisage a trip to New York as something more amusing than a gold-trek into a formalized Australian Bush.

For just a moment, before it was demonstrated that I was unable to play the role, I , who knew less of New York than any reporter of six months standing and less of its society than any hall-room boy in a Ritz stag line, was pushed into the position not only of spokesman for the time but of the typical product of that same moment. I, or rather it was "we" now, did not know exactly what New York expected of us and found it rather confusing. Within a few months after our embarkation on the Metropolitan venture we scarcely knew any more who we were and we hadn't a notion what we were. A dive into a civic fountain, a casual brush with the law, was enough to get us into the gossip columns, and we were quoted on a variety of subjects we knew nothing about. Actually our "contacts" included half a dozen unmarried college friends and a few new literary acquaintances—I remember a lonesome Christmas when we had not one friend in the city, nor one house we could go to. Finding no nucleus to which we could cling, we became a small nucleus ourselves and gradually we fitted our disruptive personalities into the contemporary scene of New York. Or rather New York forgot us and let us stay.

This is not an account of the city's changes but of the changes in this writer's feeling for the city. From the confusion of the year 1920 I remember riding on top of a taxi-cab along deserted Fifth Avenue on a hot Sunday night, and a luncheon in the cool Japanese gardens at the Ritz with the wistful Kay Laurel and George Jean Nathan, and writing all night again and again, and paying too much for minute apartments, and buying magnificent but broken-down cars. The first speakeasies had arrived, the toddle was *passé*, the Montmartre was the smart place to dance and Lillian Tashman's fair hair weaved around the floor among the enliquored college boys. The plays were *Declassée* and *Sacred and Profane Love*, and at the Midnight Frolic you danced elbow to elbow with Marion Davies and perhaps picked out the vivacious Mary Hay in the pony chorus. We thought we were apart from all that; perhaps everyone thinks they are apart from their milieu. We felt like small children in a great bright unexplored barn. Summoned out to Griffith's studio on Long Island, we trembled in the presence of the familiar faces of the *Birth of a Nation;* later I realized that behind much of the entertainment that the city poured forth into the nation there were only a lot of rather lost and lonely people. The world of the picture actors was like our own in that it was in New York and not of it. It had little sense of itself and no center: when I first met Dorothy Gish I had the feeling that we were both standing on the North Pole and it was snowing. Since then they have found a home but it was not destined to be New York.

When bored we took our city with a Huysmans-like perversity. An afternoon alone in our "apartment" eating olive sandwiches and drinking a quart of Bushmill's whiskey presented by Zoë Atkins, then out into the freshly bewitched city, through strange doors into strange apartments with intermittent swings along in taxis through the soft nights. At last we were one with New York, pulling it after us through every portal. Even now I go into many flats with the sense that I have been there before or in the one above or below—was it the night I tried to disrobe in the *Scandals,* or the night when (as I read with astonishment in the paper next morning) "Fitzgerald Knocks Officer This Side of Paradise"? Successful scrapping not being among my accomplishments, I tried in vain to reconstruct the sequence of events which led up to this dénouement in Webster Hall. And lastly from that period I remember riding in a taxi one afternoon between very tall buildings under a mauve and rosy sky; I began to bawl because I had everything I wanted and knew I would never be so happy again.

It was typical of our precarious position in New York that when our child was to be born we played safe and went home to St. Paul—it seemed inappropriate to bring a baby into all that glamor and loneliness. But in a year we were back and we began doing the same things over again and not liking them so much. We had run through a lot, though we had retained an almost theatrical innocence by preferring the role of the observed to that of the observer. But innocence is no end in itself and as our minds unwillingly matured we began to see New York whole and try to save some of it for the selves we would inevitably become.

It was too late—or too soon. For us the city was inevitably linked up with Bacchic diversions, mild or fantastic. We could organize ourselves only on our return to Long Island and not always there. We had no incentive to meet the city half way. My first symbol was now a memory, for I knew that triumph is in oneself; my second one had grown commonplace—two of the actresses whom I had worshipped from afar in 1913 had dined in our house. But it filled me with a certain fear that even the third symbol had grown dim—the tranquillity of Bunny's apartment was not to be found in the ever-quickening city. Bunny himself was married, and about to become a father, other friends had gone to Europe, and the bachelors had become cadets of houses larger and more social than ours. By this time we "knew everybody"—which is to say most of those whom Ralph Barton would draw as in the orchestra on an opening night.

But we were no longer important. The flapper, upon whose activities the popularity of my first books was based, had become *passé* by 1923—anyhow in the East. I decided to crash Broadway with a play, but Broadway sent its scouts to Atlantic City and quashed the idea in advance, so I felt that, for the moment, the city and I had little to offer each other. I would take the Long Island atmosphere that I had familiarly breathed and materialize it beneath unfamiliar skies.

It was three years before we saw New York again. As the

ship glided up the river, the city burst thunderously upon us in the early dusk—the white glacier of lower New York swooping down like a strand of a bridge to rise into uptown New York, a miracle of foamy light suspended by the stars. A band started to play on deck, but the majesty of the city made the march trivial and tinkling. From that moment I knew that New York, however often I might leave it, was home.

The tempo of the city had changed sharply. The uncertainties of 1920 were drowned in a steady golden roar and many of our friends had grown wealthy. But the restlessness of New York in 1927 approached hysteria. The parties were bigger—those of Condé Nast, for example, rivaled in their way the fabled balls of the nineties; the pace was faster—the catering to dissipation set an example to Paris; the shows were broader, the buildings were higher, the morals were looser and the liquor was cheaper; but all these benefits did not really minister to much delight. Young people wore out early—they were hard and languid at twenty-one and save for Peter Arno none of them contributed anything new; perhaps Peter Arno and his collaborators said everything there was to say about the boom days in New York that couldn't be said by a jazz band. Many people who were not alcoholics were lit up four days out of seven, and frayed nerves were strewn everywhere; groups were held together by a generic nervousness and the hangover became a part of the day as well allowed-for as the Spanish siesta. Most of my friends drank too much—the more they were in tune to the times the more they drank. And as effort *per se* had no dignity against the mere bounty of those days in New York, a depreciatory word was found for it: a successful programme became a racket—I was in the literary racket.

We settled a few hours from New York and I found that every time I came to the city I was caught up into a complication of events that deposited me a few days later in a somewhat exhausted state on the train for Delaware. Whole sections of the city had grown rather poisonous, but invariably I found a moment of utter peace in riding south through Central Park at dark toward where the façade of 59th Street thrusts its lights through the trees. There again was my lost city, wrapped cool in its mystery and promise. But that detachment never lasted long—as the toiler must live in the city's belly, so I was compelled to live in its disordered mind.

Instead there were the speakeasies—the moving from luxurious bars, which advertised in the campus publications of Yale and Princeton, to the beer gardens where the snarling face of the underworld peered through the German good nature of the entertainment, then on to strange and even more sinister localities where one was eyed by granite-faced boys and there was nothing left of joviality but only a brutishness that corrupted the new day into which one presently went out. Back in 1920 I shocked a rising young business man by suggesting a cocktail before lunch. In 1929 there was liquor in half the downtown offices, and a speakeasy in half the large buildings.

One was increasingly conscious of the speakeasy and of Park Avenue. In the past decade Greenwich Village, Washington Square, Murray Hill, the châteaux of Fifth Avenue had somehow disappeared, or become unexpressive of anything. The city was bloated, glutted, stupid with cake and circuses, and a new expression "Oh yeah?" summed up all the enthusiasm evoked by the announcement of the last super-skyscrapers. My barber retired on a half million bet in the market and I was conscious that the head waiters who bowed me, or failed to bow me, to my table were far, far wealthier than I. This was no fun—once again I had enough of New York and it was good to be safe on shipboard where the ceaseless revelry remained in the bar in transport to the fleecing rooms of France.

"What news from New York?"

"Stocks go up. A baby murdered a gangster."

"Nothing more?"

"Nothing. Radios blare in the street."

I once thought that there were no second acts in American lives, but there was certainly to be a second act to New York's boom days. We were somewhere in North Africa when we heard a dull distant crash which echoed to the farthest wastes of the desert.

"What was that?"

"Did you hear it?"

"It was nothing."

"Do you think we ought to go home and see?"

"No—it was nothing."

In the dark autumn of two years later we saw New York again. We passed through curiously polite customs agents, and then with bowed head and hat in hand I walked reverently through the echoing tomb. Among the ruins a few childish wraiths still played to keep up the pretense that they were alive, betraying by their feverish voices and hectic cheeks the thinness of the masquerade. Cocktail parties, a last hollow survival from the days of carnival, echoed to the plaints of the wounded: "Shoot me, for the love of God, someone shoot me!", and the groans and wails of the dying: "Did you see that United States Steel is down three more points?" My barber was back at work in his shop; again the head waiters bowed people to their tables, if there were people to be bowed. From the ruins, lonely and inexplicable as the sphinx, rose the Empire State Building and, just as it had been a tradition of mine to climb to the Plaza Roof to take leave of the beautiful city, extending as far as eyes could reach, so now I went to the roof of the last and most magnificent of towers. Then I understood— everything was explained: I had discovered the crowning error of the city, its Pandora's box. Full of vaunting pride the New Yorker had climbed here and seen with dismay what he had never suspected, that the city was not the endless succession of canyons that he had supposed but that *it had limits*—from the tallest structure he saw for the first time that it faded out into the country on all sides, into an expanse of green and blue that alone was limitless. And with the awful realization that New York was a city after all and not a universe, the whole shining edifice that he had reared in his imagination came crashing to the ground. That was the rash gift of Alfred E. Smith to the citizens of New York.

Thus I take leave of my lost city. Seen from the ferry boat in the early morning, it no longer whispers of fantastic success and eternal youth. The whoopee mamas who prance before its empty parquets do not suggest to me the ineffable beauty of my dream girls of 1914. And Bunny, swinging along confidently with his cane toward his cloister in a carnival, has gone over to Communism and frets about the wrongs of southern mill workers and western farmers whose voices, fifteen years ago, would not have penetrated his study walls.

All is lost save memory, yet sometimes I imagine myself reading, with curious interest, a *Daily News* of the issue of 1945:

MAN OF FIFTY RUNS AMUCK IN NEW YORK
Fitzgerald Feathered Many Love Nests Cutie Avers Bumped Off By Outraged Gunman

So perhaps I am destined to return some day and find in the city new experiences that so far I have only read about. For the moment I can only cry out that I have lost my splendid mirage. Come back, come back, O glittering and white!

RING

For a year and a half, the writer of this appreciation was Ring Lardner's most familiar companion; after that, geography made separations and our contacts were rare. When my wife and I last saw him in 1931, he looked already like a man on his deathbed—it was terribly sad to see that six feet three inches of kindness stretched out ineffectual in the hospital room. His fingers trembled with a match, the tight skin on his handsome skull was marked as a mask of misery and nervous pain.

He gave a very different impression when we first saw him in 1921—he seemed to have an abundance of quiet vitality that would enable him to outlast anyone, to take himself for long spurts of work or play that would ruin any ordinary constitution. He had recently convulsed the country with the famous kitten-and-coat saga (it had to do with a world's series bet and with the impending conversion of some kittens into fur), and the evidence of the betting, a beautiful sable, was worn by his wife at the time. In those days he was interested in people, sports, bridge, music, the stage, the newspapers, the magazines, the books. But though I did not know it, the change in him had already begun— the impenetrable despair that dogged him for a dozen years to his death.

He had practically given up sleeping, save on short vacations deliberately consecrated to simple pleasures, most frequently golf with his friends, Grantland Rice or John Wheeler. Many a night we talked over a case of Canadian ale until bright dawn, when Ring would rise and yawn: "Well, I guess the children have left for school by this time —I might as well go home."

The woes of many people haunted him—for example, the doctor's death sentence pronounced upon Tad, the cartoonist, (who, in fact, nearly outlived Ring)—it was as if he believed he could and ought to do something about such things. And as he struggled to fulfill his contracts, one of which, a comic strip based on the character of "the busher," was a terror, indeed, it was obvious that he felt his work to be directionless, merely "copy." So he was inclined to turn his cosmic sense of responsibility into the channel of solving other people's problems—finding someone an introduction to a theatrical manager, placing a friend in a job, maneuvering a man into a golf club. The effort made was often out of proportion to the situation; the truth back of it was that Ring was getting off—he was a faithful and conscientious workman to the end, but he had stopped finding any fun in his work ten years before he died.

About that time (1922) a publisher undertook to reissue his old books and collect his recent stories and this gave him a sense of existing in the literary world as well as with the public, and he got some satisfaction from the reiterated statements of Mencken and F. P. A. as to his true stature as a writer. But I don't think he cared then—it is hard to understand but I don't think he really gave a damn about anything except his personal relations with a few people. A case in point was his attitude to those imitators who lifted everything except the shirt off his back—only Hemingway has been so thoroughly frisked—it worried the imitators more than it worried Ring. His attitude was that if they got stuck in the process he'd help them over any tough place.

Throughout this period of huge earnings and an increasingly solid reputation on top and beneath, there were two ambitions more important to Ring than the work by which he will be remembered; he wanted to be a musician—sometimes he dramatized himself ironically as a thwarted composer—and he wanted to write shows. His dealings with managers would make a whole story: they were always commissioning him to do work which they promptly forgot they had ordered, and accepting librettos that they never produced. (Ring left a short ironic record of Ziegfeld.) Only with the aid of the practical George Kaufman did he achieve his ambition, and by then he was too far gone in illness to get a proper satisfaction from it.

The point of these paragraphs is that, whatever Ring's achievement was, it fell short of the achievement he was capable of, and this because of a cynical attitude toward his work. How far back did that attitude go?—back to his youth in a Michigan village? Certainly back to his days with the Cubs. During those years, when most men of promise achieve an adult education, if only in the school of war, Ring moved in the company of a few dozen illiterates playing a boy's game. A boy's game, with no more possibilities in it than a boy could master, a game bounded by walls which kept out novelty or danger, change or adventure. This material, the observation of it under such circumstances, was the text of Ring's schooling during the most formative period of the mind. A writer can spin on about his adventures after thirty, after forty, after fifty, but the criteria by which these adventures are weighed and valued are irrevocably settled at the age of twenty-five. However deeply Ring might cut into it, his cake had exactly the diameter of Frank Chance's diamond.

Here was his artistic problem, and it promised future trouble. So long as he wrote within that enclosure the result was magnificent: within it he heard and recorded the voice of a continent. But when, inevitably, he outgrew his interest in it, what was Ring left with?

He was left with his fine linguistic technique—and he was left rather helpless in those few acres. He had been formed by the very world on which his hilarious irony had released itself. He had fought his way through to knowing what people's motives are and what means they are likely to resort to in order to attain their goals. But now he had a new problem—what to do about it. He went on seeing, and the sights traveled back to the optic nerve, but no longer to be thrown off in fiction, because they were no longer sights that could be weighed and valued by the old criteria. It was never that he was completely sold on athletic virtuosity as the be-all and end-all of problems; the trouble was that he could find nothing finer. Imagine life conceived as a business of beautiful muscular organization—an arising, an effort, a good break, a sweat, a bath, a meal, a love, a sleep—imagine it achieved; then imagine trying to apply that standard to the horribly complicated mess of living, where nothing, even the greatest conceptions and workings and achievements, is else but messy, spotty, tortuous—and then one can imagine the confusion that Ring faced on coming out of the ball park.

He kept on recording but he no longer projected, and this accumulation, which he has taken with him to the grave, crippled his spirit in the latter years. It was not the fear of Niles, Michigan, that hampered him—it was the habit of silence, formed in the presence of the "ivory" with which he lived and worked. Remember it was not humble ivory— Ring has demonstrated that—it was arrogant, imperative, often megalomaniacal ivory. He got the habit of silence, then the habit of repression that finally took the form of his odd little crusade in the New Yorker against pornographic songs. He had agreed with himself to speak only a small portion of his mind.

The present writer once suggested to him that he organize some cadre within which he could adequately display his talents, suggesting that it should be something deeply personal, and something on which Ring could take his time, but he dismissed the idea lightly; he was a disillusioned idealist but he had served his Fates well, and no other ones could be casually created for him—"This is something that can be printed," he reasoned; "this, however, belongs with that bunch of stuff that can never be written."

He covered himself in such cases with protests of his inability to bring off anything big, but this was specious, for he was a proud man and had no reason to rate his abilities cheaply. He refused to "tell all" because in a crucial period

[37]

of his life he had formed the habit of not doing it—and this he had elevated gradually into a standard of taste. It never satisfied him by a damn sight.

So one is haunted not only by a sense of personal loss but by a conviction that Ring got less percentage of himself on paper than any other American of the first flight. There is *"You Know Me, Al,"* and there are about a dozen wonderful short stories (my God, he hadn't even saved them—the material of *How to Write Short Stories* was obtained by photographing old issues in the public library!), and there is some of the most uproarious and inspired nonsense since Lewis Carroll. Most of the rest is mediocre stuff, with flashes, and I would do Ring a disservice to suggest it should be set upon an altar and worshipped, as have been the most casual relics of Mark Twain. Those three volumes should seem enough—to everyone who didn't know Ring. But I venture that no one who knew him but will agree that the personality of the man overlapped it. Proud, shy, solemn, shrewd, polite, brave, kind, merciful, honorable—with the affection these qualities aroused he created in addition a certain awe in people. His intentions, his will, once in motion, were formidable factors in dealing with him—he always did every single thing he said he would do. Frequently he was the melancholy Jaques, and sad company indeed, but under any conditions a noble dignity flowed from him, so that time in his presence always seemed well spent.

On my desk, at the moment, I have the letters Ring wrote to us; here is a letter one thousand words long, here is one of two thousand words—theatrical gossip, literary shop talk, flashes of wit but not much wit, for he was feeling thin and saving the best of that for his work, anecdotes of his activities. I reprint the most typical one I can find:

"The Dutch Treat show was a week ago Friday night. Grant Rice and I had reserved a table, and a table holds ten people and no more. Well, I had invited, as one guest, Jerry Kern, but he telephoned at the last moment that he couldn't come. I then consulted with Grant Rice, who said he had no substitute in mind, but that it was a shame to waste our extra ticket when tickets were at a premium. So I called up

Jones, and Jones said yes, and would it be all right for him to bring along a former Senator who was a pal of his and had been good to him in Washington. I said I was sorry, but our table was filled and, besides, we didn't have an extra ticket. "Maybe I could dig up another ticket somewhere," said Jones. "I don't believe so," I said, "but anyway the point is that we haven't room at our table." "Well," said Jones, "I could have the Senator eat somewhere else and join us in time for the show." "Yes," I said, "but we have no ticket for him." "Well, I'll think up something," he said. Well, what he thought up was to bring himself and the Senator and I had a hell of a time getting an extra ticket and shoving the Senator in at another table where he wasn't wanted, and later in the evening, the Senator thanked Jones and said he was the greatest fella in the world and all I got was goodnight.

"Well, I must close and nibble on a carrot. R.W.L."

Even in a telegram Ring could compress a lot of himself. Here is one: WHEN ARE YOU COMING BACK AND WHY PLEASE ANSWER RING LARDNER

This is not the moment to recollect Ring's convivial aspects, especially as he had, long before his death, ceased to find amusement in dissipation, or indeed in the whole range of what is called entertainment—save for his perennial interest in songs. By grace of the radio and of the many musicians who, drawn by his enormous magnetism, made pilgrimages to his bedside, he had a consolation in the last days, and he made the most of it, hilariously rewriting Cole Porter's lyrics in the *New Yorker*. But it would be an evasion for the present writer not to say that when he was Ring's neighbor a decade ago, they tucked a lot under their belts in many weathers, and spent many words on many men and things. At no time did I feel that I had known him enough, or that anyone knew him—it was not the feeling that there was more stuff in him and that it should come out, it was rather a qualitative difference, it was rather as though, due to some inadequacy in one's self, one had not penetrated to something unsolved, new and unsaid. That is why one wishes that Ring had written down a larger proportion of what was in his mind and heart. It would have saved him longer for us, and that in itself would be something. But I would like to know what it was, and now I will go on wishing—what did Ring want, how did he want things to be, how did he think things were?

A great and good American is dead. Let us not obscure him by the flowers, but walk up and look at that fine medallion, all abraded by sorrows that perhaps we are not equipped to understand. Ring made no enemies, because he was kind, and to many millions he gave release and delight.

"SHOW MR. AND MRS. F. TO NUMBER—"

By F. Scott and Zelda Fitzgerald

May-June, 1934

We are married. The Sibylline parrots are protesting the sway of the first bobbed heads in the Biltmore panelled luxe. The hotel is trying to look older.

The faded rose corridors of the Commodore end in subways and subterranean metropolises—a man sold us a broken Marmon and a wild burst of friends spent half an hour revolving in the revolving door.

There were lilacs open to the dawn near the boarding house in Westport where we sat up all night to finish a story. We quarreled in the gray morning dew about morals; and made up over a red bathing suit.

The Manhattan took us in one late night though we looked very young and gay. Ungratefully we packed the empty suitcase with spoons and the phone book and a big square pin-cushion.

The Traymore room was gray and the chaise longue big enough for a courtesan. The sound of the sea kept us awake.

Electric fans blew the smell of peaches and hot biscuit and the cindery aroma of travelling salesmen through the New Willard halls in Washington.

But the Richmond hotel had a marble stair and long unopened rooms and marble statues of the gods lost somewhere in its echoing cells.

At the O. Henry in Greensville they thought a man and

his wife ought not to be dressed alike in white knicker-
bockers in nineteen-twenty and we thought the water in
the tubs ought not to run red mud.

Next day the summer whine of phonographs billowed out
the skirts of the southern girls in Athens. There were so
many smells in the drug stores and so much organdy and
so many people just going somewhere. . . . We left at dawn.

1921

They were respectful in the Cecil in London; disciplined
by the long majestuous twilights on the river and we were
young but we were impressed anyway by the Hindus and
the Royal Processions.

At the St. James and Albany in Paris we smelled up the
room with an uncured Armenian goat-skin and put the un-
melting "ice-cream" outside the window, and there were
dirty postcards, but we were pregnant.

The Royal Danieli in Venice had a gambling machine
and the wax of centuries over the window-sill and there
were fine officers on the American destroyer. We had fun
in a gondola feeling like a soft Italian song.

Bamboo curtains and an asthma patient complaining of
the green plush and an ebony piano were all equally em-
balmed in the formal parlors of the Hôtel d'Italie in Florence.

But there were fleas on the gilded filigree of the Grand
Hôtel in Rome; men from the British embassy scratched
behind the palms; the clerks said it was the flea season.

Claridge's in London served strawberries in a gold dish,
but the room was an inside room and gray all day, and the
waiter didn't care whether we left or not, and he was our
only contact.

In the fall we got to the Commodore in St. Paul, and
while leaves blew up the streets we waited for our child
to be born.

1922-1923

The Plaza was an etched hotel, dainty and subdued, with
such a handsome head waiter that he never minded lending

five dollars or borrowing a Rolls-Royce. We didn't travel much in those years.

1924

The Deux Mondes in Paris ended about a blue abysmal court outside our window. We bathed the daughter in the *bidet* by mistake and she drank the gin fizz thinking it was lemonade and ruined the luncheon table next day.

Goat was to eat in Grimm's Park Hotel in Hyères, and the bougainvillea was brittle as its own color in the hot white dust. Many soldiers loitered outside the gardens and brothels listening to the nickelodeons. The nights, smelling of honeysuckle and army leather, staggered up the mountain side and settled upon Mrs. Edith Wharton's garden.

At the Ruhl in Nice we decided on a room not facing the sea, on all the dark men being princes, on not being able to afford it even out of season. During dinner on the terrace, stars fell in our plates, and we tried to identify ourselves with the place by recognizing faces from the boat. But nobody passed and we were alone with the deep blue grandeur and the *filet de sole Ruhl* and the second bottle of champagne.

The Hôtel de Paris at Monte Carlo was like a palace in a detective story. Officials got us things: tickets and permissions, maps and newly portentous identities. We waited a good while in the formalized sun while they fitted us out with all we needed to be fitting guests of the Casino. Finally, taking control of the situation, we authoritatively sent the bell-boy for a tooth-brush.

Wistaria dripped in the court of the Hôtel d'Europe at Avignon and the dawn rumbled up in market carts. A lone lady in tweeds drank Martinis in the dingy bar. We met French friends at the Taverne Riche and listened to the bells of late afternoon reverberate along the city walls. The Palace of the Popes rose chimerically through the gold end of day over the broad still Rhône, while we did nothing, assiduously, under the plane trees on the opposite bank.

Like Henri IV, a French patriot fed his babies red wine in the Continental at St. Raphaël and there were no carpets because of summer, so echoes of the children's protestations fell pleasantly amidst the clatter of dishes and china. By this time we could identify a few words of French and felt ourselves part of the country.

The Hôtel du Cap at Antibes was almost deserted. The heat of day lingered in the blue and white blocks of the balcony and from the great canvas mats our friends had spread along the terrace we warmed our sunburned backs and invented new cocktails.

The Miramare in Genoa festooned the dark curve of the shore with garlands of lights, and the shape of the hills was picked out of the darkness by the blaze from the windows of high hotels. We thought of the men parading the gay arcades as undiscovered Carusos but they all assured us that Genoa was a business city and very like America and Milan.

We got to Pisa in the dark and couldn't find the leaning tower until we passed it by accident leaving the Royal Victoria on our way out. It stood stark in a field by itself. The Arno was muddy and not half as insistent as it is in the cross-word puzzles.

Marion Crawford's mother died in the Quirinal Hotel at Rome. All the chamber-maids remember it and tell the visitors about how they spread the room with newspapers afterwards. The sitting-rooms are hermetically sealed and palms conceal the way to open the windows. Middle-aged English doze in the stale air and nibble stale-salted peanuts with the hotel's famous coffee, which comes out of a calliope-like device for filling it full of grounds, like the glass balls that make snow storms when shaken.

In the Hôtel des Princes at Rome we lived on Bel Paese cheese and Corvo wine and made friends with a delicate spinster who intended to stop there until she finished a three-volume history of the Borgias. The sheets were damp and the nights were perforated by the snores of the people next door, but we didn't mind because we could always come home down the stairs to the Via Sistina, and there were jonquils and beggars along that way. We were too superior at that time to use the guide books and wanted to discover the ruins for ourselves, which we did when we had ex-

hausted the night-life and the market places and the cam-
pagna. We liked the Castello Sant'Angelo because of its round
mysterious unity and the river and the debris about its base.
It was exciting being lost between centuries in the Roman
dusk and taking your sense of direction from the Colosseum.

1925

At the hotel in Sorrento we saw the tarantella, but it was
a *real* one and we had seen so many more imaginative
adaptations. . . .

A southern sun drugged the court of the Quisisana to
somnolence. Strange birds protested their sleepiness beneath
the overwhelming cypress while Compton Mackenzie told
us why he lived in Capri: Englishmen must have an island.

The Tiberio was a high white hotel scalloped about the
base by the rounded roofs of Capri, cupped to catch rain
which never falls. We climbed to it through devious dark
alleys that house the island's Rembrandt butcher shops and
bakeries; then we climbed down again to the dark pagan
hysteria of Capri's Easter, the resurrection of the spirit of
the people.

When we got back to Marseilles, going north again, the
streets about the waterfront were bleached by the brightness
of the harbor and pedestrians gayly discussed errors of time
at little cafés on the corner. We were so damn glad of the
animation.

The hotel in Lyons wore an obsolete air and nobody ever
heard of Lyonnaise potatoes and we became so discouraged
with touring that we left the little Renault there and took
the train for Paris.

The Hôtel Florida had catacornered rooms; the gilt had
peeled from the curtain fixtures.

When we started out again after a few months, touring
south, we slept six in a room in Dijon (Hôtel du Dump, Pens.
from 2 frs. Pouring water) because there wasn't any other
place. Our friends considered themselves somewhat compromised but snored towards morning.

In Salies-de-Béarn in the Pyrenees we took a cure for coli-

[45]

tis, disease of that year, and rested in a white pine room in the Hôtel Bellevue, flush with thin sun rolled down from the Pyrenees. There was a bronze statue of Henri IV on the mantel in our room, for his mother was born there. The boarded windows of the Casino were splotched with bird droppings—along the misty streets we bought canes with spears on the end and were a little discouraged about everything. We had a play on Broadway and the movies offered $60,000, but we were china people by then and it didn't seem to matter particularly.

When that was over, a hired limousine drove us to Toulouse, careening around the grey block of Carcassonne and through the long unpopulated planes of the Côte d'Argent. The Hôtel Tivollier, though ornate, had fallen into disuse. We kept ringing for the waiter to assure ourselves that life went on somewhere in the dingy crypt. He appeared resentfully and finally we induced him to give us so much beer that it heightened the gloom.

In the Hôtel O'Connor old ladies in white lace rocked their pasts to circumspection with the lullabyic motion of the hotel chairs. But they were serving blue twilights at the cafés along the Promenade des Anglais for the price of a porto, and we danced their tangos and watched girls shiver in the appropriate clothes for the Côte d'Azur. We went to the Perroquet with friends, one of us wearing a blue hyacinth and the other an ill temper which made him buy a wagon full of roasted chestnuts and immediately scatter their warm burnt odor like largesse over the cold spring night.

In the sad August of that year we made a trip to Mentone, ordering bouillabaisse in an aquarium-like pavillion by the sea across from the Hôtel Victoria. The hills were silver-olive, and of the true shape of frontiers.

Leaving the Riviera after a third summer, we called on a writer friend at the Hôtel Continental at Cannes. He was proud of his independence in adopting a black mongrel dog. He had a nice house and a nice wife and we envied his comfortable installations that gave the effect of his having retired from the world when he had really taken such of it as he wanted and confined it.

When we got back to America we went to the Roosevelt Hotel in Washington and to see one of our mothers. The cardboard hotels, bought in sets, made us feel as if we committed a desecration by living in them—we left the brick pavements and the elms and the heterogeneous qualities of Washington and went further south.

1927

It takes so long to get to California, and there were so many nickel handles, gadgets to avoid, buttons to invoke, and such a lot of newness and Fred Harvey, that when one of us thought he had appendicitis we got out at El Paso. A cluttered bridge dumps one in Mexico where the restaurants are trimmed with tissue paper and there are contraband perfumes—we admired the Texas rangers, not having seen men with guns on their hips since the war.

We reached California in time for an earthquake. It was sunny, and misty at night. White roses swung luminous in the mist from a trellis outside the Ambassador windows; a bright exaggerated parrot droned incomprehensible shouts in an aquamarine pool—of course everybody interpreted them to be obscenities; geraniums underscored the discipline of the California flora. We paid homage to the pale aloof concision of Diana Manners' primitive beauty and dined at Pickfair to marvel at Mary Pickford's dynamic subjugation of life. A thoughtful limousine carried us for California hours to be properly moved by the fragility of Lillian Gish, too aspiring for life, clinging vine-like to occultisms.

From there we went to the DuPont in Wilmington. A friend took us to tea in the mahogany recesses of an almost feudal estate, where the sun gleamed apologetically in the silver tea-service and there were four kinds of buns and four indistinguishable daughters in riding clothes and a mistress of the house too busily preserving the charm of another era to separate out the children. We leased a very big old mansion on the Delaware River. The squareness of the rooms and the sweep of the columns were to bring us a judicious tranquility. There were sombre horse-chestnuts

[47]

in the yard and a white pine bending as graciously as a Japanese brush drawing.

We went up to Princeton. There was a new colonial inn, but the campus offered the same worn grassy parade ground for the romantic spectres of Light-Horse Harry Lee and Aaron Burr. We loved the temperate shapes of Nassau Hall's old brick, and the way it seems still a tribunal of early American ideals, the elm walks and meadows, the college windows open to the spring—open, open to everything in life—for a minute.

The Negroes are in knee-breeches at the Cavalier in Virginia Beach. It is theatrically southern and its newness is a bit barren, but there is the best beach in America; at that time, before the cottages were built, there were dunes and the moon tripped, fell, in the sandy ripples along the seafront.

Next time we went, lost and driven now like the rest, it was a free trip north to Quebec. They thought maybe we'd write about it. The Château Frontenac was built of toy stone arches, a tin soldier's castle. Our voices were truncated by the heavy snow, the stalactite icicles on the low roofs turned the town to a wintry cave; we spent most of our time in an echoing room lined with skis, because the professional there gave us a good feeling about the sports at which we were so inept. He was later taken up by the DuPonts on the same basis and made a powder magnate or something.

When we decided to go back to France we spent the night at the Pennsylvania, manipulating the new radio earphones and the servidors, where a suit can be frozen to a cube by nightfall. We were still impressed by running ice-water, self-sustaining rooms that could function even if besieged with current events. We were so little in touch with the world that they gave us an impression of a crowded subway station.

The hotel in Paris was triangular-shaped and faced Saint-Germain-des-Prés. On Sundays we sat at the Deux Magots and watched the people, devout as an opera chorus, enter the old doors, or else watched the French read newspapers. There were long conversations about the ballet over sauerkraut in Lipps, and blank recuperative hours over books and prints in the dank Allée Bonaparte.

Now the trips away had begun to be less fun. The next one to Brittany broke at Le Mans. The lethargic town was crumbling away, pulverized by the heat of the white hot summer and only travelling salesmen slid their chairs preëmptorily about the uncarpeted dining room. Plane trees bordered the route to La Baule.

At the Palace in La Baule we felt raucous amidst so much chic restraint. Children bronzed on the bare blue-white beach while the tide went out so far as to leave them crabs and starfish to dig for in the sands.

1929

We went to America but didn't stay at hotels. When we got back to Europe we spent the first night at a sun-flushed hostelry, Bertolini's in Genoa. There was a green tile bath and a very attentive valet de chambre and there was ballet to practice, using the brass bedstead as a bar. It was good to see the brilliant flowers colliding in prismatic explosions over the terraced hillside and to feel ourselves foreigners again.

Reaching Nice, we went economically to the Beau Rivage, which offered many stained glass windows to the Mediterranean glare. It was spring and was brittly cold along the Promenade des Anglais, though the crowds moved persistently in a summer tempo. We admired the painted windows of the converted palaces on the Place Gambetta. Walking at dusk, the voices fell seductively through the nebulous twilight inviting us to share the first stars, but we were busy. We went to the cheap ballets of the Casino on the jettée and rode almost to Villefranche for *Salade Niçoise* and a very special bouillabaisse.

  In Paris we economized again in a not-yet-dried cement hotel, the name of which we've forgotten. It cost us a good deal, for we ate out every night to avoid starchy table d'hôtes. Sylvia Beach invited us to dinner and the talk was all of the people who had discovered Joyce; we called on friends in better hotels: Zoë Akins, who had sought the picturesque of the open fires at Foyot's, and Esther at the Port-Royal, who took us to see Romaine Brooks' studio, a glass enclosed square of heaven swung high above Paris.

Then southward again, and wasting the dinner hour in an argument about which hotel: there was one in Beaune where Ernest Hemingway had liked the trout. Finally we decided to drive all night, and we ate well in a stable courtyard facing a canal—the green-white glare of Provence had already begun to dazzle us so that we didn't care whether the food was good or not. That night we stopped under the white-trunked trees to open the windshield to the moon and to the sweep of the south against our faces, and to better smell the fragrance rustling restlessly amidst the poplars.

At Fréjus Plage, they had built a new hotel, a barren structure facing the beach where the sailors bathe. We felt very superior remembering how we had been the first travellers to like the place in summer.

After the swimming at Cannes was over and the year's octopi had grown up in the crevices of the rocks, we started back to Paris. The night of the stock-market crash we stayed at the Beau Rivage in St. Raphaël in the room Ring Lardner had occupied another year. We got out as soon as we could because we had been there so many times before—it is sadder to find the past again and find it inadequate to the present than it is to have it elude you and remain forever a harmonious conception of memory.

At the Jules César in Arles we had a room that had once been a chapel. Following the festering waters of a stagnant canal we came to the ruins of a Roman dwelling-house. There was a blacksmith shop installed behind the proud columns and a few scattered cows ate the gold flowers off the meadow.

Then up and up; the twilit heavens expanded in the Cévennes valley, cracking the mountains apart, and there was a fearsome loneliness brooding on the flat tops. We crunched chestnut burrs on the road and aromatic smoke wound out of the mountain cottages. The Inn looked bad, the floors were covered with sawdust, but they gave us the best pheasant we ever ate and the best sausage, and the feather-beds were wonderful.

In Vichy, the leaves had covered the square about the wooden bandstand. Health advice was printed on the doors at the Hôtel du Parc and on the menu, but the salon was filled with people drinking champagne. We loved the massive trees in Vichy and the way the friendly town nestles in a hollow.

By the time we got to Tours, we had begun to feel like Cardinal Balue in his cage in the little Renault. The Hôtel de l'Univers was equally stuffy but after dinner we found a café crowded with people playing checkers and singing choruses and we felt we could go on to Paris after all.

Our cheap hotel in Paris had been turned into a girls' school—we went to a nameless one in the Rue du Bac, where potted palms withered in the exhausted air. Through the thin partitions we witnessed the private lives and natural functions of our neighbors. We walked at night past the moulded columns of the Odéon and identified the gangrenous statue behind the Luxembourg fence as Catherine de Medici.

It was a trying winter and to forget bad times we went to Algiers. The Hôtel de l'Oasis was laced together by Moorish grills; and the bar was an outpost of civilization with people accentuating their eccentricities. Beggars in white sheets were propped against the walls, and the dash of colonial uniforms gave the cafés a desperate swashbuckling air. Berbers have plaintive trusting eyes but it is really Fate they trust.

In Bou Saada, the scent of amber was swept along the streets by wide desert cloaks. We watched the moon stumble over the sand hillocks in a dead white glow and believed the guide as he told us of a priest he knew who could wreck railroad trains by wishing. The Ouled Naïls were very brown and clean-cut girls, impersonal as they turned themselves into fitting instruments for sex by the ritual of their dance, jangling their gold to the tune of savage fidelities hid in the distant hills.

The world crumbled to pieces in Biskra; the streets crept

through the town like streams of hot white lava. Arabs sold nougat and cakes of poisonous pink under the flare of open gas jets. Since *The Garden of Allah* and *The Sheik* the town has been filled with frustrate women. In the steep cobbled alleys we flinched at the brightness of mutton carcases swung from the butchers' booths.

We stopped in El Kantara at a rambling inn whiskered with wistaria. Purple dusk steamed up from the depths of a gorge and we walked to a painter's house, where, in the remoteness of those mountains, he worked at imitations of Meissonier.

Then Switzerland and another life. Spring bloomed in the gardens of the Grand Hôtel in Glion, and a panorama world scintillated in the mountain air. The sun steamed delicate blossoms loose from the rocks while far below glinted the lake of Geneva.

Beyond the balustrade of the Lausanne Palace, sailboats plume themselves in the breeze like birds. Willow trees weave lacy patterns on the gravel terrace. The people are chic fugitives from life and death, rattling their teacups in querulous emotion on the deep protective balcony. They spell the names of hotels and cities with flowerbeds and laburnum in Switzerland and even the street lights wore crowns of verbena.

1931

Leisurely men played checkers in the restaurant of the Hôtel de la Paix in Lausanne. The depression had become frank in the American papers so we wanted to get back home.

But we went to Annecy for two weeks in summer, and said at the end that we'd never go there again because those weeks had been perfect and no other time could match them. First we lived at the Beau-Rivage, a rambler rose-covered hotel, with a diving platform wedged beneath our window between the sky and the lake, but there were enormous flies on the raft so we moved across the lake to Menthon. The water was greener there and the shadows long and cool and the scraggly gardens staggered up the shelved precipice to the Hôtel Palace. We played tennis on the baked clay courts and fished tentatively from a low brick wall. The heat of summer seethed in the resin of the white pine bath-houses. We walked at night towards a café blooming with Japanese lanterns, white shoes gleaming like radium in the damp darkness. It was like the good gone times when we still believed in summer hotels and the philosophies of popular songs. Another night we danced a Wiener waltz, and just simply swep' around.

At the Caux Palace, a thousand yards in the air, we tea-danced on the uneven boards of a pavilion and sopped our toast in mountain honey.

When we passed through Munich the Regina-Palast was empty; they gave us a suite where the princes stayed in the days when royalty travelled. The young Germans stalking the ill-lit streets wore a sinister air—the talk that underscored the beer-garden waltzes was of war and hard times. Thornton Wilder took us to a famous restaurant where the beer deserved the silver mugs it was served in. We went to see the cherished witnesses to a lost cause; our voices echoed through the planetarium and we lost our orientation in the deep blue cosmic presentation of how things are.

In Vienna, the Bristol was the best hotel and they were glad to have us because it, too, was empty. Our windows looked out on the mouldy baroque of the Opera over the tops of sorrowing elms. We dined at the widow Sacher's— over the oak panelling hung a print of Franz Joseph going some happier place many years ago in a coach; one of the Rothschilds dined behind a leather screen. The city was poor already, or still, and the faces about us were harassed and defensive.

We stayed a few days at the Vevey Palace on Lake Geneva. The trees in the hotel gardens were the tallest we had ever seen and gigantic lonely birds fluttered over the surface of the lake. Farther along there was a gay little beach with a modern bar where we sat on the sands and discussed stomachs.

We motored back to Paris: that is, we sat nervously in

our six horse-power Renault. At the famous Hôtel de la Cloche in Dijon we had a nice room with a very complicated mechanical inferno of a bath, which the valet proudly referred to as American plumbing.

In Paris for the last time, we installed ourselves amidst the faded grandeurs of the Hôtel Majestic. We went to the Exposition and yielded up our imaginations to gold-lit facsimiles of Bali. Lonely flooded rice fields of lonely far-off islands told us an immutable story of work and death. The juxtaposition of so many replicas of so many civilizations was confusing, and depressing.

Back in America we stayed at the New Yorker because the advertisements said it was cheap. Everywhere quietude was sacrificed to haste and, momentarily, it seemed an impossible world, even though lustrous from the roof in the blue dusk.

In Alabama, the streets were sleepy and remote and a calliope on parade gasped out the tunes of our youth. There was sickness in the family and the house was full of nurses so we stayed at the big new elaborate Jefferson Davis. The old houses near the business section were falling to pieces at last. New bungalows lined the cedar drives on the outskirts; four-o'clocks bloomed beneath the old iron deer and arborvitae boxed the prim brick walks while vigorous weeds uprooted the pavements. Nothing had happened there since the Civil War. Everybody had forgotten why the hotel had been erected, and the clerk gave us three rooms and four baths for nine dollars a day. We used one as a sitting-room so the bell-boys would have some place to sleep when we rang for them.

1932

At the biggest hotel in Biloxi we read *Genesis* and watched the sea pave the deserted shore with a mosaic of black twigs.

We went to Florida. The bleak marshes were punctuated by biblical admonitions to a better life; abandoned fishing boats disintegrated in the sun. The Don Ce-sar Hotel in Pass-A-Grille stretched lazily over the stubbed wilderness, surrendering its shape to the blinding brightness of the gulf. Opalescent shells cupped the twilight on the beach and a stray dog's footprints in the wet sand staked out his claim to a free path round the ocean. We walked at night and discussed the Pythagorean theory of numbers, and we fished by day. We were sorry for the deep-sea bass and the amberjacks—they seemed such easy game and no sport at all. Reading the *Seven Against Thebes*, we browned on a lonely beach. The hotel was almost empty and there were so many waiters waiting to be off that we could hardly eat our meals.

1933

The room in the Algonquin was high up amidst the gilded domes of New York. Bells chimed hours that had yet to penetrate the shadowy streets of the canyon. It was too hot in the room, but the carpets were soft and the room was isolated by dark corridors outside the door and bright façades outside the window. We spent much time getting ready for theatres. We saw Georgia O'Keefe's pictures and it was a deep emotional experience to abandon oneself to that majestic aspiration so adequately fitted into eloquent abstract forms.

For years we had wanted to go to Bermuda. We went. The Elbow Beach Hotel was full of honeymooners, who scintillated so persistently in each other's eyes that we cynically moved. The Hotel St. George was nice. Bougainvillea cascaded down the tree trunks and long stairs passed by deep mysteries taking place behind native windows. Cats slept along the balustrade and lovely children grew. We rode bicycles along the wind-swept causeways and stared in a dreamy daze at such phenomena as roosters scratching amidst the sweet alyssum. We drank sherry on a veranda above the bony backs of horses tethered in the public square. We had travelled a lot, we thought. Maybe this would be the last trip for a long while. We thought Bermuda was a nice place to be the last one of so many years of travelling.

AUCTION – MODEL 1934

By F. Scott and Zelda Fitzgerald

July, 1934

OF course we asked our friends what they thought and they said it was a perfect house—though not even the California claret could induce them to admit that it was the sort of place they would have lived in. The idea was to stay there until the sheets were shredded away and the bed springs looked like the insides of broken watches: then we wouldn't have to pack any more—the usages of time would have set us free. We could travel again in a suit-case, and not be harassed by bills from a storage warehouse. So we gathered our things from here and there; all that remained from fifteen years of buying, except some faded beach umbrellas we had left at the American Express five years ago in Cannes. It was to have been very edifying to have only the things we were fond of around us again and maybe we'd like the new place so well that we'd never move any more but just sit behind the wistaria and watch the rhododendron disintegrate beneath the heat of June, July and August, and the fanfare of the dogwood over the hills.

Then we opened the packing cases.

Lot 1. The first case is oblong and enormous and about the right shape to have contained enormous family portraits —it holds a mirror bought a long time ago for practising ballet-dancing at home. It once decorated the wall of a bordello. Any bids? No! Take it to that little room in the attic.

Lot 2. A smaller crate of the same shape containing fifty

photographs of ourselves and drawings of the same by various artists and pictures of the houses we lived in and of our aunts and uncles and of where they were born and died. In some of the pictures we are golfing and swimming and posing with other people's animals, or tilting borrowed surf-boards against the spray of younger summers. There are also many impressive photographs of old and very dear friends whose names we have forgotten. These faces were very precious to us at the time, and now those times are very precious, though it is hard to imagine how we came to ask from life such an exaggerated head of Mae Murray. It must have been that summer day in Paris when we watched the children bowl the summer sun along the paths of the Jardin des Plantes—we might, late that afternoon, have begged for the photograph. And one of Pascin, whom we met over a pebble-rocked table watching the elegant ladies circle the Rondpoint attending upon the natural functions of Pekinese—Pascin already enveloped in tragedy and pursued by a doom so powerful that he could well afford the nonchalance in which lay his sombre charm. And one of Pearl White that she gave us in a spring when she was buying the Paris nights in clusters. Any bidders? No? The little room in the attic, Essie.

Lot 3. A pornographic figurine bought with great difficulty in Florence twelve years ago. *"Une statue sale*—no, we don't mean *salle* that way—we mean *sale."* Slightly damaged—any bidders? All right take this, too, Essie, while you're going up. It seems a shame after all the lascivious gesticulation it took to obtain it.

Lot 4. Two bronze busts of Shakespeare and Galileo with which the family had hoped to anchor us to permanent abodes. Slightly used in the fireplace but ineffectual as andirons. Any bids?—all right, Essie.

Lot 5. A barrel. Contents cost us something like a thousand dollars during the boom. Chipped pottery tea-set that was worth the trip to Venice—it had seemed such a pity not to buy something from that cluttered bazaar fanned by the plumy shade of the white plane trees. We didn't know what we wanted to drink; the white haunted countryside was hot; the hillsides smelled of jasmine and the hot backs of men digging the roads.

Two glass automobiles for salt and pepper stolen from the café in Saint-Paul (Alpes-Maritimes). Nobody was looking because Isadora Duncan was giving one of her last parties at the next table. She had got too old and fat to care whether people accepted her theories of life and art, and she gallantly toasted the world's obliviousness in lukewarm champagne. There were village dogs baying at a premature white exhausted August moon and there were long dark shadows folded accordion-like along the steps of the steep streets of Saint-Paul. We autographed the guest-book.

Fifty-two ash trays—all very simple because Hergesheimer warned us against pretentiousness in furnishing a house without money. A set of cocktail glasses with the roosters now washed off the sides. Carl Van Vechten brought us a shaker to go with them but nobody had opened the letter announcing his arrival—nobody knew where the mail was kept, there were so many rooms, twenty or twenty-one. Two curious vases we won in the amusement park. The fortune teller came back with us and drank too much and repeated a stanza of Vachel Lindsay to exorcise the mansion ghost. China, China, China, set of four, set of five, set of nine, set of thirteen. Any bids? Thank God! The kitchen, Essie.

Lot 5. Plaid Shawl donated by Carmel Myers. Slightly fatigued after long use as a table cover and packing wrapper for china pigs and dogs which held pennies turned out of the pockets of last year's coats. Once a beautiful Viennese affair, with memories of Carmel in Rome filming *Ben Hur* in bigger and grander papier-maché arenas than the real ones. One gong. No memory of what it was for or why we had bought it. Stick missing. Looks, however, like a Chinese pagoda and gives an impression of wide travel. Bits of brass: wobbly colonial candle-sticks with stems encircling little bells which ring when walked with *à la* Beatrix Esmond or Lady Macbeth. Two phallic symbols bought from an archeologist. One German helmet found in the trenches of Verdun. One chess set. We played it every evening before we began to quarrel about our respective mental capacities. Two china priests from Vevey. The figures are strung on springs and wag their heads lasciviously over bottles of wine and hampers of food. A whole lot of broken glass and china good for the tops of walls. All right, Essie. Go on—there's plenty of space up there, if you know how to use it.

Lot 6. Contents of an old army trunk. Nobody has ever explained where moth-balls go; moths thrive best on irreplaceable things such as old army uniforms. Then there was a pair of white flannels bought with the first money ever earned by writing—thirty dollars from Mencken's and Nathan's old *Smart Set*. The moths had also dined upon a blue feather fan paid for out of a first *Saturday Evening Post* story; it was an engagement present—that together with a southern girl's first corsage of orchids. The remains of the fan are not for sale. All right, Essie.

Lot 7. The daughter's first rubber doll, the back and front stuck together and too gummy to save for the grandchildren. Teething beads in good condition—never used. Any bids? *Pu*lease!

Lot 8. Ski pants. Guaranteed to remind the bankrupt traveller of blue snow-padded slopes, high in the Juras in Switzerland, with gargantuan discs of cheeses served by cow-herders in flowered velvet vests; of bells and the smell of coffee drifting out over the snow mountain clubs, of yodelling and blowing melancholic flats through long horn trumpets; of melting snow to drink from the roofs of isolated cabins—all these things lie deep in the pockets of these pants, together with inconsequential trains in angry red winter dawns, cluttered with skis in stacks and the discarded wrappings of Peter's chocolate. Any bids? Hey, Essie!

Lot 9. Cotton bathing trunks, full of the bright heat of the Mediterranean, bought in the sailors' quarter of Cannes. They make swell dust cloths but don't belong on an American beach. Used at present to wrap up the arsenal: a twenty-two that goes off if you stare at it hard enough, a cavalry carbine carved with the name "Seven Pines" and an uncle's name and some suspicious looking notches, an old thirty-two, and a police thirty-eight. On the whole we keep the arsenal and would like to pick up an old sub-machine gun cheap. Whisk 'em away.

Lot 10. Another barrel full of tops of things: sugar-bowls, vanished mustard pots, lovely colored lids for jars that must have been quite nice. Look, for instance, at this rose-encrusted top to the bowl for rose-leaves: a bowl for rose-leaves. There is the top of the delicate Tiffany urn from a chocolate set that was our first wedding present. The set remained on a dressing table at the Biltmore all during our honeymoon beside a fading Easter lily. On rainy afternoons we leaned into the brick area and listened to the music from *The Night Boat* swinging its plaints from one walled surface of the hotel to another. Any bids? Surely this gentleman— all right then. Essie, the trash heap.

Lot 11. A real Patou suit. It was the first garment bought after the marriage ceremony and again the moths have unsymmetrically eaten the nap off the seat of the skirt. This makes fifteen years it has been stored in trunks because of our principle of not throwing away things that have never been used. We are glad—oh, so relieved, to find it devastated at last. There was a rippling sun along Fifth Avenue the day it was bought and it seemed very odd to be charging things to Scott Fitzgerald. The thing was to look like Justine Johnson at the time and it still seems a fine way to have looked. The shopper was two days out of Alabama. From the shop we went to tea in the Plaza grill. Constance Bennett was still a flapper and had invented a new way of dancing with a pendulous head. We went to *Enter Madame* and the actors were cross because our tickets were in the front row and we laughed appreciatively at the wrong places and uproariously at the jokes we made up as the show went along. We went to the midnight roof and stood up to see Ziegfeld's taffeta pyramids. We thought the man was real who straggled into the show dressed like a student and very convincingly got himself thrown out. Anyhow—thank you, moths—Can you use this, Essie?

A white sweater next that really can't be disposed of, though the front is clotted with darns and the back all pulled apart to make the worn places elsewhere meet; it was used while writing three books when the house grew cold at night after the heat went off. Sixty-five stories were forced through its sagging meshes. It was a job of years to wash it—that and the socks from England of Gargantuan wool. We have often thought seriously of having other feet knit into these; we can't see them go. We remember that late afternoon in Bond Street where we bought them from stores looking like Dickens' forehead, and how we had had to hurry because we had taken so much time seeking the Half Moon Crescent that appeared in Mackenzie's *Sinister Street*. These socks made us late for a dinner with Galsworthy while the twilight turned purple and Turneresque over the Thames. These socks have wrinkled above the parquets of Lady Randolph Churchill's London house and waltzed in a sad Savoy Hotel to the envy of women in black at twenty-one, because a lot of men had forgot to come home. Of course, such wool is fine for polishing mirrors—but there are other considerations. No sale. Wake up, Essie!

Lot 12. Twelve scrap books, telling us what wonderful or horrible or mediocre people we were. Try and get them. What's that? No, not for twice that. Four dollars you say? Sold!

Lot 13. Here is a jug, a beautiful black milk jug—the dairyman left it years ago when it was cheaper to make your own ice-cream. Anyway, it once looked lovely filled with rambler roses, and now it looks nice with calla lilies. You can hardly tell it wasn't made for such a purpose in the first place. We have mixed punch inside it for so many parties before we inherited the cut-glass bowls. We fermented our first California grape-juice in something exactly like it. These ten-cent store plates we bought for the kitchen did very well for the table the summer we tried eating outdoors. That sort of thing never works in America, but remembering how happy we were over how it ought to have been, we like these dishes. No sale.

Lot 14. Remains of a service set shot to pieces by Charlie MacArthur in target practice on the lawn at Ellerslie, the day we invented croquet-polo on plow horses borrowed of a farmer. Also this Lalique turtle which once nested in a shop across from Vantine's, when there was such a place. Nobody bought him but he remained as expensive as ever until finally he lost one foot in the crush of modern window display, and *we* bought him and a joiner put him together again. It is the turtle who held the white violets the first night Ernest Hemingway came to our house, it is the turtle who hid the burned-out bulbs from so many Christmas trees over the holidays. He is out of style and no longer holds water but is good for old keys that don't fit anything. Any bids? The attic, Essie. Lalique in the attic!

Lot 15. A silver cake basket and a table that belonged to Francis Scott Key and a bed we had copied from a design in *House and Garden*—but on the whole we have decided to keep all these things forever, and put them up in the attic. The house is full and comfortable. We have five phonographs, including the pocket one, and no radio, eleven beds and no bureau. We shall keep it all—the tangible remnant of the four hundred thousand we made from hard words and spent with easy ones these fifteen years. And the collection, after all, is just about as valuable now as the Polish and Peruvian bonds of our thriftier friends.

SLEEPING AND WAKING

December, 1934

W HEN some years ago I read a piece by Ernest Hemingway called *Now I Lay Me,* I thought there was nothing
further to be said about insomnia. I see now that that was
because I had never had much; it appears that every man's
insomnia is as different from his neighbor's as are their
daytime hopes and aspirations.

Now if insomnia is going to be one of your naturals, it
begins to appear in the late thirties. Those seven precious
hours of sleep suddenly break in two. There is, if one is
lucky, the "first sweet sleep of night" and the last deep sleep
of morning, but between the two appears a sinister, ever
widening interval. This is the time of which it is written in
the Psalms: *Scuto circumdabit te veritas eius: non timebis a
timore nocturno, a sagitta volante in die, a negotio perambu-
lante in tenebris.*

With a man I knew the trouble commenced with a mouse;
in my case I like to trace it to a single mosquito.

My friend was in course of opening up his country house
unassisted, and after a fatiguing day discovered that the
only practical bed was a child's affair—long enough but
scarcely wider than a crib. Into this he flopped and was
presently deeply engrossed in rest *but* with one arm irre-
pressibly extending over the side of the crib. Hours later he
was awakened by what seemed to be a pin-prick in his

finger. He shifted his arm sleepily and dozed off again—to be again awakened by the same feeling.

This time he flipped on the bed-light—and there attached to the bleeding end of his finger was a small and avid mouse. My friend, to use his own words, "uttered an exclamation," but probably he gave a wild scream.

The mouse let go. It had been about the business of devouring the man as thoroughly as if his sleep were permanent. From then on it threatened to be not even temporary. The victim sat shivering, and very, very tired. He considered how he would have a cage made to fit over the bed and sleep under it the rest of his life. But it was too late to have the cage made that night and finally he dozed, to wake in intermittent horrors from dreams of being a Pied Piper whose rats turned about and pursued him.

He has never since been able to sleep without a dog or cat in the room.

My own experience with night pests was at a time of utter exhaustion—too much work undertaken, interlocking circumstances that made the work twice as arduous, illness within and around—the old story of troubles never coming singly. And ah, how I had planned that sleep that was to crown the end of the struggle—how I had looked forward to the relaxation into a bed soft as a cloud and permanent as a grave. An invitation to dine *à deux* with Greta Garbo would have left me indifferent.

But had there been such an invitation I would have done well to accept it, for instead I dined alone, or rather was dined upon by one solitary mosquito.

It is astonishing how much worse one mosquito can be than a swarm. A swarm can be prepared against, but *one* mosquito takes on a personality—a hatefulness, a sinister quality of the struggle to the death. This personality appeared all by himself in September on the twentieth floor of a New York hotel, as out of place as an armadillo. He was the result of New Jersey's decreased appropriation for swamp drainage, which had sent him and other younger sons into neighboring states for food.

The night was warm—but after the first encounter, the

vague slappings of the air, the futile searches, the punishment of my own ears a split second too late, I followed the ancient formula and drew the sheet over my head.

And so there continued the old story, the bitings through the sheet, the sniping of exposed sections of hand holding the sheet in place, the pulling up of the blanket with ensuing suffocation—followed by the psychological change of attitude, increasing wakefulness, wild impotent anger—finally a second hunt.

This inaugurated the maniacal phase—the crawl under the bed with the standing lamp for torch, the tour of the room with final detection of the insect's retreat on the ceiling and attack with knotted towels, the wounding of oneself —my God!

—After that there was a short convalescence that my opponent seemed aware of, for he perched insolently beside my head—but I missed again.

At last, after another half hour that whipped the nerves into a frantic state of alertness came the Pyrrhic victory, and the small mangled spot of blood, *my* blood, on the head-board of the bed.

As I said, I think of that night, two years ago, as the beginning of my sleeplessness—because it gave me the sense of how sleep can be spoiled by one infinitesimal incalculable element. It made me, in the now archaic phraseology, "sleep-conscious." I worried whether or not it was going to be allowed me. I was drinking, intermittently but generously, and on the nights when I took no liquor the problem of whether or not sleep was specified began to haunt me long before bedtime.

A typical night (and I wish I could say such nights were all in the past) comes after a particularly sedentary work-and-cigarette day. It ends, say without any relaxing interval, at the time for going to bed. All is prepared, the books, the glass of water, the extra pajamas lest I awake in rivulets of sweat, the luminol pills in the little round tube, the note book and pencil in case of a night thought worth recording. (Few have been—they generally seem thin in the morning, which does not diminish their force and urgency at night.)

I turn in, perhaps with a night-cap—I am doing some comparatively scholarly reading for a coincident work so I choose a lighter volume on the subject and read till drowsy on a last cigarette. At the yawning point I snap the book on a marker, the cigarette at the hearth, the button on the lamp. I turn first on the left side, for that, so I've heard, slows the heart, and then—coma.

So far so good. From midnight until two-thirty peace in the room. Then suddenly I am awake, harassed by one of the ills or functions of the body, a too vivid dream, a change in the weather for warm or cold.

The adjustment is made quickly, with the vain hope that the continuity of sleep can be preserved, but no—so with a sigh I flip on the light, take a minute pill of luminol and reopen my book. The *real* night, the darkest hour, has begun. I am too tired to read unless I get myself a drink and hence feel bad next day—so I get up and walk. I walk from my bedroom through the hall to my study, and then back again, and if it's summer out to my back porch. There is a mist over Baltimore; I cannot count a single steeple. Once more to the study, where my eye is caught by a pile of unfinished business: letters, proofs, notes, etc. I start toward it, but No! this would be fatal. Now the luminol is having some slight effect, so I try bed again, this time half circling the pillow on edge about my neck.

"Once upon a time" (I tell myself) "they needed a quarterback at Princeton, and they had nobody and were in despair. The head coach noticed me kicking and passing on the side of the field, and he cried: 'Who is *that* man—why haven't we noticed *him* before?' The under coach answered, 'He hasn't been out,' and the response was: 'Bring him to me.'

". . . we go to the day of the Yale game. I weigh only one hundred and thirty-five, so they save me until the third quarter, with the score—"

—But it's no use—I have used that dream of a defeated dream to induce sleep for almost twenty years, but it has worn thin at last. I can no longer count on it—though even now on easier nights it has a certain lull . . .

The war dream then: the Japanese are everywhere victorious—my division is cut to rags and stands on the defensive in a part of Minnesota where I know every bit of the ground. The headquarters staff and the regimental battalion commanders who were in conference with them at the time have been killed by one shell. The command devolved upon Captain Fitzgerald. With superb presence . . .

—but enough; this also is worn thin with years of usage. The character who bears my name has become blurred. In the dead of the night I am only one of the dark millions riding forward in black buses toward the unknown.

Back again now to the rear porch, and conditioned by intense fatigue of mind and perverse alertness of the nervous system—like a broken-stringed bow upon a throbbing fiddle —I see the real horror develop over the roof-tops, and in the strident horns of night-owl taxis and the shrill monody of revelers' arrival over the way. Horror and waste—

—Waste and horror—what I might have been and done that is lost, spent, gone, dissipated, unrecapturable. I could have acted thus, refrained from this, been bold where I was timid, cautious where I was rash.

I need not have hurt her like that.

Nor said this to him.

Nor broken myself trying to break what was unbreakable.

The horror has come now like a storm—what if this night prefigured the night after death—what if all thereafter was an eternal quivering on the edge of an abyss, with everything base and vicious in oneself urging one forward and the baseness and viciousness of the world just ahead. No choice, no road, no hope—only the endless repetition of the sordid and the semi-tragic. Or to stand forever, perhaps, on the threshold of life unable to pass it and return to it. I am a ghost now as the clock strikes four.

On the side of the bed I put my head in my hands. Then silence, silence—and suddenly—or so it seems in retrospect —suddenly I am asleep.

Sleep—real sleep, the dear, the cherished one, the lullaby. So deep and warm the bed and the pillow enfolding me, letting me sink into peace, nothingness—my dreams now, after the catharsis of the dark hours, are of young and lovely people doing young, lovely things, the girls I knew once, with big brown eyes, real yellow hair.

In the fall of '16 in the cool of the afternoon
I met Caroline under a white moon
There was an orchestra—Bingo-Bango
Playing for us to dance the tango
And the people all clapped as we arose
For her sweet face and my new clothes—

Life *was* like that, after all; my spirit soars in the moment of its oblivion; then down, down deep into the pillow . . .

". . . Yes, Essie, yes.—Oh, My God, all right, I'll take the call myself."

Irresistible, iridescent—here is Aurora—here is another day.

THE CRACK-UP

February, 1936

O<small>F</small> course all life is a process of breaking down, but the blows that do the dramatic side of the work—the big sudden blows that come, or seem to come, from outside—the ones you remember and blame things on and, in moments of weakness, tell your friends about, don't show their effect all at once. There is another sort of blow that comes from within—that you don't feel until it's too late to do anything about it, until you realize with finality that in some regard you will never be as good a man again. The first sort of breakage seems to happen quick—the second kind happens almost without your knowing it but is realized suddenly indeed.

Before I go on with this short history, let me make a general observation—the test of a first-rate intelligence is the ability to hold two opposed ideas in the mind at the same time, and still retain the ability to function. One should, for example, be able to see that things are hopeless and yet be determined to make them otherwise. This philosophy fitted on to my early adult life, when I saw the improbable, the implausible, often the "impossible," come true. Life was something you dominated if you were any good. Life yielded easily to intelligence and effort, or to what proportion could be mustered of both. It seemed a romantic business to be a successful literary man—you were not ever going to be as famous as a movie star but what note you had was probably

[69]

longer-lived—you were never going to have the power of a man of strong political or religious convictions but you were certainly more independent. Of course within the practice of your trade you were forever unsatisfied—but I, for one, would not have chosen any other.

As the twenties passed, with my own twenties marching a little ahead of them, my two juvenile regrets—at not being big enough (or good enough) to play football in college, and at not getting overseas during the war—resolved themselves into childish waking dreams of imaginary heroism that were good enough to go to sleep on in restless nights. The big problems of life seemed to solve themselves, and if the business of fixing them was difficult, it made one too tired to think of more general problems.

Life, ten years ago, was largely a personal matter. I must hold in balance the sense of the futility of effort and the sense of the necessity to struggle; the conviction of the inevitability of failure and still the determination to "succeed"—and, more than these, the contradiction between the dead hand of the past and the high intentions of the future. If I could do this through the common ills—domestic, professional and personal—then the ego would continue as an arrow shot from nothingness to nothingness with such force that only gravity would bring it to earth at last.

For seventeen years, with a year of deliberate loafing and resting out in the center—things went on like that, with a new chore only a nice prospect for the next day. I was living hard, too, but: "Up to forty-nine it'll be all right," I said. "I can count on that. For a man who's lived as I have, that's all you could ask."

—And then, ten years this side of forty-nine, I suddenly realized that I had prematurely cracked.

II

Now a man can crack in many ways—can crack in the head—in which case the power of decision is taken from you by others! or in the body, when one can but submit to the white hospital world; or in the nerves. William Seabrook in an unsympathetic book tells, with some pride and a movie ending, of how he became a public charge. What led to his alcoholism or was bound up with it, was a collapse of his nervous system. Though the present writer was not so entangled—having at the time not tasted so much as a glass of beer for six months—it was his nervous reflexes that were giving way—too much anger and too many tears.

Moreover, to go back to my thesis that life has a varying offensive, the realization of having cracked was not simultaneous with a blow, but with a reprieve.

Not long before, I had sat in the office of a great doctor and listened to a grave sentence. With what, in retrospect, seems some equanimity, I had gone on about my affairs in the city where I was then living, not caring much, not thinking how much had been left undone, or what would become of this and that responsibility, like people do in books; I was well insured and anyhow I had been only a mediocre caretaker of most of the things left in my hands, even of my talent.

But I had a strong sudden instinct that I must be alone. I didn't want to see any people at all. I had seen so many people all my life—I was an average mixer, but more than average in a tendency to identify myself, my ideas, my destiny, with those of all classes that I came in contact with. I was always saving or being saved—in a single morning I would go through the emotions ascribable to Wellington at Waterloo. I lived in a world of inscrutable hostiles and inalienable friends and supporters.

But now I wanted to be absolutely alone and so arranged a certain insulation from ordinary cares.

It was not an unhappy time. I went away and there were fewer people. I found I was good-and-tired. I could lie around and was glad to, sleeping or dozing sometimes twenty hours a day and in the intervals trying resolutely not to think—instead I made lists—made lists and tore them up, hundreds of lists: of cavalry leaders and football players and cities, and popular tunes and pitchers, and happy times, and hobbies and houses lived in and how many suits since I left the army and how many pairs of shoes (I didn't count the suit I bought in Sorrento that shrunk, nor the pumps and dress shirt and collar that I carried around for years and never wore, because the pumps got damp and grainy and the shirt and collar got yellow and starch-rotted). And lists of women I'd liked, and of the times I had let myself be snubbed by people who had not been my betters in character or ability.

—And then suddenly, surprisingly, I got better.

—And cracked like an old plate as soon as I heard the news.

That is the real end of this story. What was to be done about it will have to rest in what used to be called the "womb of time." Suffice it to say that after about an hour of solitary pillow-hugging, I began to realize that for two years my life had been a drawing on resources that I did not possess, that I had been mortgaging myself physically and spiritually up to the hilt. What was the small gift of life given back in comparison to that?—when there had once been a pride of direction and a confidence in enduring independence.

I realized that in those two years, in order to preserve something—an inner hush maybe, maybe not—I had weaned myself from all the things I used to love—that every act of life from the morning tooth-brush to the friend at dinner had become an effort. I saw that for a long time I had not liked people and things, but only followed the rickety old pretense of liking. I saw that even my love for those closest to me was become only an attempt to love, that my casual relations—with an editor, a tobacco seller, the child of a friend, were only what I remembered I *should* do, from other days. All in the same month I became bitter about such things as the sound of the radio, the advertisements in the magazines, the screech of tracks, the dead silence of the country—contemptuous at human softness, immediately (if secretively) quarrelsome toward hardness —hating the night when I couldn't sleep and hating the day because it went toward night. I slept on the heart side now because I knew that the sooner I could tire that out, even a little, the sooner would come that blessed hour of nightmare which, like a catharsis, would enable me to better meet the new day.

There were certain spots, certain faces I could look at. Like most Middle Westerners, I have never had any but the vaguest race prejudices—I always had a secret yen for the lovely Scandinavian blondes who sat on porches in St. Paul but hadn't emerged enough economically to be part of what was then society. They were too nice to be "chickens" and too quickly off the farmlands to seize a place in the sun, but I remember going round blocks to catch a single glimpse of shining hair—the bright shock of a girl I'd never know. This is urban, unpopular talk. It strays afield from the fact that in these latter days I couldn't stand the sight of Celts, English, Politicians, Strangers, Virginians, Negroes (light or dark), Hunting People, or retail clerks, and middlemen in general, all writers (I avoided writers very carefully because they can perpetuate trouble as no one else can)—and all the classes as classes and most of them as members of their class . . .

Trying to cling to something, I liked doctors and girl children up to the age of about thirteen and well-brought-up boy children from about eight years old on. I could have peace and happiness with these few categories of people. I forgot to add that I liked old men—men over seventy, sometimes over sixty if their faces looked seasoned. I liked Katharine Hepburn's face on the screen, no matter what was said about her pretentiousness, and Miriam Hopkins' face, and old friends if I only saw them once a year and could remember their ghosts.

All rather inhuman and undernourished, isn't it? Well, that, children, is the true sign of cracking up.

It is not a pretty picture. Inevitably it was carted here and there within its frame and exposed to various critics. One of them can only be described as a person whose life makes other people's lives seem like death—even this time when she was cast in the usually unappealing role of Job's comforter. In spite of the fact that this story is over, let me append our conversation as a sort of postscript:

"Instead of being so sorry for yourself, listen—" she said.

(She always says "Listen," because she thinks while she talks—*really* thinks.) So she said: "Listen. Suppose this wasn't a crack in you—suppose it was a crack in the Grand Canyon."

"The crack's in me," I said heroically.

"Listen! The world only exists in your eyes—your conception of it. You can make it as big or as small as you want to. And you're trying to be a little puny individual. By God, if I ever cracked, I'd try to make the world crack with me. Listen! The world only exists through your apprehension of it, and so it's much better to say that it's not you that's cracked—it's the Grand Canyon."

"Baby et up all her Spinoza?"

"I don't know anything about Spinoza. I know—" She spoke, then, of old woes of her own, that seemed, in the telling, to have been more dolorous than mine, and how she had met them, over-ridden them, beaten them.

I felt a certain reaction to what she said, but I am a slow-thinking man, and it occurred to me simultaneously that of all natural forces, vitality is the incommunicable one. In days when juice came into one as an article without duty, one tried to distribute it—but always without success; to further mix metaphors, vitality never "takes." You have it or you haven't it, like health or brown eyes or honor or a baritone voice. I might have asked some of it from her, neatly wrapped and ready for home cooking and digestion, but I could never have got it—not if I'd waited around for a thousand hours with the tin cup of self-pity. I could walk from her door, holding myself very carefully like cracked crockery, and go away into the world of bitterness, where I was making a home with such materials as are found there—and quote to myself after I left her door:

"Ye are the salt of the earth. But if the salt hath lost its savour, wherewith shall it be salted?"

Matthew 5-13.

PASTING IT TOGETHER

March, 1936

In a previous article this writer told about his realization that what he had before him was not the dish that he had ordered for his forties. In fact—since he and the dish were one, he described himself as a cracked plate, the kind that one wonders whether it is worth preserving. Your editor thought that the article suggested too many aspects without regarding them closely, and probably many readers felt the same way—and there are always those to whom all self-revelation is contemptible, unless it ends with a noble thanks to the gods for the Unconquerable Soul.

But I had been thanking the gods too long, and thanking them for nothing. I wanted to put a lament into my record, without even the background of the Euganean Hills to give it color. There weren't any Euganean hills that I could see.

Sometimes, though, the cracked plate has to be retained in the pantry, has to be kept in service as a household necessity. It can never again be warmed on the stove nor shuffled with the other plates in the dishpan; it will not be brought out for company, but it will do to hold crackers late at night or to go into the ice box under left-overs . . .

Hence this sequel—a cracked plate's further history.

Now the standard cure for one who is sunk is to consider those in actual destitution or physical suffering—this is an all-weather beatitude for gloom in general and fairly salutory day-time advice for everyone. But at three o'clock in the morning, a forgotten package has the same tragic importance as a death sentence, and the cure doesn't work— and in a real dark night of the soul it is always three o'clock in the morning, day after day. At that hour the tendency is to refuse to face things as long as possible by retiring into an infantile dream—but one is continually startled out of this by various contacts with the world. One meets these occasions as quickly and carelessly as possible and retires once more back into the dream, hoping that things will adjust themselves by some great material or spiritual bonanza.

But as the withdrawal persists there is less and less chance of the bonanza—one is not waiting for the fade-out of a single sorrow, but rather being an unwilling witness of an execution, the disintegration of one's own personality . . .

Unless madness or drugs or drink come into it, this phase comes to a dead-end, eventually, and is succeeded by a vacuous quiet. In this you can try to estimate what has been sheared away and what is left. Only when this quiet came to me, did I realize that I had gone through two parallel experiences.

The first time was twenty years ago, when I left Princeton in junior year with a complaint diagnosed as malaria. It transpired, through an X-ray taken a dozen years later, that it had been tuberculosis—a mild case, and after a few months of rest I went back to college. But I had lost certain offices, the chief one was the presidency of the Triangle Club, a musical comedy idea, and also I dropped back a class. To me college would never be the same. There were to be no badges of pride, no medals, after all. It seemed on one March afternoon that I had lost every single thing I wanted—and that night was the first time that I hunted down the spectre of womanhood that, for a little while, makes everything else seem unimportant.

Years later I realized that my failure as a big shot in college was all right—instead of serving on committees, I took a beating on English poetry; when I got the idea of what it was all about, I set about learning how to write. On Shaw's principle that "If you don't get what you like, you better like what you get," it was a lucky break—at the moment it was a harsh and bitter business to know that my career as a leader of men was over.

Since that day I have not been able to fire a bad servant, and I am astonished and impressed by people who can. Some old desire for personal dominance was broken and gone. Life around me was a solemn dream, and I lived on the letters I wrote to a girl in another city. A man does not recover from such jolts—he becomes a different person and, eventually, the new person finds new things to care about.

The other episode parallel to my current situation took

place after the war, when I had again over-extended my flank. It was one of those tragic loves doomed for lack of money, and one day the girl closed it out on the basis of common sense. During a long summer of despair I wrote a novel instead of letters, so it came out all right, but it came out all right for a different person. The man with the jingle of money in his pocket who married the girl a year later would always cherish an abiding distrust, an animosity, toward the leisure class—not the conviction of a revolutionist but the smouldering hatred of a peasant. In the years since then I have never been able to stop wondering where my friends' money came from, nor to stop thinking that at one time a sort of *droit de seigneur* might have been exercised to give one of them my girl.

For sixteen years I lived pretty much as this latter person, distrusting the rich, yet working for money with which to share their mobility and the grace that some of them brought into their lives. During this time I had plenty of the usual horses shot from under me—I remember some of their names—*Punctured Pride, Thwarted Expectation, Faithless, Show-off, Hard Hit, Never Again.* And after awhile I wasn't twenty-five, then not even thirty-five, and nothing was quite as good. But in all these years I don't remember a moment of discouragement. I saw honest men through moods of suicidal gloom—some of them gave up and died; others adjusted themselves and went on to a larger success than mine; but my morale never sank below the level of self-disgust when I had put on some unsightly personal show. Trouble has no necessary connection with discouragement—discouragement has a germ of its own, as different from trouble as arthritis is different from a stiff joint.

When a new sky cut off the sun last spring, I didn't at first relate it to what had happened fifteen or twenty years ago. Only gradually did a certain family resemblance come through—an over-extension of the flank, a burning of the candle at both ends; a call upon physical resources that I did not command, like a man over-drawing at his bank. In its impact this blow was more violent than the other two but it was the same in kind—a feeling that I was standing at twilight on a deserted range, with an empty rifle in my hands and the targets down. No problem set—simply a silence with only the sound of my own breathing.

In this silence there was a vast irresponsibility toward every obligation, a deflation of all my values. A passionate belief in order, a disregard of motives or consequences in favor of guess work and prophecy, a feeling that craft and industry would have a place in any world—one by one, these and other convictions were swept away. I saw that the novel, which at my maturity was the strongest and supplest medium for conveying thought and emotion from one human being to another, was becoming subordinated to a mechanical and communal art that, whether in the hands of Hollywood merchants or Russian idealists, was capable of reflecting only the tritest thought, the most obvious emotion. It was an art in which words were subordinate to images, where personality was worn down to the inevitable low gear of collaboration. As long past as 1930, I had a hunch that the talkies would make even the best selling novelist as archaic as silent pictures. People still read, if only Professor Canby's book of the month—curious children nosed at the slime of Mr. Tiffany Thayer in the drugstore libraries—but there was a rankling indignity, that to me had become almost an obsession, in seeing the power of the written word subordinated to another power, a more glittering, a grosser power . . .

I set that down as an example of what haunted me during the long night—this was something I could neither accept nor struggle against, something which tended to make my efforts obsolescent, as the chain stores have crippled the small merchant, an exterior force, unbeatable—

(I have the sense of lecturing now, looking at a watch on the desk before me and seeing how many more minutes—).

Well, when I had reached this period of silence, I was forced into a measure that no one ever adopts voluntarily: I was impelled to think. God, was it difficult! The moving about of great secret trunks. In the first exhausted halt, I wondered whether I had ever thought. After a long time I came to these conclusions, just as I write them here:

(1) That I had done very little thinking, save within the problems of my craft. For twenty years a certain man had been my intellectual conscience. That was Edmund Wilson.

(2) That another man represented my sense of the "good life," though I saw him once in a decade, and since then he might have been hung. He is in the fur business in the Northwest and wouldn't like his name set down here. But in difficult situations I had tried to think what *he* would have thought, how *he* would have acted.

(3) That a third contemporary had been an artistic conscience to me—I had not imitated his infectious style, because my own style, such as it is, was formed before he published anything, but there was an awful pull toward him when I was on a spot.

(4) That a fourth man had come to dictate my relations with other people when these relations were successful: how to do, what to say. How to make people at least momentarily happy (in opposition to Mrs. Post's theories of how to make everyone thoroughly uncomfortable with a sort of systematized vulgarity). This always confused me and made me want to go out and get drunk, but this man had seen the game, analyzed it and beaten it, and his word was good enough for me.

(5) That my political conscience had scarcely existed for ten years save as an element of irony in my stuff. When I became again concerned with the system I should function under, it was a man much younger than myself who brought it to me, with a mixture of passion and fresh air.

So there was not an "I" any more—not a basis on which I could organize my self-respect—save my limitless capacity for toil that it seemed I possessed no more. It was strange to have no self—to be like a little boy left alone in a big house, who knew that now he could do anything he wanted to do, but found that there was nothing that he wanted to do—

(The watch is past the hour and I have barely reached my thesis. I have some doubts as to whether this is of general interest, but if anyone wants more, there is plenty left, and your editor will tell me. If you've had enough, say so—but not too loud, because I have the feeling that someone, I'm not sure who, is sound asleep—someone who could have helped me to keep my shop open. It wasn't Lenin, and it wasn't God.)

HANDLE WITH CARE

April, 1936

I have spoken in these pages of how an exceptionally optimistic young man experienced a crack-up of all values, a crack-up that he scarcely knew of until long after it occurred. I told of the succeeding period of desolation and of the necessity of going on, but without benefit of Henley's familiar heroics, "my head is bloody but unbowed." For a check-up of my spiritual liabilities indicated that I had no particular head to be bowed or unbowed. Once I had had a heart but that was about all I was sure of.

This was at least a starting place out of the morass in which I floundered: "I felt—therefore I was." At one time or another there had been many people who had leaned on me, come to me in difficulties or written me from afar, believed implicitly in my advice and my attitude toward life. The dullest platitude monger or the most unscrupulous Rasputin who can influence the destinies of many people must have some individuality, so the question became one of finding why and where I had changed, where was the leak through which, unknown to myself, my enthusiasm and my vitality had been steadily and prematurely trickling away.

One harassed and despairing night I packed a brief case and went off a thousand miles to think it over. I took a dollar room in a drab little town where I knew no one and sunk all the money I had with me in a stock of potted meat, crackers and apples. But don't let me suggest that the change from a rather overstuffed world to a comparative asceticism was any Research Magnificent—I only wanted absolute quiet to think out why I had developed a sad attitude toward sadness, a melancholy attitude toward melancholy and a tragic attitude toward tragedy—*why I had become identi-fied with the objects of my horror or compassion.*

Does this seem a fine distinction? It isn't: identification such as this spells the death of accomplishment. It is something like this that keeps insane people from working. Lenin did not willingly endure the sufferings of his proletariat, nor Washington of his troops, nor Dickens of his London poor. And when Tolstoy tried some such merging of himself with the objects of his attention, it was a fake and a failure. I mention these because they are the men best known to us all.

It was dangerous mist. When Wordsworth decided that "there had passed away a glory from the earth," he felt no compulsion to pass away with it, and the Fiery Particle Keats never ceased his struggle against t. b. nor in his last moments relinquished his hope of being among the English poets.

My self-immolation was something sodden-dark. It was very distinctly not modern—yet I saw it in others, saw it in a dozen men of honor and industry since the war. (I heard you, but that's too easy—there were Marxians among these men.) I had stood by while one famous contemporary of mine played with the idea of the Big Out for half a year; I had watched when another, equally eminent, spent months in an asylum unable to endure any contact with his fellow men. And of those who had given up and passed on I could list a score.

This led me to the idea that the ones who had survived had made some sort of clean break. This is a big word and is no parallel to a jail-break when one is probably headed for a new jail or will be forced back to the old one. The famous "Escape" or "run away from it all" is an excursion in a trap even if the trap includes the south seas, which are only for those who want to paint them or sail them. A clean break is something you cannot come back from; that is irretrievable because it makes the past cease to exist. So, since I could no longer fulfill the obligations that life had set for me or that I had set for myself, why not slay the empty shell who had been posturing at it for four years? I must continue to be a writer because that was my only way of life, but I would cease any attempts to be a person—to be kind, just or generous. There were plenty of counterfeit coins around that would pass instead of these and I knew where I could get them at a nickel on the dollar. In thirty-nine years an observant eye has learned to detect where the milk is watered and the sugar is sanded, the rhinestone passed for diamond and the stucco for stone. There was to be no more giving of myself—all giving was to be outlawed henceforth under a new name, and that name was Waste.

The decision made me rather exuberant, like anything that is both real and new. As a sort of beginning there was a whole shaft of letters to be tipped into the waste basket when I went home, letters that wanted something for nothing—to read this man's manuscript, market this man's poem, speak free on the radio, indite notes of introduction, give this interview, help with the plot of this play, with this domestic situation, perform this act of thoughtfulness or charity.

The conjuror's hat was empty. To draw things out of it had long been a sort of sleight of hand, and now, to change the metaphor, I was off the dispensing end of the relief roll forever.

The heady villainous feeling continued.

I felt like the beady-eyed men I used to see on the commuting train from Great Neck fifteen years back—men who didn't care whether the world tumbled into chaos tomorrow if it spared their houses. I was one with them now, one with the smooth articles who said:

"I'm sorry but business is business." Or:

"You ought to have thought of that before you got into this trouble." Or:

"I'm not the person to see about that."

And a smile—ah, I would get me a smile. I'm still working on that smile. It is to combine the best qualities of a hotel manager, an experienced old social weasel, a headmaster on visitors' day, a colored elevator man, a pansy pulling a profile, a producer getting stuff at half its market value, a trained nurse coming on a new job, a body-vender in her first rotogravure, a hopeful extra swept near the camera, a ballet dancer with an infected toe, and of course the great beam of loving kindness common to all those from Washington to Beverly Hills who must exist by virtue of the contorted pan.

The voice too—I am working with a teacher on the voice. When I have perfected it the larynx will show no ring of conviction except the conviction of the person I am talking to. Since it will be largely called upon for the elicitation of the word "Yes," my teacher (a lawyer) and I are concentrating on that, but in extra hours. I am learning to bring into it that polite acerbity that makes people feel that far from being welcome they are not even tolerated and are under continual and scathing analysis at every moment. These times will of course not coincide with the smile. This will be reserved exclusively for those from whom I have nothing to gain, old worn-out people or young struggling people. They won't mind—what the hell, they get it most of the time anyhow.

But enough. It is not a matter of levity. If you are young and you should write asking to see me and learn how to be a sombre literary man writing pieces upon the state of emotional exhaustion that often overtakes writers in their prime —if you should be so young and so fatuous as to do this, I would not do so much as acknowledge your letter, unless you were related to someone very rich and important indeed. And if you were dying of starvation outside my window, I would go out quickly and give you the smile and the voice (if no longer the hand) and stick around till somebody raised a nickel to phone for the ambulance, that is if I thought there would be any copy in it for me.

I have now at last become a writer only. The man I had persistently tried to be became such a burden that I have "cut him loose" with as little compunction as a Negro lady cuts loose a rival on Saturday night. Let the good people function as such—let the overworked doctors die in harness, with one week's "vacation" a year that they can devote to straightening out their family affairs, and let the underworked doctors scramble for cases at one dollar a throw; let the soldiers be killed and enter immediately into the Valhalla of their profession. That is their contract with the gods. A writer need have no such ideals unless he makes them for himself, and this one has quit. The old dream of being an entire man in the Goethe-Byron-Shaw tradition, with an opulent American touch, a sort of combination of J. P. Morgan, Topham Beauclerk and St. Francis of Assisi, has been relegated to the junk heap of the shoulder pads worn for one day on the Princeton freshman football field and the overseas cap never worn overseas.

So what? This is what I think now: that the natural state of the sentient adult is a qualified unhappiness. I think also that in an adult the desire to be finer in grain than you are, "a constant striving" (as those people say who gain their bread by saying it) only adds to this unhappiness in the end —that end that comes to our youth and hope. My own happiness in the past often approached such an ecstasy that I could not share it even with the person dearest to me but had to walk it away in quiet streets and lanes with only fragments of it to distil into little lines in books—and I think that my happiness, or talent for self-delusion or what you will, was an exception. It was not the natural thing but the unnatural—unnatural as the Boom; and my recent experience parallels the wave of despair that swept the nation when the Boom was over.

I shall manage to live with the new dispensation, though it has taken some months to be certain of the fact. And just as the laughing stoicism which has enabled the American Negro to endure the intolerable conditions of his existence has cost him his sense of the truth—so in my case there is a price to pay. I do not any longer like the postman, nor the grocer, nor the editor, nor the cousin's husband, and he in turn will come to dislike me, so that life will never be very pleasant again, and the sign *Cave Canem* is hung permanently just above my door. I will try to be a correct animal though, and if you throw me a bone with enough meat on it I may even lick your hand.

EARLY SUCCESS

October, 1937

Seventeen years ago this month I quit work or, if you prefer, I retired from business. I was through—let the Street Railway Advertising Company carry along under its own power. I retired, not on my profits, but on my liabilities, which included debts, despair, and a broken engagement and crept home to St. Paul to "finish a novel."

That novel, begun in a training camp late in the war, was my ace in the hole. I had put it aside when I got a job in New York, but I was as constantly aware of it as of the shoe with cardboard in the sole, during all one desolate spring. It was like the fox and goose and the bag of beans. If I stopped working to finish the novel, I lost the girl.

So I struggled on in a business I detested and all the confidence I had garnered at Princeton and in a haughty career as the army's worst aide-de-camp melted gradually away. Lost and forgotten, I walked quickly from certain places—from the pawn shop where one left the field glasses, from prosperous friends whom one met when wearing the suit from before the war—from restaurants after tipping with the last nickel, from busy cheerful offices that were saving the jobs for their own boys from the war.

Even having a first story accepted had not proved very exciting. Dutch Mount and I sat across from each other in a car-card slogan advertising office, and the same mail brought each of us an acceptance from the same magazine—the old *Smart Set*.

"My check was thirty—how much was yours?"

"Thirty-five."

The real blight, however, was that my story had been written in college two years before, and a dozen new ones hadn't even drawn a personal letter. The implication was that I was on the down-grade at twenty-two. I spent the thirty dollars on a magenta feather fan for a girl in Alabama.

My friends who were not in love or who had waiting arrangements with "sensible" girls, braced themselves patiently for a long pull. Not I—I was in love with a whirlwind and I must spin a net big enough to catch it out of my head, a head full of trickling nickels and sliding dimes, the incessant music box of the poor. It couldn't be done like that, so when the girl threw me over I went home and finished my novel. And then, suddenly, everything changed, and this article is about that first wild wind of success and the delicious mist it brings with it. It is a short and precious time— for when the mist rises in a few weeks, or a few months, one finds that the very best is over.

It began to happen in the autumn of 1919 when I was an empty bucket, so mentally blunted with the summer's writing that I'd taken a job repairing car roofs at the Northern Pacific shops. Then the postman rang, and that day I quit work and ran along the streets, stopping automobiles to tell friends and acquaintances about it—my novel *This Side of Paradise* was accepted for publication. That week the postman rang and rang, and I paid off my terrible small debts, bought a suit, and woke up every morning with a world of ineffable toploftiness and promise.

While I waited for the novel to appear, the metamorphosis of amateur into professional began to take place—a sort of stitching together of your whole life into a pattern of work, so that the end of one job is automatically the beginning of another. I had been an amateur before; in October, when I strolled with a girl among the stones of a southern graveyard, I was a professional and my enchantment with certain things that she felt and said was already paced by an anxiety to set them down in a story—it was called *The Ice Palace* and it was published later. Similarly, during

[86]

Christmas week in St. Paul, there was a night when I had stayed home from two dances to work on a story. Three friends called up during the evening to tell me I had missed some rare doings: a well-known man-about-town had disguised himself as a camel and, with a taxi-driver as the rear half, managed to attend the wrong party. Aghast with myself for not being there, I spent the next day trying to collect the fragments of the story.

"Well, all I can say is it was funny when it happened." "No, I don't know where he got the taxi-man." "You'd have to know him well to understand how funny it was."

In despair I said:

"Well, I can't seem to find out exactly what happened but I'm going to write about it as if it was ten times funnier than anything you've said." So I wrote it, in twenty-two consecutive hours, and wrote it "funny," simply because I was so emphatically told it was funny. *The Camel's Back* was published and still crops up in the humorous anthologies.

With the end of the winter set in another pleasant pumped-dry period, and, while I took a little time off, a fresh picture of life in America began to form before my eyes. The uncertainties of 1919 were over—there seemed little doubt about what was going to happen—America was going on the greatest, gaudiest spree in history and there was going to be plenty to tell about it. The whole golden boom was in the air—its splendid generosities, its outrageous corruptions and the tortuous death struggle of the old America in prohibition. All the stories that came into my head had a touch of disaster in them—the lovely young creatures in my novels went to ruin, the diamond mountains of my short stories blew up, my millionaires were as beautiful and damned as Thomas Hardy's peasants. In life these things hadn't happened yet, but I was pretty sure living wasn't the reckless, careless business these people thought—this generation just younger than me.

For my point of vantage was the dividing line between the two generations, and there I sat—somewhat self-consciously. When my first big mail came in—hundreds and hundreds of letters on a story about a girl who bobbed her hair—it seemed rather absurd that they should come to me about it. On the other hand, for a shy man it was nice to be somebody except oneself again: to be "the Author" as one had been "the Lieutenant." Of course one wasn't really an author any more than one had been an army officer, but nobody seemed to guess behind the false face.

All in three days I got married and the presses were pounding out *This Side of Paradise* like they pound out extras in the movies.

With its publication I had reached a stage of manic depressive insanity. Rage and bliss alternated hour by hour. A lot of people thought it was a fake, and perhaps it was, and a lot of others thought it was a lie, which it was not. In a daze I gave out an interview—I told what a great writer I was and how I'd achieved the heights. Heywood Broun, who was on my trail, simply quoted it with the comment that I seemed to be a very self-satisfied young man, and for some days I was notably poor company. I invited him to lunch and in a kindly way told him that it was too bad he had let his life slide away without accomplishing anything. He had just turned thirty and it was about then that I wrote a line which certain people will not let me forget: "She was a faded but still lovely woman of twenty-seven."

In a daze I told the Scribner Company that I didn't expect my novel to sell more than twenty thousand copies and when the laughter died away I was told that a sale of five thousand was excellent for a first novel. I think it was a week after publication that it passed the twenty thousand mark, but I took myself so seriously that I didn't even think it was funny.

These weeks in the clouds ended abruptly a week later when Princeton turned on the book—not undergraduate Princeton but the black mass of faculty and alumni. There was a kind but reproachful letter from President Hibben, and a room full of classmates who suddenly turned on me with condemnation. We had been part of a rather gay party staged conspicuously in Harvey Firestone's car of robin's-egg blue, and in the course of it I got an accidental black eye trying to stop a fight. This was magnified into an orgy and in spite of a delegation of undergraduates who went to the board of Governors, I was suspended from my club for a couple of months. The *Alumni Weekly* got after my book and only Dean Gauss had a good word to say for me. The unctuousness and hypocrisy of the proceedings was exasperating and for seven years I didn't go to Princeton. Then a magazine asked me for an article about it and when I started to write it, I found I really loved the place and that the experience of one week was a small item in the total budget. But on that day in 1920 most of the joy went out of my success.

But one was now a professional—and the new world couldn't possibly be presented without bumping the old out of the way. One gradually developed a protective hardness against both praise and blame. Too often people liked your things for the wrong reasons or people liked them whose dislike would be a compliment. No decent career was ever founded on a public and one learned to go ahead without precedents and without fear. Counting the bag, I found that in 1919 I had made $800 by writing, that in 1920 I had made $18,000, stories, picture rights and book. My story price had gone from $30 to $1,000. That's a small price to what was paid later in the Boom, but what it sounded like to me couldn't be exaggerated.

The dream had been early realized and the realization carried with it a certain bonus and a certain burden. Premature success gives one an almost mystical conception of destiny as opposed to will power—at its worst the Napoleonic delusion. The man who arrives young believes that he exercises his will because his star is shining. The man who only asserts himself at thirty has a balanced idea of what will power and fate have each contributed, the one who gets there at forty is liable to put the emphasis on will alone. This comes out when the storms strike your craft.

The compensation of a very early success is a conviction that life is a romantic matter. In the best sense one stays young. When the primary objects of love and money could be taken for granted and a shaky eminence had lost its fascination, I had fair years to waste, years that I can't honestly regret, in seeking the eternal Carnival by the Sea. Once in the middle twenties I was driving along the High Corniche Road through the twilight with the whole French Riviera twinkling on the sea below. As far ahead as I could see was Monte Carlo, and though it was out of season and there were no Grand Dukes left to gamble and E. Phillips Oppenheim was a fat industrious man in my hotel, who lived in a bathrobe—the very name was so incorrigibly enchanting that I could only stop the car and like the Chinese whisper: "Ah me! Ah me!" It was not Monte Carlo I was looking at. It was back into the mind of the young man with cardboard soles who had walked the streets of New York. I was him again—for an instant I had the good fortune to share his dreams, I who had no more dreams·of my own. And there are still times when I creep up on him, surprise him on an autumn morning in New York or a spring night in Carolina when it is so quiet that you can hear a dog barking in the next county. But never again as during that all too short period when he and I were one person, when the fulfilled future and the wistful past were mingled in a single gorgeous moment—when life was literally a dream.

The Note-Books

FITZGERALD *had been from his college days a great admirer of Samuel Butler's* Note-Books, *and he undertook at some point in his later life to do for his own accumulations of material what Festing Jones had done for Butler's. He carefully sorted them out and grouped them under alphabetical headings in such a way as to impose upon them a certain coherence and general design, almost as if he were preparing a book to be read as well as a storehouse for his own convenience.*

They do make, in fact, extremely good reading. There are among them many passages on the level of brilliant and precise expression which is characteristic of Fitzgerald's best work. Certain of them were evidently intended to be used in the short stories of his later years; but, actually, he seems rarely so to have used them; and this was perhaps because they belonged to a plane of the activity of his mind and his craft so much higher than that represented by this rather inferior magazine fiction that it was difficult for him to incorporate them in it. It was only—as in The Last Tycoon—*when he was attempting something artistically more serious that he drew much upon this collection; and these note-books really ought to be read with* Tender Is the Night, The Last Tycoon *and the pieces in the first part of this volume for their record of the final phases of the milieux in which Fitzgerald lived and of his sensations, emotions and ideas in the last years before his death.*

The manuscript is here presented in a considerably abbreviated form. It has been necessary for personal reasons to suppress a certain amount of matter which would otherwise be included, and the editor has had to use his best judgment in weeding out entries which were of value to Fitzgerald as suggestions or reminders for his work, but which seem otherwise unintelligible or uninteresting. A number of notes that have already been printed with the manuscript of The Last Tycoon *have not been reprinted here, and two jottings that were found with that manuscript but do not relate to the story have been added on page* 181 *at the end of the section called* Literary.*

The Basil and Josephine sometimes referred to in these notes are the central figures of two series of stories included in* Taps at Reveille; *the Philippe was to have figured as the hero of a mediaeval novel. Four episodes dealing with this last character were published in the* Redbook *magazine (October,* 1924; *June and August,* 1935; *and November,* 1941); *but the requirements of the fiction market compelled Fitzgerald to depart from his original conception, and he eventually lost interest in the story.*

THE NOTE-BOOKS

A

ANECDOTES

℃ René had never before searched for a colored man in the Negro residential quarter of an American city. As time passed, he had more and more a sense that he was pursuing a phantom; it began to shame him to ask the whereabouts of such ghostly, blatantly immaterial lodgings as the house of Aquilla's brother.

℃ But he came back because the herd (society) is all we have and we cannot stray without shortly finding that the wolves have to eat us, too. He preached his special gospel to the herd. They (let us assume) liked it or half liked it. It worked.

℃ Then there's Emily. You know what happened to her; one night her husband came home and told her she was acting cold to him, but that he'd fix that up. So he built a bonfire under her bed, made up of shoes and things, and set fire to it. And if the leather hadn't smelled so terrible, she'd have been burned to death.

℃ The absent-minded gentleman on the train started to get off at the wrong station. As he walked back to his seat he assumed a mirthless smile and said aloud as though he were talking to himself: "I thought this was Great Neck."

But he couldn't smooth over his mistake—we all knew that he had made a fool of himself and looked upon him with distaste and contempt.

℃ A man wrapped up some domestic rats in small blankets cut from an old carpet, lest they should spread germs. A few months after he had turned them loose he found young rats around the house with carpet patterns on their fur.

"How peculiar!" he exclaimed. "I didn't suspect it would turn out that way when I wrapped up those rats."

But it did.

℃ Story of the ugly aunt in album.

℃ Jimmy the 95 pd. center.

℃ The girl who fell off the shelf.

℃ Once there was a whole lot of bird seed around the room because an author had adopted a chicken. It was impossible to explain to anyone just why he had adopted the chicken, but still more impossible to know why he had bought the bird-seed for the chicken. The chicken was later broiled and the bird-seed thrown out, but the question of whether the man was an author or a lunatic was still unsolved in the minds of the hotel servants who had to deal with the situation. The hotel servants didn't understand it. They didn't understand how months later the author could write a story about it, but they all bought the magazine.

B

BRIGHT CLIPPINGS

℃ "Snowladen evergreens will decorate the stairway and foyer leading to the ballroom, where a reproduction of the boat in which the Viking princes, at the invitation of the

Russians, came to rule Russia in the ninth century, will be arranged against a mirrored background. Its huge golden sails will bear the imperial insignia, the double-headed eagle, and Joss Moss and his orchestra, in Russian garb, will be seated in the craft.

"Flags of old Russia will recall the imperial regime. The ancient Russian custom of welcoming guests will be invoked by six young Russian girls, in costume, who will serve to those arriving, at a table near the ballroom entrance, tiny squares of black bread dipped in salt and small tumblers of vodka.

"Prince Alexis Obolensky will sing during the midnight supper in the oval restaurant and will present the Siberian Singers, a male ensemble, on their first appearance in New York, in a selection of Russian folk songs. Several dance numbers will feature the entertainment."

❲ *Blossom Time*—the greatest musical romance ever written." Cleveland: *"One of the best musical sows written in modern times."*

❲ "Men of Genius are great as certain ethereal Chemicals operating on the Mass of neutral intellect—but they have not any individuality, and determined Character."—Keats.

❲ Egyptian Proverb: The worst things:
To be in bed and sleep not,
To want for one who comes not.
To try to please and please not.

C

CONVERSATIONS AND THINGS OVERHEARD

❲ "I'm having them all psychoanalyzed," he said. "I got a guy down from Zürich, and he's doing one a day. I never saw such a gloomy bunch of women; always bellyaching wherever I take 'em. A man I knew told me he had his wife psychoanalyzed and she was easier to be with afterward."

❛ "When I hear people bragging about their social position and who they are, and all that, I just sit back and laugh. Because I happen to be descended directly from Charlemagne. What do you think of that?" Josephine blushed for him.

❛ "I like poetry and music better than anything in the world," she said. "They're wonderful."
He believed her, knowing that she spoke of her liking for him.

❛ "Yes, he has a position with the Dolleh Line, has a position with the Dolleh Line."
"Sweetie, he just scratched and scratched and scratched all night. Scratched and scratched and—"

❛ "Of course I'm afraid of horses. They try to bite me."
"I've never met a horse—socially, that is—who didn't try to bite me. They used to do it when I put the bridle on; then, when I gave up putting the bridle on, they began reaching their heads around trying to get at my calves."
"When I went to Southampton, I was—thrown at him."
"Thrown from a horse?"

❛ "She's really radiunt," she said, "really radiunt."

❛ "You meig me sick to my stomach."
"S'Chris' Watisis—a ship?"

❛ "Perfectly respectable girl, but only been drinking that day. No matter how long she lives she'll always know she's killed somebody."

❛ "Well, isn't it true? I told him how American education was terrible and you thought mine ought to be different."
"Oh-h-h! And then to finish it off you slapped him?"

"Well, I thought the best thing was to be partly American and slap him."

¢ "What nice words," she teased him. "If you keep on, I'm going to throw myself under the wheels of the cab."

¢ "Call me Micky Mouse," she said suddenly.
"Why?"
"I don't know—it was fun when you called me Micky Mouse."

¢ "I am willing to die with my boots on—I just want to be sure that they are my own boots and that they're all on."

¢ "Showing off."
"Well, then, so was Christ showing off."

¢ "Prowling the rattlers"—robbing freight cars.

¢ Beginning of a story, *Incorrigible.*
Father: Who do you admire?
Son: Andy Gump. Who do you think I admire—George Washington? Grow up!

¢ "With a piquant face and all the chic in the world. This is because I was educated in Paris and this in turn I owe to someone's chance remark to Cousin Arletta that she had a nice big daughter who was only twenty-two or three at the time. It took three bromides to calk Cousin Arletta and I started for the Convent of the Sacré-Coeur next day."

¢ Kitty, if you write on that pillow with my lipstick!

¢ People's home—a lovely home.

¢ "Am I right or wrong?" he asked the head waiter. The answer was obvious—he was right—gloriously and everlastingly right. Interesting, too.

¢ "I'm giving a dinner tonight, some very fine cultivated people. I want you to come. I sent a note to your cabin."

[97]

"For God's sake," Lew groaned, "I don't want to meet any people. I know some people."

C "Look me up in the Social Register."

C "You hate people, don't you?"
"Yes, and you do, too."
"I hate them like hell."
"What are you going to do about it?"
"I don't know. But not that anyhow. If I'm cold I'm not always going to use it to learn their secrets by finding them off guard and vulnerable. And I'm not going around saying I'm fond of people when I mean I'm so damned used to their reactions to my personal charm that I can't do without it. Getting emptier and emptier. Love is shy. I thought from the first that no one who thought about it like you did ever had it."

C "Oh, have you got an engagement with your drug-taking friend in Monte Carlo?"
He sat down and began putting on his shoes.
"I shouldn't have told you that. I suppose you think he'll convert me to the habit."
"I certainly don't think it's a very profitable association."
"Oh, yes it is. It's not everybody who can get the dope habit from a prominent moving picture director. In fact, it's begun already. At this very moment I'm full of dope. He started me on cocaine, and we're working slowly up to heroin."
"That isn't really funny, Francis."
"Excuse me. I was trying to be funny and I know you don't like my way of being funny."
She countered his growing bitterness by adopting a tone of calm patience.

C In Virginia the Italian children say:
"Lincoln threw blacks out; now they're back."
"The white people fit the Yankees."
"Yankees *are* white people."
"Not I ever hear tell of."

[98]

❡ I really loved him, but of course it wore out like a love affair. The fairies have spoiled all that.

❡ "Just a couple of old drunks, just a couply of ol-l-ld circus clowns."

❡ "I'm in a hurry.
  "I'm in a hurry — I'm in a hurry."
  "What are you in a hurry about?"
  "I can't explain — I'm in a hurry."

❡ "This is a tough girl and I'm taking her to a tough place."

❡ Three hundred a day die in auto accidents in the U. S. A.

❡ Man looking at aeroplane: "That's one of them new gyro-practors."

❡ Bijou, regarding her cigarette fingers: "Oh, Trevah! Get me the pumice stone."

❡ His life was a sort of dream, as are most lives with the mainspring left out.

❡ Suddenly her face resumed that expression which can only come from studying moving picture magazines over and over, and only be described as one long blond wish toward something—a wish that you'd have a wedlock with the youth of Shirley Temple, the earning power of Clark Gable; the love of Clark Gable and the talent of Charles Laughton—and with a bright smile the girl was gone.

❡ Feel wide awake—no, but at least I feel born, which is more than I did the first time I woke up.

❡ The cartoon cat licked the cartoon kitten and a girl behind me said, "Isn't that sweet?"

❡ We can't just let our worlds crash around us like a lot of dropped trays.

❦ Q. What did he die of? A. He died of jus' dieability.

❦ "Hello, Sam." When you were a good guest, you knew the names of the servants, the smallest babies, and the oldest aunts. "Is Bonny in?"

❦ "I like writers. If you speak to a writer, you often get an answer."

❦ Woman says about husband that he keeps bringing whole great masses of dogs back from the pound.

❦ "We haven't got any more gin," he said. "Will you have a bromide?" he added hopefully.

❦ Long engagement: nothing to do but to marry or quarrel, so I decided to quarrel.

❦ "*I* didn't do it," he said, using the scented "I."

❦ "Remember you're physically repulsive to me."

❦ "Learn young about hard work and good manners—and you'll be through the whole dirty mess and nicely dead again before you know it."

❦ Now it's all as useless as repeating a dream.

❦ "I'm going to break that stubborn stupid part of you that thinks that any American woman who has met Brancusi is automatically a genius and entitled ever after to leave the dishes and walk around with her head in the clouds."

❦ "You look to me like a very ordinary three-piece suit."

❦ Man to Woman: "You look as if you wanted excitement— is that true?"

❦ "Go and sleep with a cheapskate—go on—it'd do you

good. It would take another little tuck in your soul and you'd fit better, be more comfortable."

C "Francis says he wants to go away and try his personality on a lot of new people."

C "You went out of your way to make a preposterous attack on an old gentlewoman who had given you nothing but courtesy and consideration."

C "I have decided that the office cannot continue to hold both you and me. One of us must go—which shall it be?"
"Well, Mr. Wrackham, your name is painted on the doors—I suppose it would be simpler if you stayed."

C "My last husband was thrown from his horse. You must learn to ride." He takes one look around uneasily for a horse.

C "We throw in one of these flowers. You know how frails are—if a stone sails in, they put up a yelp—if it's a rose, they think there's the Prince of Wales at last."

C "That one about the four girls named Meg who fall down the rabbit hole."

C "He wants to make a goddess out of me and I want to be Mickey Mouse."

C "Yes mam, if necessary. Look here, you take a girl and she goes into some café where she's got no business to go. Well, then, her escort he gets a little too much to drink an' he goes to sleep an' then some fella comes up and says, 'Hello, sweet mamma,' or whatever one of those mashers says up here. What does she do? She can't scream, on account of no real lady will scream nowadays—no—she just reaches down in her pocket and slips her fingers into a pair of Powell's defensive brass-knuckles, debutante's size, executes what I call the Society Hook, and Wham! that big fella's on his way to the cellar."

ℭ "Well-what—What's the guitar for?" whispered the awed Amanthis. "Do they have to knock somebody over with the guitar?"

"No, mam!" exclaimed Jim in horror. "No mam. In my course no lady would be taught to raise a guitar against anybody. I teach 'em to play. Shucks! you ought to hear 'em. Why, when I've given 'em two lessons, you'd think some of 'em was colored."

ℭ "What are they doing?" whispered Amanthis to Jim.

"That there's a course in southern accent. Lot of young men up here want to learn southern accent—so we teach it —Georgia, Florida, Alabama, Eastern Shore, Ole Virginian. Some of 'em even want straight nigger—for song purposes."

ℭ "The time I fell off a closet shelf."

"You what?"

"I fell off a shelf—and he put it in the paper."

"Well, what were you doing?"

"I just happened to be up on a shelf and I fell off."

"Oh, don't say it."

"I've stopped giving any further explanations. Anyhow, father said it was news."

D

DESCRIPTIONS OF THINGS AND ATMOSPHERES

ℭ The wind shivered over the leaves, over the white casements—then as if it was beauty it could not stand, jumped out the window and climbed down from the cornice on the corner.

Then it came to ground. All that had happened was that green had blown through the wind and back and returned to settle on the same red walls, waving it forever after as a green flag, a heavy, ever bearded, ever unshaven flag, like water when you drop a petal in it, like a woman's dress, and

then the little trickles that wound about the casements—
faint, somnescent and gone.

After that silence—the wind blowing the curtains. The
cross child you had to scold. The moment had gone. The
moment had come and existed for a minute. A lacy light
played once more—a scherzo, no, a new prelude to ever
blooming, ever greening, and he was sorry for what he had
ever said or thought.

Once more the wind was dead. There was only one leaf
flickering against the white casement. Perhaps there was
someone back of it being happy.

₵ The pleasant, ostentatious boulevard was lined at prosperous intervals with New England Colonial houses—
without ship models in the hall. When the inhabitants
moved out here, the ship models had at last been given to
the children. The next street was a complete exhibit of the
Spanish-bungalow phase of West Coast architecture; while
two streets over, the cylindrical windows and round towers
of 1897—melancholy antiques which sheltered swamis,
yogis, fortune tellers, dressmakers, dancing teachers, art
academies and chiropractors—looked down now upon brisk
busses and trolley cars. A little walk around the block could,
if you were feeling old that day, be a discouraging affair.

On the green flanks of the modern boulevard children,
with their knees marked by the red stains of the mercuro-
chrome era, played with toys with a purpose—beams that
taught engineering, soldiers that taught manliness, and
dolls that taught motherhood. When the dolls were so
banged up that they stopped looking like real babies and
began to look like dolls, the children developed affection for
them. Everything in the vicinity—even the March sunlight—was new, fresh, hopeful and thin, as you would
expect in a city that had tripled its population in fifteen
years.

₵ Days of this February were white and magical, the nights
were starry and crystalline. The town lay under a cold
glory.

❲ Dyed Siberian horses.

❲ As thin as a repeated dream.

❲ The sea was coming up in little intimidating rushes.

❲ The island floated, a boat becalmed, upon the almost perceptible curve of the world.

❲ Lost in the immensity of surfaceless blue sky like air piled on air.

A sudden gust of rain blew over them and then another— as if small liquid clouds were bouncing along the land. Lightning entered the sea far off and the air blew full of crackling thunder.

The table cloths blew around the pillars. They blew and blew and blew. The flags twisted around the red chairs like live things, the banners were ragged, the corners of the table tore off through the burbling, billowing ends of the cloths. There was Pat O'Mara, his hands, adequate enough, smoothing hair. Blow, banners, blow. You in ermine slow down, you, slow, whip, no snap, only whip wind in the corners of the tables. Can I have a flower if they don't want one.

❲ On the great swell of the *Blue Danube*, the summer ball rocked into motion.

❲ A circus ring for ponies in country houses.

❲ A tense, sunny room seemed romantic to Becky, with its odor of esoteric gases, the faint perfumes of future knowledge, the low electric sizz in the glass cells.

❲ A rambling frame structure that had been a residence in the 80's, the country poorhouse in the 1900's, and now was a residence again.

❲ The groans of moribund plumbing.

❲ The silvery "Hey!" of a telephone.

❡ The curious juxtapositions made him feel the profound waves of change that were already washing this country— the desperate war that had rendered the plantation house obsolete, the industrialization that had spoiled the easy-going life centering around the old court house. And then the years yielding up eventually in the backwater of those curious young products who were neither peasants, nor bourgeois, nor scamps, but a little of all three, gathered there in front of the store.

❡ New York's flashing, dynamic good looks, its tall man's quick-step.

❡ Afterward they would drive around until they found the center of the summer night and park there while the enchanted silence spread over them like leaves over the babes in the wood.

❡ Stevedores appeared momentarily against the lighted hold of a barge and jerked quickly out of sight down an invisible incline.

❡ The moon came up rosy gold with a haze around.

❡ Whining, tinkling hoochie-coochie show.

❡ The first lights of the evening were springing into pale existence. The Ferris wheel, pricked out now in lights, revolved leisurely through the dusk; a few empty cars of the roller coaster rattled overhead.

❡ Metropolitan days and nights that were tense as singing wires.

❡ The late sun glinted on the Mississippi flats a mile away.

❡ When the stars were bright enough to compete with the bright lamps.

❡ The limousine crawled crackling down the pebbled drive.

❡ Three frail dock lights glittered dimly upon innumerable fishing boats heaped like shells along the beach. Farther out in the water there were other lights where a fleet of slender yachts rode the tide with slow dignity, and farther still a full ripe moon made the water bosom into a polished dancing floor.

❡ That stream of silver that waved like a wide strand of curly hair toward the moon.

❡ The club lay in a little valley, almost roofed over by willows, and down through their black silhouettes, in irregular blobs and patches, dripped the light of a huge harvest moon. As they parked the car, Basil's tune of tunes, *Chinatown*, drifted from the windows and dissolved into its notes, which thronged like elves through the glade.

❡ Deep autumn had set in, with a crackling wind from the west.

❡ Next door they were scrubbing a building upon a lit-up platform. It was fun to see it come out all bright and new.

❡ The hotel we selected—The *Hôtel de la Morgue*—was small and silent enough to suit even the most refined taste.

❡ The droning of frogs in the Aislette Valley covered the sound of the bringing up of our artillery.

❡ In the afternoon they came to a lake. It was a cup of a lake with lily pads for dregs and a smooth surface of green cream.

❡ You can order it in four sizes: *demi* (half a litre), *distingué* (one litre), *formidable* (three litres), and *catastrophe* (five litres).

❡ In the deep locker-room of the earth.

⁅ The rear wall was formed by a wide flag of water, falling from a seam in the rock ceiling, and afterwards draining into some lower level cave beyond.

⁅ Seen in a Junk Yard. Dogs, chickens with few claws, brass fittings, T's elbow, rust everywhere, bales of metal 1800 lbs., plumbing fixtures, bathtubs, sinks, water pumps, wheels, Fordson tractor, acetylene lamps for tractors, sewing machine, bell on dinghy, box of bolts, (No. 1), van, stove, auto stuff (No. 2), army trucks, cast iron body, hot dog stand, dinky engines, sprockets like watch parts, hinge all taken apart on building side, motorcycle radiators, George on the high army truck.

⁅ Across the street from me in Hendersonville, N. C., is a movie sign, usually with a few bulbs out in the center. It reads tonight: *The Crusades: The Flaming Passion of a Woman Torn Between Two Camps.*
    This is the right idea, and to aid in the campaign to prove that a woman (not *women* mind you—that point is granted) is at the tiller in every storm, I submit the following suggestions to draw in the elder gadgets and their tokens: *Huckleberry Finn—How a Girl Changed the Life of a Missouri Boy.*

⁅ A strip of straw, half-braided, that fell across another desk.

⁅ A region of those monotonous apartment rows that embody the true depths of the city—darkly mysterious at night, drab in the afternoon.

⁅ Memory of coming into Washington.

⁅ All of a sudden the room struck like a clock.

⁅ For a while the big liner, so sure and proud in the open sea, was shoved ignominiously around by the tugs, like a helpless old woman.

[107]

❡ There were Roman legionaries with short, bright swords and helmets and shields shining with gilt, a conqueror in his chariot with six horses, and an entourage of sparkling, plumed Roman knights, captured Gauls in chains, Greeks in buskins and tunics of Ionian blue, black Egyptians in flashing desert reds with images of Isis and Osiris, a catapult, and, in person, Hannibal, Caesar, Rameses and Alexander.

❡ The evening gem-play of New York was already taking place outside the window. But as Charlie gazed at it, it seemed to him tawdry and theatrical, a great keeping up of appearances after the reality was gone. Each new tower was something erected in defiance of obvious and imminent disaster; each beam of light a final despairing attempt to pretend that all was well.

"But they had their time. For a while they represented a reality. These things are scarcely built; not a single generation saw them and passed away before we ceased to believe."

❡ The rhythm of the weekend, with its birth, its planned gaieties, and its announced end, followed the rhythm of life and was a substitute for it.

❡ The blurred world seen from a merry-go-round settled into place; the merry-go-round suddenly stopped.

❡ The city's quick metropolitan rhythm of love and birth and death that supplied dreams to the unimaginative, pageantry and drama to the drab.

❡ Spring came sliding up the mountains in wedges and spear-points of green.

❡ Far out past the breakers he could survey the green-and-brown line of the Old Dominion with the pleasant impersonality of a porpoise. The burden of his wretched marriage fell away with the buoyant tumble of his body among the swells, and he would begin to move in a child's dream of space. Sometimes remembered playmates of his youth swam with him; sometimes, with his two sons beside him, he seemed to be setting off along the bright pathway to the moon. Americans, he liked to say, should be born with fins, and perhaps they were—perhaps money was a form of fin. In England, property begot a strong place sense, but Americans, restless and with shallow roots, needed fins and wings. There was even a recurrent idea in America about an education that would leave out history and the past, that should be a sort of equipment for aerial adventure, weighed down by none of the stowaways of inheritance or tradition.

❦ The nineteen wild green eyes of a bus were coming up to them through the dark.

❦ The mingling and contrast of the silver lines of car track and the gold of the lamps, the streams of light rippling on the old road and the lamps on the bridge, and then when the rain had stopped, the shadows of the maple leaves on the picket fence.

❦ The train gave out a gurgle and a forlorn burst of false noise, and with a clicking strain of couplers pulled forward a few hundred yards.

❦ When the freight stopped next the stars were out, so sudden that Chris was dazzled. The train was on a rise. About three miles ahead he saw a cluster of lights fainter and more yellow than the stars, that he figured would be Dallas.

❦ The music indoors was strange in the summer; it lay uneasily upon the pulsing heat, disturbed by the loud whir of the fans.

❦ There were only the colleges and the country clubs. The parks were cheerless, without beer and mostly without music. They ended at the monkey house or at some imitation French vista. They were for children—for adults there was nothing.

❲ A half-displayed packet of innocuous post cards warranted to be very dirty indeed.

❲ Against the bar a group of ushers was being photographed, and the flash-light surged through the room in a stifling cloud.

❲ In one corner of the ballroom an arrangement of screens like a moving-picture stage had been set up and photographers were taking official pictures of the bridal party. The bridal party, still as death and pale as wax under the bright lights, appeared, to the dancers circling the modulated semi-darkness of the ballroom, like those jovial or sinister groups that one comes upon in The Old Mill at an amusement park.

❲ Drawing away from the little valley, past pink pines and fresh, diamond-strewn snow.

❲ A sound of clinking waiters.

❲ The music started again. Under the trees the wooden floor was red in the sun.

❲ Phonograph roared new German tangoes into the smoke and clatter.

❲ Cannes in the season—he was filling the café, the light which blazed against the white poplar bark and green leaves, with sprightlier motes of his own creation—he saw it vivid with dresses just down from Paris and giving off a sweet pungent odor of flowers and chartreuse and fresh black coffee and cigarettes, and mingled with these another scent, the mysterious thrilling scent of love. Hands touched jewelled hands over the white tables; the vivid gowns and the shirt fronts swayed together and matches were held, trembling a little, for slow-lighting cigarettes.

❲ Parts of New Jersey, as you know, are under water, and other parts are under continual surveillance by the authorities. But here and there lie patches of garden country dotted with old-fashioned frame mansions, which have wide shady porches and a red swing on the lawn. And perhaps, on the widest and shadiest of the porches there is even a hammock left over from the hammock days, stirring gently in a Victorian wind.

(The battered hacks waiting at the station; the snow-covered campus, the big open fires in the club houses.

(Not long after noon—he could tell by the thin shadow of the shutter.

(Duty, Honor, Country, West Point—the faded banners on the chapel walls.

(No one has ever seen Richerees, near Asheville, because the windows fog with smoke just before you get there.

(But while the crowd surged into the bright stadium like lava coming down a volcano from the craters of the runways—

(The * * * * Hotel was planned to give rest and quiet to tired and overworked business men and overwrought and over-societied women.

(When opened up, the fish smelled like a very stuffy room.

(Trolley running on the crack of dawn.

(An old-style flivver crushed the obliterated borders of the path.

(It was not at all the remodelled type of farmhouse favored by the wealthy; it was pristine. No wires, and one was sure no pipes, led to it.

(Occasionally two yellow disks would top a rise ahead of

them and take shape as a late-returning automobile. Except for that, they were alone in a continual rushing dark. The moon had gone down.

C The decks were bright and restless, but bow and stern were in darkness, so the boat had no more outline than an accidental cluster of stars. Francis took the trip one lonely evening.

C One of those places they used to call somebody's "Folly." All ready for a whole slew of people who weren't there—hopeful little shops built into the hotel, some open and some closed.

C There was rosy light still on that big mountain, the Pic de Something or the Dent de Something, because the world was round or for some such reason. Bundled up children were splattering in for tea as if the outdoors were tired of them and wanted to change its dress in quiet dignity. Down in the valley there were already bright windows and misty glows from the houses and hotels of the town.

C The sun was already waving gold, green and white flags on the Wildstrubel.

C Its familiar light and books and last night's games always pushed just out of sight under something, the piano with last night's songs still open on it.

C A toiling sweating sun stoked the sky overhead.

C It was nice out—still as still.

C Green jars and white magnolias.

C Clairmont Avenue.

C Shallows in the lake of day.

❦ Colors at Oregon: gold, dark green, little white buoys on safety rope, background white figures, grey underpinnings —all seen through foliage dark and light green.

❦ Bird call: Weecha, weecha, weecha, weecha *eat?*

❦ Suddenly the room rang like a diamond in all four corners.

❦ Josephine picked them out presently below a fringe by their well-known feet—Travis de Coppet's deft, dramatic feet; Ed Bement's stern and uncompromising feet; the high, button shoes of some impossible girl.

❦ He passed an apartment house that jolted his memory. It was on the outskirts of town, a pink horror built to represent something, somewhere, so cheaply and sketchily that whatever it copied the architect must have long since forgotten.

❦ The two orchestras moaned in pergolas lit with fireflies, and many-colored spotlights swept the floor, touching a buffet where dark bottles gleamed.

❦ Abruptly it became full summer. After the last April storm someone came along the street one night, blew up the trees like balloons, scattered bulbs and shrubs like confetti, opened a cage full of robins, and, after a quick look around, signaled up the curtain upon a new backdrop of summer sky.

❦ White chestnut blossoms slanted down across the tables and dropped impudently into the butter and the wine. Julia Ross ate a few with her bread.

❦ The stench of cigars in small houses. (Remember it with Old Mill.)

❦ Zelda's worn places in yard and hammock.

❦ The river flowed in a thin scarlet gleam between the public baths and the massed tracks upon the other side. Booming, whistling, far-away railroad sounds reached them from down there; the voices of children playing tennis in Prospect Park sailed frailly overhead.

℄ Out the window the snow on the pine trees had turned rosy and lilac in the early dusk and bundled up children were splattering back to their hotels to tea.

℄ God's whitest whiskers dissolved before a roaring plane bound for Corsica.

℄ The corpses of a million blue fish.

℄ Bryn Mawr coverlet.

℄ Her face flushed with cold, etc. (more to this.)

℄ It was a crisp cold night with frost shooting along the grass.

℄ The familiar, unforgotten atmosphere of many Negroes and voices pleasing-calm and girls painted bright as savages to stand out against the tropical summer.

℄ The Grand Duc had just begun its slow rattling gasp for life in the inertness of the weakest hour.

℄ The lights of many battleships drifting like water jewels upon the dark Hudson.

℄ We looked out at the port where the rocking masts of boats pointed at the multitudinous stars.

℄ The wind searched the walls for old dust.

℄ Cluster of murky brown doors so alike that to be identified it seemed that her's must be counted off from the abutting blackness of an alley.

❡ Listless disorder.

❡ On the sky-blue sky, the clouds low above the prairie, the grand canyonesque architecture of the cliffs, the cactus penguins extending conciliatory arms.

❡ The new trees, the new quivering life, the new shadows that designed new terrain on the old.

❡ The main room, for which no adequate name has yet been found in the Republic.

❡ Hot Springs. In a Spring vacation hotel the rain is bad news indeed. The hundred French windows of the great galleries led the eye out to ink-and-water pines snivelling listlessly on to raw brown tennis courts, to desolate hills against soiled white sky. There was "nothing to do," for hotel and resort were one and the same, and no indoor activity was promised on the bulletin-board until the concert of the Princeton Glee Club Easter Monday. Women who had come to breakfast in riding clothes rushed to the hair-dresser instead; at eleven the tap-k'tap of ping-pong balls was the only sound of life in the enormous half-empty hotel.

The girl was one of a pair in white skirts and yellow sweaters who walked down the long gallery after breakfast. Her face reflected the discontent of the weather, reflected it darkly and resentfully. Looking at her, De Forest Colman thought: "Bored and fierce," and then as his eyes continued to follow her: "No, proud and impatient. Not that either, but what a face—vitality and hand-cuffs—where's this getting me?—liver and bacon, Damon and Pythias, Laurel and Hardy."

❡ The gaunt scaffolding of Coney Island slid by.

❡ Save for two Russian priests playing chess, their party was alone in the smoking room.

❡ Everybody in the room was hot. There was a faint flavor of starch on the air that leaked out to the lovely garden.

❡ One of those huge spreading hotels of the capital, built to shelter politicians, retired officers suddenly discovering themselves without a native town, foreigners with axes to grind, legation staffs, and women fascinated by one of the outer rings of officialdom—everyone could have their Congressman or Minister, if not their Senator or Ambassador—

❡ The terrible way the train had seemed to foreshorten and hurry as it got into motion.

❡ It was already eight o'clock when they drove off into a windy twilight. The sun had gone behind Naples, leaving a sky of pigeon's blood and gold, and as they rounded the bay and climbed slowly toward Torre Annunziata, the Mediterranean momentarily toasted the fading splendor in pink wine. Above them loomed Vesuvius and from its crater a small persistent fountain of smoke contributed darkness to the gathering night.

"We ought to reach our destination about twelve," said Nosby. No one answered. The city had disappeared behind a rise of ground and now they were alone, where the Maffia sprang out of rank human weeds and the Black Hand rose to throw its ominous shadow across two continents. There was something eerie in the sound of the wind over these gray mountains, crowned with decayed castles. Hallie suddenly shivered.

❡ Motor boat like a clock tick.

❡ The sky that looks like smoke on Charles Street.

❡ He heard them singing and looked down toward the lights. There was a trembling of the leaves before they passed.

❡ Night at Fair: Eyes awakening.

❡ March: The crêpe myrtle was under corn stalks.

❡ "I'm glad I'm American," she said. "Here in Italy I feel

[116]

that everybody's dead. Carthaginians and old Romans and Moorish pirates and medieval princes with poisoned rings."

℃ The solemn gloom of the countryside communicated itself to all of them.

℃ The wind had come up stronger and was groaning through the dark-massed trees along the way.

℃ White and inky night.

℃ A soft bell hummed midnight.

℃ In children's books forests are sometimes made out of all-day suckers, boulders out of peppermints and rivers out of gently flowing, rippling molasses taffy. Such books are less fantastic than they sound, for such localities exist, and one day a girl, herself little more than a child, sat dejected in the middle of one. It was all hers, she owned it; she owned Candy Town.

℃ The red dusk was nearly gone, but she had advanced into the last patch of it.

℃ Yellow and lavender filled her eyes, yellow for the sun through lavender shades and lavender for the quilt, swollen as a cloud and drifting in soft billows over the bed. Suddenly she remembered her appointment, and, uncovering her arms, she squirmed into a violet negligee, flipped back her hair with a circular movement of her head, and melted into the color of the room.

℃ Lying awake in bed that night, he listened endlessly to the long caravan of a circus moving through the street from one Paris fair to another. When the last van had rumbled out of hearing and the corners of the furniture were pastel blue with the dawn, he was still thinking.

℃ The road was lined sparsely with a row of battered houses, some of them repainted a pale unhealthy blue and all of them situated far back in large plots of shaggy and unkempt land.

℃ It was a collapsed house, a retired house, set far back from the road and sunned and washed to the dull color of old wood.

One glance told him it was no longer a dwelling. The shutters that remained were closed tight, and from the tangled vines arose, as a single chord, a rich shrill sound of a hundred birds. John Jackson left the road and stalked across the yard, knee-deep in abandoned grass.

℃ Stifling as curtain dust.

℃ The pavements grew sloppier and the snow in the gutters melted into dirty sherbet.

℃ The sea was dingy grey and swept with rain. Canvas sheltered all the open portions of the promenade deck, even the ping-pong table was wet.

℃ It was the Europa—a moving island of light. It grew larger minute by minute, swelled into a harmonious fairy-land with music from its deck and searchlights playing on its own length. Through field-glasses they could discern figures lining the rail, and Evelyn spun out the personal history of a man who was pressing his pants in a cabin. Charmed they watched its sure matchless speed.

"Oh, Daddy, buy me that!" Evelyn cried.

℃ She climbed a network of steel, concrete and glass, walked under a high echoing dome and came out into New York.

℃ The hammock was of the particularly hideous yellow peculiar to hammocks.

℃ Adorned in front by an enormous but defunct motometer and behind by a mangy pennant bearing the legend "Tarleton, Ga."

[118]

❦ In the dim past someone had begun to paint the hood yellow but unfortunately had been called away when but half through the task.

❦ On all sides faintly irregular fields stretched away to a faintly irregular unpopulated horizon.

❦ In the light of four strong pocket flashlights, borne by four sailors in spotless white, a gentleman was shaving himself, standing clad only in athletic underwear upon the sand. Before his eyes an irreproachable valet held a silver mirror, which gave back the soapy reflection of his face. To right and left stood two additional menservants, one with a dinner coat and trousers hanging from his arm and the other bearing a white stiff shirt, whose studs glistened in the glow of the electric lamps. There was not a sound except the dull scrape of the razor along its wielder's face and the intermittent groaning sound that blew in out of the sea.

❦ But here beside the warm friendly rain that tumbled from his eaves onto the familiar lawn—

❦ Next morning, walking with Knowleton under starry frosted bushes in one of the bare gardens, she grew quite light-hearted.

❦ "Ballroom," for want of a better word. It was that room, filled by day with wicker furniture, which was always connotated by the phrase, "Let's go in and dance." It was referred to as "inside" or "downstairs." It was that nameless chamber wherein occur the principal transactions of all the country clubs in America.

❦ They were there. The Cherbourg breakwater, a white stone snake, glittered along the sea at dawn; behind it red roofs and steeples, and then small, neat hills traced with a warm orderly pattern of toy farms. "Do you like this French arrangement?" it seemed to say. "It's considered very charming, but if you don't agree just shift it about—set this road here, this steeple there. It's been done before, and it always comes out lovely in the end."

℃ It was Sunday morning, and Cherbourg was in flaring collars and high lace hats. Donkey carts and diminutive automobiles moved to the sound of incessant bells.

℃ Those were the dog days. Out at the lake there was a thin green scum upon the water and in the city a last battering exhausting heat wave softened the asphalt till it retained the ghastly prints of human feet. In those days there was one auto for every 200 inhabitants, so in the evening—

℃ A large but quick restaurant.

℃ Aeolian or Wind-built Islands.

℃ They all went to the porch, where the children silhouetted themselves in silent balance on the railing and unrecognizable people called greetings as they passed along the dark dusty street.

℃ The first lights of the evening were springing into pale existence.

℃ At three o'clock in the morning, grey broken old women scrub the floors of the great New York Hotels.

℃ Great flatness of American life when everything had the same value.

℃ The run to the purple mountains and back.

℃ Spring had come early to the Eastern seaboard—thousands of tiny black surprise berries on every tree were shining with anticipation and a fresh breeze wafted them south all day.

℃ Is there anything more soothing than the quiet whir of a lawnmower on a summer afternoon?

❡ A mid-Victorian wind.

❡ This restaurant with a haunted corner.

❡ Lunar Rainbow.

❡ New Jersey villages where even Sunday is only a restless lull between the crash of trains.

❡ Elevators look like two big filing cabinets.

❡ Out in the suburbs, chalk white windows looked down indifferently at them in sleeping roads.

❡ The abundant waiters at Dartmouth seemed to me rather comedy characters—I mean not in themselves but in their roles. They go all out of character and begin to talk to the guests just like the man who hires himself out to do that.

❡ St. Paul in 1855 (or '66): The rude town was like a great fish just hauled out of the Mississippi and still leaping and squirming on its bank.

❡ The lobby of the Hôtel Roi d'Angleterre was as desolate as a schoolhouse after school. In the huge, scarcely completed palace a few servants scurried about like rabbits, a few guests sidled up to the concierge, spoke in whispers and vanished with a single awed look around at the devastating emptiness. They were mostly women escaped from the deep melancholy at home, and finding that the torture chamber was preferable to the tomb.

❡ Passing the building which housed the Negro wards. The patients were singing always. Among the voices that lay suspended in sweet melancholy on the August air in the early summer night, Owen recognized the deep bass of Doofus, who had been there two years—an interne on that ward had told him that Doofus was due to die; his place in the chorus would be hard to fill.

[121]

E

EPIGRAMS, WISECRACKS AND JOKES

(A man says to another man: "I'd certainly like to steal your girl." Second man: "I'd give her to you, but she's part of a set."

("Has D. P. injured you any way?" "No, but don't remind her. Maybe she hasn't done her bad deed for the day."

(The movies are the only court where the judge goes to the lawyer for advice.

(Show me a hero and I will write you a tragedy.

(Not a word in the Roosevelt inaugural was as logical as Zangara saying he shot at Roosevelt because he had a stomach ache.

(Agility (vitality)—pleasing people you perversely shouldn't please and can't reach.

(Her unselfishness came in pretty small packages well wrapped.

(After all, the portrait of an old shoe by Van Gogh hangs in the Louvre, but where is there a portrait of Van Gogh by an old shoe?

(Berry Wall. He doesn't dare go back. He was drafted for the Civil War and he doesn't know it's over.

(Optimism is the content of small men in high places.

(She's bashful. She has small-pox. She stumbles so she couldn't get up.

❡ Wouldn't a girl rather have half of *him* than a whole Spic with a jar of pomade thrown in? Life was so badly arranged —better no women at all than only one woman.

❡ One of those tragic efforts like repainting your half of a delapidated double house.

❡ Bryan to Darrow. Fellow Apes of the Scopes trial.

❡ Trying to support a large and constantly increasing French family who jokingly referred to themselves as "our servants."

❡ Sent a girl flowers on Mothers' Day.

❡ You don't write because you want to say something; you write because you've got something to say.

❡ Genius is the ability to put into effect what is in your mind. There's no other definition of it.

❡ Get a man for Elspeth, a man for Elspeth, was the cry. This was difficult because Elspeth had had so many men. Two of her sisters rode, so to speak, Elspeth's discarded mounts.

❡ Switzerland is a country where very few things begin, but many things end.

❡ Cotton manufacturer who worries because African chiefs go in for rayon.

❡ No grand idea was ever born in a conference, but a lot of foolish ideas have died there.

❡ Ye Old Hooke Shoppe.

❡ Genius goes around the world in its youth incessantly apologizing for having large feet. What wonder that later in life it should be inclined to raise those feet too swiftly to fools and bores.

❡ No such thing as a man willing to be honest—that would be like a blind man willing to see.

❡ Hospitality is a wonderful thing. If people really want you, they'll have you even if the cook has just died in the house of small-pox.

❡ Suddenly he turned in bed and put his arms around her arm. Her free hand touched his hair.

"You've been bad," she said.

"I can't help it."

She sat with him silently for half an hour; then she changed her position so that her arm was under his head. Stooping over him, she kissed him on the brow. (See *Two Wrongs*.)

❡ Any walk through a park that runs between a double line of mangy trees and passes brazenly by the ladies' toilet is invariably known as "Lover's Lane."

❡ Gynecologist to trace his pedigree.

❡ Women are going to refuse to build with anything but crushed brick.

❡ Shy beaten man named Victor.

Clumsy girls named Grace.

Great truck drivers named Earl and Cecil.

❡ She was one of those people who would just as soon starve in a garret with a man—if she didn't have to.

❡ Beatrice Lillie broke up the British Empire with *March to the Roll of the Drums*.

❡ Mencken forgives much to the Catholic church—perhaps because it has an index.

℃ All my characters killed each other off in the first act because I couldn't think of any more hard boiled things for them to say.

℃ They thought a child would be nice, too, because they had a nursery and the Harold Lloyds had one.

℃ They have more money. (Ernest's wisecrack.)*

℃ She's got to be a loyal, frank person if she's got to bitch everyone in the world to do it.

℃ For a statesman—any school child knows that hot air rises to the top.

℃ Suicide and wife arrive in Cuba.

℃ Debut: the first time a young girl is seen drunk in public.

℃ He repeated to himself an old French proverb that he had made up that morning.

℃ A sleeping porch is a back room with no pictures on the walls. It should contain at least one window.

℃ Forgotten is forgiven.

℃ If all your clothes are worn to the same state, it means you go out too much.

℃ American actresses now use European convents as a sort of female Muldoon's.

℃ The guy that played Sergeant Quirt in *Romeo and Juliet*.

℃ Three men better known as Christ's nails.

* Fitzgerald had said, "The rich are different from us." Hemingway had replied, "Yes, they have more money."

❦ The spiritual stomach of the race was ruined those fifty years when Mid-Western women didn't go to the toilet.

❦ To bring on the revolution it may be necessary to work inside the Communist Party.

❦ They try to be Jesus (Forsythe)* while I only attempt to be God, which is easier.

❦ To most women art is a form of scandal.

❦ Impersonating 46 presidents at once.

❦ "What kind of man was he?"
    "Well, he was one of those men who come in a door and make any woman with them look guilty."

❦ Grown up, and that is a terribly hard thing to do. It is much easier to skip it and go from one childhood to another.

❦ Dieticians: They have made great progress in the last few years. They know pretty definitely that bichloride of mercury or arsenic in the right dose will kill you and that food should probably be eaten rather than taken in gas form or over the radio.

❦ Honi soit qui Malibu.

❦ Trained nurses who eat as if they didn't own the food but it was just lent them.

❦ Parked his pessimism in her sun-parlour.

❦ No such thing as graceful old age.

❦ Vitality shows in not only the ability to persist but the ability to start over.

* Kyle Crichton, who wrote for the *New Masses* under the name of Robert Forsythe.

❦ What is the point at which loan becomes property of loanee and at the offer of a refund one says, "But I don't like to take your money"? What is the point when one accepts return of loan with most profuse thanks?

❦ The inevitable shallowness that goes with people who have learned everything by experience.

❦ Somebody's specimen hijacked on way to doctor's.

❦ The biggest temptation we can offer people to let *us* talk is to cry "say" (or *dites*) to them.

❦ This isn't the South. This is the center of the country. We're only polite half the time.

❦ I'm going through the crisis of my life like railroad ties.

❦ For Esther M.: In memory of an old friendship or a prolonged quarrel that has gone on so long and accumulated so much moss that it is much the same thing.

❦ Mr. and Mrs. Jay O'Brien moving like the center of population.

❦ "I can't pay you much," said the editor to the author, "but I can give you some good publicity."
   "I can't pay you much," said the advertiser to the editor, "but I can give you some beautiful ads."

❦ When he buys his ties he has to ask if gin will make them run.

❦ Very bad jokes should be known as "employer's jokes" or "creditor's jokes." The listener has to laugh, so it seems wasteful to use up a good story on him.

❦ The kiss originated when the first male reptile licked the first female reptile, implying in a subtle, complimentary way that she was as succulent as the small reptile he had for dinner the night before.

℄ You are contemplating a gigantic merger between J. P. Morgan and the Queensboro Bridge.

℄ Beware of him who would give his last sou to a beggar in the street. He would also give it to you and that is something you would not be able to endure.

℄ Fashion's Blessing: Think how many flappers would have been strangled like Porphyria except for bobbed hair.

℄ Don't get thinking it's a real country because you can get a lot of high school kids into gym suits and have them spell out "bananas" for the news reels.

℄ I used to whip you up to a nervous excitement that bore a resemblance to intelligence.

℄ It grows harder to write, because there is much less weather than when I was a boy and practically no men and women at all.

F

FEELINGS AND EMOTIONS (WITHOUT GIRLS)

℄ Ah, it was a great feeling to relax—the best feeling, unlike any sinking down he had ever known before.
"I have half an hour, an hour, two hours, ten hours, a hundred hours. God Almighty, I have even time to take a drink of water from the cooler in the hall; I can sleep eight full hours tonight, with a piece of paper stuffed in the telephone buzzer; I can face everybody in the office knowing they'll be paid again this week, the week after, the week after next!"

But most of all—he had that first half an hour. Having no one to communicate with, Andrew Fulton made sounds. One was like Whee-ee-ooo, but though it was expressive for awhile it palled presently, and he tried a gentle yawning sigh, but that was not enough. Now he knew what he wanted to do—he wanted to cry. He wanted to drink but there was nothing to drink, or to take his office force for an aeroplane ride or wake up his parents out of their graves and say, "Look—I too can rest."

℃ He might find the ecstasy and misery, the infatuation that he wanted.

℃ The thrilling staccato joy of the meeting.

℃ "I feel as if I had a cannon ball in my stomach."

℃ Wait for what? Wait while he swam off into a firmament of his own, so far off that she could. only see his feathers gleaming in the distance, only hear distintly the clamor of war or feel the vacuum that he created when sometimes he fell through space. He came back eventually with spoils, but for her there was always another larger waiting—for the end of youth, the blurring of her uniqueness: her two menacing deaths beside which mortal death was no more than sleep

℃ She looked lovely, but he thought of a terrible thing she had said once when they were first married—that if he were away she could sleep with another man and it wouldn't really affect her, or make her really unfaithful to him. This kept him awake for another hour, but he had a little fine deep restful sleep toward morning.

℃ The blind luck that had attended the industry, and he knew croupiers who raked in the earning of that vast gambling house. And he knew that the Europeans were impressed with it as they were impressed with the sky- scrapers, as something without human rhythm or movement. They had left rhythm behind them and it was their rhythm he wanted. He was tired of his own rhythm and the rhythms of the people in Hollywood. He wanted to see people with more secrets than the necessity of concealing a proclivity for morphine.

❡ Two Dreams: (1) A trip to Florida with Howard Garrish and many bathing beauties. Asleep standing on the prow, the beach and girls dancing. The one with skates like skiis. Like Switzerland, far castles and palaces. The horseman in the sea, the motor truck on sand, the horsemen coming ashore, the Bishop rears, falls, the horse saves him. My room, suits and ties, the view, the soldiers drilling under arcs in khaki, the wonderful water man is now Tom Taylor, I buy ties and wake in strange room. Blunder into Mother, who nags me. My mean remarks.
   (2) The colored burglar. Found clothes in hotel—underwear, suit; I discover pocket book, Echenard, my accusation.

❡ By the next morning she realized that she was the only one who cared, the only one who had the time and youth for the luxury of caring. Her aunt, her old cousins, were mercifully anaesthetized against death—her brother was already worrying about his wife and children back in West Virginia. She and her father were alone; since the funeral had been held over for her, the others somehow looked to her to summarize their grief. They were thin-drawn, worn-out Anglo-Saxon stock and all that remained of their vitality seemed to have flowed by a mysterious distillation into her. They were chiefly interested in her. They wanted boldly to know whether it was true about the Prince of—.

❡ Slaves may love their bondage, but all those in slavery are not slaves. What joy in the threat that the solid wall surrounding us is falling to rack and ruin—the whispers of measles running through the school on Monday morning, the news that the supply officer has run away with the mess fund, the rumor that the floor manager has appendicitis and won't be downtown for two weeks! "Break it up! Tear it down!" shouted the *sans culottes*, and I can distinguish my voice among the others. Stripes and short rations tomorrow, but for God's sake, give us our measure of hysteria today.

❢ Fed up with it—he wanted to deal again in the vapid, to deliver a drop of material solid out of the great gaseous world of men, and never again waste his priceless hours watching nothing and nothing with nothing.

❢ She was alone at last. There was not even a ghost left now to drift with through the years. She might stretch out her arms as far as they could reach into the night without fear that they would brush friendly cloth.

❢ Liking a man when he's tired.

❢ Felt utterly forlorn and defeated and outlasted by circumstances.

❢ She wanted to crawl into his pocket and be safe forever.

❢ She fronted the appalling truth. She could never love him, never while he lived. It was as if he had charged her to react negatively and so long as the current flowed she had no choice. Passionately she tried to think back to a few minutes before when the world had been tragic and glorious, but the moment was gone. He was alive, and as she heard his feet take up the chase again, the wings of her mind were already preening themselves for flight.

G

DESCRIPTIONS OF GIRLS

❢ She turned her slender smile full upon Lew for a moment, and then aimed it a little aside, like a pocket torch that might dazzle him.

C She was the dark Gunther—dark and shining and driven.

C He had not realized that flashing fairness could last so far into the twenties.

C Nevertheless, the bright little apples of her cheeks, the blue of the Zuyder Zee in her eyes, the braided strands of golden corn on the wide forehead, testified to the purity of her origin. She was the school beauty.

C Her beauty was as poised and secure as a flower on a strong stem; her voice was cool and sure, with no wayward instruments in it that played on his emotions.

C She was not more than eighteen—a dark little beauty with the fine crystal gloss over her that, in brunettes, takes the place of a blond's bright glow.

C Becky was nineteen, a startling little beauty, with her head set upon her figure as though it had been made separately and then placed there with the utmost precision. Her body was sturdy, athletic; her head was a bright, happy composition of curves and shadows and vivid color, with that final kinetic jolt, the element that is eventually sexual in effect, which made strangers stare at her. (Who has not had the excitement of seeing an apparent beauty from afar; then, after a moment, seeing that same face grow mobile and watching the beauty disappear moment by moment, as if a lovely statue had begun to walk with the meager joints of a paper doll?) Becky's beauty was the opposite of that. The facial muscles pulled her expressions into lovely smiles and frowns, disdains, gratifications and encouragements; her beauty was articulated, and expressed vividly whatever it wanted to express.

C Anyone looking at her then, at her mouth which was simply a kiss seen very close up, at her head that was a gorgeous detail escaped from the corner of a painting, not mere formal beauty but the beholder's unique discovery, so that it evoked different dreams to every man, of the mother, of the nurse, of the lost childish sweetheart or whatever had formed his first conception of beauty—anyone looking at her would have conceded her a bisque on her last remark.

❲ She was a stalk of ripe corn, but bound not as cereals are but as a rare first edition, with all the binder's art. She was lovely and expensive, and about nineteen.

❲ A lovely dress, soft and gentle in cut, but in color a hard, bright, metallic powder blue.

❲ An exquisite, romanticized little ballerina.

❲ He imagined Kay and Arthur Busch progressing through the afternoon. Kay would cry a great deal and the situation would seem harsh and unexpected to them at first, but the tender closing of the day would draw them together. They would turn inevitably toward each other and he would slip more and more into the position of the enemy outside.

❲ Her face, flushed with cold and then warmed again with the dance, was a riot of lovely, delicate pinks, like many carnations, rising in many shades from the white of her nose to the high spot of her cheeks. Her breathing was very young as she came close to him—young and eager and exciting.

❲ The intimacy of the car, its four walls whisking them along toward a new adventure, had drawn them together.

❲ A beauty that had reached the point where it seemed to contain in itself the secret of its own growth, as if it would go on increasing forever.

❲ Her body was so assertively adequate that someone remarked that she always looked as if she had nothing on underneath her dress, but it was probably wrong.

❰ A few little unattached sections of her sun-warm hair blew back and trickled against the lobe of the ear closest to him, as if to indicate that she was listening.

❰ A square-chinned, decided girl with fleshy white arms and a white dress that reminded Basil domestically of the lacy pants that blew among the laundry in the yard.

❰ He saw she was lying, but it was a brave lie. They talked from their hearts—with the half truths and evasions peculiar to that organ, which has never been famed as an instrument of precision.

❰ "I look like a *femme fatale*."

❰ After a certain degree of prettiness, one pretty girl is as pretty as another.

❰ Shimmering with unreality for the fancy-dress party.

❰ Popularly known as the "Death Ray." She was an odd little beauty with a skull-like face and hair that was a natural green-gold—the hair of a bronze statue by sunset.

❰ He rested a moment on the verandah—resting his eyes on a big honeysuckle that cut across a low sickle moon—then as he started down the steps his abstracted glance fell upon a trailer from it sleeping in the moonlight.

❰ She was the girl from foreign places; she was so asleep that you could see the dream of those places in the faint lift of her forehead. He struck the inevitable creaky strip and promptly the map of wonderland written on the surface of women's eyebrows creased into invisibility.

❰ His brisk blond sidelocks scratched her cheek while a longer tenuous end of gold silk touched him in the corner of his eye.

❰ She wore the usual little dishpan cover.

❲ She was small with a springy walk that would have been aggressive if it had been less dainty.

❲ Her mouth was made of two small intersecting cherries pointing off into a bright smile.

❲ What's a girl going to do with herself on a boat — fish?

❲ The girl hung around under the pink sky waiting for something to happen. There were strange little lines in the trees, strange little insects, unfamiliar night cries of strange small beasts beginning.

Those are frogs, she thought, or no, those are *crillons*—what is it in English?—those are crickets up by the pond.—That is either a swallow or a bat, she thought; then again, the difference of trees—then back to love and such practical things. And back again to the different trees and shadows, skies and noises—such as the auto horns and the barking dog up by the Philadelphia turnpike. . . .

❲ Her face, flowing out into the world under an amazing Bersaglieri bonnet, was epicene; as they disembarked at the hotel the sight of her provoked a curious sigh-like sound from a dense mass of women and girls who packed the sidewalk for a glimpse of her, and Bill realized that her position, her achievement, however transient and fortuitous, was neither a little thing nor an inheritance. She was beauty for a hundred afternoons, its incarnation in millions of aspiring or fading lives. It was impressive, startling and almost magnificent.

❲ Half an hour later, sitting a few feet from the judgment dais, he saw a girl detach herself from a group who were approaching it in threes—it was a girl in a white evening dress with red gold hair and under it a face so brave and tragic that it seemed that every eye in the packed hall must be fixed and concentrated on its merest adventures, the faintest impression upon her heart.

❦ Women having only one role—their own charm—all the rest is mimicry.

❦ If you keep people's blood in their heads it won't be where it should be for making love.

❦ Men get to be a mixture of the charming mannerisms of the women they have known.

❦ Her air of saying, "This is my opportunity of learning something," beckoned their egotism imperatively near.

❦ A frown, the shadow of a hair in breadth, appeared between her eyes.

❦ The little fourteen-year-old nymph in the Vagabonds.

❦ Wearing a kimono bright with big blue moons, she sat up among the pillows, drawing her lips by a hand-glass.

❦ He had thought of her once as a bubble and had told her about it—an iridescent soap-blown bubble with a thin delicate film over all the colors of the rainbow. He had stopped abruptly at that point but he was conscious, too, of the sun panning gold from the clear brooks of her hair, of her tawny skin—hell! he had to stop thinking of such things.

❦ She was eighteen, with such a skin as the Italian painters of the decadence used for corner angels, and all the wishing in the world glistening in her grey eyes.

❦ Wherever she was became a beautiful and enchanted place to Basil, but he did not think of it that way. He thought the fascination was inherent in the locality, and long afterward a commonplace street or the mere name of a city would exude a peculiar glow, a sustained sound, that struck his soul alert with delight. In her presence he was too absorbed to notice his surroundings; so that her absence never made them empty, but, rather, sent him seeking for her through haunted rooms and gardens that he had never really seen before.

C The glass doors hinged like French windows, shutting them in on all sides. It was hot. Down through three more compartments he could see another couple—a girl and her brother, Minnie said—and from time to time they moved and gestured soundlessly, as unreal in these tiny human conservatories as the vase of paper flowers on the table. Basil walked up and down nervously.

C Life burned high in them both; the steamer and its people were at a distance and in darkness.

C What was it they said? Did you hear it? Can you remember?

C She was a thin burning flame, colorless yet fresh. Her smile came first slowly, shy and bold, as if all the life of that little body had gathered for a moment around her mouth and the rest of her was a wisp that the least wind would blow away. She was a changeling whose lips were the only point of contact with reality.

C Came up to him taking his hand as though she was stepping into the circle of his arm.

C The tilted shadow of her nose on her cheek, the point of dull fire in her eyes.

C Mae's pale face and burning lips faded off, faded out, against the wild dark background of the war.

C The copper green eyes, greener than the green-brown foliage around them.

C She gave him a side smile, half of her face, like a small white cliff.

C Flustered, Johanna fumbled for an apology. Nell jumped up and was suddenly at the window, a glitter of leaves in a quick wind, a blond glow of summer lightning. Even in her

state of intimidation, Johanna noticed that she seemed to
bear with her, as she moved, a whole dream of women's
future; bore it from the past into the present, as if it were
a precious mystery she held in the carriage of her neck
and arms.

❲ A girl who could send tear-stained telegrams.

❲ The lady was annoyed, and so intense was her personality
that it had taken only a fractional flexing of her eyes to
indicate the fact. She was a dark, pretty girl with a figure
that would be full-blown sooner than she wished. She was
just eighteen.

❲ Hallie Bushmill was young and vivid and light, with a
boy's hair and a brow that bulged just slightly, like a baby's
brow.

❲ Sat a gold-and-ivory little beauty with dark eyes and a
moving childish smile that was like all the lost youth in the
world.

❲ He bent and kissed her braided forehead.

❲ Helen Avery's voice and the drooping of her eyes, when
she finished speaking, like a sort of exercise in control,
fascinated him. He had felt that they both tolerated something, that each knew half of some secret about people and
life, and that if they rushed toward each other, there would
be a romantic communication of almost unbelievable intensity. It was this element of promise and possibility that had
haunted him for a fortnight and was now dying away.

❲ Standing at the gate with that faint glow behind her,
Dinah was herself the garden's last outpost, its most representative flower.

❲ Lola Shisbe had never wrecked a railroad in her life.
But she was just sixteen and you had only to look at her to

know that her destructive period was going to begin any day now.

❡ He saw now, framing her face in the crook of his arm, her resemblance to Kay Phillips, or rather the genus to which they both belonged. The hard little chin, the small nose, the taut, wan cheeks—it was the way actresses made up to play the woman wronged and tubercular: a matter of structure and shadows of course, for they had fresh cheeks. Again, in Dinah the created lines were firmness—in Kay they had an aesthetic value alone.

❡ Your eyes always shining as if you had fever.

❡ Passing within the radius of the girl's perfume.

❡ Then for a moment they faded into the sweet darkness so deep that they were darker than the darkness, so that for a while they were darker than the black trees—then so dark that when she tried to look up at him she could but look at the wild waves of the universe over his shoulder and say, "Yes, I guess I love you, too."

❡ Nymph of the harvest.

❡ She was the tongue of flame that made the firelight vivid.

❡ "Sometimes I'd see you in the distance, moving along like a golden chariot." After twenty minutes of such eloquence, Alida began to feel exceedingly attractive. She was tired and rather happy, and eventually she said: "All right, you can kiss me if you want to, but it won't mean anything. I'm just not in that mood."

❡ Long white gloves dripping from her forearms.

❡ Her eyes shone at Bill with friendly interest, and then, just before the car shot away, she did something else with them—narrowed them a little and then widened them, recognizing by this sign the uniqueness of their relationship. "I see you," it seemed to say. "You registered. Everything's possible."

C Emily, who was twenty-five and carried space around with her into which he could step and be alone with their two selves.

C She was a bundle of fur next to Caros Moros, and he saw the latter drop his arm around her till they were one mass of fur together.

C He took them each in one arm, like a man in a musical comedy, and kissed the rouge on their cheeks.

C Her low voice wooed him casually from some impersonal necessity of its own.

C It was fine hearing Nora say that she never looked behind.

C A woman's laughter when it's like a child—just· one syllable, eager and approving, a crow and a cry of delight.

C She took it to the rocker and settled herself to a swift seasick motion which she found soothing.

C Her voice seemed to hesitate after consonants and then out came resonant and clear vowels—ahs and ohs and joyful ees lingering on the air.

C Her hair was soft as silk and faintly curling. Her hair was stiff fluff, her hair was a damp, thick shiny bank. It was not this kind or that kind, it was all hair.
Her mouth was (different things about her mouth, contrary things, impossible to reconcile—and always with:) It was not this kind or that kind of mouth, it was all mouths.
Also nose, eyes, legs, etc., same ending.

C Always a glisten of cold cream under her eyes, of wet rouge on her lips.

[140]

❲ Griselda was now unnaturally calm; as a woman becomes when she feels that, in the man, she has fulfilled her intuitive role and is passing along the problem to the man.

❲ Her lovely straggled hair.

❲ She felt nice and cool after a dip in the lake, felt her pink dress where it touched her, frothy as pink soda water, all fresh in the new wind. When Roger appeared, she would make him sorry for his haughtiness of the last twenty-four hours.

❲ He had once loved a girl with a blight (describe) on her teeth, who hid it by reaching down her upper lip when any emotion was in sight—laughter or tears—and laughing with a faint bowing of her head—and then, being absolutely sure she had not exposed her scar, laughing quite freely and exposing it. He had adopted the mannerism, and, to get on with what happened and why, he was still doing the same thing, etc.

❲ * * * *'s gay, brave, stimulating, "Tighten up your belt, baby, let's get going. To any Pole." I am astonished sometimes by the fearlessness of women, the recklessness like * *, * *, * *. In each case, it's partly because they are all three spoiled babies who never felt the economic struggle on their shoulders. But it's heartening when it stays this side of recklessness. In each case, I've had to strike a balance and become the cautious *petit bourgeois*, after, in each case, throwing them off their initial balance. Yet consider * * * *, who was a clergyman's daughter—and equally with the others had everything to lose and nothing to gain economically. She had the same recklessness. It's a question of age and the times to a great extent....

❲ * * * * looks like a trinket.

❲ Some impressions of the Carnival. What made everyone walk all through the train to get out; the boys smashing baggage at the station; the high snowdrifts; the girls' faces in the car windows drifting ghost-like past the watchers; the yell of recognition as a last watcher found some last girl; the figures in the dark passing the frat houses on their way to the carnival. The comparative bareness of the scene where the queens were chosen. How did some of those girls get there—some must have been accidents or at least chosen by pull or the wrong girl tapped—they weren't the twenty prettiest girls there. Some pretty girls must have ducked it.

℃ A young woman came out of the elevator and wavered uneasily across the lobby.

℃ Myron Selznick's, "Beautiful—she'll lose that pudgy baby fat."

℃ Beggar's lips that would not beg in vain.

℃ * * * * is still a flapper. Fashions, names, manners, customs and morals change, but for * * * * it is still 1920. This concerns me, for there is no doubt that she originally patterned herself upon certain immature and unfortunate writings of mine, so I have a special indulgence for * * * * as for one who has lost an arm or leg in one's service.

℃ She was a ripe grape, ready to fall for the mere shaking of a vine.

℃ The sunlight dodged down to her hair through bright red maple and bronze eucalyptus leaves that bent down low to say to the young men: "See, we are nothing beside her cheeks, her russet hair."

℃ One of those girls who straighten your necktie to show that in her lay the spirit of the eternal mother.

℃ A girl who thought the whole thing was awfully overestimated.

⟨ She's all tied up in knots, that girl.

⟨ Anything added to beauty has to be paid for—that is, the qualities that pass as substitutes can be liabilities when added to beauty itself.

⟨ The car was gay with girls, whose excited chatter filled the damp rubbery air like smoke.

⟨ Women are fragile that way. You do something to them at certain times and literally nothing can ever change what you've done.

⟨ Your voice with the lovely pathetic little peep at the crescendo of the stutter.

⟨ * * * * comes up to people when she meets them as if she were going to kiss them on the mouth, or walk right through them, looking them straight in the eyes—then stops a bare foot away and says her Hello, in a very disarming understatement of a voice. This approach is her nearest to Zelda's personality. Zelda's was always a vast surprise.

⟨ She kissed him several times then in the mouth, her face getting big as it came up to him, her hands holding him by the shoulders, and still he kept his arms by his side.

⟨ Among the very few domestics in sight that morning was a handsome young maid sweeping the steps of the biggest house on the street. She was a large simple Mexican girl with the large simple ambitions of the time and the locality, and she was already conscious of being a luxury—she received one hundred dollars a month in return for her personal liberty.

⟨ Who with every instant was dancing further and further off with Caros Moros into a youthful Spanish dream.

⟨ At [her] voice full of husky laughter his stomach froze.

[143]

⟨ Josephine's lovely face with its expression of just having led the children from a burning orphan asylum did the rest.

⟨ She admired him; she was used to clasping her hands together in his wake and heaving audible sighs.

⟨ She wore a blue crêpe-de-chine dress sprinkled with soft brown leaves that were the color of her eyes.

⟨ Instead, she let the familiar lift and float and flow of love close around them, pulling him back from his far-away uniqueness.

⟨ It was a harvest night, bright enough to read by. Josephine sat on the verandah steps listening to the tossing of sleepless birds, the rattle of a last dish in the kitchen, the sad siren of the Chicago-Milwaukee train.

⟨ She saw through to his profound woundedness, and something quivered inside her, died out along the curve of her mouth and in her eyes.

⟨ Their hearts had in some way touched across two feet of Paris sunlight.

⟨ Of a despairing afternoon in a little speakeasy on Forty-eighth Street in the last sad months.

⟨ Crackly yellow hair.

⟨ A girl with a bright red dress and a friendly dog jumping at her under the arcs.

⟨ Her face was a contrast between herself looking over a frontier—and a silhouette, an outline seen from a point of view, something finished—white, polite, unpolished—it was a destiny, scarred a little with young wars, worried with old white faiths . . . And out of it looked eyes so green that they were like phosphorescent marbles, so green that the scarcely dry clay of the face seemed dead beside it.

❡ The white glints in her eyes cracked the heavens as a diamond would crack glass, and let stream down a whiter light than he had ever seen before; it shone over a wide beautiful mouth, set and frightened.

❡ Looking for a last time into her eyes, full of cool secrets.

❡ Pushing a strand of indefinite hair out of her eyes.

❡ They swayed suddenly and childishly together.

❡ Mae Purley, without the involuntary quiver of an eyelash, fitted the young man into her current dream.

❡ For some years there had been the question as to whether or not Boops was going to have a nose. There was a sort of button between her big dark eyes, eyes that were round at the bottom, half moons hinting that half a person lay undivulged—but at eleven the button was still rudimentary and so unnoticeable that of a winter her elders were often driven frantic by its purls and mutterings, its gurgles, hisses and back-firings, before it occurred to them to say, "Blow it."

❡ He had passed the wire to her, to a white rose blooming without reason at the end of a cross-bar on the edge of space and time like a newly created tree.

❡ She was desperately adaptable, desperately sweet-natured.

❡ Her face was heart-shaped, an impression added to by honey-colored pointed-back hair which accentuated the two lovely rounds of her temples.

❡ She was a key-board all resonant and gleaming.

❡ He smoothed down her plain brown hair, knowing for the thousandth time that she had none of the world's dark magic for him, and that he couldn't live without her for six consecutive hours.

❦ Her childish beauty was wistful and sad about being so rich and sixteen.

❦ Much as the railroad kings of the pioneer West sent their waitress sweethearts to convents in order to prepare them for their high destinies.

❦ Basil's heart went bobbing around the ballroom in a pink silk dress.

H

DESCRIPTIONS OF HUMANITY (PHYSICAL)

❦ They rode through those five years in an open car with the sun on their foreheads and their hair flying. They waved to people they knew, but seldom stopped to ask a direction or check on the fuel, for every morning there was a gorgeous new horizon and it was blissfully certain that they would find each other there at twilight. They missed collisions by inches, wavered on the edge of precipices, and skidded across tracks to the sound of the warning bell. Their friends tired of waiting for the smash and grew to accept them as sempiternal, forever new as Michael's last idea or the gloss on Amanda's hair. One could almost name the day when the car began to splutter and slow up; the moment found them sitting in a Sea Food place on the water-front in Washington; Michael was opening his letters, his long legs thrust way under the table to make a footstool for Amanda's little slippers. It was only May but they were already bright brown and glowing. Their clothes were few and sort of pink in general effect like the winter cruise advertisements.

❦ The uni-cellular child effect—short dress.

❦ Cordell Hull—Donald Duck eyes?

❡ His hair was grey at thirty-five, but people said the usual things—that it made him handsomer and all that, and he never thought much about it, even though early grey hair didn't run in his family.

❡ When Jill died at last, resentful and bewildered to the end, Cass Erskine closed up his house, cancelled his contracts and took a boat around the world as far as Constantinople—no further because he and Jill had once been to Greece and the Mediterranean was heavy with memories of her. He turned back, loitered in the Pacific Isles and came home with a dread of the years before him.

❡ Attractive people are always getting into cars in a hurry or standing still and statuesque, or out of sight.

❡ * * * *'s expression, as if he could hardly wait till you did something else funny—even when I was ordering soup.

❡ His mannerisms were all girls' mannerisms, rather gentle considerations got from [—] girls, or restrained and made masculine, a trait that, far from being effeminate, gave him a sort of Olympian stature that, in its all-kindness and consideration, was masculine and feminine alike.

❡ Captain Saltonville—the left part of his hair flying.

❡ For better or worse, the awkward age has become shorter, and this youth seemed to have escaped it altogether. His tone was neither flip nor bashful when he said:

❡ Ernest—until we began trying to walk over each other with cleats.

❡ His features were well-formed against the flat canvas of his face.

❡ Dr. X's story about the Emperor of the World.

[147]

℃ Big fingers catching lisps from unintended notes. Arms crowded against his sides.

℃ Max Eastman—like all people with a swaying walk, he seemed to have some secret.

℃ Romanticism is really a childish throwback horror of being alone at the top—which is the real horror.

℃ Photographed through gauze.

℃ Women read a couple of books and see a few pictures because they haven't got anything else to do, and then they say they're finer in grain than you are, and to prove it they take the bit in their teeth and tear off for a fare-you-well—just about as sensitive as a fire horse.

℃ Pretty girl with dandruff in Rome.

℃ A long humorous pimply chin.

℃ A panama hat, under which burned fierce, undefeated Southern eyes.

℃ His heart made a dizzy tour of his chest.

℃ A gleam of patent Argentine hair.

℃ A lady whose lips, in continual process of masking buck teeth, gave her a deceptively pleasant expression.

℃ He was a tall, even a high young man.

℃ His old clothes with their faint smell of old clothes.

℃ The boy's defence of his mother's innocence in the Lausanne Palace Bar. His mother sleeping with the son of the Consul.

[148]

(Single way of imitating: distend nostrils, wave his head from side to side and talk through his nose.

(Francis' excitability, nerves, eyes, against calm atmosphere.

(They went to sleep easily on other people's pain.

(The air seemed to have distributed the applejack to all the rusty and unused corners of his body.

(His long, lanky body, his little lost soul in the universe, sat there on the bathroom window seat.

(The young man with a sub-Cro-Magnon visage.

(She did not plan; she merely let herself go, and the overwhelming life in her did the rest. It is only when youth is gone and experience has given us a sort of cheap courage that most of us realize how simple such things are.

(The oily drug store sweat that glistens on battle and struggle in films.

(He swelled out the muscles of his forehead but the perfect muscles of his legs and arms rested always quiescent, tranquil.

(Her dress wrapped around her like a wrinkled towel unnecessarily exposing her bottom.

(Always seems to be one deaf person in every room I'm in now.

(Receiving line—girls pirouette, men shifting from one foot to the other. Very gracious man shaking hands like crawl.

(The continual "don't remember" of amateur singers is annoying.

❲ Small black eyes buttoned to her face.

❲ * * * *   * * * *,* bound as Gulliver, vomiting on tread-mill, etc., 1932.

❲ Gus first learned to laugh, not because he had any sense of humor, but because he had learned it was fun to laugh—think of other types in society—as a girl learns it's pretty.

❲ Deep belly-laughs of H. L. M.

❲ He was not the frock-coated and impressive type of millionaire which has become so frequent since the war. He was rather the 1910 model—a sort of cross between Henry VIII and "our Mr. Jones will be in Minneapolis on Friday."

❲ He was one of those unfortunate people who are always constrained to atone for their initial aggressiveness by presently yielding a more important point.

❲ A white handsome face aghast—imprisoned eyes that had been left out and stepped on and a mouth [—] at the outrage.

❲ She held her teeth in the front of her mouth as if on the point of spitting them delicately out.

❲ Harlot in glasses.

❲ South—aviation caps, southern journalism, men's faces.

❲ Glass fowl eyes.

❲ A hand-serrated blue vein climbing the ridges of the knuckles and continuing in small tributaries along the fingers.

❲ Girls pushed by their arm in movies.

* A Hollywood writer.

❡ Thornton Wilder glasses in the rosy light.

❡ He was dressed in a tight and dusty readymade suit which evidently expected to take flight at a moment's notice, for it was secured to his body by a line of six preposterous buttons.
    There were supernumerary buttons upon the coat-sleeves, also, and Amanthis could not resist a glance to determine whether or not more buttons ran up the side of his trouser leg.

❡ Rather like a beachcomber who had wandered accidentally out of a movie of the South Seas.

❡ The good-looking, pimply young man with eyes of a bright marbly blue who was asleep on a dunnage bag a few feet away was her husband—

❡ Fat women at vaudeville or the movies repeating the stale wisecracks aloud and roaring at them.

❡ The steam heat brings out Aquilla's bouquet.

❡ Jews lose clarity. They get to look like old melted candles, as if their bodies were preparing to waddle. Irish get slovenly and dirty. Anglo-Saxons get frayed and worn.

❡ There was no hint of dissipation in his long warm cheeks.

❡ She carried a sceptre and wore a crown made by the local costumer, but due to the cold air the crown had undergone a peculiar chemical change and faded to an inconspicuous roan.

❡ Those terrible sinister figures of Edison, of Ford and Firestone—in the rotogravures.

❡ Round sweet smiling mouth like the edge of a great pie plate.

❡ She took an alarming photograph in which she looked rather like a marmoset.

❡ The bulbs, save for two, were dimmed to a pale glow; the faces of the passengers as they composed themselves for slumber were almost universally yellow-tired.

❡ He saw that they made a design, the faces profile upon profile, the heads blond and dark, turning toward Mr. Scofield, the erect yet vaguely lounging bodies, never tense but ever ready under the flannels and the soft angora wool sweaters, the hands placed on other shoulders, as if to bring each one into the solid freemasonry of the group. Then suddenly, as though a group of models posing for a sculptor were being dismissed, the composition broke and they all moved toward the door.

❡ His restless body, which never spared itself in sport or danger, was destined to give him one last proud gallop at the end.

❡ He had leaned upon its glacial bosom like a trusting child, feeling a queer sort of delight in the diamonds that cut hard into his cheek. He had carried his essential boyishness of attitude in a milieu somewhat less stable than gangdom and infinitely less conscientious about taking care of its own.

❡ Aquilla's brother—a colored boy who had some time ago replaced a far-wandering houseman, but had never quite acquired a name of his own in the household.

❡ Her buck teeth always made her look mildly, shyly pleasant.

❡ Then, much as a postwar young man might consult the George Washington Condensed Business Course, he sat at his desk and slowly began to turn the pages of *Bound to Rise*.

❡ So poor they could never even name their children after themselves but always after some rich current patron.

❡ The chin wabbling like a made-over chin, in which the

paraffin had run—it was a face that both expressed and inspired disgust.

℃ Men mouthed cigars grotesquely.

℃ A handsome girl with a dirty neck and furtive eyes.

℃ As an incorrigible masturbator, he was usually in a state of disgust with life. It came through, however, etc.

℃ For the first time a dim appreciation of the problems which Dr. Hines was called upon to face brought a dim, sympathetic sweat to his temples.

℃ The ones who could probably drive looked as if they couldn't type; the ones who looked as if they could type looked as if they couldn't drive with any safety—and the overwhelming majority of both these classes looked as though, even if they liked children, the child might not respond.

℃ "The German Prince is the horse-faced man with white eyes. This one—" He took a passenger list from his pocket, "—is either Mr. George Ives, or Mr. Jubal Early Robbins and valet, or Mr. Joseph Widdle with Mrs. Widdle and six children."

℃ A young man with one of those fresh red complexions ribbed with white streaks, as though he had been slapped on a cold day.

℃ Family like the last candies left in dish.

℃ She was so thin that she was no longer a girl, scarcely a human being—so she had to be treated like a *grande dame.*

℃ His face over his collar was like a Columbia salmon that had flopped halfway out of a can.

❡ A thin young man walking in a blue coat that was like a pipe.

❡ Run like an old athlete.

❡ She reminds me of a turned dress by Molyneux.

❡ They look like brother and sister, don't they? Except that her hair is yellow with a little red in it and his is yellow with a little green in it.

❡ He sat so low in the car that his bullet head was like a machine gun between the propellers of a plane.

I

IDEAS

❡ Play in which revolutionist in big scene—"Kill me," etc.—displays all bourgeois talents hitherto emphasized, paralyzes them with his superiority, and then shoots them.

❡ Lois and the bear hiding in the Yellowstone.

❡ *For Play.*
    Personal charm.
    Elsa Maxwell.
    Bert.
    Hotels.
    Pasts—great maturity of characters.
    Children—their sex and incomprehension of others.
    Serious work and worker involved. No more patience with idlers unless *about* them.

❡ Helpmate: Man running for Congress gets hurt in line of other duty and while he's unconscious his wife, on bad advice, plans to run in his stead. She makes a fool of herself. He saves her face.

❲ Family breaks up. It leaves mark on three children, two of whom ruin themselves keeping a family together and a third who doesn't.

❲ A young woman bill collector undertakes to collect a ruined man's debts. They prove to be moral as well as financial.

❲ * * * * * * * * running away from it all and finding that new ménage is just the same.

❲ Widely separated family inherit a house and have to live there together.

❲ Fairy who fell for wax dummy.

❲ Three people caught in triangle by desperation. Don't resolve it geographically, so it is crystallized and they have to go on indefinitely living that way.

❲ Andrew Fulton, a facile character who can do anything, is married to a girl who can't express herself. She has a growing jealousy of his talents. The night of her musical show for the Junior League comes and is a great failure. He takes hold and saves the piece and can't understand why she hates him for it. She has interested a dealer secretly in her pictures (or designs or sculptures) and plans to make an independent living. But the dealer has only been sold on one specimen. When he sees the rest he shakes his head. Andrew in a few minutes turns out something in putty and the dealer perks up and says, "That's what we want." She is furious.

❲ A Funeral: His own ashes kept blowing in his eyes. Everything was over by six and nothing remained but a small man to mark the spot. There were no flowers requested or proffered. The corpse stirred faintly during the evening but otherwise the scene was one of utter quietude.

℃ Story of a man trying to live down his crazy past and encountering it everywhere.

℃ A tree, finding water, pierces roof and solves a mystery.

℃ Father teaches son to gamble on fixed machine; later the son unconsciously loses his girl on it.

℃ A criminal confesses his crime methods to a reformer, who uses them that same night.

℃ Girl and giraffe.

℃ Marionettes during dinner party meeting and kissing.

℃ Play opens with man run over.

℃ Play about a whole lot of old people—terrible things happen to them and they don't really care.

℃ The man who killed the idea of tanks in England—his after life.

℃ Play: *The Office*—an orgy after hours during the boom.

℃ A bat chase. Some desperate young people apply for jobs at Camp, knowing nothing about wood lore but pretending, each one.

℃ The Tyrant Who Had To Let His Family Have Their Way For One Day.

℃ The Dancer Who Found She Could Fly.

℃ There was once a moving picture magnate who was shipwrecked on a desert island with nothing but two dozen cans of film.

❲ Angered by a hundred rejection slips, he wrote an extraordinarily good story and sold it privately to twenty different magazines. Within a single fortnight it was thrust twenty times upon the public. The headstone was contributed by the Authors' League.

❲ Driving over the rooftops on a bet.

❲ Girl whose ear is so sensitive she can hear radio. Man gets her out of insane asylum to use her.

❲ Boredom is not an end-product, is comparatively rather an early stage in life and art. You've got to go by or past or through boredom, as through a filter, before the clear product emerges.

❲ A man hates to be a prince, goes to Hollywood and has to play nothing but princes. Or a general—the same.

❲ Girl marries a dissipated man and keeps him in healthy seclusion. She meanwhile grows restless and raises hell on the side.

J

JINGLES AND SONGS

ONE SOUTHERN GIRL

Lolling down on the edge of time
    Where the flower months fade as the days move over,
Days that are long like lazy rhyme,
    Nights that are pale with the moon and the clover,

Summer there is a dream of summer
    Rich with dusks for a lover's food—
Who is the harlequin, who is the mummer,
    You or time or the multitude?

Still does your hair's gold light the ground
    And dazzle the blind till their old ghosts rise?
Then, all you care to find being found,
    Are you yet kind to their hungry eyes?
Part of a song, a remembered glory—
    Say there's one rose that lives and might
Whisper the fragments of our story:
    Kisses, a lazy street—and night.

FOR A LONG ILLNESS

Where did we store the summer of our love?
    Come here and help me find it.
Search as I may there is no trove,
    Only a dusty last year's calendar.
Without your breath in my ear,
    Your light in my eye to blind it,
        I cannot see in the dark.
            Oh, tender
Was your touch in spring, your barefoot voice—
In August we should find graver music and rejoice.

A long Provence of time we saw
    For the end—to march together
Through the white dust.
            The wines are raw—
Still that we will drink
    In the groves by the old walls in the old weather.
Two who were hurt in the first dawn
    Of battle; first to be whole again (let's think)
        If the wars grow faint, sweep over . . .
Come, we will rest in the shade of the *Invalides*, the lawn
Where there is luck only in three-leaf clover.

[158]

In the fall of sixteen
 In the cool of the afternoon
I saw Helena
 Under a white moon—
I heard Helena
 In a haunted doze
Say: "I know a gay place
 Nobody knows."

Her voice promised
 She'd live with me there,
She'd bring everything—
 I needn't care:
Patches to mend my clothes
 When they were torn,
Sunshine from Maryland,
 Where I was born.

My kind of weather,
 As wild as wild,
And a funny book
 I wanted as a child;
Sugar and, you know,
 Reason and Rhyme,
And water like water
 I had one time.

There'd be an orchestra
 Bingo! Bango!
Playing for us
 To dance the tango,
And people would clap
 When we arose,
At her sweet face
 And my new clothes.

But more than all this
    Was the promise she made
That nothing, nothing,
    Ever would fade—
Nothing would fade
    Winter or fall,
Nothing would fade,
    Practically nothing at all.

Helena went off
    And married another,
She may be dead
    Or some man's mother.
I have no grief left
    But I'd like to know
If she took him
    Where she promised we'd go.

CLAY FEET

Clear in the morning I can see them sometimes:
    Men, gods and ghosts, slim girls and graces—
Then the light grows, noon burns, and soon there come times
    When I see but the pale and ravaged places
Their glory long ago adorned.—And seeing
    My whole soul falters as an invalid
Too often cheered. Did something in their being
    Of worth go from them when my ideal did?

Men, gods and ghosts, cast down by that young damning,
    You have no answer; I but heard you say,
"Why, we are weak. We failed a bit in shamming."
    —So I am free! Will freedom always weigh
So much around my heart? For your defection,
    Break! You who had me in your keeping, break! Fall
From that great height to this great imperfection!
    Yet I must weep.—Yet can I hate you all?

[160]

FIRST LOVE*

All my ways she wove of light,
　　Wove them all alive,
Made them warm and beauty bright...
　　　So the trembling ambient air
　　　Clothes the golden waters where
　　The pearl fishers dive.

When she wept and begged a kiss
　　Very close I'd hold her,
And I know so well in this
　　　Fine fierce joy of memory
　　　She was very young like me
　　Though half an aeon older.

Once she kissed me very long,
　　Tiptoed out the door,
Left me, took her light along,
　　　Faded as a music fades...
　　　Then I saw the changing shades,
　　Color-blind no more.

THE POPE AT CONFESSION

The gorgeous Vatican was steeped in night,
　　The organs trembled on my heart no more,
But with a blend of colors on my sight
　　I loitered through a somber corridor;
When suddenly I heard behind a screen
　　The faintest whisper as from one in prayer;
I glanced about, then passed, for I had seen
　　A hushed, dim-lighted room—and two were there.

* Earlier versions of *First Love, The Pope at Confession* and *Marching Streets* appeared in *A Book of Princeton Verse II*, 1909, published by the Princeton University Press. *First Love* was there called *My First Love.*

A ragged friar, half in dream's embrace,
　Leaned sideways, soul intent, as if to seize
　　The last grey ice of sin that ached to melt
　　And faltered from the lips of him who knelt,
A little bent old man upon his knees
　With pain and sorrow in his holy face.

MARCHING STREETS

Death shrouds the moon and the long dark deepens,
　Hastens to the city, to the great stone heaps,
Blinds all eyes and lingers on the corners,
　Whispers on the corners that the last soul sleeps.

Gay grow the streets now, torched by yellow lamp-light,
　March all directions with a staid, slow tread;
East West they wander through the sodden city,
　Rattle on the windows like the wan-faced dead.

Ears full of throbbing, a babe awakens startled,
　Lends a tiny whimper to the still, dark doom;
Arms of the mother tighten round it gently,
　Deaf to the marching in the far-flung gloom.

Old streets hoary with dead men's footsteps,
　Scarred with the coach-wheels of a gold old age;
Young streets, sand-white, fresh-cemented, soulless,
　Virgin with the pallor of the fresh-cut page.

Black mews and alleys, stealthy-eyed and tearless,
　Shoes patched and coats torn, torn and dirty old;
Mire-stained and winding, poor streets and weary,
　Trudge along with curses, harsh as icy cold.

White lanes and pink lanes, strung with purple roses,
　Dancing from a meadow, weaving from a hill,
Beckoning the boy streets with stray smiles wanton,
　Strung with purple roses that the dawn must chill.

Soon will they meet, tiptoe on the corners,
    Kiss behind the foliage of the leaf-filled dark.
Avenues and highroads, bridlepaths and parkways,
    All must trace the pattern that the street-lamps mark.

Steps stop sharp! A clamor and a running!
    Light upon the corner spills the milk of dawn.
Now the lamps are fading and a blue-winged silence
    Settles like a swallow on a dew-drenched lawn.

LAMP IN THE WINDOW *

Do you remember, before keys turned in the locks,
When life was a close-up, and not an occasional letter,
That I hated to swim naked from the rocks
While you liked absolutely nothing better?

Do you remember many hotel bureaus that had
Only three drawers? But the only bother
Was that each of us got holy, then got mad
Trying to give the third one to the other.

East, west, the little car turned, often wrong
Up an erroneous Alp, an unmapped Savoy river.
We blamed each other, wild were our words and strong,
And, in an hour, laughed and called it liver.

And, though the end was desolate and unkind:
To turn the calendar at June and find December
On the next leaf; still, stupid-got with grief, I find
These are the only quarrels that I can remember.

* This poem appeared in the *New Yorker* of March 23, 1935, from
which it is reprinted here. Fitzgerald did not include it in his note-books,
but indicated that he wanted to correct the third line of the second
stanza to read as above.

We don't want visitors, we said:
　　They come and sit for hours and hours;
They come when we have gone to bed;
　　They are imprisoned here by showers;
They come when they are low and bored—
　　Drink from the bottle of your heart.
Once it is emptied, the gay horde,
　　Shouting the *Rubaiyat*, depart.

I balked: I was at work, I cried;
　　Appeared unshaven or not at all;
Was out of gin; the cook had died
　　Of small-pox—and more tales as tall.
On boor and friend I turned the same
　　Dull eye, the same impatient tone—
The ones with beauty, sense and fame
　　Perceived we wished to be alone.

But dull folk, dreary ones and rude—
　　Long talker, lonely soul and quack—
Who hereto hadn't dare intrude,
　　Found us alone, swarmed to attack,
Thought silence was attention; rage
　　An echo of their own home's war—
Glad we had ceased to "be upstage."
　　—But the nice people came no more.

OUR APRIL LETTER

❡ This is April again. Roller skates rain slowly down the street.

Your voice far away on the phone.

Once I would have jumped like a clown through a hoop —but.

"Then the area of infection has increased? . . . Oh . . . What can I expect after all—I've had worse shocks, anyhow, I *know* and that's something." (Like hell it is, but it's what you say to an X-ray doctor.)

Then the past whispering faint now on another phone:
"Is there any change?"
"Little or no change."
"I see."

The roller skates rain down the streets,
The black cars shine between the leaves,
Your voice far away:
"I am going with my daughter to the country. My husband left today . . . No he knows nothing."
"Good."
I have asked a lot of my emotions—one hundred and twenty stories. The price was high, right up with Kipling, because there was one little drop of something—not blood, not a tear, not my seed, but me more intimately than these, in every story, it was the extra I had. Now it has gone and I am just like you now.
Once the phial was full—here is the bottle it came in.
Hold on, there's a drop left there . . . No, it was just the way the light fell.
But your voice on the telephone. If I hadn't abused words so, what you said might have meant something. But one hundred and twenty stories . . .
April evening spreads over everything, the purple blur left by a child who has used the whole paint-box.

FRAGMENT

Every time I blow my nose I think of you
   And the mellow noise it makes
      Says I'll be true —
With beers and wines
With Gertrude Steins,
   With all of that
      I'm through—
'Cause every time I blow my no-o-ose
   I—think—of—you.

[165]

K

KARACTERS

(A Portrait: She will never be able to build a house. She hops herself up on crazy arrogance at intervals and wanders around in the woods chopping down everything that looks like a tree (*vide:* sixteen or twenty short stories in the last year, *all of them* about as interesting as the average high-school product and yet all of them "talented"). When she comes near to making a clearing, it looks too much to her like all the other clearings she's ever seen, so she fills it up with rubbish and debris and is ashamed even to speak of it afterwards. Driven, ordered, organized from without, she is a very useful individual—but her dominant idea and goal is freedom without responsibility, which is like gold without metal, spring without winter, youth without age, one of those maddening, coo-coo mirages of wild riches which make her a typical product of our generation. She is by no means lazy, yet when she chops down a tree she calls it work —whether it is in the clearing or not. She makes no distinction between *work* and mere sweat—less in the last few years since she has had arbitrarily to be led or driven.

(Someone who was as if heart and brain had been removed and were kept in a canopic vase.

(Lonsdale: "You don't want to drink so much because you'll make a lot of mistakes and develop sensibility and that's a bad trait for business men."

(He had once been a pederast and he had perfected a trick of writing about all his affairs as if his boy friends had been girls, thus achieving feminine types of a certain spurious originality.

(A dignity that would have been heavy save that behind it and carefully overlaid with gentleness, something bitter and bored showed through.

❡ There was, for instance, Mr. Percy Wrackham, the branch manager, who spent his time making lists of the Princeton football team, and of the second team and the third team; one busy morning he made a list of all the quarterbacks at Princeton for thirty years. He was utterly unable to concentrate. His drawer was always full of such lists.

❡ He abandoned the younger generation which had treated him so shabbily, and, using the connections he had made, blossomed out as a man of the world. His apprenticeship had been hard, but he had served it faithfully, and now he walked surefooted through the dangerous labyrinths of snobbery. People abruptly forgot everything about him except that they liked him and that he was usually around; so, as it frequently happens, he attained his position less through his positive virtues than through his ability to take it on the chin.

❡ He was a warrior; for him, peace was only the interval between wars, and peace was destroying him.

❡ "Against my better judgment," he would say, having no judgment, and "obviously" and "precisely."

❡ From the moment when, as a boy of twenty, his handsome eyes had gazed off into the imaginary distance of a Griffith Western, his audience had been really watching the progress of a straightforward, slow-thinking, romantic man through an accidentally glamorous life.

❡ A young lady "in pictures" who once, in the boom days of 1919, had been almost a star. It had been announced in the movie magazines that she was to "have her own company," but the company had never materialized. The second girl did interviews with "cinema personalities"—interviews which began, "When one thinks of Lottie Jarvis, one pictures a voluptuous tigress of a woman."

❡ He has a dark future. He hates everything.

❆ But if they haven't, it all comes out the same. Only if they control themselves, they forget their emotion, and so they think they haven't missed anything.

❆ "Don't get the idea that Seth doesn't ask anything. He's lived all his life off better minds than his own."

❆ Nicole's attitude toward sickness was either a sympathy toward a tired or convalescent relation who didn't need it—a sympathy which therefore was mere sentimentality, or else a fear when they were absolutely threatened with death. Toward real sickness—dirty, boring, unsympathetic—she could control no attitude—she had been brought up selfish in that regard. Often this was a source of anger and contempt to Dick.

❆ Idea about Nicole [that she] can do everything, extroverts toward everything save people. So earth, flowers, pictures, voices, comparisons. [She] seems to writhe—no rest wherever she turns, like a tom-tom beat. Escapes over the line, where in fantasy alone she finds rest.

❆ No first old man in an amateur production of a Victorian comedy was ever more pricked and prodded by the daily phenomena of life than was—

❆ Mrs. Rogers' voice drifted off on an indefinite note. She had never in her life compassed a generality until it had fallen familiarly on her ear from constant repetition.

❆ Instinct of Peggy Joyce collecting jewelry instead of bonds.

❆ *List of Troubles:*
  Heart burn
  Eczema
  Piles
  Flu
  Night Sweats

Alcoholism
Infected Nose
Insomnia
Ruined Nerves
Chronic Cough
Aching Teeth
Shortness of Breath
Falling Hair
Cramps in Feet
Tingling Feet
Constipation
Cirrhosis of the Liver
Stomach Ulcers
Depression and Melancholia

❢ He was wearing old white duck trousers with a Spanish flare and a few strange coins nodding at their seams, and a striped Riviera sweater, and straw shoes from the Bahamas, and an ancient Mexican hat. It was, for him, a typical costume, Diana thought. Always at Christmas she arranged to get him some odd foreign importation from parts as far away as possible from Loudoun County.

❢ When I like men I want to be like them—I want to lose the outer qualities that give me my individuality and be like them. I don't want the man; I want to absorb into myself all the qualities that make him attractive and leave him out. I cling to my own innards. When I like women I want to own them, to dominate them, to have them admire me.

❢ Like so many "men's women," she hid behind girls when available, as if challenging a man to break through and rescue her. Any group she was with became automatically a little club, protected by her frail, almost ethereal strength —tensile strength of thin fine wires.

❢ The old woman afraid of aeroplanes.

❦ When he was despised, it was rather more than usually annoying,—the last stages of throwing him over, I mean. For he knew it as soon as, if not sooner, than you, and seemed to hang about analyzing your actual method of accomplishing the business.

❦ Fatality of Beauty: Man who instinctively with people he liked turned the left side of face, the ugly half, had corresponding reaction on brain, spinal chord, etc., and had charm.

Contrariwise, right side of face exact opposite. Perfect— made him self-conscious, paralyzed mental and nervous etc.

To be worked out.

❦ The nervous quarrel between husband and wife, which had already caused sensitive passengers to have their tables changed in the dining salon.

❦ He had a knowledge of the interior of Skull and Bones.

❦ "You were so brave about people, George. Whoever it was, you walked right up to them and tore something aside as if it was in your way and began to know them. I tried to make love to you, just like the rest, but it was difficult. You drew people right up close to you and held them there, not able to move either way."

❦ Addresses in his pocket—mostly bootleggers and psychiatrists.

❦ Inescapable racial childishness. In the act of enjoying anything, wanted to tell. Sandy, Annabel, etc., trying to get everything out of first meeting.

❦ He seldom exuded liquor because now he had tuberculosis and couldn't breathe very freely.

[170]

❡ Just when somebody's taken him up and making a big fuss over him, he pours the soup down his hostess' back, kisses the serving maid and passes out in the dog kennel. But he's done it too often. He's run through about everybody, until there's no one left.

❡ "You mustn't do that, Abe," protested Mary. "Abe spends half his time living up to engagements he makes when he's tight. This spring in Paris he used to take dozens of cards and scraps of paper out of his pockets every morning, all scrawled with dates and obligations. He'd sit and brood over them for an hour before he dared tell me who was coming to lunch."

❡ "I've given parties that have made Indian rajahs green with envy. I've had prima donnas break $10,000 engagements to come to my smallest dinners. When you were still playing button back in Ohio, I entertained on a cruising trip that was so much fun that I had to sink my yacht to make the guests go home."

❡ Mother had explained his faults to Seth and found him extremely understanding.

❡ She wanted to be ringmaster—for a while. In somebody else's circus—a father's circus. "Look here, my father owns this circus. Give me the whip. I don't know how or why I snap it, but my father owns this circus. Give me your mask, clown—acrobat, your trapeze, etc."

❡ * * * * was a social impressario of considerable ability but her ambition had driven her to please so many worthless people that she had become, so to speak, a sort of lowest common denominator of all her clients.

❡ Zelda on Gerald's Irishness, face moving first.

❡ Hates old things, the past, Provence. A courtier.

℃ Constance Talmadge on my middle-class snobbishness. Also Fanny Brice.

℃ There is undoubtedly something funny about not being a lady, or rather about being a gold digger. You've got to laugh a lot like * * * * and * * * *

℃ Once tried to get up a ship's party on a ferry boat.

℃ You had to have a head of lettuce and mayonnaise, and she realized vaguely that the latter was seldom found in a wild state. Brought up in apartment hotels and married at the beginning of the delicatessen age, Vivian had not learned to cook anything save a strange fluid that in emergencies she evolved from coffee bean; she was most familiar with the product of the soil in such highly evolved forms as "triple combination sandwiches." A farm to her was a place where weary butterflies retired with their lovers after the last fade-out in the movies.

℃ Vivian Barnaby was just what her husband had made her, no masterpiece. She was pretty in a plaintive key, so was the child, and momentarily when you first met them you liked them for a certain innocence, a blowy immaturity— momentarily, that was all.

℃ Perhaps a drunk with great bursts of sentimentality or resentment or maudlin grief.

℃ He saw men acutely and he saw them small, and he was not invariably amused—it was obvious that his occasional dry humor was washed over the brim of an over-full vessel. Francis' first instinct was to defer to him as to an older man, a method of not bothering him, but he saw that Herkimer turned away from delicacy even more than from the commonness to which he was adjusted.

℃ Roscoe's gestures increasingly large and increasingly fall short. Again he "hates old things."

❦ Greatest vitality goes into displeasure and discontent.

❦ Irving—on the bust at fifty.

❦ He said that, no matter what happened, he always carried about his own can of olive oil. He had a large collection of lead soldiers and considered Ludendorf's memoirs one of the greatest books ever written. When McKisco said that history was already ruined by too much about war, Monsieur Brugerol's mouth twisted fiercely under his hooked nose, and he answered that history is a figured curtain, hiding that terrible door into the past through which we all must go.

❦ Capable of imaginative rudeness.

❦ Mother always waiting in waiting-rooms an hour early, etc., pulled forward by an irresistible urge of boredom and vitality.

❦ * * * * talks in several more syllables than she thinks in.

❦ He was one of those men who had a charger; she always knew it was tethered outside, chafing at its bit. But now, for once, she didn't hear it, though she listened for the distant snort and fidgeting of hoofs.

❦ Like most men who do not smoke, he was seldom still, and his moments of immobility were more taut and noticeable.

❦ Someone with a low voice who feels humble about it.

❦ About a man looking as if he was made up for a role he couldn't play.

❦ Mrs. Smith had been born on the edge of an imaginary precipice and had lived there ever since, looking over the precipice every half hour in horror, and yet unable to get herself away.

[173]

(Surprised that a creature so emotionally tender and torn as himself should have been able to set up such strong defenses around his will.

(My father is very much alive at something over a hundred, and always resents the fact that the fathers of most of the principal characters in my books are dead before the book begins. To please him, I once had a father stagger in and out at the end of the book, but he was far from flattered— however, this is a short word on money-lending. Father passed on to me certain ineradicable tastes in poetry: *The Raven* and *The Bells*, *The Prisoner of Chillon*.

(One button always showed at the front of his trousers.

(Family explained or damned by its dogs.

(Girl's tenderness against man's bogus humility.

(The drunk on *Majestic* and his hundred yard dash.

(Bogus girl who reads *Ulysses*—Wharton gives her a pain in the eye.

(As to Ernest as a boy: reckless, adventurous, etc. Yet it is undeniable that the dark was peopled for him. His bravery and acquired characteristics.

(All girls know some way to kill time, but * * * * knows all the ways.

(I never know what * * * * is—I only know what she's like. This year she seems to have a certain community of purpose with the Scarlet Pimpernel.

(For * * * * Communism is a spiritual exercise. He's making it his own.

[174]

(* * * *: An intellectual simpleton: He pleases you, not by direct design, but because his desire to please is so intense that it is disarming. He pleases you most perhaps when his very words are irritants.

(Boy from the Tropics: That wonderful book *Soldiers of Fortune* was a "gross misrepresentation." He was least objectionable when he talked about what they did to Igorrotes and how there were natives in the backhills of Luzon who had tails of real fur.

L

LITERARY

(* * * * * * * *'s Book: It was wonderful. I couldn't lay it down, was impelled on the contrary to hurry through it. In fact I finished it in six and a half minutes while getting shaved in the Continental Hotel. It is what we call a book written at a fine pace. As for the high spots, there are so many that it is difficult to pick them, but I could select.

(Nothing is any more permitted in fiction like stage convention of keeping people on stage by coincidences.

(Edgar Wallace—G. A. Henty.

(Must listen for conversation *à la* Joyce.

(Livid, demean, jejune—all misused.

(In a transition from, say fight or action interest to love and woman interest, the transition *cannot* be abrupt. The man must be *before* or *after* an event to be interested in women; that is, if he *is* a man and not a weakwad.

℃ Fault in transition in Musa Dagh book. After battle, right to Julia. Sometimes clumsy. Better an interval. You cannot tie two so different masculine emotions by the same thread.

℃ Nevertheless, value of Ernest's feeling about the pure heart when writing—in other words, the comparatively pure heart, the "house in order."

℃ Zelda's style formed on her letters to her mother—an attempt to make visual, etc.

℃ *This Side of Paradise:* A Romance and a Reading List.
   The Sun Also Rises: A Romance and a Guide Book.

℃ Resent the attempt of the boys and girls who tried to bury me before I was dead.

℃ Books are like brothers. I am an only child. Gatsby my imaginary eldest brother, Amory my younger, Anthony my worry, Dick my comparatively good brother, but all of them far from home. When I have the courage to put the old white light on the home of my heart, then . . .

℃ Shakespeare—whetting, frustrating, surprising and gratifying.

℃ Forbearance, good word.

℃ I can never remember the times when I wrote anything—*This Side of Paradise* time or *Beautiful and Damned* and *Gatsby* time, for instance. Lived in story.

℃ Idea for an essay on the "Lilies that fester" sonnet.

℃ That Willa Cather's poem shall stand at the beginning of Mediaeval* and that it shall be the story of Ernest.

* See editor's note at the beginning of *Note-Books.*

❲ What are successful backgrounds nowadays—think—
Coquette?

❲ Shows in which you forget background, remember no help
from description. Gas stations is the type.

❲ Just as Stendhal's portrait of a Byronic man made *Le
Rouge et le Noir,* so couldn't my portrait of Ernest as
Philippe make the real modern man?

❲ But there was one consolation:
They could never use any of Mr. Hemingway's four-letter
words, because that was for fourth class and fourth class has
been abolished—
(The first class was allowed to cheat a little on the matter.)
But on the other hand, they could never use any two-
letter words like NO. They *had* to use three-letter words like
YES!

❲ A character who spends all his time trying to break down
stray and careless aphorisms of great men. Give him a name
and list him under characters and note aphorisms as they
pop up in reading.

❲ There never was a good biography of a good novelist.
There couldn't be. He is too many people, if he's any good.

❲ The great hitch-hike to glory that's going to make them
good artisans—able to repair the car much in the manner
of the cars in this jacket frieze.

❲ And such condescension toward the creative life—Tol-
stoi caught the sense of the Napoleonic wars out in the street
from the man in the street; his comments on fiction, which
would make any old 1864 copy of *Leslie's* more humanly
valuable than *The Red Badge of Courage;* the idealization of
all that passes through his empty mind; his hatred of all
people who formed the world in which he lives; a political
Oscar Wilde peddling in the provinces the plums he took

from our pudding; his role of Jesus cursing. You can see him going from prize fight to first night to baseball game— maybe even to women—[people?] trying to put back into movement the very things Lenin regretted that he might have destroyed—gracelessness and ugliness, for its own sake. Gentlemen, proletarians—for a prize skunk I give you Mr. * * * *.

❲ D. H. Lawrence's great attempt to synthesize animal and emotional—things he left out. Essential pre-Marxian. Just as I am essentially Marxian.

❲ She had written a book about optimism called *Wake Up and Dream*, which had the beautiful rusty glow of a convenient half-truth—a book that left out illness and death, war, insanity, and all measure of achievement, with titillating comfortability. She had also written a wretched novel and a subsequent volume telling her friends how to write fiction, so she was on her way to being a prophet in the great American Tradition.

❲ When Whitman said "O Pioneers," he said all.

❲ Byron's mountains warm.

❲ Didn't Hemingway say this in effect: If Tom Wolfe ever learns to separate what he gets from books from what he gets from life, he will be an original. All you can get from books is rhythm and technique. He's half-grown artistically—this is truer than what Ernest said about him. But when I've criticized him (several times in talk), I've felt mad afterwards. Putting sharp weapons in the hands of his inferiors.

❲ Reporting the extreme things as if they were the average things will start you on the art of fiction.

❲ Work out my hard-luck season—my most productive seasons, etc.

❡ Conrad's secret theory examined: He knew that things do transpire about people. Therefore he wrote the truth and transposed it to parallel to give that quality, adding confusion however to his structure. Nevertheless, there is in his scheme a desire to imitate life which is in all the big shots. Have I such an idea in the composition of this book?

❡ Conrad influenced by *Man Without a Country*.

❡ No English painting because of their putting everything into words.

❡ Chapter in slow motion.

❡ Right to pretty heroines.

❡ Exact equivalent of escape mechanism in Little Colonel books is in escape mechanism of Greta Garbo films.

❡ Art invariably grows out of a period when, in general, the artist admires his own nation and wants to win its approval. This fact is not altered by the circumstance that his work may take the form of satire, for satire is the subtle flattery of a certain minority in a nation. The greatest grow out of these periods as the tall head of the crop. They may seem not to be affected, but they are.

❡ Great art is the contempt of a great man for small art.

❡ Tarkington: I have a horror of going into a personal debauch and coming out of it devitalized with no interest except an acute observation of the behavior of colored people, children and dogs.

❡ The queer slanting effect of the substantive, the future imperfect, a matter of intuition or ear to O'Hara, is unknown to careful writers like Bunny and John.

❡ My feelings on rereading *Imagination and a Few Mothers* and realizing that it had probably influenced Mrs. Swann's whole life.

❲ I thought Waldo Frank was just the pen name that a whole lot of other writers used for symposiums.

❲ When the first-rate author wants an exquisite heroine or a lovely morning, he finds that all the superlatives have been worn shoddy by his inferiors. It should be a rule that bad writers must start with plain heroines and ordinary mornings, and, if they are able, work up to something better.

❲ Man reads good reviews of his book so many times that he begins finally to remodel his style on them and use their rhythms.

❲ Realistic details like Dostoievsky glasses.

❲ *Re* Cole Porter: *vide* the ending of Mrs. Lowesboro Something, which does not bother even to be a paraphrase of Tchaikovsky's *Chanson Triste.*

❲ The Scandal of "English Teaching."

❲ The two basic stories of all times are *Cinderella* and *Jack the Giant Killer*—the charm of women and the courage of men. The Nineteenth Century glorified the merchant's cowardly son. Now a reaction.

❲ Taking things hard—from * * * * to * * * *:* That's the stamp that goes into my books so that people can read it blind like Braille.

❲ The Steinbeck scene. Out of touch with that life. The exact observation there.

❲ Bunny Wilson writing his Renan before Christ is deified.

❲ Analysis of *Tender:*
   I Case History 151-212: 61 pp. (change moon, p. 212)

* He mentions here his first great love and a Hollywood producer whom he considered to have spoiled one of his best scripts.

[180]

⊄ *Hope of Heaven* [a novel by John O'Hara]: He didn't bite off anything to chew on. He just began chewing with nothing in his mouth.

⊄ I talk with the authority of failure—Ernest with the authority of success. We could never sit across the same table again.

M

MOMENTS (WHAT PEOPLE DO)

⊄ Dogs:

We went through a routine, with a lot of false starts, charges, leg and throat holds, rolling over, and escapes.

I only barked a little in the bass to stretch my throat— I'm not one of the kind always shooting off their muzzle.

We followed a tall lady for awhile—no particular reason except she had a parcel with meat in it—we knew we wouldn't get any, but you never can tell. Sometimes I just feel like shutting my eyes and just following somebody pretending they're yours or that they're taking you somewhere.

The Brain wasn't there yet but the Beard was. He got out that damn pole and tried to kid me again, holding it out and jabbering—a long time ago I figured out that his object is to see if I'm fool enough to jump over it. But I don't bite, just walk around it. Then he tried the trick they all do— held my paws and tried to balance me up on the end of my spine. I never could figure out the point of that one.

I wanted to lick him, but when I came really close he snarled, "Scram!", and got half up on his haunches. He thought I was going to eat him just because he was down.

[181]

The little boy said, "Get away, you!", and it made me feel bad because I've never eaten a dog in my life and would not unless I was very hungry.

I must have had a hundred bones around here and I don't know why I save them. I never find them again unless accidentally, but I just can't stand leaving them around.

Ⅽ Thinking the world was going to start over with the things they could make of cellophane. Because for a moment everyone was making things of cellophane.

Ⅽ The idea of the *grande dame* slightly tight is one of the least impressive in the world. You know: "The foreign office will hear about this, hic!"

Ⅽ I once financed the great grandson of the great Morgan.

Ⅽ It was an old pistol, for as he took it away from her a slice of pearl came off the handle and fell on the floor.

Ⅽ Some kind of small animal that looked all wrong, "as if it were turned inside out," had emerged from the forest, regarded them curiously for a moment and hurried mysteriously away.

Ⅽ They were all hungry now, and sitting jaded beside the stream they developed individual tendencies to look around for a sign "Restaurant" or strain their ears for the tinkle of a dinner bell.

Ⅽ In Manila Mr. Barnaby had struck her with a whisk broom because she had ruined his life.

Ⅽ Nurses clucking. As if that confirmed some idea of life that they had held for long.

Ⅽ Dorothy Parker going Victorian, making up for the past by weeping—a sort of deliberate retrogression.

❦ He put out a mosquito on the paper and erased its body with the rubber.

❦ Her mouth fell open comically, she balanced a moment.

❦ She was asleep—he stood for a moment beside her bed, sorry for her, because she was asleep, and because she had set her slippers beside her bed.

❦ Everyone suddenly stiffened—after a terrible moment, Mrs. Littleton, by making herself figuratively into oil, managed to ooze a few words through.

❦ Only a fat Victorian pin-cushion filled with an assorted variety of many-colored-headed pins seemed to assure her that a well-brought-up girl would do the right thing.

❦ They ran for it through a blinding white hot crash.

❦ He cocked one miserable eye at the bright tropical stars.

❦ Belina, the young Corsican, yelled with glory as he bounced his aeroplane across the sky.

❦ The inebriated American who had invited him to lunch thought at first that Val was a son of the czar.

❦ "Dramatic club! Oh gosh!" cried the girl. "Did you hear that? She thinks it's a dramatic club, like Miss Pinkerton's school." In a moment her uninfectious laughter died away.

❦ Back in the sitting room, he resumed his walking; unconsciously he was walking with his father, the judge, dead thirty years ago; he was parading his dead father up and down the room.

❦ The cuff-button dropped to the floor; he stooped to pick it up and then said "Helen!" urgently into the mouth-piece to cover the fact that he had momentarily been away.

❦ The water went into his nose and started a raw stinging; it blinded him; it lingered afterward in his ears, rattling back and forth like pebbles for hours.

❦ The silence was coming from some deep place in Mrs. Ives' heart.

❦ The almost regular pat-smack, smack-pat-pat of the balls, the thud of a jump, and the overtone of the umpire's "Fault"; "Out"; "Game and set, 6—2, Mr. Oberwalter."

❦ Our fathers died. Suddenly in the night they died and in the morning we knew.

❦ They laughed, ending with yawning gurgles that were not laughed out but sucked in.

❦ She yet spoke somewhat sharply, as people will with a bitter refusal to convey.

❦ To ride off into the sunset in such a chariot, into the very husn and mystery of night, beside him the mystery of that baby-faced girl.

❦ Couple treading water dancing.

❦ Wiping his chin with a long rag which he took from some obscure section of his upholstery.

❦ When he left the house, their engagement was over, but her love for him was not over and her hope was not gone, and her actions had only begun.

❦ If Teddy had played the current sentimental song from *Erminie*, and had played it with feeling, she would have understood and been moved, but he was plunging her suddenly into a world of mature emotions, whither her nature neither could nor wished to follow.

❲ A chorus of pleasant envy followed in the wake of their effortless glamour.

❲ He threw his hands up so high it seemed as if they left his wrists and were caught again on their descent.

❲ Hesitation before name doesn't displease.

❲ Behind them a long haired Nebraska pederast told the plot in mournful numbers.

❲ He went back into the bathroom and swallowed a draught of rubbing alcohol guaranteed to produce violent gastric disturbances.

❲ He put his mind in order with a short résumé of the history of music, beginning with some chords from *The Messiah* and ending with Debussy's *La Plus que Lente*, which had an evocative quality for him, because he had first heard it the day his cat died.

❲ Clubbing him with his taller fist, his head side-swiped a fence, with blood tasting on his mouth and going cold on his ear lobes.

❲ Trying to dismiss him as a sort of inspired fairy.

❲ Opens magazine several times at the fact that poetry is at crossroads.

❲ A beam, soft and pleasant, fell across his spirit. Those two beings, tender and cloud-like, unreal, with the little sins of little people. They were no more than sick-room flowers where he lay.

❲ But at the look of childish craftiness in her eyes he took it back quickly.

❲ She leaned back comfortably against the water pipe, as one enjoying the moment at leisure. He lit her cigarette impatiently and waited.

❲ She walked toward the dressing table as though her own reflection was the only decent company with which to foregather.

❲ De Sano tearing the chair.

❲ The funeral carriages—a man smoking in the last.

❲ Two brown port bottles appeared ahead, developed white labels, turned into starched nuns, who seared us with holy eyes as we went by.

❲ We left him there dancing with a fluttering waiter.

❲ Dog arrives. I call him. Doesn't like me. Expressionless, he passes on.

❲ Her voice trying to blow life into the dead number 2-0-1-1.

❲ Mother majestically dipping her sleeves in the coffee.

❲ His ecstasy made him use the cane. He pointed it at little patches of snow that still remained on the ground and then raised it overhead, dragging it through the lower limbs of the trees.

❲ There was a flick of the lip somewhere, a bending of the smile toward some indirection, a momentary lifting and dropping of the curtain over a hidden passage.

❲ He sat back robbed and glowering.

❲ Hats coming off, thought it was his head.

❲ Went into the bathroom and sat on the seat, crying because it was more private than anywhere she knew.

❲ When he urinated, it sounded like night prayer.

❲ The feeling that she was (his) began between his shoulders and spread over him like a coat going on.

[186]

℃ A thing called the *Grand Canyon Suite*, which seemed to me to lean heavily on *Horses Horses Horses*.

℃ Breaking into an *Off to Buffalo* against a sudden breath of wet wind.

℃ Shocked at five razor blades instead of twelve.

℃ Shuddering with pleasure at the difficult idiom.

℃ The young people got back into the boat—they all felt fine and quietly passionate.

℃ When she heard his footsteps again, she turned frankly and held his eyes for a moment until his turned away, as a woman can when she has the protection of other men's company.

℃ An idea ran back and forth in his head like a blind man, knocking over the solid furniture.

℃ He had written a complimentary letter to Mr. X, the humorist, for an autograph and had received Mr. X's form letter, which was a joke. "About bunions, Dear Sir," the letter said, "My advice to you is to—"

℃ Her mother handed the passenger list across the table— her fingers so meticulously indicating the name that Rosemary had to pry it up to read.

℃ Person driving away after seeing friend off—"I'm glad you've gone John," and does a takem, glancing back.

℃ "Bring me a box of Elizabeth Arden," you'd wired me, and how our love shone through any old trite phrase in a telegram.

℃ After a while a skittish lady with an air of being pursued slipped in and not without a few wary glances around achieved sanctuary in the front row.

❡ The moment of closeness between savagery and civilization never closer than in the self-consciousness of truces and surrenders of men in love with the same girl, or in common life when we handle money. Scene to show this—paying Flora, setting down money on bureau—"No, you keep it," etc.

❡ I have known and analyzed too much charm to be impressed by ladies who recompose their features after an interdict.

N

NONSENSE AND STRAY PHRASES

❡ King's Own Leopards.

❡ "I've arranged that if anything should happen to you, the remains will be kept in cold storage until I return."

❡ They were startled—that was inevitable; one couldn't crash right in on people without tearing a little bit of diaphanous material.

❡ The car waited tenderly for a minute.

❡ All around her he could feel the vast Mortmain fortune melting down, seeping back into the matrix whence it had come.

❡ Scott Fitzgerald climax runner for the Cal. "Courtesans" today passed his zenith. It was rushed after him to Peoria, Indiana, but by that time the soap on the nursery floor had become a shambles.

❡ He had long forgotten whether Darrow called Scopes a monkey or Bryan called Darrow a scope or why Leopold-Loeb was ever tried in the first place.

❈ Burlesque on Molly Pitcher in Dos Passos Manner: Continentals starving for want of coal finally get some, but can't digest it because it's hard coal. After the war—hollow victory—they lost Montreal and it's wet. Profiteers in daguerreotypes. Everybody tired of *Yankee Doodle.* Men seasick crossing the Delaware. Rammed her petticoat down cannon, she was restrained. British walked away with hands over their eyes.

❈ Ernest Hemingway, while careful to avoid clichés in his work, fairly revels in them in his private life, his favorite being *"Parbleu!"* ("So what?"—French), and "Yes, We Have No Bananas." Contrary to popular opinion, he is not as tall as Thomas Wolfe, standing only six feet five in his health belt. He is naturally clumsy with his body, but shooting from a blind or from adequate cover, makes a fine figure of a man. We are happy to announce that his work will appear in future exclusively on United States postage stamps.

❈ Thomas Wolfe or "Loup" (*Anthony Adverse, Time and the River, N. Y. Telephone Directory,* 1935) is a newcomer to American Skulduggery. Born during a premium contest.

❈ Name: Luna Gineva.

❈ Backwoods Names: Olsie, Hassie, Coba, Bleba, Onza (Ozma —my own), Retha, Otella, Tatrina, Delphia, Wedda, Zan-nis, Avaline, Burtryce, Chalme, Glenola, Turla, Verlie, Legitta, Navilla, Oha, Verla, Blooma, Inabeth, Versia, Gomeria, Valaria, Berdine, Olabeth, Adelloyd.
   Niggers: Glee, Earvial, Aerial, Roayna, Margerilla, Paro-lee, Ferdiliga, Abolena, Iodine, Tooa, Negolna.
   Name: Tycoonskins.

❈ *The Barnyard Boys* or *Fun on the Soil:*
   George Barnyard
   Thomas Barnyard
   Glenway Barnyard

Lladislas Barnyard, their uncle
Knut Barnyard, their father
Burton Smalltown, the hired man
Chambers, a city dude
Ruth Kitchen
Martha Kitchen
Willa Kitchen, their mother
Little Edna, an orphan
Margaret Kitchen

"How Hamsun you are looking!" cried the fan.

Chambers dressed 1903.

It was winter, summer, spring, anything you like, and
the Barnyard Boys were merrily at work getting together
epics of the American soil in time for the next publishing
season. All day long they dug around in the great Hardy
fields, taking what would come in handy in the next winter
(or spring, summer—the seasons follow one another, tearing
up growths of [—] by the roots.)

❲ To dine at a "serious" restaurant.

❲ Proximity of her tan legs.

❲ Economy Statements:
    They're much less expensive to run.
    It's all right to run around in.
    It'll do to wear around the house.
    It'll keep us from being extravagant and inviting too
many people to dinner.
    It'll do till we have another.
    We're saving that up so we'll have something to look
forward to.
    That's good for the moths.
    It (a carpet) just gets worn out in this house.
    We want to wait until we get a really nice one.

[190]

⊂ A weak heart, a sick heart, a broken heart or a chicken heart?

⊂ Shot through bald forehead—like where a picture and its nail had been removed from wall.

⊂ The Thyroid Islands.

⊂ He would be part of that great army divided by the dark storm.

⊂ Listen, little Elia: draw your chair up close to the edge of the precipice and I'll tell you a story.

⊂ Drifting towards some ignoble destiny they could not evade.

⊂ Then I was drunk for many years, and then I died.

⊂ It would have been a bigger picture if he could have had everyone gilded.

⊂ Since his wife ran off one windy night and gave him back the custody of his leisure hours.

⊂ He had hit her before and she him.

⊂ Far gone, far called, far crowned.

⊂ We gave the corpse twenty-four hours to leave town.

⊂ *Esprit frondeur.*

⊂ As twice as a double bumble bee.

⊂ The aristocratic nose and the vulgar heart.

⊂ Superfluous as a Gideon Bible in the Ritz.

℃ Given at his birth a spoonful of noxema just brought from Palestine.

℃ One can do little more than deny the persistent rumors that hover about him; for instance that he was born in a mole cave near Schenectady, in a state of life-long coma—conversely, that his father was a certain well-known international munitions manufacturer of pop-guns, a notorious blatherskite who earned a precarious living in the dives of Zion City or, as others say, a line coach at a famous correspondence school.

℃ Simile about paper they paste on glass during building.

℃ I have never wished there was a God to call on—I have often wished there was a God to thank.

℃ "Sure—you did a sequence for Collins with a watch face and some little cardboard silhouettes. It was very interesting."

℃ Better Hollywood's bizarre variations on the normal, with * * * * * * * * on the phone ordering twelve girls for dinner, none over eighteen.

℃ We'll find you a pooch that'll say "Arp."

℃ Dive back, Aphrodite, dive back and try for the fish undersea.

℃ The blue-green unalterable dream.

℃ A day full of imaginary telegrams.

℃ Wit born in darkness of college movie houses.

℃ The "Wyn" in Metro-Goldwyn-Mayer. Explain its presence.

℃ I think I'd better go out and stay too long—don't you?

(At two-thirty this afternoon the Countess of Fréjus will be fired out of this cannon.

(Antibes before the merchants came.

(I may as well spend this money now. Hell, I may never get it.

TURKEY REMAINS AND HOW TO INTER THEM
WITH NUMEROUS SCARCE RECIPES

(At this post holiday season, the refrigerators of the nation are overstuffed with large masses of turkey, the sight of which is calculated to give an adult an attack of dizziness. It seems, therefore, an appropriate time to give the owners the benefit of my experience as an old gourmet, in using this surplus material. Some of the recipes have been in the family for generations. (This usually occurs when rigor mortis sets in.) They were collected over years, from old cook books, yellowed diaries of the Pilgrim Fathers, mail order catalogues, golf-bats and trash cans. Not one but has been tried and proven—there are headstones all over America to testify to the fact.

Very well then: here goes:

1. *Turkey Cocktail:* To one large turkey add one gallon of vermouth and a demijohn of angostura bitters. Shake.

2. *Turkey à la Française:* Take a large ripe turkey, prepare as for basting and stuff with old watches and chains and monkey meat. Proceed as with cottage pudding.

3. *Turkey and Water:* Take one turkey and one pan of water. Heat the latter to the boiling point and then put in the refrigerator. When it has jelled, drown the turkey in it. Eat. In preparing this recipe it is best to have a few ham sandwiches around in case things go wrong.

4. *Turkey Mongole:* Take three butts of salami and a large turkey skeleton, from which the feathers and natural

stuffing have been removed. Lay them out on the table and call up some Mongole in the neighborhood to tell you how to proceed from there.

5. *Turkey Mousse:* Seed a large prone turkey, being careful to remove the bones, flesh, fins, gravy, etc. Blow up with a bicycle pump. Mount in becoming style and hang in the front hall.

6. *Stolen Turkey:* Walk quickly from the market, and, if accosted, remark with a laugh that it had just flown into your arms and you hadn't noticed it. Then drop the turkey with the white of one egg—well, anyhow, beat it.

7. *Turkey à la Crême:* Prepare the crême a day in advance. Deluge the turkey with it and cook for six days over a blast furnace. Wrap in fly paper and serve.

8. *Turkey Hash:* This is the delight of all connoisseurs of the holiday beast, but few understand how really to prepare it. Like a lobster, it must be plunged alive into boiling water, until it becomes bright red or purple or something, and then before the color fades, placed quickly in a washing machine and allowed to stew in its own gore as it is whirled around. Only then is it ready for hash. To hash, take a large sharp tool like a nail-file or, if none is handy, a bayonet will serve the purpose—and then get at it! Hash it well! Bind the remains with dental floss and serve.

9. *Feathered Turkey:* To prepare this, a turkey is necessary and a one pounder cannon to compel anyone to eat it. Broil the feathers and stuff with sage-brush, old clothes, almost anything you can dig up. Then sit down and simmer. The feathers are to be eaten like artichokes (and this is not to be confused with the old Roman custom of tickling the throat.)

10. *Turkey à la Maryland:* Take a plump turkey to a barber's and have him shaved, or if a female bird, given a

facial and a water wave. Then, before killing him, stuff with old newspapers and put him to roost. He can then be served hot or raw, usually with a thick gravy of mineral oil and rubbing alcohol. (Note: This recipe was given me by an old black mammy.)

11. *Turkey Remnant:* This is one of the most useful recipes for, though not "chic," it tells us what to do with turkey after the holiday, and how to extract the most value from it. Take the remnants, or, if they have been consumed, take the various plates on which the turkey or its parts have rested and stew them for two hours in milk of magnesia. Stuff with moth-balls.

12. *Turkey with Whiskey Sauce:* This recipe is for a party of four. Obtain a gallon of whiskey, and allow it to age for several hours. Then serve, allowing one quart for each guest. The next day the turkey should be added, little by little, constantly stirring and basting.

13. *For Weddings or Funerals:* Obtain a gross of small white boxes such as are used for bride's cake. Cut the turkey into small squares, roast, stuff, kill, boil, bake and allow to skewer. Now we are ready to begin. Fill each box with a quantity of soup stock and pile in a handy place. As the liquid elapses, the prepared turkey is added until the guests arrive. The boxes delicately tied with white ribbons are then placed in the handbags of the ladies, or in the men's side pockets.

There I guess that's enough turkey talk. I hope I'll never see or hear of another until—well, until next year.

O

OBSERVATIONS

℃ * * * * trying to carry with him the good of every age—one must discard, no matter from how unworthy a motive. Trying to see good in everyone, he saw only his own good.

❡ Drunk at 20, wrecked at 30, dead at 40.
  Drunk at 21, human at 31, mellow at 41, dead at 51.

❡ Like all men who are fundamentally of the group, of the herd, he was incapable of taking a strong stand with the inevitable loneliness that it implied.

❡ Voices: American doubtful—"Well, I don't know"; English saying, "Extraordinary," refusing to think; French saying, "Well, there you are."

❡ Apropos of Cocteau—perverts' love of perverted children m[asculine] or f[eminine], is compensation for missing women, who are, in their social aspect, children with guile and sometimes wisdom, but still children.

❡ Like all self-controlled people, the French talk to themselves.

❡ She knew that she herself was superior in something to the girls who criticized her—though she often confused her superiority with the homage it inspired.

❡ Too soon they were responding to Josephine with a fatal sameness, a lack of temperament that blurred their personalities.

❡ Cocktails before meals like Americans, wines and brandies like Frenchmen, beer like Germans, whiskey-and-soda like the English, and, as they were no longer in the twenties, this preposterous mélange, that was like some gigantic cocktail in a nightmare.

❡ Do you know what your affair was founded on? On sorrow. You got sorry for each other.

❡ Young people do not perceive at once that the giver of wounds is the enemy and the quoted tattle merely the arrow.

[196]

❲ Arbitrary groups formed by the hazards of money or geography may be sufficiently quarrelsome and dull, but for sheer unpleasantness the condition of young people who have been thrust together by a common unpopularity can be compared only with that of prisoners herded in a cell. In Basil's eyes the guests at the little dinner the following night were a collection of cripples.

❲ I can even live with a lie (even someone else's lie—can always spot them because imaginative creation is my business and I am probably one of the most expert liars in the world and expect everybody to discount nine-tenths of what I say), but I have made two rules in attempting to be both an intellectual and a man of honor simultaneously—that *I do not tell myself lies that will be of value to myself*, and secondly, *I do not lie to myself*.

❲ They went on to the party. It was a housewarming, with Hawaiian musicians in attendance, and the guests were largely of the old crowd. People who had been in the early Griffith pictures, even though they were scarcely thirty, were considered to be of the old crowd; they were different from those coming along now and they were conscious of it.

❲ The combination of a desire for glory and an inability to endure the monotony it entails puts many people in the asylum. Glory comes from the unchanging din-din-din of one supreme gift.

❲ France was a land, England was a people, but America, having about it still that quality of the idea, was harder to utter—it was the graves at Shiloh and the tired, drawn, nervous faces of its great men, and the country boys dying in the Argonne for a phrase that was empty before their bodies withered. It was a willingness of the heart.

❲ The real plot of all Little Theatre plays, the one that transpires through whatever play they're officially acting, is how the young gosling actor of fourteen ever managed to be in love with the leading woman of forty and what's going to come of the situation. The reality of this gives that blurred air that the performances always have.

☾ It is difficult for young people to live things down. We will tolerate vice, grand larceny and the quieter forms of murder in our contemporaries, because we think of ourselves as so strong and incorruptible, but our children's friends must show a blank service record.

☾ What would you rather be loved for, your beauty, your intrinsic worth, your money?
    First two vanish and are replaced by their equivalents: beauty, by charm and tact; spirituality and energy, by experience and intelligence. Third never knows any change.

☾ Why do whores have husky voices?

☾ After all, any given moment has its value; it can be questioned in the light of after-events, but the moment remains. The young prince in velvet gathered in lovely domesticity around the queen amid the hush of rich draperies may presently grow up to be Pedro the Cruel or Charles the Mad, but the moment of beauty was there.

☾ Perhaps that life is constantly renewed, and glamour and beauty make way for it.

☾ "A pair of thoroughbreds, those two," said the other woman complacently, meaning that she admitted them to be her equals.

☾ Family quarrels are bitter things. They don't go according to any rules. They're not like aches or wounds; they're more like splits in the skin that won't heal because there's not enough material.

☾ One advantage of politeness is to be able to deal with women on their own grounds, to please or to torture the enemy, as it may prove necessary. And not to fire random shots and flowers from the pure male camp many miles away.

℃ Advantage of politeness: Extending out of ordinary world, etc.

℃ Actors the clue to much.

℃ It is in the thirties that we want friends. In the forties we know they won't save us any more than love did.

℃ But the world is always curious, and people become valuable merely for their inaccessibility.

℃ You can usually scare a certain amount of brains into a woman but usually you can't make them stick.

℃ Force of a proverb in another language.

℃ He felt then that if the pilgrimage eastward of the rare poisonous flower of his race was the end of the adventure which had started westward three hundred years ago, if the long serpent of the curiosity had turned too sharp upon itself, cramping its bowels, bursting its shining skin, at least there had been a journey; like to the satisfaction of a man coming to die—one of those human things that one can never understand unless one has made such a journey and heard the man give thanks with the husbanded breath. The frontiers were gone—there were no more barbarians. The short gallop of the last great race, the polyglot, the hated and the despised, the crass and scorned, had gone—at least it was not a meaningless extinction up an alley.

℃ Despairingly and miserably, to what purpose neither knew, as people in fires save things they don't want and have long disliked.

℃ He had one of those minds so incomprehensible to the literary man, which are illiterate not through insensibility but through the fact that the past and future are with them contemporary with the present, having no special value or pathos of their own.

❧ No learning without effort—educational movies.

❧ When we do something mean to a friend we think of it as an exception in our relations with him, but as a matter of fact it has immediately become the type thing. We have just one time.

❧ My sometimes reading my own books for advice. How much I know sometimes—how little at others.

❧ This being in love is great—you get a lot of compliments and begin to think you're a great guy.

❧ Very strong personalities must confine themselves in mutual conversation to very gentle subjects. Everything eventually transpires—but if they start at a high pitch as at the last meeting of Ernest, Bunny and me, their meeting is spoiled. It does not matter who sets the theme or what it is.

❧ If you're strong enough, there *are* no precedents.

❧ Gertrude Harris about pleasure of giving. The excess.

❧ Didn't finish idea today that lack of success of physical sheer power in my life made trouble. Fighting through intellectual power—parallel in life of modern woman—courage in Zelda, etc.

❧ They had a dignity and straightforwardness about them from the fact that they had worked in pictures before pictures were bathed in a golden haze of success. They were still rather humble before their amazing triumph, and thus, unlike the new generation, who took it all for granted, they were constantly in touch with reality. Half a dozen or so of the women were especially aware of being unique. No one had come along to fill their places; here and there a pretty face had caught the public imagination for a year, but those of the old crowd were already legends, ageless and disembodied. With all this they were still young enough to believe that they would go on forever.

C Like a bad play where there is nothing to do but pick out the actors that look most like real people and watch them until, like amateurs, their true existence has become speculatively interesting.

C Something in his nature never got over things, never accepted his sudden rise to fame, because all the steps weren't there.

C Francis says he's tired of a life like a full glass of water, relations with people a series of charades, you never do the whole world.

C Is snubbed when he dramatizes himself as victim of American failure.

C De Sano: If you use both logic and imagination you can destroy everything in the world between them.

C Men hate to stay in hotel run by woman.
   Women *vice versa*.

C The American capitol, not being New York, was of enormous importance in our history. It had saved the Union from the mobs in '63—but, on the other hand, the intellectual drifted to the Metropolis and our politics were childish from lack of his criticism.

C Each of us thinks his own life has been, etc.

C Fairy can only stand young girls on stage, where they're speaking other people's lines.

℃ The laugh generated by Fred Stone's "I'm so nervous," in *The Wizard of Oz* justified a whole generation in cultivating nerves.

℃ Subject of control: British pitch—from strength easy, from nervous effort hard—therefore a moral question?

℃ It seemed to her that the dance was woman's interpretation of music; instead of strong fingers, one had limbs with which to render Tschaikowsky and Stravinsky; and feet could be as eloquent in *Chopiniana* as voices in *The Ring*. At the bottom, it was something sandwiched in between the acrobats and the trained seals; at the top, it was Pavlova and art.

℃ To record one must be unwary.

℃ They would like to have been her, but not to have paid the price in self-control.

℃ Your first most typical figure in any new place turns out to be a bluff or a local nuisance.

℃ Afternoons came in retrospect to have a more enduring value of their own. Nights are their own fulfillment—we possess them and not their memory, save for certain nights that open out into a novel and startling dawn. But perhaps it is only that it is easier to remember afternoons.

℃ "They come over so the children can learn French," said Abe gloomily. "They all just slip down through Europe like nails in a sack, until they stick out of it a little into the Mediterranean Sea."

℃ I heard a child called Venice in a movie theatre at night. First Michael Arlen generation. The sort of picture you'd expect, and it was night.

℃ I've noticed that the children of other nations always seem precocious. That's because the strange manners of their elders have caught our attention most and the children echo those manners enough to seem like their parents.

℄ Once a change of direction has begun, even though it's the wrong one, it still tends to clothe itself as thoroughly in the appurtenances of rightness as if it had been a natural all along.

℄ A large personality is built on such a structure that we scarcely realize its dimensions while it is being built; it keeps up its monstrous development, flinging out as many unaccountable commitments as the limbs on an octopus, growing until we scarcely recognize its shadows—so large has it become beyond that of ordinary people. Except we can recognize the dimensions of the shadow in the horizontal twilight of the coffin.

It becomes such a valuable thing that it is a pity when it is killed, and those nature lovers among us should watch its growth; it is difficult to reproduce scientifically; and if allowed to die, may not re-occur for many years.

℄ You and Seth can be radicals and show your children how you look in the bathtub, because you're both so good, but people who really experiment with themselves find out that all the old things are true.

℄ My theory of partial arbitrary covering of skin as protection from cold—furred Dolmans, Roman shin-guards, etc.

℄ "You can be nice to someone without falling into their arms" almost always means "You can be awful to somebody without their knowing it."

℄ She never realized that, whenever she mustered all the cold cruelty with which she could dominate over the wide-open sensitivity that she lived on but could never know—she never knew that, later, in a form of revenge, when his wounds were well, his sores closed, he would inevitably crush down on her with a pressure she could no more comprehend than his sensitivity. It contained the same elements —only his suffering was now made over into suffering for her—even more fatal for not being deliberate.

C She was plagued by the devastating small one-ring selfishness of some women. For instance, to a statement that a man had been on sentry duty all night, she would oppose the fragment of truth that he had somewhere snatched two legitimate hours of sleep, and thus discredit his ability to take the punishment of a twenty-one hour day. This seems to be one of the last achievements women are likely to wrest from men, but, having made the confusion of mere patience with work, they are not inclined to surrender the point graciously.

C The word "manly" ruined by commercial use.

C On Operations: Being a soldier takes the life out of you, as was the experience of Philip Sidney; being a good poet removes or invalidates the nervous system; being a politician or statesman operates only on the conscience, and is as simple as the removal of the heart which too often goes with doctoring. The removal of the soul consequent on being a successful merchant is accomplished practically without pain.

C Idea that on the higher levels of human achievement— writing, Thalberg, etc.—difference is so slight, etc.

C Awful disillusion of arriving at center of supposed authority and finding need of flattery so as to be reinforced in that authority.

C The grand triumph of the people who don't care over the people who do—the well in the sick room, nurse over patient, doctor's jokes, their exquisite attention to my egotism, the advantage of the beloved over the lover, and the lender over the borrower, but also the sponge over the softy.

C Personality precludes inspection by vis-à-vis.

❪ Wanting to mother a man—wanting to keep him from spending his money on some other woman.

❪ The words gentleman and lady only have a concise meaning to a person just learning to be one or just having ceased to be one.

❪ A woman's sense of men conspiring together and *vice versa*.

❪ You can take your choice between God and Sex. If you choose both, you're a smug hypocrite; if neither, you get nothing.

❪ Fairies: Nature's attempt to get rid of soft boys by sterilizing them.

❪ Some discussion of the facts that, in general: *Haute bourgeoisie* training is so much more enlightened that more stuffed shirts survive. *Esprit de corps. Petite bourgeoisie* training is rougher and selects the fittest. But *proletarian* training is the roughest of all, and has poorest education and least *esprit de corps*, is hampered by race prejudices, etc.

❪ Artistic temperament is like a king with vigor and unlimited opportunity. You shake the structure to pieces by playing with it.

❪ In any given individual life or situation, things progress from good toward less good. But life itself never does.

❪ Mankind has lived through three ideas: (1) That the capacity for leadership is hereditary, (2) that the soul is immortal, (3) that he [man] can govern as a mass and is fit and able to choose his leaders—and into a fourth, i.e. that ethics are attractive in themselves.

❪ Zelda's idea: the bad things are the same in everyone; only the good are different.

❡ It is necessary to emphasize the individual differences between men. If you are high enough in the air, you can't even see the leader of the parade, sometimes you can't even see the way it's going—and it's necessary to know. Al Capone.

❡ Women took over political-religious thought, with their lack of education, their almost universal lack of knowledge of things as they are, and turned this delegated prerogative inward, cultivating all tendencies in children as individualism. This can best be looked at in the case of a conscious mother and a conscious son, such as your mother and you, where the dead or senile grandfather was still the head of the family.

❡ Does anyone think an angel of God appeared to George Washington and suddenly informed him that if he gave up all the allegiances that he had in Virginia, and the entire caste to which he had been born, he would become a model hero of all the school children of 1933?

❡ The very elements of disintegration seemed to him romantic—the vague unrest that went on back of the big tranquil lawn, the incessant small bickering that seemed to prove that in their magnificence they had no need of solidarity. Actually it meant that the old Millers, having nothing to teach, had taught their children no common good, having traded their Bavarian field-wisdom for a sort of wisdom that was current in the Middle West twenty to forty years ago, which was of no value at all. Evolved under one set of conditions, the settlement and development of the West, it seemed as academic to children growing up in a static city as the morals of the Samurai.

❡ He was in the safety zone. In a man this is the period between twenty-four and twenty-eight, and, however precarious for a man to rely upon and belied by marriage statistics, such a safety-zone is a reality. At that age a good man will not mistake the wide-eyed attention of eighteen

[206]

for the wisdom of thirty, nor forgive thirty for lacking the freshness of eighteen. Let it even be insisted upon: a bachelor of twenty-six in his right mind is not a serious prospect.

❤ Women's continual reacting reacting reacting, almost to a point of self-immolation, to forces that they haven't caused and can't do anything about.

❤ On such occasions as this, thought Scott, as his eyes still sought casually for Yanci, occurred the matings of the leftovers, the plainer, the duller, the poorer of the social world; matings actuated by the same urge toward perhaps a more glamorous destiny, yet, for all that, less beautiful and less young. Scott himself was feeling very old.

❤ Learning of a word or place, etc., and then seeming to run across the word or place in your reading constantly in the next few weeks.
Use as simile: "as when one," etc.

❤ You can stroke people with words.

❤ Advantages of children whose mother is dead.

❤ Weaknesses of medium point of view: (1) not attractive, (2) always borne along in practise in the trial of extreme points of view, etc.

❤ A man being only the sum of his initials.

❤ There are certain ribald stories that I heard at ten years old and never again, for I heard a new and more sophisticated set at eleven. Many years later I heard a ten-year-old boy telling another one of those old stories, and it occurred to me that it had been handed on from one ten-year-old generation to the next for an incalculable number of centuries. So with the set I learned at eleven. Each set of stories, like a secret ritual, stays always within its age-class, never growing older, because there is always a new throng of ten-year-olds to learn them, and never growing stale because these same boys will forget them at eleven. One can almost believe that there is a conscious theory behind this unofficial education.

❡ The easiest way to get a reputation is to go outside the fold, shout around for a few years as a violent atheist or a dangerous radical, and then crawl back to the shelter. The fatted calf is killed for Spargo, Papini, Chesterton and Henry Arthur Jones. There is a bigger temporary premium put on losing your nerve in this regard than in any other.

❡ When men agree on a subject of controversy, they love to tell or listen to personal stories that seem to strengthen their side of the question. They laugh deliberately and enjoy a warm feeling that the case is won.

❡ His mind full of the odd ends of all he had read, dim tracings of thoughts whose genesis was already far away when (their dim carbons) reached his ears.

❡ The reason morons can stand good entertainment is that they don't like to understand all the time. Like a nurse or child at a sophisticated lunch table. Something they could follow all through is a stirring nervous experience for them. Through a good picture they can drowse—as morons always drowse mentally through great events.

❡ Fifty years ago we Americans substituted melodrama for tragedy, violence for dignity under suffering. That became a quality that only women were supposed to exhibit in life or fiction—so much so that there are few novels or biographies in which the American male, tangled in an irreconcilable series of contradictions, is considered as anything but an unresourceful and cowardly weakwad.

❡ All the sucks on the Astor and Whitney fortunes.

❡ Time marches on—ruthlessly—until the Russians tried to replace their artists and scientists—then time stood still and only the pendulum functioned.

❲ I can watch a cigarette burn, like *Esquire's* streamlines. Charly Petty's lines are all from a cigarette, even the hair where the smoke breaks.

❲ Never noticed Mother's eyes after living with her twenty years. Mrs. O. says they are like mine.

❲ Like all "final" people—judges, doctors, great artists, etc.

❲ You began by pretending to be kind (politeness). It pays so well that it becomes second nature. Some people like Jews can't get past the artificiality of the first step.

❲ When people get mixed up, they try to throw out a sort of obscuring mist, and then the sharp shock of a fact—a collision!—seems to be the only thing to make them sober-minded again.

❲ The luxuriance of your emotions under the strict discipline which you habitually impose on them, makes that tensity in you that is the secret of all charm—when you let that balance become disturbed, don't you become just another victim of self-indulgence?—breaking down the solid things around you and, moreover, making yourself terribly vulnerable?

❲ But scratch a Yale man with both hands and you'll be lucky to find a coast-guard. Usually you find nothing at all. Or else eleven bought iron men and 3000 ninnies. God preserve you from *that* vacuum foundry!

❲ There is this to be said for the Happy Ending: that the healthy man goes from love to love.

❲ Reversion to childhood typical of the only child.

❲ Nine girls out of ten can stand good looks without going to pieces, though only one boy out of ten ever comes out from under them.

[209]

❧ American farmer as a fighter comes of desperate stock as well as adventurous.

❧ Remember that women are ostriches about themselves; and that all men—and by this I mean *every* man—will tell everything, and usually more, within three months from date. Remember the daughter of * * * * who owned the * * * * Street apartment. I heard her story long before she'd left Baltimore.

❧ You could tell a * * * * boy by his table manners. You see they ate with the servants while their parents divorced and remarried.

❧ Some men have a necessity to be mean, as if they were exercising a faculty which they had to partially neglect since early childhood.

❧ In the beginning, we are the split and splintered pieces of the basket in which we are all contained. At the end, the basket, turned upside down, has become a haystack in which we search for our own smooth identity—as if it had ever existed.

❧ Remember this—if you shut your mouth, you have your choice.

❧ The flapper never really disappeared in the twenties—she merely dropped her name, put on rubber heels and worked in the dark.

❧ The tackles, good or bad, are a necessary fact in life. The Tiger Inn type, little nervous system, Dickinson, McGraw, etc. Their recognition of each other.

❧ About finding I am not a rational type—finding it in Hollywood, I mean, in script writing. How every director *must* be, for instance.

℀ Justification of happy ending. My father and Oscar Wilde born in the same year. One ruined at forty—one "happy" at seventy. So Becky and Amelia are, in fact, *true*.

℀ A precociously tough boy makes jokes like an old man. Like saying (referring to twenty years ago): "So you laughed at me, eh?" Utterly safe kidding of people who don't want to hurt or be hurt.

℀ "I explained to you that waiting is just part of the picture business. Everybody's so much overpaid that, when something finally happens, you realize that you were making money all the time. The reason it's slow is because one man's keeping it all in his head, and fighting the weather and actors and accidents."

℀ Beginnings of a bad education—when, from Myers' *Ancient History* and concentrated attention on Roman columns, I assumed that that was standard and solid and indicative of mind and taste—and therefore was puzzled years later when Western bank architecture was deserted for more modern forms.

℀ I didn't have the two top things: great animal magnetism or money. I had the two second things, though: good looks and intelligence. So I always got the top girl.

℀ In 1908 our Pacific and Caribbean adventures were as romantic as the G-men exploits of today.

R

ROUGH STUFF

℀ A man giving up the idea of himself as a hero. Perhaps picking his nose in a can.

❦ You can't take the son of a plough manufacturer, clip off his testicles and make an artist of him.

❦ "Did you ever see squirrels yincing?" he asked her suddenly.

❦ Scenario hacks, having removed all life from a story, substituting the stink of life—a fart, a loose joke, a dirty jeer. How do they do it?

❦ Apology to Ogden Nash:
Every California girl has lost at least one ovary
And none of them has read *Madame Bovary*.

S

SCENES AND SITUATIONS

❦ Sir Francis Elliot, King George, the barley water and champagne.

❦ The big toy banks with candles inside that were really the great fashionable hotels, the lighted clock in the old town, the blurred glow of the Café de Paris, the pricked-out points of villa windows on slow hills toward the dark sky.

"What is everyone doing there?" she whispered. "It looks as though something gorgeous was going on, but what it is I can't quite tell."

"Everyone there is making love," said Val quietly.

❦ Blind man's buff and fiancée with no chin.

❦ Colored woman and dead Jewish baby.

❦ "There's no use looking at things, because you don't like things," remarked Raines, in answer to his polite interest.

"No," said Charlie frankly, "I don't."

"You like only rhythms, with things marking the beats, and now your rhythm is broken."

❢ The orchestra was playing a Wiener Walzer, and suddenly she had the sensation that the chords were extending themselves, that each bar of three-four time was bending in the middle, dropping a little and thus drawing itself out, until the waltz itself, like a phonograph running down, became a torture.

❢ She stood there in the middle of an enormous quiet. The pursuing feet that had thundered in her dream had stopped. There was a steady, singing silence.

❢ Perhaps that slate we looked at once, that was all the grey blue we'd ever know in life—where the dark brown tide receded, the slate came. It was indescribable as the dress beside him (the color of hours of a long human day)—blue like misery, blue for the shy-away from happiness—"If I could [touch?] that shade everything would be all right forever. . . ." Touch it? Touch.

❢ For me an unhappy day on the Rivera, 1926:
   The bouillabaisse.
   The baby gar.
   (Maurice—the first Peter Arno cartoons about Hic and Whoops.)
   Who would save the weakest swimmer.
   (The quarrel.)
   Isolation of two in end of boat.
   Gerald and Walker at Villefranche.
   Archie and the car on my eyebrow.
   The swim *au naturel,* but not.

❢ Didn't evenings sometimes end on a high note and not fade out vaguely in bars? After ten o'clock every night she felt she was the only real being in a colony of ghosts, that she was surrounded by utterly intangible figures who retreated whenever she stretched out her hand.

❈ When he gets sober for six months and can't stand any of the people he's liked when drunk.

❈ The two young men could only groan and play sentimental music on the phonograph, but presently they departed; the fire leaped up, day went out behind the window, and Forrest had rum in his tea.

❈ Josephine Baker's chocolate arabesques. Chorus from her show.

❈ In front of the shops in the Rue de Castiglione, proprietors and patrons were on the sidewalk gazing upward, for the Graf Zeppelin, shining and glorious, symbol of escape and destruction—of escape, if necessary, through destruction—glided in the Paris sky. He heard a woman say in French that it would not astonish her if that commenced to let fall the bombs.

(Not funny now—1939.)

❈ Why didn't they back away? Why didn't they back right up, walking backward down the Rue de Castiglione, across the Rue de Rivoli, through the Tuileries Gardens, still walking backward as fast as they could till they grew vague and faded out across the river?

❈ Lying awake in bed that night, he listened endlessly to the long caravan of a circus moving through the street from one Paris fair to another. When the last van had rumbled out of hearing, the corners of the furniture were pastel blue with the dawn.

❈ Almost at once Josephine realized that everybody there except herself was crazy. She knew it incontrovertibly, although the only person of outward eccentricity was a robust woman in a frock coat and grey morning trousers. Their frightened eyes lifted to the young girl's elegant clothes, her confident, beautiful face, and they turned from her rudely in self-protection.

❡ "Well, what do you want to do?"

"Kiss you."

A spasm of timidity, quickly controlled, went over her face.

"I'm all dirty."

"Don't you kiss people when they're all dirty?"

"I don't kiss people. I'm just before that generation. We'll find you a nice young girl you can kiss."

"There aren't any nice young girls—you're the only one I like."

"I'm not nice. I'm a hard woman."

❡ The woman who snatched her children away on the boat just to be exclusive—exclusive from what?

❡ She laughed sweetly.

"Where you been?"

"Skiing. But every time I go away that doesn't mean you can go dance with a whole lot of gigolo numbers from Cairo. Why does he hold his hand parallel to the floor when he dances? Does he think he's stilling the waves? Does he think the floor's going to swing up and crack him?"

"He's a Greek, honey."

❡ A small car, red in color and slung at that proximity to the ground which indicated both speed of motion and speed of life. It was a Blatz Wildcat. Occupying it, in the posture of aloof exhaustion exacted by the sloping seat, was a blond, gay, baby-faced girl.

❡ They floated off, immediately entering upon a long echoing darkness. Somewhere far ahead a group in another boat were singing, their voices now remote and romantic, now nearer and yet more mysterious, as the canal doubled back and the boats passed close to each other with an invisible veil between. The continual bump-bump of the boat against the wooden sides. They slid into a red glow—a stage set of hell, with grinning demons and lurid paper fires—then again into the darkness, with the gently lapping water and the passing of the singing boat now near, now far away.

[215]

❦ He paused speculatively to vault the high hydrant in front of the Van Schellinger house, wondering if one did such things in long trousers and if he would ever do it again.

❦ "Do away with yourself," he demanded, startled. "You? Why on earth—"

"Oh, I've almost done it twice. I get the horrors—usually when something goes wrong with my art. Once they said I fell in the bathtub when I only jumped in, and another time somebody closed a window before I could get to it."

"You ought to be careful."

"I am careful. I keep a lady with me always—but she couldn't come East because she was going to be married."

❦ Sending orchestra second rate champagne—never, *never* do it again.

❦ Gerald walking Paris.

❦ Once in his room and reassured by the British stability of them, the ingenuity of the poor asserted itself. He began literally to wind himself up in his clothes. He undressed, put on two suits of underwear and over that four shirts and two suits of clothes, together with two white piqué vests. Every pocket he stuffed with ties, socks, studs, gold-backed brushes and a few toilet articles. Panting audibly, he struggled into an overcoat. His derby looked empty, so he filled it with collars and held them in place with some handkerchiefs. Then, rocking a little on his feet, he regarded himself in the mirror.

He might possibly manage it—if only a steady stream of perspiration had not started to flow from somewhere up high in the edifice and kept pouring streams of various temperatures down his body, until they were absorbed in the heavy blotting paper of three pairs of socks that crowded his shoes.

Moving cautiously, like Tweedledum before the battle, he traversed the hall and rang for the elevator. The boy looked at him curiously, but made no comment, though another passenger made a dry reference to Admiral Byrd.

Through the lobby he moved, a gigantic figure of a man. Perhaps the clerks at the desk had a subconscious sense of something being wrong, but he was gone too quickly for them to do anything about it.

"Taxi, sir?" the doorman inquired, solicitous at Val's pale face.

Unable to answer, Val tried to shake his head, but, this also proving impossible, he emitted a low negative groan. The sun was attracted to his bulk as lightning is attracted to metal, as he staggered out toward a bus. Up on top, he thought; it would be cooler up on top.

His training as a hall-room boy stood him in good stead now; he fought his way up the winding stair as if it had been the social ladder. Then, drenched and suffocating, he sank down upon a bench, the bourgeois blood of many Mr. Joneses pumping strong in his heart. Not for Val to sit upon a trunk and kick his heels and wait for the end; there was fight in him yet.

€ * * * * married into a family of boarding house aristocrats in Charleston and they didn't like him. But outside of Charleston their prestige depended on him, so that they took it out in mild abuse. There was a coast guard officer in the family that was always going to jump down his throat with a loaded revolver. When his wife broke down, the father used to go to the hospital, and after getting his prestige with the doctors from poor * * * *'s shows, he'd tear into him. * * * * ducking around Europe at the time, sleeping with chambermaids and raising hell on the quiet generally. "Jesus Christ," he used to say, "they climb up on your shoulders and then pull your nose."

€ A lot of young girls together is a romantic secret thing like the first sight of wild ducks at dawn (enlarge—Hotel Don Ce-sar at pink dawn—the gulf.)

€ Children's Hour: "Kiddies, I'd be the last one to ask you to begin smoking before, say, six, but remember we are in the depths of a depression—the depths of a depression from four to six, through the courtesy of the American Cigarette Company—and you represent a potential market of forty million smokers."

❧ The city had been merely an unfamiliar rhythm persisting outside the windows of an American Express Hotel, with days composed of such casual punctuation marks as going for the mail or taking auto rides that did not go back and forth but always in a circle.

❧ Dogs appraising buildings.

❧ A taxi tipping over on a nervous night.

❧ Throwing away jewelry, burning clothes.

❧ She told him a wonderful plot she had for a "Scenario," and then repeated to him the outline of *The Miracle Man.* He gave her the address of Joe Gibney in Hollywood as someone who might be interested. Joe was the studio bootlegger. Perhaps she suspected his evasion, for now she cast him an angry glance and whispered to her companions. She would go to his next six pictures to see if he had stolen her idea.

❧ In the corner a huge American negro with his arms around a lovely French tart, roared a song to her in a rich beautiful voice and suddenly Melarky's Tennessee instincts were remembered and aroused.

❧ Man fascinated by girl finds she's showing off for someone else.

❧ The missing raft hurried desolately before a light wind with its sail tied, until the rotten canvas suddenly split and shredded away. When night came, it went off on its own again, speeding along the dark tide as if driven by a ghostly propellor.

❧ Scene equivalent to my last afternoon with Gerald, for benefit of two women. Portentousness.

❡ How I scared away a customer from the Hôtel de la Paix.

❡ The problem as to whether it was a duty or a favor when she helped the English nurse down the steps with the perambulator. The English nurse always said "Please," and "Thanks very much," but Dolores hated her and would have liked without any special excitement to beat her insensible. Like most Latins under the stimulus of American life, she had irresistible impulses toward violence.

❡ Jules had dark circles under his eyes. Yesterday he had closed out the greatest problem of his life by settling with his ex-wife for two hundred thousand dollars. He had married too young, and the former slavey from the Quebec slums had taken to drugs upon her failure to rise with him. Yesterday, in the presence of lawyers, her final gesture had been to smash his finger with the base of a telephone.

❡ Before her eyes would pass in turn a prodigious, prodigal Latin American or a lady whose title blazed with history or that almost mythological figure, an international banker, or even a great Hollywood star with her hat pulled down over her face lest it be apparent that no one recognized her— all these being great figures to her—and Dick would say something kind, really kind, about them, and they would recede out of the far vista as a stark naked Argentine, a stuffed chemise of the society column, Dinah's uncle, or an actress pleased to see Seth—when we really possessed him, when he preferred us.

❡ "I'm pretty tired," he said—unfortunately, because this gave her an advantage: she wasn't tired; while his mind and body moved in a tedious half-time like a slow moving picture, her nerves were crowded with feverish traffic. She tried to think of some mischief.

❡ * * * * in the limousine at Meadowbrook, getting as small as the man he was arguing with.

❡ Scene toward end of déménagement—distressing amount of goods, five phonographs, eight pairs of dark glasses, wasteful reduplication, etc.

❡ During the ride the young man held his attention coolly away from his mother, unwilling to follow her eyes in any direction or even to notice his surroundings except when at a revealing turn the sky and sea dropped before them and he said, "It's hot as hell," in a decided voice.

❡ She sat down on the water closet with a coquettish smile. Her eyes, glazed a few minutes since, were full of impish malice.

❡ "I would like to enjoy," said the man, "but I can only hope and remember. What the hell—leave me my reactions even though they're faint beside yours. Let me see things my own way."

"You mean you don't want me to talk?"

"I mean we come up here, and before I can register, before I can realize that this *is* the Atlantic Ocean, you've analyzed it like a chemist, like a chemist who painted, or a painter who studied chemistry, and it's all diminished, and I say 'Yes it does remind me of a delicatessen shop—' "

"Let you alone—"

❡ He lived his life, then, as an honored man. But from time to time he would indulge his habit of eating mountain grass in preference to valley grass, a habit formed during those early days outside the herd.

"Oke!" said the herd.

Some of them would watch his curious munching and shake their heads. Some of them, though, grouped together and said: "If we eat that grass, that will make us honored like him."

They tried it and it had the negative result of such follies.

❡ "Why, she's your wife—I can't imagine touching your wife." Having heard this said to a husband ten minutes before the most passionate attempts to maneuver the wife into bed.

❦ He ran a low fever that evening and the mosquito netting bound him down into a little stifling space. But the morning was fresh and fair, and he remembered that with a little vigilance there is seldom the necessity of being alone with oneself.

❦ He got up suddenly, stumbling through the shrubbery, and followed an almost obliterated path to the house, starting at the whirring sound of a blackbird which rose out of the grass close by. The front porch sagged dangerously at his step as he pushed open the door. There was no sound inside, except the steady slow throb of silence.

❦ "Let's not talk about such things now. I'll tell you something funny instead." Her look was not one of eager anticipation, but he continued, "By merely looking around, you can review the largest battalion of the Boys I've seen collected in one place. This hotel seems to be a clearing house for them—" He returned the nod of a pale and shaky Georgian who sat down at a table across the room. "That young man looks somewhat retired from life. The little devil I came down to see is hopeless. You'd like him—if he comes in, I'll introduce him."

As he was speaking, the flow into the bar began. Nicole's fatigue accepted Dick's ill-advised words and mingled with the fantastic Koran that presently appeared. She saw the males gathered down at the bar: the tall gangling ones; the little pert ones with round thin shoulders; the broad ones with the faces of Nero and Oscar Wilde, or of senators— faces that dissolved suddenly into girlish fatuity, or twisted into leers; the nervous ones who hitched and twitched, jerking open their eyes very wide, and laughed hysterically; the handsome, passive and dumb men who turned their profiles this way and that; the pimply, stodgy men with delicate gestures; or the raw ones with very red lips and frail curly bodies, their shrill voluble tones piping their favorite word "treacherous" above the hot volume of talk; the ones over-self-conscious who glared with eager politeness toward every noise; among them were English types with great racial self-control, Balkan types, one small cooing Siamese. "I think now," Nicole said, "I think I'm going to bed."

"I think so, too."

—Goodby, you unfortunates. Goodby, Hotel of Three Worlds.

❡ In a moving automobile sat a Southern gentleman accompanied by his body-servant. He was on his way, after a fashion, to New York, but he was somewhat hampered by the fact that the upper and lower portions of his automobile were no longer in exact juxtaposition. In fact, from time to time the two riders would dismount, shove the body on to the chassis, corner to corner, and then continue onward, vibrating slightly in involuntary unison with the motor.

❡ Only a few apathetic stags gathered one by one in the doorways, and to a close observer it was apparent that the scene did not attain the gayety which was its aspiration. These girls and men had known each other from childhood, and though there were marriages incipient upon the floor tonight, they were marriages of environment, of resignation, or even of boredom.

❡ Almost a whole chapter on the man's attempt to educate his children without knowing where he stands himself— amid difficulties.

❡ A chapter in which their kid comes to him for homosexuality, and a consequent long consideration of homosexuality from some such attitude as a Groton father thinking it's maybe all right for social reasons.

❡ Tremendous American generosity, without comment.

❡ In the shadow of the Pope's palace at Avignon our Greek guide, an exile from the butcheries in Smyrna, told us with wild enthusiasm of his cousin, a restaurateur and an Elk of Terre Haute, Indiana.

"He wears a high hat and a blue coat with epaulettes and blue braid and green trousers, and carries a gold sword in his hand, and marches down the main street once a year behind a big band, and—"

℃ Meeting Cole Porter in Ritz.

℃ We all went to hear Chaliapin that night; after the second act, he stayed out in the bar talking to the barmaids and then joined us afterwards, a tall unsteady figure, pale as the phantom of the opera himself descending the great staircase.

℃ Imagine saying to * * * *, apropos of his brother's death: "Well, he must have been an awful pig."

℃ "They don't allow us and the other rich boys to go to anything except comedies and kidnappings and things like that. The comedies are the things I like."
  "Who? Chaplin?"
  "Who?"
  "Charlie Chaplin."
  Obviously the words failed to record.
  "No, the—you know, the comedies."
  "Who do you like?" Bill asked.
  "Oh—" The boy considered, "Well, I like Garbo and Dietrich and Constance Bennett."
  "Their things are *com*edies?"
  "They're the funniest ones."
  "Funniest what?"
  "Funniest comedies."
  "Why?"
  "Oh, they try to do this passionate stuff all the time."

℃ "Then somebody told us about 'party girls.' Business men with clients from out of town sometimes wanted to give them a big time—singing and dancing and champagne, all that sort of thing, make them feel like regular fellows seeing New York. So they'd hire a room in a restaurant and invite a dozen party girls. All it required was to have a good evening dress and to sit next to some middle-aged man for two hours and laugh at his jokes and maybe kiss him goodnight. Sometimes you'd find a fifty dollar bill in your napkin when you sat down at table."

❈ Most Pleasant Trips:
  Auto Paris-Zürich
  Auto Zelda and Sap and I
  Auto Ernest and I North
  P.L.M. going North, 1925
  Cherbourg-Paris
  Havre-Paris
  South to Norfolk
  Around Lake Geneva

❈ Most Unpleasant Trips:
  Auto Zelda and I South
  Around Lake Como
  Mentone
  California
  Quebec
  North from Norfolk
  * * * * and * * * *

❈ "The somewhat nervous little man at the desk," after a long conversation as to whether the celebrity is "just folks," "just like anybody else," etc., with the nervous little man caustic and resentful, divulges himself suddenly as the celebrity.

❈ She had never done anything for love before. She didn't know what it meant. When her hand struck the bulb she still didn't know it, nor while the shattered glass made a nuisance by the bedside.

NOSTALGIA OR THE FLIGHT OF THE HEART

❈ Young St. Paul
  Florida
  Norfolk

Burgundy
Montgomery as it was
Paris Left Bank
New York 1911, 1917, 1920
Hopkins
Bermuda a little
Chicago
Wheatley Hills
Capri
Old boarding house or summer hotel
Place across from Niagara
Annecy
The First Ships
First London
Second Paris
Provence
Riviera (Antibes, St. Raphaël, St. Tropez, Nice, Monte
   Carlo, Cannes, St. Paul)
Gstaad
Randolph
Placid
Frontenac
Early White Bear
Woodstock
Princeton 1st and 2nd years
Yale
Newman as grad.
Deal Beach
Athens, Georgia
Sorrento
Marseilles
Battlefields
Virginia Beach
Orvieto
Bou Saada
Territet
Other Playgrounds: Rockville and Charleston, Montana
Washington
Deal, Ellerslie.

❡ The Sport Roadster: When I was a boy I dreamed that I sat always at the wheel of a magnificent Stutz—in those days the Stutz was the stamp of the romantic life—a Stutz as low as a snake and as red as an Indiana barn. But in point of fact, the best I could manage was the intermittent use of the family car. If I were willing to endure the most unaristocratic groanings and vibrations, I could torture it up to fifty miles an hour.

But no matter how passionately I slouched down in the seat, I couldn't make it look like a Stutz. One day I lowered the top and opened the windshield, and with the car thus pathetically jazzed up, took my mother and another lady down town shopping.

It was a scorching day. The sun blazed down upon us, the molten air blew like the breath of a furnace into our faces—through the open windshield. I could literally feel the sunburn deepening on me, block by block. It was appalling.

The two ladies fanned themselves uneasily. I don't believe either of them quite realized what the trouble was. But I, even with the perspiration pouring into my eyes, found sight to envy the owner of a peagreen cut-down flivver which oozed by us through the heat.

My passengers visited a series of stores. I waited in the sun, still slouched down, and with that sort of half-sneer on my face which I had noted was peculiar to drivers of racing cars. The heat continued to be terrific.

Finally my mother's friend came out of the store and I helped her into the car. She sank down into the seat—then rose quickly up again.

"Ah!" she said wildly.

She had burned herself.

When we reached home, I offered—most unusually—to take them both for a long ride—anywhere they wished to go. They said politely that they were going for a little walk to cool off!

❡ As they turned into Crest Avenue, the new cathedral, immense and unfinished in imitation of a cathedral left

unfinished by accident in some little Flemish town, squatted
just across the way like a plump white bulldog on its
haunches. The ghost of four moonlit apostles looked down
at them wanly from wall niches still littered with the white
dusty trash of the builders. The cathedral inaugurated Crest
Avenue. After it came the great brownstone mass built by
R. R. Comerford, the flour king, followed by a half mile of
pretentious stone houses built in the gloomy 90's. These
were adorned with monstrous driveways and porte-cochères
which had once echoed to the hoofs of good horses and with
high circular windows that corseted the second stories.

The continuity of these mausoleums was broken by a
small park, a triangle of grass where Nathan Hale stood ten
feet tall, with his hands bound behind his back by stone
cord, and stared over a great bluff at the slow Mississippi.
Crest Avenue ran along the bluff, but neither faced it nor
seemed aware of it, for all the houses fronted inward toward
the street. Beyond the first half mile it became newer,
essayed ventures in terraced lawns, in concoctions of stucco
or in granite mansions which imitated through a variety of
gradual refinements the marble contours of the Petit
Trianon. The houses of this phase rushed by the roadster for
a succession of minutes; then the way turned and the car
was headed directly into the moonlight, which swept toward
it like the lamp of some gigantic motorcycle far up the
avenue.

Past the low Corinthian lines of the Christian Science
Temple, past a block of dark frame horrors, a deserted row
of grim red brick—an unfortunate experiment of the late
90's—then new houses again, bright blinding flowery
lawns. These swept by, faded past, enjoying their moment
of grandeur; then waiting there in the moonlight to be outmoded as had the frame, cupolaed mansions of lower down
and the brownstone piles of older Crest Avenue in their
turn.

The roofs lowered suddenly, the lots narrowed, the houses
shrank up in size and shaded off into bungalows. These
held the street for the last mile, to the bend in the river
which terminated the prideful avenue at the statue of

Chelsea Arbuthnot. Arbuthnot was the first governor—and almost the last of Anglo-Saxon blood.

All the way thus far Yanci had not spoken, absorbed still in the annoyance of the evening, yet soothed somehow by the fresh air of Northern November that rushed by them. She must take her fur coat out of storage next day, she thought.

"Where are we now?"

As they slowed down, Scott looked up curiously at the pompous stone figure, clear in the crisp moonlight, with one hand on a book and the forefinger of the other pointing, as though with reproachful symbolism, directly at some construction work going on in the street.

"This is the end of Crest Avenue," said Yanci, turning to him. "This is our show street."

"A museum of American architectural failures."

❆ Once upon a time Princeton was a leafy campus where the students went in for understatement, and if they had earned a P, wore it on the inside of the sweater, displaying only the orange seams, as if the letter were only faintly deserved. The professors were patient men who prudently kept their daughters out of contact with the students. Half a dozen great estates ringed the township, which was inhabited by townsmen and darkies—these latter the avowed descendents of body servants brought north by southerners before the Civil War.

Nowadays Princeton is an "advantageous residential vicinity"—in consequence of which young ladies dressed in riding habits, with fashionable manners, may be encountered lounging in the students' clubs on Prospect Avenue. The local society no longer has a professional, almost military homogeneity—it is leavened with many frivolous people, and has "sets" and antennae extending to New York and Philadelphia.

❆ The constant endeavor of trained nurses in a patient's room is to get all movable articles out before the doctor arrives, approximating as closely as possible the stripped look of an operating chamber. The result is like that obtained in the case of a dog burying a bone: it is the burying that matters, not the bone.—In the meantime, after the nurses' departure, missed or forgotten objects turn up in the corners of strange drawers and escritoires. The hanging of trousers is another matter the technique of which must be part of the nurses' course. From the decorums of Hopkins to the casualness of the Pacific, they are seized by both cuffs, twisted several times in reverse, placed in one corner of the hanger and left to dangle rather like a man hanged. The same nurse may go home and put away a pair of slacks in perfect shape for future wearing, but no man ever left a hospital with the same crease that he had when he went in.

❬ They had been run into by a school bus, which lay, burning from the mouth, half on its side against a tall bank of the road, with the little girls screaming as they stumbled out the back.

❬ A young man phoned from a city far off, then from a city near by, then from downtown, informing me that he was coming to call, though he had never seen me. He arrived eventually with a great ripping up of garden borders, a four-ply rip in a new lawn, a watch pointing accurately and unforgivably at 3 A.M. But he was prepared to disarm me with the force of his compliment, the intensity of the impulse that had brought him to my door. "Here I am at last," he said, teetering triumphantly. "I had to see you. I feel I owe you more than I can say. I feel that you formed my life."

❬ Hearing Hitler's speech while going down Sunset Boulevard in a car.

T

TITLES

C *Journal of a Pointless Life.*
Red and yellow villas, called *Fleur du Bois, Mon Nid,*
   or *Sans Souci.*
Wore Out His Welcome.
"Your Cake."
Jack a Dull Boy.
Dark Circles.
The Parvenu Hat.
Talks to a Drunk.
The firing of Jasbo Merribo. Sketch.
Tall Women.
Birds in the Bush.
Travels of a Nation.
Don't You Love It?
All Five Senses.
Napoleon's Coat.
Tavern music, Boat trains.
Dated.
Thumbs Up.
The Bed in the Ball Room.
Book of burlesque entitled *These My Betters.*
Title for bad novel: *God's Convict.*
Skin of His Teeth.
Picture-Minded.
Love of a Lifetime.
Gwen Barclay in the Twentieth Century.
Result—Happiness.
Murder of My Aunt.
Police at the Funeral.
The District Eternity.

U

UNCLASSIFIED

❧ My extraordinary dream about the Crimean War.

❧ The improper number of *Life* and the William's *Purple Cow* cover beginning something.

❧ *Time:* Henry VIII cut from a halitosis ad.

❧ Just before quarrel had been talking about the best and what it was founded on.

❧ She and her husband and all their friends had no principles. They were good or bad according to their natures; often they struck attitudes remembered from the past, but they were never sure, as her father and her grandfather had been sure. Confusedly she supposed it was something about religion. But how could you get principles just by wishing for them?

❧ The war had become second-page news.

❧ Meeting Princetonians in the army as buglers, etc.

❧ Diary of the God Within: They got half of it—this is the other half.

❧ Before breakfast, their horses' hoofs sedately scattered the dew in sentimental glades, or curtained them with dust as they raced on dirt roads. They bought a tandem bicycle and pedaled all over Long Island—which a contemporary Cato considered "rather fast" for a couple not yet married.

❧ About three pieces of the truth (specific) fitted into one of the most malicious and troublesome lies she'd ever told. These latter are permitted this indiscretion within limits as about the only surcease they will ever find in this world.

❰ We took a place in the great echoing salon as far away from the other clients as possible, much as theatrical managers "dress a thin house," distributing the crowd to cover as much ground as possible.

❰ In Hendersonville: * I am living very cheaply. Today I am in comparative affluence, but Monday and Tuesday I had two tins of potted meat, three oranges and a box of Uneedas and two cans of beer. For the food, that totalled eighteen cents a day—and when I think of the thousand meals I've sent back untasted in the last two years. It was fun to be poor —especially you haven't enough liver power for an appetite. But the air is fine here, and I liked what I had—and there was nothing to do about it anyhow because I was afraid to cash any checks, and I had to save enough for postage for the story. But it was funny coming into the hotel and the very deferential clerk not knowing that I was not only thousands, nay tens of thousands in debt, but had less than forty cents cash in the world and probably a deficit at my bank. I gallantly gave Scotty my last ten when I left her and of course the Flynns, etc., had no idea and wondered why I didn't just "jump into a taxi" (four dollars and tip) and run over for dinner.

Enough of this bankrupt's comedy—I suppose it has been enacted all over the U. S. in the last four years, plenty of times.

Nevertheless, I haven't told you the half of it—i.e., my underwear I started with was a pair of pyjama pants— *just that*. It was only today I could replace them with a union suit. I washed my two handkerchiefs and my shirt every night, but the pyjama trousers I had to wear all the time, and I am presenting it to the Hendersonville Museum. My socks would have been equally notorious save there was not enough of them left, for they served double duty as slippers at night. The final irony was when a drunk man in the shop where I bought my can of ale said in a voice obviously intended for me, "These city dudes from the East

* Hendersonville, North Carolina. This note was probably written in 1936 or 1937.

come down here with their millions. Why don't they support us?"

❲ My great grandmother visited Dolly Madison.

❲ It appeared on the page of great names and was illustrated by a picture of a cross-eyed young lady holding the hand of a savage gentleman with four rows of teeth. That was how their pictures came out, anyhow, and the public was pleased to know that they were ugly monsters for all their money, and everyone was satisfied all around. The society editor set up a column telling how Mrs. Van Tyne started off in the Aquitania wearing a blue traveling dress of starched felt with a round square hat to match.

❲ From a little distance one can perceive an order in what at the time seemed confusion. The case in point is the society of a three generation Middle Western city before the war. There were the two or three enormously rich, nationally known families—outside of them rather than below them the hierarchy began. At the top came those whose grandparents had brought something with them from the East, a vestige of money and culture; then came the families of the big self-made merchants, the "old settlers" of the sixties and seventies, American-English-Scotch, or German or Irish, looking down somewhat in the order named—upon the Irish less from religious difference—French Catholics were considered rather distinguished—than from their taint of political corruption in the East. After this came certain well-to-do "new people"—mysterious, out of a cloudy past, possibly unsound. Like so many structures, this one did not survive the cataract of money that came tumbling down upon it with the war.

❲ This preamble is necessary to explain the delicate social relation, so incomprehensible to a European, between Gladys Van Schillinger, aged fourteen, and her senior by one year, Basil Duke Lee. Basil's father had been an unsuccessful young Kentuckian of good family and his mother,

[233]

Alice Reilly, the daughter of a "pioneer" wholesale grocer. As Tarkington says, American children belong to their mother's families, and Basil was "Alice Reilly's son." Gladys Van Schillinger, on the contrary—

Way Down in Cotton Town (Rogers Bros.).
Teasing
Coax Me
Kiss Me Goodnight, Dear Love
Don't Get Married Anymore, Love
Waiting at the Church (Vesta Victoria). ·
Tale of a Kangaroo
Dearie, My Dearie
If It Takes My Whole Week's Pay
Roosevelt and Big Stick
Princeton Glee Club
Nora Bayes and *Harvest Moon*

V

VERNACULAR

❡ Man saying, "This is Jack O'Brien," "This is Florence Fuller."

❡ "Sleep, male cabbage."

❡ " 'Cause I just came home from there and they told me one of their mos' celebrated heartbreakers was visiting up here, and meanwhile her suitors were shooting themselves all over the city. That's the truth. I used to help pick 'em up myself sometimes when they got littering the streets."

❡ Freeman: Grease in the transcommission—What are you scused of?

❧ Man on pier pronouncing *dessert* as *desert*.

❧ Those dumguards.

❧ The McCoy.

❧ Modern Slang, 1932:
    Pushover
    Grand
    Bag
    Lay
    Sugar
    Life preserver
    A Hell
    A Dick
    A Natural
    On the Lose (not loose)
    A Punk
    Kee-ooot

❧ Well you're not exactly in the saoth or the soth or the suth or even the sith.

❧ A phrenograstic-stenographer (Freeman).
    A toomer—a tournament.

❧ Ring's friend: Retire, Expectorate, Wish some potatoes.

❧ "Put it down there" for "sit down."

❧ Cliché: In spite of them perhaps because of them.

❧ Obsolete expression: Confound it!

❧ Unusual—Babbitt's word very, very fine.

❧ Unbeknownst.

❧ Italian woman who stole my boat at Placid.

ℂ "Ai feel ez if eme being kpt," said the English lady.

ℂ "Admired mentality" of Mrs. Richards.

ℂ Slang: Branegan (party), conk (kill), klink (jail).

ℂ Too much shiftin' of the vessels for the movin' of the vittles.

ℂ It burns her up—in the movies.

ℂ No dice, no soap.

ℂ Comes in a pa-a-akige, so conven-i-e-n't (ending all clauses and sentences.)

Y

YOUTH AND ARMY

ℂ Bobby's motorcycle and cigarette case.

ℂ Club elections in 1915 were in the worst snow storm in years. Found that out twenty years afterwards, but remember chasing Sap through snow.

ℂ The forced march.

ℂ The rides to see Zelda.

ℂ The thief at Leavenworth.

ℂ The missing material.

ℂ The scene with sergeants.

ℂ Once in his youth he had been a boy scout for a month,

but all he remembered was the scout call, "Zinga, Zinga Bom-Bom."

❦ There was a flurry of premature snow in the air and the stars looked cold. Staring up at them, he saw that they were his stars as always—symbols of ambition, struggle and glory. The wind blew through them, trumpeting that high white note for which he always listened, and the thin-brown clouds, stripped for battle, passed in review. The scene was of an unparalleled brightness and magnificence, and only the practised eye of the commander saw that one star was no longer there.

❦ Who called me Fitzboomski during Russo-Jap war?

❦ Children's lack of emotion as we know it is healthy.

❦ The days of blazers and two sorts of telephones.

❦ Scott Fitzgerald so they say,
　 Goes a-courting night and day.

❦ Playing with yo-yos in the drug store, walking the dog ditto.

❦ *Dearie*
　 Stay in Your Own Backyard
　 Waiting at the Church
　 Tropic Color
　 Kiss Me Goodnight
　 I'm Romeo
　 Oh, Moonbeam Light and Airy
　 Bamboo Tree

❦ My Buckboard.

❦ Alley's razor.

❦ Banjo lessons.

❦ The Mormon who came to see me at Aunt A's in St. Paul.

❦ *Everybody Works* and *I'm the Guy*.

❦ "Dear old fellow

"I may inform you that I received your note. But can also inform you that the place where I stay is Le Poildu and not La Poildu. Amen. I play every afternoon in the garden with a little girl who lives in the hotel. When we climbed on the top of a tall sort of thing we had a magnificent view of the country all around. Brittany is a really very pretty place. Very many laboureurs, workers, farmers with their wives, farmers and washers. You can see rocks and rocks with the night-capped waves attacking them. I hope you have the same exquisite site. I am learning tennis with a very good teacher at the Union sportive de la poel.

"Oug! Aie! there is the cat Dicky who is putting his claws into my innocent skin of my delicious self."

There followed a portrait of Dicky "seen of face and of side" and the letter bore the signature "Iris, your delicious daughter."

"P.S. I just left this note on Mlle's bureau 'puisque vous me faîtes le supplice des Pruneaux délivrez-moi des gouttes dans le nez.' I hope she will have pity." (Scotty)

❦ Morgan opened one of the "weekly newspapers" that Iris had made for him when she was away in Brittany last summer:

THE 100 PIECES OF NEW NEWS

India is in a bad case.

Yesterday the english king spoke of a complete defeat among the indians the defeat of Calicut is terrible for us.

We will sadly announce that Mrs. Iris Parkling's reverend daughter, Miss Marie-Antoinette Parkling, who came from Bellegio, Italy, had to go yesterday to the doll hospital. Her arm came straight off during her school recess while she was tumbling over a pile of comrades.

The new fantasy of Miss Iris Parkling.

The well-known actress has had a fantasy these last days and has wanted to buy clay to undertake sculpture. She wants to model a head of Mlle. her most complaisant poser.

❲ Fitzgerald's livery stable.

❲ Jimmie and me kissing Marie and Elizabeth, and the sprained ankle.

❲ Gave up spinach for Lent.

❲ "Idioglossia" what Driscoll twins had.

❲ May I take the key?

❲ Sing Song at Yacht Club.

❲ Candy being distributed in youth—"Oh, come on, you know me."

❲ You're liable to get a bullet in the side of the head.

❲ Foxy Grampa.

❲ Sis Hopkins.

❲ Mrs. Wiggs.

❲ My lady sips from her satin shoe.

❲ Since he rode into Brussels in a staff car in October, 1918.

❲ It all seemed very familiar to me, probably it was like some hay ride in my youth.

❲ Thirteen: Me: What? Did they separate the sexes at the play?

Scotty: Daddy—don't be vulgar!

℩ Curious nostalgia about *Pam, Anne of Green Gables,* etc.

℩ Her eyes, dark and intimate, seemed to have wakened at the growing brilliance of the illuminations overhead; there was the promise of excitement in them now, like the promise of the cooling night.

℩ With a bad complexion brooding behind a mask of cheap pink powder.

℩ As the car rose, following the imagined curve of the sky, it occurred to Basil how much he would have enjoyed it in other company, or even alone, the fair twinkling beneath him with new variety, the velvet quality of the darkness that is on the edge of light and is barely permeated by its last attenuations. Again they reached the top of the wheel and the sky stretched out overhead, again they lapsed down through gusts of music from remote calliopes.

℩ When I was young, the boys in my street still thought that Catholics drilled in the cellar every night with the idea of making Pius the Ninth autocrat of this republic.

℩ She and I used to sit at the piano and sing. We were eighteen, so whenever we came to the embarrassing words "lovey-dovey" or "tootsie-wootsie" or "passion" in the lyric, we would obliterate the indelicacy by hurried humming.

℩ Among the more jazzy of the themes in Annabel's convent composition book, I found *Earthquakes, Italy, St. Francis Xavier.* The subjects had a familiar ring.

℩ Father Barrow told me of a pious nun who opened the regents' examinations in advance and showed it to her class so that Catholic children might make a good showing to the glory of God.

℩ Young Alec Seymore wrote a story and read it to me. It was about a murderer who, after the crime, was "greatly abashed at what he had done."

[240]

℃ Notes of Childhood:
Make a noise like a hoop and roll away.
She's neat ha ha.
Grandfather's whiskers.
Aha, she laughed.
Annex rough house.
Hume against Locke.
Changing Voice.
Snow.
Hot dogs.
Hair oily and pumps from notes.
Miss Sweet's school.
Folwell Paulson.
Each Bath.
Writing in class.
Debates.
It's one thing to call a man.
Story of dirty shirt.
Trick show lemonade stand.

℃ *Baby's Arms*
Tulip Time
Dardenella
Hindustan
After You've Gone
I'm Glad I Could Make
Smiles
Down to Meet You in a Taxi
Shimmee
Wait Till the Cows Come Home
Shimmee Shake or Tea
So Long, Letty
Why Do They Call Them Babies
Goodbye, Alexander
Nobody Knows
Bubbles
Dear Heart
Pretty Girl Like Melody (1920)
Buttercup

Rose of No Man's Land
How You Going to Keep 'em
Long, Long Trail
Mlle. from Armentieres
My Buddy
Home Fires
Want to Go Home
Madelon
Joan of Arc
Over There
We Don't Want the Melon
God Help Kaiser Bill
Belgium Rose
All Around the Barnyard Rag

The Letters

*It is to be hoped that Scott Fitzgerald's letters will
be eventually collected and published. Those that
follow are merely a handful that happened to be
easily obtainable and which throw light on Fitzgerald's literary activities and interests. The first
group consists of letters to friends; the second of
letters to his daughter. In most of the letters of the
first group, the spelling and punctuation have been
left as they were in the originals, except for the
uniform italicization of titles of books and magazines
and the insertion of missing ends of parentheses.*

LETTERS TO FRIENDS

TO EDMUND WILSON

September 26th, 1917
593 Summit Ave
St. Paul, Minn.

Dear Bunny:

You'll be surprised to get this but it's really begging for an answer. My purpose is to see exactly what effect the war at close quarters has on a person of your temperament. I mean I'm curious to see how you're point of view has changed or not changed—

I've taken regular army exams but haven't heard a word from them yet. John Bishop is in the second camp at Fort Benjamin Harrison in Indiana. He expects a 1st Lieutenancy. I spent a literary month with him (July) and wrote a terrific lot of poetry mostly under the Masefield-Brooke influence.

Here's John's latest.

BOUDOIR*

The place still speaks of worn-out beauty of roses,
   And half retrieves a failure of Bergamotte,
Rich light and a silence so rich one all but supposes
   The voice of the clavichord stirs to a dead gavotte

* Later published in a different form in Bishop's first book of poems, *Green Fruit*.

For the light grows soft and the silence forever quavers,
    As if it would fail in a measure of satin and lace,
Some eighteenth century madness that sighs and wavers
    Through a life exquisitely vain to a dying grace.

This was the music she loved; we heard her often
    Walking alone in the green-clipped garden outside.
It was just at the time when summer begins to soften
    And the locust shrills in the long afternoon that she died.

The gaudy macaw still climbs in the folds of the curtain;
    The chintz-flowers fade where the late sun strikes them
        aslant.
Here are her books too: Pope and the earlier Burton,
    A worn Verlaine; *Bonheur* and the *Fêtes Galantes*.

Come—let us go—I am done. Here one recovers
    Too much of the past but fails at the last to find
Aught that made it the season of loves and lovers;
    Give me your hand—she was lovely—mine eyes blind.

Isn't that good? He hasn't published it yet. I sent twelve
poems to magazines yesterday. If I get them all back I'm
going to give up poetry and turn to prose. John may publish
a book of verse in the Spring. I'd like to but of course there's
no chance. Here's one of mine.

To Cecilia*

When Vanity kissed Vanity
    A hundred happy Junes ago,
He pondered o'er her breathlessly,
    And that all time might ever know
He rhymed her over life and death,
    "For once, for all, for love," he said . . .
Her beauty's scattered with his breath
    And with her lovers she was dead.

* Later incorporated in a different form and set as prose in Book Two,
Chapter III, of *This Side of Paradise*.

Ever his wit and not her eyes,
  Ever his art and not her hair.
"Who'd learn a trick in rhyme be wise
  And pause before his sonnet there."
So all my words however true
  Might sing you to a thousandth June
And no one ever know that you
  Were beauty for an afternoon.

It's pretty good but of course fades right out before John's. By the way I struck a novel that you'd like *Out of Due Time* by Mrs. Wilfred Ward. I don't suppose this is the due time to tell you that, though. I think that *The New Machiavelli* is the greatest English novel of the century. I've given up the summer to drinking (gin) and philosophy (James and Shoepenhaur and Bergson).

Most of the time I've been bored to death—Wasn't it tragic about Jack Newlin*—I hardly knew poor Gaily.* Do write me the details.

I almost went to Russia on a commission in August but didn't so I'm sending you one of my passport pictures—if the censor doesn't remove it for some reason—It looks rather Teutonic but I can prove myself a Celt by signing myself
                    Very sincerely
                          F. Scott Fitzgerald

TO EDMUND WILSON

                    [Autumn of 1917]
                    Cottage Club,
                    Princeton, N. J.

Dear Bunny:

I've been intending to write you before but as you see I've had a change of scene and the necessary travail there-off has stolen time.

* Princetonians who died in the War.

Your poem came to John Biggs, my room-mate, and we'll put it in the next number—however it was practically illegible so I'm sending you my copy (hazarded) which you'll kindly correct and send back—

I'm here starting my senior year and still waiting for my commission. I'll send you the *Litt.** or no—you've subscribed haven't you. . . .

Do write John Bishop and tell him not to call his book *Green Fruit*.

Alec is an ensign. I'm enclosing you a clever letter from Townsend Martin which I wish you'd send back.

Princeton is stupid but Gauss and Gerrould are here. I'm taking naught but Philosophy & English—I told Gauss you'd sailed (I'd heard as much) but I'll contradict the rumor.

Have you read Well's *Boon, the Mind of the Race*, (Doran —1916) It's marvellous! (Debutante expression.)

The Litt is prosperous—Biggs & I do the prose—Creese and Keller (a junior who'll be chairman) and I the poetry. However any contributions would be ect. ect.

Young Benêt (at New Haven) is getting out a book of verse before Xmas that I fear will obscure John Peale's. His subjects are less precieuse & decadent. John is really an anachronism in this country at this time—people want ideas and not fabrics.

I'm rather bored here but I see Shane Leslie occasionally and read Wells and Rousseau. I read Mrs. Geroulds *British Novelists Limited* & think she underestimates Wells but is right in putting McKenzie at the head of his school. She seems to disregard Barry and Chesterton whom I should put above Bennet or in fact anyone except Wells.

Do you realize that Shaw is 61, Wells 51, Chesterton 41, Leslie 31 and I 21. (Too bad I haven't a better man for 31. I can hear your addition to this remark). . . .

Yes—Jack Newlin is dead—killed in ambulance service. He was, potentially, a great artist.

Here is a poem I just had accepted by *Poet Lore*

* *The Nassau Literary Magazine,* the Princeton undergraduate magazine.

The Way of Purgation*

A fathom deep in sleep I lie
   With old desires, restrained before;
To clamor life-ward with a cry
   As dark flies out the greying door.
And so in quest of creeds to share
   I seek assertive day again;
But old monotony is there—
   Long, long avenues of rain.

Oh might I rise again! Might I
   Throw off the throbs of that old wine—
See the new morning mass the sky,
   With fairy towers, line on line—
Find each mirage in the high air
   A symbol, not a dream again!
But old monotony is there—
   Long, long avenues of rain.

No—I have no more stuff of Johns—I ask but never receive.

If Hillquit gets the mayoralty of New York it means a new era. Twenty million Russians from South Russia have come over to the Roman Church.

I can go to Italy if I like as private secretary of a man (a priest) who is going as Cardinal Gibbons representative to discuss the war with the Pope (American Catholic point of view—which is most loyal—barring the Sien-Fien—40% of Pershing's army are Irish Catholics). Do write.

News jottings (unofficial)

Gaelicly yours
Scott Fitzgerald

I remind myself lately of Pendennis, Sentimental Tommy (who was not sentimental and whom Barrie never understood) Michael Fane, Maurice Avery & Guy Hazelwood.†

* This poem in slightly different form and without the title appears at the beginning of Book Two, Chapter V, of *This Side of Paradise*.
† The last three of these names refer to characters in Compton Mackenzie's early novels.

TO EDMUND WILSON

Jan. 10th, 1917 [1918]

Dear Bunny:

Your last refuge from the cool sophistries of the shattered world, is destroyed!* I have left Princeton. I am now Lieutenant F. Scott Fitzgerald of the 45th Infantry (regulars). My present address is

co Q. P.O.B.
Ft. Leavenworth
Kan.

After Feb 26th

593 Summit Ave.
St. Paul
Minnesota

will always find me forwarded.

—So the short, swift chain of the Princeton intellectuals, Brooke's clothes, clean ears and, withall, a lack of mental prigishness . . . Whipple, Wilson, Bishop, Fitzgerald . . . have passed along the path of the generation—leaving their shining crown upon the gloss and unworthiness of John Bigg's head.

One of your poems I sent on to the Litt. and I'll send the other when I've read it again. I wonder if you ever got the Litt. I sent you . . . So I enclosed you two pictures,† well give one to some poor motherless Poilu fairy who has no dream. This is smutty and forced but in an atmosphere of cabbage...

John's book came out in December and though I've written him rheams (Rhiems) of praise, I think he's made poor use of his material. It is a thin Green Book.

GREEN FRUIT
by JOHN PEALE BISHOP
1st Lt. Inf. R.C.
SHERMAN FRENCH CO.
BOSTON

* I had graduated from college in 1916 and had written him from France that my last solace was to think of those of our literary group who were still at Princeton. E.W.

† I had mentioned in my reply to his previous letter that he had enclosed two prints of his passport picture. E.W.

[250]

In section one *(Souls and Fabrics)* are *Boudoir, The Nassau Inn* and of all things *Fillipo's Wife*, a relic of his decadent sophomore days. *Claudius* and other documents in obscurity adorn this section.

Section two contains the Elspeth poems—which I think are rotten. Section three is *Poems out of Jersey and Virginia* and has *Campbell Hall, Millville* and much sacharine sentiment about how much white bodies pleased him and how, nevertheless, he was about to take his turn with crushed brains (this slender thought done over in poem after poem). This is my confidential opinion, however; if he knew what a nut I considered him for leaving out *Ganymede* and *Salem Water* and *Francis Thompson* and *Prayer* and all the things that might have given body to his work, he'd drop me from his writing list. The book closed with the dedication to Townsend Martin which is on the circular I enclose. I have seen no reviews of it yet.

* * * * * * * *

THE ROMANTIC EGOTIST

by F. Scott Fitzgerald

" . . . the Best is over
You may complain and sigh
    Oh Silly Lover . . ."
            Rupert Brooke

"Experience is the name Tubby gives to his mistakes."
            Oscar Wilde

Chas. Scribners Sons (Maybe!)
MCMXVIII

* * * * * * * *

There are twenty-three chapters, all but five are written and it is poetry, prose, vers libre and every mood of a temperamental temperature. It purports to be the picaresque ramble of one Stephen Palms [Dalius?] from the San Francisco fire thru school, Princeton, to the end where at twenty-one he writes his autobiography at the Princeton aviation school. It shows traces of Tarkington, Chesterton, Chambers, Wells, Benson (Robert Hugh), Rupert Brooke and includes Compton-McKenzielike love-affairs and three psychic adventures including an encounter with the devil in a harlot's apartment.

It rather damns much of Princeton but its nothing to what it thinks of men and human nature in general. I can most nearly describe it by calling it a prose, modernistic Childe Harolde and really if Scribner takes it I know I'll wake some morning and find that the debutantes have made me famous over night. I really believe that no one else could have written so searchingly the story of the youth of our generation.

In my right hand bunk sleeps the editor of *Contemporary Verse* (ex) Devereux Joseph, Harvard '15 and a peach—on my left side is G. C. King a Harvard crazy man who is dramatizing *War and Peace;* but you see I'm lucky in being well protected from the Philistines.

The *Litt* continues slowly but I haven't received the December issue yet so I cant pronounce on the quality.

This insolent war has carried off Stuart Wolcott in France, as you may know and really is beginning to irritate me—but the maudlin sentiment of most people is still the spear in my side. In everything except my romantic Chestertonian orthodoxy I still agree with the early Wells on human nature and the "no hope for Tono Bungay" theory.

God! How I miss my youth—that's only relative of course but already lines are beginning to coarsen *in other people* and that's the sure sign. I don't think you ever realized at Princeton the childlike simplicity that lay behind all my petty sophistication and my lack of a real sense of honor. I'd be a wicked man if it wasn't for that and now that's disappearing.

[252]

Well I'm overstepping and boring you and using up my novel's material. So Goodbye. Do write and lets keep in touch if you like.

God bless you.

Celticly

F. Scott Fitzgerald

Bishop's adress

Lieut. John Peale Bishop (He's a 1st Lt.)
   334th Infantry
   Camp Taylor
    Kentucky

TO EDMUND WILSON

[1920]
599 Summit Ave.
St. Paul, Minn
August 15th

Dear Bunny:

Delighted to get your letter. I am deep in the throes of a new novel.

Which is the best title

(1) *The Education of a Personage*
(2) *The Romantic Egotist*
(3) *This Side of Paradise*

I am sending it to Scribner. They liked my first one. Am enclosing two letters from them that might amuse you. Please return them.

I have just finished the story for your book.* It's not written yet. An American girl falls in love with an officer Francais at a southern camp.

Since I last saw you I've tried to get married & then tried to drink myself to death but foiled, as have been so many good men, by the sex and the state I have returned to literature.

---

* I was trying to get together a collection of realistic stories about the war. E.W.

Have sold three or four cheap stories to American magazines.

Will start on story for you about 25th d'Auout (as the French say or do not say) (which is about 10 days off)

I am ashamed to say that my Catholicism is scarcely more than a memory—no that's wrong it's more than that; at any rate I go not to the church nor mumble stray nothings over chrystaline beads.

Maybe in N'York in Sept or early Oct.

Is John Bishop in hoc terrain? ...

For God's sake Bunny write a novel & don't waste your time editing collections. It'll get to be a habit.

That sounds crass & discordant but you know what I mean.

Yours in the Holder* group
Scott Fitzgerald

TO EDMUND WILSON

[1920]
599 Summit Ave.
St. Paul, Minn.

Dear Bunny:

Scribner has accepted my book for publication late in the winter. You'll call it sensational but it really is niether sentimental nor trashy.

I'll probably be East in November & I'll call you up or come to see you or something. Haven't had time to hit a story for you yet. Better not count on me as the w. of i. or the E.S. are rather dry.

Yrs. faithfully
Francis S. Fitzgerald

* This refers to Holder Hall, one of the Princeton dormitories.

TO JOHN V. A. WEAVER

[1921]
626 Goodrich Ave.
St. Paul, Minn

Dear John:

I was tickled to write the review.* I saw Broun's & F.P.A.'s reviews but you know how they love me & how much attention I pay to their dictums.

This is my new style of letter writing.† It is to make it easy for comments & notes to be put in when my biographer begins to assemble my collected letters.

The Metropolitan isn't here yet. I shall certainly read *Enamel.* I wish to Christ I could go to Europe.

Thine

F. Scott Fitzgerald

TO EDMUND WILSON

[Postmarked November 25, 1921]
626 Goodrich Avenue
St. Paul, Minn.

Dear Bunny:

Thank you for your congratulations.‡ I'm glad the damn thing's over. Zelda came through without a scratch & I have awarded her the croix-de-guerre with palm. Speaking of France, the great general with the suggestive name is in town today.

I agree with you about Mencken—Weaver & Dell are both something awful. . . .

* Of John V. A. Weaver's book of poems, *In American.*

† This note was written in a very small hand in the middle of a sheet of paper.

‡ On the birth of his daughter.

[255]

I have almost completely rewritten my book.* Do you remember you told me that in my midnight symposium scene I had sort of set the stage for a play that never came off—in other words when they all began to talk none of them had anything important to say. I've interpolated some recent ideas of my own and (possibly) of others. See inclosure at end of letter.† . . . Having disposed of myself I turn to you. I am glad you and Ted Paramore are together. . . I like Ted immensely. He is a little too much the successful Eli to live comfortably in his mind's bed-chamber but I like him immensely.

What in hell does this mean? My control must have dictated it. His name is Mr. Ikki and he is an Alaskan orange-grower. . . .

If the baby is ugly she can retire into the shelter of her full name Frances Scott.

St. Paul is dull as hell. Have written two good short stories and three cheap ones.

I like *Three Soldiers* immensely & reviewed it for the *St. Paul Daily News*. I am tired of modern novels & have just finished Paine's biography of Clemens. It's excellent. Do let me see if you do me for the *Bookman*. Isn't *The Triumph of the Egg* a wonderful title. I liked both John's‡ and Don's§ articles in *Smart Set*. I am lonesome for N. Y. May get there next fall & may go to England to live. Yours in this hell-hole of life & time, the world.

F. Scott Fitz

---

* *The Beautiful and Damned*.

† These enclosures included the greater part of Maury Noble's monologue in the chapter called *Symposium*, pp. 252-258.

‡ John Peale Bishop.

§ Donald Ogden Stewart.

[Postmarked January 24, 1922]
626 Goodrich Ave.
St. Paul, Minn.

Dear Bunny:

Farrar tells a man here that I'm to be in the March *Literary Spotlight*.* I deduce that this is your doing. My curiosity is at fever heat—for God's sake send me a copy immediately.

Have you read Upton Sinclair's *The Brass Check?*

Have you seen Hergeshiemer's movie *Tol'able David?*

Both are excellent. I have written two wonderful stories & get letters of praise from six editors with the addenda that "our readers, however, would be offended." Very discouraging. Also discouraging that Knopf has put off the *Garland†* till fall. I enjoyed your da-daist article in *Vanity Fair*—also the free advertising Bishop gave us. Zelda says the picture of you is "beautiful and bloodless."

I am bored as hell out here. The baby is well—we dazzle her exquisite eyes with gold pieces in the hopes that she'll marry a millionaire. We'll be east for ten days early in March. . . .

What are you doing? I was tremendously interested by all the data in your last letter. I am dying of a sort of emotional aenemia like the lady in Pound's poem. *The Briary Bush* is stinko.

Cytherea is Hergeshiemer's best but its not quite.

Yours

John Grier Hibben‡

---

* A series of portraits of contemporary writers published in *The Bookman*.

† *The Undertaker's Garland*, by John Peale Bishop and Edmund Wilson.

‡ John Grier Hibben was president of Princeton at this time.

[Probably written in the spring of 1922]
626 Goodrich Avenue
[St. Paul, Minn.]

Dear John:

I'll tell you frankly what I'd rather you'd do. Tell specifically what you like about the book* and don't — —. The
characters—Anthony, Gloria, Adam Patch, Maury, Bleek-
man, Muriel Dick, Rachael, Tana ect ect ect. Exactly
whether they are good or bad, convincing or not. What you
think of the style, too ornate (if so quote) good (also quote)
rotten (also quote). What emotion (if any) the book gave
you. What you think of its humor. What you think of its
ideas. If ideas are bogus hold them up specifically and laugh
at them. Is it boring or interesting. How interesting. What
recent American books are more so. If you think my "Flash
Back in Paradise" in Chap I is like the elevated moments of
D. W. Griffith say so. Also do you think it is imitative and
of whom.

What I'm angling for is a specific definite review. I'm
tickled both that they have asked for such a lengthy thing
and that you are going to do it. You cannot hurt my feelings
about the book—tho I did resent in your Baltimore article
being definitely limited at 25 years old to a place between
McKenzie who wrote 2½ good (but not wonderful) novels
and then died—and Tarkington who if he has any talent has
the mind of a schoolboy. I mean, at my age, they'd done
nothing.

As I say I'm delighted that you're going to do it and as
you wrote asking me to suggest a general mode of attack I
am telling you frankly what I would like. I'm so afraid of
all the reviews being general and I devoted so much more
care myself to the *detail* of the book than I did to thinking
out the *general* scheme that I would appreciate a detailed
review. If it is to be that length article it could scarcely be
all general anyway.

* *The Beautiful and Damned.*

I'm awfully sorry you've had the flue. We arrive east on the 9th. I enjoy your book page in Vanity Fair and think it is excellent—

The baby is beautiful.

As Ever
Scott

TO EDMUND WILSON

[Probably written in the spring of 1922]
626 Goodrich Ave.
St. Paul, Minn.

Dear Bunny:

From your silence I deduce that either you decided that the play* was not in shape to offer to the Guild or that they refused it.

I have now finished the revision. I am forwarding one copy to Harris &, if you think the Guild would be interested, will forward them the other. Your play should be well along by now. Could you manage to send me a carbon?

I'm working like a dog on some movies at present. I was sorry our meetings in New York were so fragmentary. My original plan was to contrive to have long discourses with you but that interminable party began and I couldn't seem to get sober enough to be able to tolerate being sober. In fact the whole trip was largely a failure.

My compliments to Mary Blair, Ted Paramour and whomsoever else of the elect may cross your path.

We have no plans for the summer.

Scott Fitz—

* *The Vegetable.*

June 25th, 1922

Dear Bunny:

Thank you for giving the play to Craven—and again for your interest in it in general. I'm afraid I think you overestimate it—because I have just been fixing up *Mr. Icky** for my fall book and it does not seem very good to me. I am about to start a revision of the play—also to find a name. I'll send it to Hopkins next. So far it has only been to Miller, Harris & the Theatre Guild. I'd give anything if Craven would play that part. I wrote it, as the text says, with him in mind. I agree with you that *Anna Christie* was vastly overestimated. . . .

Am going to write another play whatever becomes of this one. *The Beautiful & Damned* has had a very satisfactory but not inspiring sale. We thought it'd go far beyond *Paradise* but it hasn't. It was a dire mistake to serialize it. *Three Soldiers* and *Cytherea* took the edge off it by the time it was published. . . .

Did you like *The Diamond as Big as the Ritz* or did you read it. It's in my new book anyhow. . . .

I have *Ullyses* from the Brick Row Bookshop & am starting it. I wish it was laved in America—there is something about middle-class Ireland that depresses me inordinately—I mean gives me a sort of hollow, cheerless pain. Half of my ancestors came from just such an Irish strata or perhaps a lower one. The book makes me feel appallingly naked. Expect to go either South or to New York in October for the Winter.

Ever thine,
F. Scott Fitz

* I had been telling him how funny I thought this burlesque, which first appeared in *The Smart Set* and was afterwards included in *Tales of the Jazz Age*. E.W.

TO EDMUND WILSON

> [Postmarked August 1, 1922]
> The Yatch Club
> White Bear Lake, Minn.

Dear Bunny:

Just a line to tell you I've finished my play & am sending it to Nathan to give to Hopkins or Selwyn. It is now a wonder. I'm going to ask you to destroy the 2 copies you have as it makes me sort of nervous to have them out. This is silly but so long as a play is in an actors office and is unpublished as my play at Cravens I feel lines from it will soon begin to appear on B'way....

Write me any gossip if you have time. No news or plans have I.

> Thine
> Fitz

TO EDMUND WILSON

> F. Scott Fitzgerald
> Hack Writer and Plagiarist
> St. Paul Minnesota*

> [Postmarked August 5, 1922]

Dear Bunny:

Fitzgerald howled over *Quintilian*.† He is glad it was reprinted as he couldn't get the *Double Dealer* and feared he had missed it. It's excellent especially the line about Nero and the one about Dr. Bishop.

The play with an absolutely new second act has gone to Nathan who is giving it to Hopkins or Selwynn. Thank you for taking it to Ames & Elkins. I'm rather glad now that none of them took it as I'd have been tempted to let them do

---

* This was a printed letterhead.

† A nonsense poem of mine published in the New Orleans *Double Dealer*. E.W.

it—and my new version is much better. Please do not bother to return the 2 mss. you have as its a lot of trouble. I have copies of them & no use for them. Destruction will save the same purpose—it only worries me to have them knocking around.

I read sprigs of the old oak that grew from the marriage of Mencken & Margaret Anderson (Christ! What a metaphor!) and is known as the younger genitals. It bored me. I didn't read yours—but * * * * is getting worse than Frank Harris with his elaborate explanations and whitewashings of himself. There's no easier way for a clever writer to become a bore. It turns the gentle art of making enemies into the East Aurora Craft of making people indifferent . . . in the stunned pause that preceded this epigram Fitzgerald bolted his aspic and went to a sailor's den.

"See here," he said, "I want some new way of using the great Conradian vitality, the legend that the sea exists without Polish eyes to see it. Masefield has spread it on iambics and downed it; O'Niell has sprinkled it on Broadway; McFee has added an evenrude motor—"

cribbed from Harry Leon Wilson

But I could think of no new art form in which to fit him. So I decided to end the letter. The little woman, my best pal and I may add, my severest critic, asked to be remembered.

Would you like to see the new play? Or are you fed up for awhile. Perhaps we better wait till it appears. I think I'll try to serialize it in Scribners—would you?

Scott F.

Am undecided about *Ullyses* application to me—which is as near as I ever come to forming an impersonal judgement.

[Postmarked August 28, 1922]
The Yatch Club
White Bear Lake
Minnesota

Dear Bunny—

The *Garland* arrived and I have re-read it. Your preface is perfect—my only regret is that it wasn't published when it was written almost two years ago. *The Soldier* of course I read for about the fifth time. I think it's about the best short war story yet—but I object violently to "pitched forward" in the lunch-putting anecdote. The man would have said "fell down" or "sorta sank down." Also I was delighted as usual by the Efficiency Expert. Your poems I like less than your prose—*The Lake* I do not particularly care for. I like the Centaur and the Epilogue best—but all your poetry seems to flow from some source outside or before the romantic movement even when its intent is most lyrical.

I like all of John's except the play which strikes me as being obvious and *Resurrection* which despite its excellent idea & title & some spots of good writing is pale and without any particular vitality.

Due to you, I suppose, I had a wire from Langner. I referred him to Geo. Nathan.

Many thinks for the book. Would you like me to review it? If so suggest a paper or magazine and I'll be glad to.

Thine

F. Scott Fitz.

The format of the book is most attractive. I grow envious every time I see a Knopf binding.

> [Postmarked October 7, 1924]
> Villa Marie, Valescure,
> St. Raphael, France

Dear Bunny:

The above will tell you where we are as you proclaim yourself unable to find it on the map.* We enjoyed your letter enormously, collossally, stupendously. It was epochal, acrocryptical, categorical. I have begun life anew since getting it and Zelda has gone into a nunnery on the Pelleponesus. . . .

The news about the play is grand & the ballet too. I gather from your letter that O'Niell & Mary had a great success. But you are wrong about Ring's book.† My title was the best possible. You are always wrong—but always with the most correct possible reasons. (This statement is merely acrocrytical, hypothetical, diabolical, metaphorical). . . .

I had a short curious note from the latter‡ yesterday, calling me to account for my *Mercury* story.§ At first I couldn't understand this communication after seven blessedly silent years—behold: he was a Catholic. I had broken his heart. . . .

I will give you now the Fitz touch without which this letter would fail to conform to your conception of my character.

Sinclair Lewis sold his new novel to the *Designer* for $50,000 (950,000.00 francs)—I never did like that fellow. (I do really).

My book is wonderful,‖ so is the air & the sea. I have got my health back—I no longer cough and itch and roll from one side of the bed to the other all night and have a hollow ache in my stomach after two cups of black coffee. I really

---

* He had drawn a map of the French coast between Hyères and Nice.
† Ring Lardner's *How to Write Short Stories*.
‡ A friend whom he has just mentioned in a passage not printed here.
§ *Absolution*.
‖ *The Great Gatsby*.

worked hard as hell last winter—but it was all trash and it nearly broke my heart as well as my iron constitution.

Write to me of all data, gossip, event, accident, scandal, sensation, deterioration, new reputation—and of yourself.

Our love

Scott

TO JOHN PEALE BISHOP

> [Winter of 1924-25]
> I am quite drunk
> I am told fhat this is Capri;
> though as I remember Capri
> was quieter

Dear John:

As the literary wits might say, your letter received and contents quoted. Let us have more of the same—I think it showed a great deal of power and the last scenc— the dinner at the young Bishops—was handled with admirable restraint. I am glad that at last Americans are producing letters of their own. The climax was wonderful and the exquisite irony of the "sincerely yours" has only been equalled in the work of those two masters Flaubert and Ferber. . . .

I will now have two copies of Westcott's *Apple* as in despair I ordered one—a regular orchard. I shall give one to Brooks whom I like. Do you know Brooks? He's just a fellow here. . . .

Excuse the delay. I have been working on the envelope. . . .

That was a caller. His name was Musselini, I think, and he says he is in politics here. And besides I have lost my pen so I will have to continue in pencil* . . . It turned up— I was writing with it all the time and hadn't noticed. That is because I am full of my new work, a historical play based on the life of Woodrow Wilson.

---

* This sentence is written in pencil. The rest of the letter is in ink.

Act I At Princeton

Woodrow seen teaching philosophy. Enter Pyne. Quarrel scene—Wilson refuses to recognize clubs. Enter woman with Bastard from Trenton. Pyne reenters with glee club and trustees. Noise outside "We have won—Princeton 12-Lafayette 3." Cheers. Football team enter and group around Wilson. Old Nassau. Curtain.

Act. II. Gubernatorial Mansion at Patterson

Wilson seen signing papers. Tasker Bliss and Marc Connelly come in with proposition to let bosses get control. "I have important papers to sign—and none of them legalize corruption." Triangle Club begins to sing outside window. . . . Enter women with Bastard from Trenton. President continues to sign papers. Enter Mrs. Galt, John Grier Hibben, Al Jolsen and Grantland Rice. Song "The call to Larger Duty." Tableau. Coughdrop.

Act III. (Optional)

The Battle front 1918

Act IV.

The peace congress. Clemenceau, Wilson and Jolsen at table. . . . The junior prom committee comes in through the skylight. Clemenceau: "We want the Sarre." Wilson: "No, sarre, I won't hear of it." Laughter. . . . Enter Marylyn Miller, Gilbert Seldes and Irish Meusel. Tasker Bliss falls into cuspidor.

Oh Christ! I'm sobering up! Write me the opinion you may be pleased to form of my chef d'oevre and others opinion. *Please!* I think its great but because it deals with much debauched materials, quick-deciders like Rasco may mistake it for Chambers. To me its fascinating. I never get tired of it. . . .

Zelda's been sick in bed for five weeks, poor child, and is only now looking up. No news except I now get 2000 a story and they grow worse and worse and my ambition is to get where I need write no more but only novels. Is Lewis' book any good. I imagine that mine is infinitely better— what else is well-reviewed this spring? Maybe my book* is rotten but I don't think so.

What are you writing? Please tell me something about your novel. And if I like the idea maybe I'll make it into a short story for the Post to appear just before your novel and steal the thunder. Who's going to do it? Bebé Daniels? She's a wow!

How was Townsend's first picture. Good reviews? What's Alec doing? And Ludlow? And Bunny? Did you read Ernest Boyd's account of what I might ironically call our "private" life in his "*Portraits?*" Did you like it? I rather did.

Scott

I am quite drunk again and enclose a postage stamp.

TO JOHN PEALE BISHOP

[Winter of 1924-25]
American Express Co.
Rome, Italy.

Dear John:

Your letter was perfect. It told us everything we wanted to know and the same day I read your article (very nice too) in *Van. Fair* about cherching the past. But you disappointed me with the quality of some of it (the news)—for instance that Bunny's play failed and that you and Margaret find life dull and depressing there. We want to come back but we want to come back with money saved and so far we haven't saved any—tho I'm one novel ahead and book of pretty good (seven) short stories. I've done about 10 pieces

* *The Great Gatsby.*

of horrible junk in the last year tho that I can never republish or bear to look at—cheap and without the spontaneity of my first work. But the novel I'm sure of. It's marvellous.

We're just back from Capri where I sat up (tell Bunny) half the night talking to my old idol Compton Mackenzie. Perhaps you met him. I found him cordial, attractive and pleasantly mundane. You get no sense from him that he feels his work has gone to pieces. He's not pompous about his present output. I think he's just tired. The war wrecked him as it did Wells and many of that generation.

To show how well you guessed the gossip I wanted we were wondering where the * * * *s got the money for Havana, whether the Film Guild finally collapsed (Christ! You should have seen their last two pictures.) But I don't doubt that * * * * and * * * * will talk themselves into the cabinet eventually. I'd do it myself if I could but I'm too much of an egoist and not enough of a diplomat ever to succeed in the movies. You must begin by placing the tongue flat against the posteriors of such worthys as * * * * and * * * * and commence a slow caressing movement. Say what they may of Cruze—Famous Players is the product of two great ideas Demille and Gloria Swanson and it stands or falls not by their "conference methods" but on those two and the stock pictures that imitate them. The Cruze winnings are usually lost on such expensive experiments as * * * *.

Is Dos Passos novel any good? And what's become of Cummings work. I haven't read *Some Do Not* but Zelda was crazy about it. I glanced through it and kept wondering why it was written backward. At first I thought they'd sewn the cover on upside down. Well—these people *will* collaborate with Conrad.

Do you still think Dos Passos is a genius? My faith in him is somehow weakened. There's so little time for faith these days.

* * * * * * * * is a damned attractive woman and while the husbands a haberdasher he's at least a Groton haberdasher (he went there, I mean, to school)....

The Wescott book will be eagerly devoured. A personable

young man of that name from Atlantic introduced himself to me after the failure of the *Vegetable*. I wonder if he's the same. At any rate your Wescott, so Harrison Rhodes tells me, is coming here to Rome.

I've given up Nathan's books. I liked the 4th series of *Prejudices*. Is Lewis new book any good. Hergesheimers was awful. He's all done....

The cheerfulest things in my life are first Zelda and second the hope that my book has something extraordinary about it. I want to be extravagantly admired again. Zelda and I sometimes indulge in terrible four day rows that always start with a drinking party but we're still enormously in love and about the only truly happily married people I know.

Our Very Best to Margaret

Please write!
Scott

(OVER)

In the Villa d'Este at Tivoli [Como] all that ran in my brain was:

> "An alley of dark cypresses
>   Hides an enrondured pool of light
> And there the young musicians come
>   With instruments for her delight
> ....locks are bowed
>   Over dim lutes that sigh aloud
> Or else with heads thrown back they tease
>   Reverberate echoes from the drum
> The still folds *etc*"

It was wonderful that when you wrote that you'd never seen Italy—or, by God, now that I think of it, never lived in the 15th century.

But then I wrote *T. S. of P.* without having been to Oxford.

[1925]
14 Rue de Tillsit
Paris, France

Dear Bunny:

Thanks for your letter about the book.* I was awfully happy that you liked it and that you approved of the design. The worst fault in it, I think is a BIG FAULT: I gave no account (and had no feeling about or knowledge of) the emotional relations between Gatsby and Daisy from the time of their reunion to the catastrophe. However the lack is so astutely concealed by the retrospect of Gatsby's past and by blankets of excellent prose that no one has noticed it—though everyone has felt the lack and called it by another name. Mencken said (in a most enthusiastic letter received today) that the only fault was that the central story was trivial and a sort of anecdote (that is because he has forgotten his admiration for Conrad and adjusted himself to the sprawling novel) and I felt that what he really missed was the lack of any emotional backbone at the very height of it.

Without making any invidious comparisons between Class A and Class C, if my novel is an anecdote so is *The Brothers Karamazoff*. From one angle the latter could be reduced into a detective story. However the letters from you and Mencken have compensated me for the fact that of all the reviews, even the most enthusiastic, not one had the slightest idea what the book was about and for the even more depressing fact that it was in comparison with the others a financial failure (after I'd turned down fifteen thousand for the serial rights!) I wonder what Rosenfeld thought of it.

I looked up Hemminway. He is taking me to see Gertrude Stein tomorrow. This city is full of Americans—most of them former friends—whom we spend most of our time dodging, not because we don't want to see them but because Zelda's only just well and I've got to work; and they seem to be incapable of any sort of conversation not composed of semi-malicious gossip about New York courtesy celebrities.

* *The Great Gatsby.*

I've gotten to like France. We've taken a swell apartment
until January. I'm filled with disgust for Americans in
general after two weeks sight of the ones in Paris—these
preposterous, pushing women and girls who assume that
you have any personal interest in them, who have all (so
they say) read James Joyce and who simply adore Mencken.
I suppose we're no worse than anyone, only contact with
other races brings out all our worse qualities. If I had anything to do with creating the manners of the contemporary
American girl I certainly made a botch of the job.

I'd love to see you. God. I could give you some laughs.
There's no news except that Zelda and I think we're pretty
good, as usual, only more so.

Scott

Thanks again for your cheering letter.

TO JOHN PEALE BISHOP

[Postmarked, August 9, 1925]
Rue de Tilsitt
Paris, France

Dear John:

Thank you for your most pleasant, full, discerning and
helpful letter about *The Great Gatsby*. It is about the only
criticism that the book has had which has been intelligible,
save a letter from Mrs. Wharton. I shall only ponder, or
rather I have pondered, what you say about accuracy—I'm
afraid I haven't quite reached the ruthless artistry which
would let me cut out an exquisite bit that had no place in
the context. I can cut out the almost exquisite, the adequate,
even the brilliant—but a true accuracy is, as you say, still
in the offing. Also you are right about Gatsby being blurred
and patchy. I never at any one time saw him clear myself—
for he started out as one man I knew and then changed into
myself—the amalgam was never complete in my mind.

Your novel sounds fascinating and I'm crazy to see it. I'm beginning a new novel next month on the Riviera. I understand that MacLeish is there, among other people (at Antibes where we are going). Paris has been a mad-house this spring and, as you can imagine, we were in the thick of it. I don't know when we're coming back—maybe never. We'll be here till Jan. (except for a month in Antibes), and then we go Nice for the Spring, with Oxford for next summer. Love to Margaret and many thanks for the kind letter.

Scott

TO JOHN PEALE BISHOP

[1925]

Dear Sir:

The enclosed explains itself.* Meanwhile I went to Antibes and liked Archie MacLeish enormously. Also his poem, though it seems strange to like anything so outrageously derivative. *T. S. of P.* was an original in comparison.

I'm crazy to see your novel. I'm starting a new one myself. There was no one at Antibes this summer except me, Zelda, the Valentinos, the Murphy's, Mistinguet, Rex Ingram, Dos Passos, Alice Terry, the MacLeishes, Charles Bracket, Maude Kahn, Esther Murphy, Marguerite Namara, E. Phillips Openheim, Mannes the violinist, Floyd Dell, Max and Chrystal Eastman, ex-Premier Orlando, Etienne de Beaumont—just a real place to rough it and escape from all the world. But we had a great time. I don't know when we're coming home—

The Hemminways are coming to din..er so I close with best wishes

Scott

* The enclosure was, as I recall it, a letter of introduction to me. But who was being introduced I cannot recall. J.P.B.

[Probably spring, 1928]
"Ellerslie"
Edgemoor, Delaware

Dear Bunny: ...

All is prepared for February 25th. The stomach pumps
are polished and set out in rows, stale old enthusiasms are
being burnished with that zeal peculiar only to the Brittish
Tommy. My God, how we felt when the long slaughter of
Paschendale had begun. Why were the generals all so old?
Why were the Fabian society discriminated against when
positions on the general staff went to Dukes and sons of
profiteers. Agitators were actually hooted at in Hyde Park
and Anglican divines actually didn't become humanitarian
internationalists over night. What is Briton coming to—
where is Milton, Cromwell, Oates, Monk? Where are Shafts-
bury, Athelstane, Thomas a Becket, Margot Asquith, Iris
March. Where are Blackstone, Touchstone, Clapham-Hope-
wellton, Stoke-Poges? Somewhere back at G.H.Q. handsome men with grey whiskers murmured "We will charge
them with the cavalry" and meanwhile boys from Bovril and
the black country sat shivering in the lagoons at Ypres writing memoirs for liberal novels about the war. What about the
tanks? Why did not Douglas Haig or Sir John French (the
big smarties) (Look what they did to General Mercer) invent tanks the day the war broke out, like Sir Phillip Gibbs
the weeping baronet, did or would, had he thought of it.

This is just a *sample* of what you will get on the 25th of
Feb. There will be small but select company, coals, blankets,
"something for the inner man."

Please don't say you can't come the 25th but would like
to come the 29th. We never receive people the 29th. It is
the anniversary of the 2nd Council of Nicea when our
Blessed Lord, our Blessed Lord, our Blessed Lord, our Blessed
Lord—

It always gets stuck in that place. Put on "Old Man
River" or something of Louis Bromfields.

[273]

Pray gravity to move your bowels. Its little we get done for us in this world. Answer.

Scott

Enjoyed your Wilson article enormously. Not so Thompson affair.*

TO JOHN PEALE BISHOP

[Probably January
or February, 1929]
% Guaranty Trust

Dear John:

My depression over the badness of the novel† as novel had just about sunk me, when I began the novellette‡—John, it's like two different men writing. The novellette is one of the best war things I've ever read—right up with the very best of Crane and Bierce—intelligent, beautifully organized and written—oh, it moved me and delighted me—the Charlestown country, the night in town, the old lady—but most of all, in the position I was in at 4 this afternoon when I was in agony about the novel, the really fine dramatic handling of the old lady—and—silver episode and the butchering scene. The preparation for the latter was adroit and delicate and just enough.

Now, to be practical—*Scribner's Magazine* will, I'm sure, publish the novellette, if you wish, and pay you from 250-400 therefore. This price is a guess but probably accurate. I'd be glad to act as your amateur agent in the case. It is

* This was an article by Mr. W. G. Thompson, counsel for Sacco and Vanzetti, called *Vanzetti's Last Statement*, which appeared in *The Atlantic Monthly* of February 1928.

† An unpublished novel by Bishop.

‡ *The Cellar*, a short story by Bishop, published in his collection, *Many Thousands Gone*.

[274]

almost impossible without a big popular name to sell a two-part story to any higher priced magazine than that, as I know from my experience with *Diamond Big as the Ritz, Rich Boy*, ect. Advise me as to whether I may go ahead—of course authority confined only to American serial rights.

The novel is just something you've learned from and profited by. It has occasional spurts—like the conversations frequently of Brakespeare, but it is terribly tepid—I refrain —rather I don't refrain but here set down certain facts which you are undoubtedly quite as aware of as I am.* . . .

I'm taking you for a beating, but do you remember your letters to me about *Gatsby*. I suffered, but I got something like I did out of your friendly tutelage in English poetry.

A big person can make a much bigger mess than a little person and your impressive stature converted a lot of pottery into pebbles during the three years or so you were in the works. Luckily the pottery was never very dear to you. Novels are not written, or at least begun with the idea of making an ultimate philosophical system—you tried to atone for your lack of confidence by a lack of humility before the form.

The main thing is: no one in our language possibly excepting Wilder has your talent for "the world," your culture and acuteness of social criticism as upheld by the story. There the approach (2nd and 3rd person ect) is considered, full scope in choice of subject for your special talents (descriptive power, sense of "le pays," ramifications of your special virtues such as loyalty, concealment of the sensuality that is your bête noire to such an extent that you can no longer see it black, like me in my drunkenness.

Anyhow the story is marvellous. Don't be mad at this letter. I have the horrors tonight and perhaps am taking it out on you. Write me when I could see you here in Paris in the afternoon between 2.30 and 6.30 and talk—and name a day and a café at your convenience—I have no dates save on Sunday, so any day will suit me. Meanwhile I will make one more stab at your novel to see if I can think of anyway

* There follow several pages of detailed criticism of the novel, which can be of no interest to anyone but myself. J.P.B.

by a miracle of cutting it could be made presentable. But I fear there's neither honor nor money in it for you

Your old and Always
Affectionate Friend
Scott

Excuse Christ-like tone of letter. Began tippling at page 2 and am now positively holy (like Dostoevsky's non-stinking monk)

TO JOHN PEALE BISHOP

[Received May 5, 1931]
Grand Hôtel de la Paix
Lausanne

Dear John:

Read *Many Thousands* over again (2nd time) and like it enormously. I think it hangs together as a book too. I like the first story—I think its damn good. I'd never read it before. *Death and Young Desire* doesn't come off—as for instance the handling of the same theme in *The Story of St. Michele*. Why I don't know. My favorite is *The Cellar*—I am still fascinated by the Conradean missing man—that's real fiction. *Bones* seems even better in the respect-inspiring light thrown by Bunny's opinion. I'm taking it to Zelda tomorrow.

Ever your Friend
Scott

TO EDMUND WILSON

[Probably February 1933]
La Paix (My God!)
Towson Md.

Dear Bunny:

Your letter with the head of Vladimir Ulianov* just received. Please come here the night of the inauguration &

* This refers to a stamp with Lenin's head, which I had put on a letter I had written him.

[276]

stay at least the next day. I want to know with what resignation you look forward to your rôle of Lunatcharsky & whether you decided you had nothing further worth saying in prose fiction or whether there was nothing further to say. Perhaps I should draw the answer to the last question from *Axel's Castle* yet I remember stories of yours that anticipated so much that was later said that it seemed a pity. (Not that I don't admire your recent stuff—particularly I liked Hull House.)

We had a most unfortunate meeting. I came to New York to get drunk . . . and I shouldn't have looked up you and Ernest in such a humor of impotent desperation. I assume full responsibility for all unpleasantness—with Ernest I seem to have reached a state where when we drink together I half bait, half truckle to him. . . . Anyhow, plenty of egotism for the moment.

Dos was here, & we had a nice evening—we never quite understand each other & perhaps that's the best basis for an enduring friendship. Alec came up to see me at the Plaza the day I left (still in awful shape but not conspicuously so). He told me to my amazement that you had explained the fundamentals of Leninism, even Marxism the night before, & Dos tells me that it was only recently made plain thru the same agency to the *New Republic*. I little thought when I left politics to you & your gang in 1920 you would devote your time to cutting up Wilson's shroud into blinders! Back to Mallarmé!

—Which reminds me that T. S. Eliot and I had an afternoon & evening together last week. I read him some of his poems and he seemed to think they were pretty good. I liked him fine. . . .

However come in March. Don't know what time the inauguration takes place but you find out & tell us the approximate time of your arrival here. Find out *in advance* for we may go to it too & we might all get lost in the shuffle.

Always Your Friend
Scott . . .

TO EDMUND WILSON

[Postmarked March 12, 1934]
1307 Park Avenue
Baltimore, Maryland

Dear Bunny:

Despite your intention of mild criticism* in our conversation, I felt more elated than otherwise—if the characters got real enough so that you disagreed with what I chose for their manifest destiny the main purpose was accomplished (by the way, your notion that Dick should have faded out as a shyster alienist was in my original design, but I thot of him, in reconsideration, as an "homme epuisé," not only an "homme manqué." I thought that, since his choice of a profession had accidentally wrecked him, he might plausibly have walked out on the profession itself.)

Any attempt by an author to explain away a partial failure in a work is of course doomed to absurdity—yet I could wish that you, and others, had read the book version rather than the mag. version which in spots was hastily put together. The last half for example has a *much* more polished facade now. Oddly enough several people have felt that the surface of the first chapters was *too* ornate. One man even advised me to "coarsen the texture," as being remote from the speed of the main narrative!

In any case when it appears I hope you'll find time to look it over again. Such irrevelancies as * * * *'s nosedive and Dick's affair in Ohnsbruck are out, together with the scene of calling on the retired bootlegger at Beaulieu, & innumerable minor details. I have driven the Scribner proofreaders half nuts but I think I've made it incomparably smoother.

Zelda's pictures go on display in a few weeks & I'll be meeting her in N. Y. for a day at least. Wouldn't it be a good time for a reunion?

It was good seeing you & good to think that our squabble, or whatever it was, is ironed out.

With affection always,
Scott Fitzgerald

* Of *Tender is the Night.*

[278]

September 7, 1934
1307 Park Avenue
Baltimore, Maryland,

Dear Bunny:

I've had a big reaction from your last two articles in the *New Republic.** In spite of the fact that we always approach material in different ways there is some fast-guessing quality that, for me, links us now in the work of the intellect. Always the overtone and the understatement.

It was fun when we all believed the same things. It was more fun to think that we were all going to die together or live together, and none of us anticipated this great loneliness, where one has dedicated his remnants to imaginative fiction and another his slowly dissolving trunk to the Human Idea. Nevertheless the stress that you put upon this in your *New Republic* article—of forces never still, of rivers never ending, of clouds shifting their prophecies at evening, afternoon or morning—this sense of things has kept our courses loosely parallel, even when our references to data have been so disparate as to throw us miles apart.

The purport of this letter is to agree passionately with an idea that you put forth in a discussion of Michelet: that conditions irretrievably change men and that what looks purple in a blue light looks, in another spectrum, like green and white bouncing snow. I want you to know that one among many readers is absolutely alert to the implications and substrata of meaning in this new work.

Ever affectionately yours,
Scott

TO BEATRICE DANCE [?]

September, 1936

I have never had so many things go wrong and with such defiant persistence. By an irony which quite fits into the

* Articles on Michelet, afterwards included in *To The Finland Station*.

picture, the legacy which I received from my mother's death (after being too ill to go to her death bed or her funeral) is the luckiest event of some time. She was a defiant old woman, defiant in her love for me in spite of my neglect of her and it would have been quite within her character to have died that I might live.

Thank you for your wire today. People have received this *Esquire* article with mingled feelings—not a few of them think it was a terrific mistake to have written any of them from *Crack-Up*. On the other hand, I get innumerable "fan letters" and requests to republish them in the *Reader's Digest*, and several anthologists' requests, which I prudently refused.

My Hollywood deal (which, as it happened, I could not have gone through with because of my shoulder) was seriously compromised by their general tone. It seems to have implied to some people that I was a complete moral and artistic bankrupt.

Now—I come to some things I may have written you before. Did I tell you that I got the broken shoulder from diving from a fifteen-foot board, which would have seemed modest enough in the old days, and the shoulder broke before I hit the water—a phenomenon which has diverted the medicos hereabout to some extent; and that when it was almost well, I tripped over the raised platform of the bath room at four o'clock one morning when I was still surrounded by an extraordinary plaster cast and I lay on the floor for forty-five minutes before I could crawl to the telephone and get rescued by Mac. It was a hot night, and I was soaking wet in the cast so I caught cold on the tile floor of the bath room, and a form of arthritis called "miotosis" developed, which involved all of the joints on that side of the body, so back to the bed I went and I have been groaning and cursing without cessation until about three days ago, when the devil began to abandon me. During this time Mother died in the North and a dozen other things seemed to happen at once, so that it will take me several months to clear the wreckage of a completely wasted summer, productive of one mediocre short story and two or three shorts.

May 16, 1939
5521 Amestoy Avenue
Encino, California

Dear Bunny:

News that you and Mary had a baby reached me rather late because I was out of California for several months. Hope he is now strong and crawling. Tell him if he grows up any bigger I shall be prepared to take him for a loop when he reaches the age of twenty-one at which time I shall be sixty-three. . . .

Believe me, Bunny, it meant more to me than it could possibly have meant to you to see you that evening. It seemed to renew old times learning about Franz Kafka and latter things that are going on in the world of poetry, because I am still the ignoramus that you and John Bishop wrote about at Princeton. Though my idea is now, to learn about a new life from Louis B. Mayer who promises to teach me all about things if he ever gets around to it.

Ever your devoted friend,

TO GERALD MURPHY

TWENTIETH CENTURY-FOX FILM CORPORATION
Studios
Beverly Hills, California
September 14, 1940

Dear Gerald:

I suppose anybody our age suspects what is emphasized —so let it go. But I was flat in bed from April to July last year with day and night nurses. Anyhow as you see from the letterhead I am now in official health.

I find, after a long time out here, that one develops new

attitudes. It is, for example, such a slack *soft* place—even its pleasure lacking the fierceness or excitement of Provence —that withdrawal is practically a condition of safety. The sin is to upset anyone else, and much of what is known as "progress" is attained by more or less delicately poking and prodding other people. This is an unhealthy condition of affairs. Except for the stage-struck young girls people come here for negative reasons—all gold rushes are essentially negative—and the young girls soon join the vicious circle. There is no group, however small, interesting as such. Everywhere there is, after a moment, either corruption or indifference. The heroes are the great corruptionists or the supremely indifferent—by whom I mean the spoiled writers, Hecht, Nunnally Johnson, Dotty,* Dash Hammet etc. That Dotty has embraced the church and reads her office faithfully every day does not affect her indifference. So is one type of commy Malraux didn't list among his categories in *Man's Hope*—but nothing would disappoint her so vehemently as success.

I have a novel pretty well on the road. I think it will baffle and in some ways irritate what readers I have left. But it is as detached from me as *Gatsby* was, in intent anyhow. The new Armegeddon, far from making everything unimportant, gives me a certain lust for life again. This is undoubtedly an immature throw-back, but it's the truth. The gloom of all causes does not affect it—I feel a certain rebirth of kinetic impulses—however misdirected. . . .

I *would* like to have some days with you and Sara. I hear distant thunder about Ernest and Archie and their doings but about you not a tenth of what I want to know.

With affection,
Scott

TO GERALD AND SARA MURPHY

Honey—that goes for Sara too:

I have written a dozen people since who mean nothing to

* Dorothy Parker.

me—writing you I was saving for good news. I suppose pride was concerned—in that personally and publicly dreary month of Sept. last about everything went to pieces all at once and it was a long uphill pull.

To summarize: I don't have to tell you anything about the awful lapses and sudden reverses and apparent cures and thorough poisoning effect of lung trouble. Suffice to say there were months with a high of 99.8, months at 99.6 and then up and down and a stabilization at 99.2 every afternoon when I could write in bed—and now for 2½ months and one short week that may have been grip—nothing at all. With it went a psychic depression over the finances and the effect on Scotty and Zelda. There was many a day when the fact that you and Sara did help me at a desperate moment . . . seemed the only pleasant human thing that had happened in a world where I felt prematurely passed by and forgotten. The thousands that I'd given and loaned—well, after the first attempts I didn't even worry about that. There seem to be the givers and the takers and that doesn't change. So you were never out of my mind—but even so no more present than always because this was only one of so many things.

In the land of the living again I function rather well. My great dreams about this place are shattered and I have written half a novel* and a score of satiric pieces that are appearing in the current *Esquires* about it. After having to turn down a bunch of well paid jobs while I was ill there was a period when no one seemed to want me for duck soup —then a month ago a producer asked me to do a piece of my own for a small sum ($2000) and a share in the profits. The piece is *Babylon Revisited* and an old and not bad *Post* story of which the child heroine was named Honoria! I'm keeping the name.

It looks good. I have stopped being a prophet (3rd attempt at spelling this) but I think I may be solvent in a month or so if the fever keeps subservient to what the doctors think is an exceptional resistance. . . .

So now you're up to date on me and it won't be so long

* *The Last Tycoon.*

again. I might say by way of counter-reproach that there's no word of any of *you* in your letter. It is sad about * * * *. Writing you today has brought back so much and I could weep very easily.

With dearest Love,
Scott

TO ERNEST HEMINGWAY

November 8, 1940

Dear Ernest:

It's a fine novel,* better than anybody else writing could do. Thanks for thinking of me and for your dedication. I read it with intense interest, participating in a lot of the writing problems as they came along and often quite unable to discover how you brought off some of the effects, but you always did. The massacre was magnificent and also the fight on the mountain and the actual dynamiting scene. Of the sideshows I particularly liked the vignette of Karkov and Pilar's Sonata to death—and I had a personal interest in the Moseby guerilla stuff because of my own father. The scene in which the father says goodbye to his son is very powerful. I'm going to read the whole thing again.

I never got to tell you how I like *To Have and to Have Not* either. There is observation and writing in that that the boys will be imitating with a vengeance—paragraphs and pages that are right up with Dostoiefski in their undeflected intensity.

Congratulations too on your new book's great success. I envy you like hell and there is no irony in this. I always liked Dostoiefski with his wide appeal more than any other European—and I envy you the time it will give you to do what you want.

With Old Affection,

---

* *For Whom the Bell Tolls.*

P.S. I came across an old article by John Bishop about how you lay four days under dead bodies at Caporetto and how I flunked out of Princeton (I left on a stretcher in November—you can't flunk out in November) . . . What I started to say was that I do know something about you on the Italian front, from a man who was in your unit—how you crawled some hellish distance pulling a wounded man with you and how the doctors stood over you wondering why you were alive with so many perforations. Don't worry—I won't tell anybody. Not even Allan Campbell who called me up and gave me news of you the other day.

P.S. (2) I hear you are marrying one of the most beautiful people I have ever seen. Give her my best remembrance.

TO EDMUND WILSON

> 1403 N. Laurel Avenue
> Hollywood, Cal.
> November 25, 1940

Dear Bunny:. . .

I think my novel* is good. I've written it with difficulty. It is completely upstream in mood and will get a certain amount of abuse but it is first hand and I am trying a little harder than I ever have to be exact and honest emotionally. I honestly hoped somebody else would write it but nobody seems to be going to.

> With best to you both,
> (signed) Scott

P.S. This sounds like a bitter letter†—I'd rewite it except for a horrible paucity of time. Not even time to be bitter.

---

* *The Last Tycoon.*
† This refers to the first part of the letter, omitted here.

LETTERS TO
FRANCES SCOTT FITZGERALD

August 8, 1933
La Paix, Rodgers' Forge,
Towson, Maryland,

Dear Pie:

I feel very strongly about you doing duty. Would you give me a little more documentation about your reading in French? I am glad you are happy—but I never believe much in happiness. I never believe in misery either. Those are things you see on the stage or the screen or the printed page, they never really happen to you in life.

All I believe in in life is the rewards for virtue (according to your talents) and the *punishments* for not fulfilling your duties, which are doubly costly. If there is such a volume in the camp library, will you ask Mrs. Tyson to let you look up a sonnet of Shakespeare's in which the line occurs *Lilies that fester smell far worse than weeds.*

Have had no thoughts today, life seems composed of getting up a *Saturday Evening Post* story. I think of you, and always pleasantly; but if you call me "Pappy" again I am going to take the White Cat out and beat his bottom *hard, six times for every time you are impertinent.* Do you react to that?

I will arrange the camp bill.

Half-wit, I will conclude. Things to worry about:

    Worry about courage

    Worry about cleanliness

    Worry about efficiency

    Worry about horsemanship . . .

Things not to worry about:

    Don't worry about popular opinion

Don't worry about dolls
Don't worry about the past
Don't worry about the future
Don't worry about growing up
Don't worry about anybody getting ahead of you
Don't worry about triumph
Don't worry about failure unless it comes through your own fault
Don't worry about mosquitoes
Don't worry about flies
Don't worry about insects in general
Don't worry about parents
Don't worry about boys
Don't worry about disappointments
Don't worry about pleasures
Don't worry about satisfactions
Things to think about:
   What am I really aiming at?
   How good am I really in comparison to my contemporaries in regard to:
     (a) Scholarship
     (b) Do I really understand about people and am I able to get along with them?
     (c) Am I trying to make my body a useful instrument or am I neglecting it?

With dearest love,

Autumn, 1937*

I shall somehow manage not to appear in a taxicab on Thanksgiving and thus disgrace you before all those "nice" girls. Isn't it somewhat old-fashioned to describe girls in expensive backgrounds as "nice?" I will bet two-thirds of

* Scott Fitzgerald was in Hollywood, working for the moving pictures, during 1937, 1938, 1939 and 1940, and most of the letters that follow must have been written from there. He made, however, a few short trips to the East, and this letter may have been written from an Eastern address.

the girls at Miss Walker's School have at least one grand-
parent that peddled old leather in the slums of New York,
Chicago, or London, and if I thought you were accepting
the standards of the cosmopolitan rich, I would much rather
have you in a Southern school, where scholastic standards
are not so high and the word "nice" is not debased to such a
ludicrous extent. I have seen the whole racket, and if there
is any more disastrous road than that from Park Avenue to
the Rue de la Paix and back again, I don't know it.

They are homeless people, ashamed of being American,
unable to master the culture of another country; ashamed,
usually, of their husbands, wives, grandparents, and unable
to bring up descendants of whom they could be proud, even
if they had the nerve to bear them, ashamed of each other
yet leaning on each other's weakness, a menace to the social
order in which they live—oh, why should I go on? You know
how I feel about such things. If I come up and find you gone
Park Avenue, you will have to explain me away as a Georgia
cracker or a Chicago killer. God help Park Avenue.

July 7, 1938

I am certainly glad that you're up and around, and sorry
that your selection of Post-Flaubertian realism depressed
you. I certainly wouldn't begin Henry James with *The
Portrait of a Lady*, which is in his "late second manner" and
full of mannerisms. Why don't you read *Roderick Hudson*
or *Daisy Miller* first? *Lord Jim* is a great book—the first
third at least and the conception, though it got lost a little
bit in the law-courts of Calcutta or wherever it was. I wonder
if you know why it is good? *Sister Carrie*, almost the first
piece of American realism, is damn good and is as easy
reading as a True Confession.

Summer, 1939

I want to have you out here for part of the summer. I have
a nice cottage in the country, but very *far* out in the country,

and utterly inaccessible if one doesn't drive well. Whether a piano here would be practical or not I don't know (remember how I felt about radio) but all that might be arranged if the personal equation were not doubtful (a situation for which for the moment I take full blame). Since I stopped picture work three months ago, I have been through not only a T.B. flare-up but also a nervous breakdown of such severity that for a time it threatened to paralyze both arms—or to quote the doctor: "The Good Lord tapped you on the shoulder." While I am running no fever above 99, I don't know what this return to picture work is going to do, and when and if my health blows up, you know what a poor family man I am. . . .

I am of course not drinking and haven't been for a long time, but any illness is liable to have a certain toxic effect on the system and you may find me depressing, over-nervous about small things and dogmatic—all these qualities more intensified than you have previously experienced them in me. Beyond this I am working very hard and the last thing I want at the end of the day is a problem, while, as it is natural at your age, what you want at the end of the day is excitement. I tell you all this because lately we had planned so many meetings with anticipation and they have turned out to be flops. Perhaps forewarned will be forearmed. . . .

If the experiment proves upsetting, I will have no further choice than to pack you off East somewhere again, but there are several friends here whom you could visit for a time if we failed to make a satisfactory household. So the trip will be worthwhile. Also I am more of a solitary than I have ever been, but I don't think that will worry you, because you had your dosages of motion picture stars on two other trips. To describe how humorless I feel about life at this point you have simply to read the Tarkington story called *Sinful Dadda Little* in the *Post* issue of July 22 (still current I believe), and remember that I read it without a particle of amusement, but with a complete disgust at *Dadda* for not drowning the two debutantes, at the end.

I think it was you who misunderstood my meaning about the comrades. The important thing is this: they had best be treated, not as people holding a certain set of liberal or conservative opinions, but rather as you might treat a set of intensely fanatical Roman Catholics among whom you might find yourself. It is not that you should not disagree with them—the important thing is that you should not argue with them. The point is that Communism has become an intensely dogmatic and almost mystical religion, and whatever you say, they have ways of twisting it into shapes which put you in some lower category of mankind ("Fascist," "Liberal," "Trotskyist"), and disparage you both intellectually and personally in the process. They are amazingly well organized. The pith of my advice is: think what you want, the less said the better. . . .

You must have some politeness toward ideas. You can neither cut through, nor challenge nor beat the fact that there is an organized movement over the world before which you and I as individuals are less than the dust. Some time when you feel very brave and defiant and haven't been invited to one particular college function, read the terrible chapter in *Das Kapital* on *The Working Day*, and see if you are ever quite the same.

Spring, 1940

Spring was always an awful time for me about work. I always felt that in the long boredom of winter there was nothing else to do but study. But I lost the feeling in the long, dreamy spring days and managed to be in scholastic hot water by June. I can't tell you what to do about it—all my suggestions seem to be very remote and academic. But if I were with you and we could talk again like we used to, I might lift you out of your trouble about concentration. It really isn't so hard, even with dreamy people like you and me—it's just that we feel so damned secure at times as long as there's enough in the bank to buy the next meal, and enough moral stuff in reserve to take us through the next ordeal. Our danger is imagining we have resources—material and moral—which we haven't got. One of the reasons I find myself so consistently in valleys of depression is that every few years I seem to be climbing uphill to recover from some bankruptcy. Do you know what bankruptcy exactly means? It means drawing on resources which one does not possess. I thought I was so strong that I never would be ill and suddenly I was ill for three years, and faced with a long, slow uphill climb. Wiser people seem to manage to pile up a reserve—so that if on a night you had set aside to study for a philosophy test, you learned that your best friend was in trouble and needed your help, you could skip that night and find you had a reserve of one or two days preparation to draw on. But I think that, like me, you will be something of a fool in that regard all your life, so I am wasting my words.

Spring, 1940

Anyhow I am alive again—getting by that October did something—with all its strains and necessities and humiliations and struggles. I don't drink. I am not a great man but sometimes I think the impersonal and objective quality of my talent and the sacrifices of it, in pieces, to preserve its essential value has some sort of epic grandeur. Anyhow after hours I nurse myself with delusions of that sort. . . .

And I think when you read this book,* which will encompass the time when you knew me as an adult, you will understand how intensively I knew your world—not *ex*tensively because I was so ill and unable to get about. If I live long enough, I'll hear your side of things, but I think your own instincts about your limitations as an artist are possibly best: you might experiment back and forth among the arts and find your niche as I found mine—but I do not believe that so far you are a "natural."

* *The Last Tycoon.*

[291]

April 12, 1940

You are doing exactly what I did at Princeton. I wore myself out on a musical comedy there for which I wrote book and lyrics, organized and mostly directed while the president played football. Result: I slipped way back in my work, got T.B., lost a year in college—and, irony of ironies, because of a scholastic slip I wasn't allowed to take the presidency of the Triangle. . . .

From your letter I guess you are doing exactly the same thing and it just makes my stomach fall out to think of it. Amateur work is fun but the price for it is just simply tremendous. In the end you get "Thank you" and that's all. You give three performances which everybody promptly forgets and somebody has a breakdown—that somebody being the enthusiast.

April 27, 1940

Musical comedy is fun—I suppose more "fun" than anything else a literary person can put their talents to and it always has an air of glamor around it. . . .

I was particularly interested in your line about "feeling that you had lost your favorite child." God, haven't I felt that so many times. Often I think writing is a sheer paring away of oneself, leaving always something thinner, barer, more meagre. However, that's not anything to worry about in your case for another twenty years. I am glad you are going to Princeton with whom you are going. I feel you have now somehow jumped a class. Boys like * * * * and * * * * are on a guess more "full of direction" than most of the happy-go-luckies in Cap and Gown. I don't mean more ambition, which is a sort of general attribute at youth and is five parts hope to five parts good will, but I mean some calculated path, stemming from a talent or money or a careful directive or all of these things, to find your way through the bourgeois maze—if you feel it is worth finding. Remember this, though, among those on both sides of the fence there are a lot of slow developers, people of quality and distinction whom you should not overlook.

You are always welcome in California, though. We are even opening our arms to Chamberlain in case the British oust him. We need him for Governor, because we are afraid the Asiatics are going to land from Chinese parasols. Never mind—Santa Barbara will be our Narvik and we'll defend it to our last producer. And remember, even England still has Noel Coward.

I actually have a formulating plan for part of your summer—if it pleases you—and I think I'll have the money to make it good. I'm working hard, guiding by the fever which now hovers quietly around the 99.2 level, which is fairly harmless. Tell Frances Kilpatrick that, though I never met her father, he is still one of my heroes, in spite of the fact that he robbed Princeton of a football championship single-handed—he was probably the greatest end who ever played football. In the future please send me clippings even though you do crack at me in the course of your interviews. I'd rather get them than have you send me accounts of what literary sourbellies write about me in their books. I've been criticized by experts including myself.

I think I've about finished a swell flicker piece. Did you read me in the current *Esquire* about Orson Welles? Is it funny? Tell me. You haven't answered a question for six letters. Better do so or I'll dock five dollars next week to show you I'm the same old meany.

You asked me whether I thought that in the Arts it was greater to originate a new form or to perfect it. The best answer is the one that Picasso made rather bitterly to Gertrude Stein:

"You do something first and then somebody else comes along and does it pretty." ...

In the opinion of any real artist, the inventor—which is

to say Giotto or Leonardo—is infinitely superior to the finished Tintoretto, and the original D. H. Lawrences are infinitely greater than the Steinbecks.

May 11, 1940

I'm glad you didn't start going to Princeton at sixteen or you'd be pretty jaded by this time. Yale is a good year ahead of Princeton in sophistication, though—it should be good for another year. Though I loved Princeton, I often felt that it was a by-water, that its snobby institutions were easy to beat and to despise, and unless a man was a natural steeple-chaser or a society groom, you'd find your own private intellectual and emotional life. Given that premise, it is a lovely quiet place, gentle and dignified, and it will let you alone. Of course, it is at its absolute worst in the * * * * atmosphere you described. Some time go down with a boy on one of those weekends when there's almost nothing to do.

June 12, 1940

I could agree with you as opposed to Dean Thompson if you were getting "B's." Then I would say: As you're not going to be a teacher or a professional scholar, don't try for "A's"—don't take the things in which you can get "A," for you can learn them yourself. Try something hard and new, and try it hard, and take what marks you can get. But you have no such margin of respectability, and this borderline business is a fret to you. Doubt and worry—you are as crippled by them as I am by my inability to handle money or my self-indulgences of the past. It is your Achilles' heel—and no Achilles' heel ever toughened by itself. It just gets more and more vulnerable. What little I've accomplished has been by the most laborious and uphill work, and I wish now I'd *never* relaxed or looked back—but said at the end of *The Great Gatsby:* "I've found my line—from now on this comes first. This is my immediate duty—without this I am nothing."

June 15, 1940

Meanwhile I have another plan which may yield a bonanza but will take a week to develop, so there's nothing to do for a week except try to cheer up your mother and derive what consolation you can in explaining the Spenglerian hypotheses to Miss * * * * and her fellow feebs of the Confederacy. Maybe you can write something down there. It is a grotesquely pictorial country as I found out long ago, and as Mr. Faulkner has since abundantly demonstrated.

June 20, 1940

I wish I were with you this afternoon. At the moment I am sitting rather dismally contemplating the loss of a three year old Ford and a thirty-three year old tooth. The Ford (heavily mortgaged) I shall probably get back, according to the police, because it is just a childish prank of the California boys to steal them and then abandon them. But the tooth I had grown to love. . . .

In recompense I found in *Collier's* a story by myself. I started it just before I broke my shoulder in 1936 and wrote it in intervals over the next couple of years. It seemed terrible to me. That I will ever be able to recover the art of the popular short story is doubtful. At present I'm doing a masterpiece for *Esquire* and waiting to see if my producer can sell the *Babylon Revisited* screen play to Shirley Temple. If this happens, everything will look very much brighter. . . .

The police have just called up telling me they've recovered my car. The thief ran out of gas and abandoned it in the middle of Hollywood Boulevard. The poor lad was evidently afraid to call anybody to help him push it to the curb. I hope next time he gets a nice big producer's car with plenty of gas in it and a loaded revolver in each side pocket and he can embark on a career of crime in earnest. I don't like to see any education left hanging in the air.

Haven't you got a carbon of the *New Yorker* article? I've heard that John Mason Brown is a great favorite as a lecturer and I think it's very modern to be taking dramatic criticism, though it reminds me vaguely of the school for Roxy Ushers. It seems a trifle detached from drama itself. I suppose the thing's to get *really* removed from the subject, and the final removal would be a school for teaching critics of teachers of dramatic criticism. . . .

Isn't the world a lousy place—I've just finished a copy of *Life* and I'm dashing around to a Boris Karloff movie to cheer up. It is an inspirational thing called "The Corpse in the Breakfast Food." . . .

Once I thought that Lake Forest was the most glamorous place in the world. Maybe it was.

I wonder if you've read anything this summer—I mean any one good book like *The Brothers Karamazov* or *Ten Days That Shook the World* or Renan's *Life of Christ*. You never speak of your reading except the excerpts you do in college, the little short bits that they must perforce give you. I know you have read a few of the books I gave you last summer—then I have heard nothing from you on the subject. Have you ever, for example, read *Père Goriot* or *Crime and Punishment* or even *The Doll's House* or *St. Matthew* or *Sons and Lovers*? A good style simply doesn't *form* unless you absorb half a dozen top-flight authors every year. Or rather it forms but instead of being a subconscious amalgam of all that you have admired, it is simply a reflection of the last writer you have read, a watered-down journalese.

This job has given me part of the money for your tuition and it comes so hard that I hate to see you spend it on a course like English Prose since 1800. Anybody that can't read modern English prose by themselves is subnormal—and you know it. The chief fault in your style is its lack of distinction—something which is inclined to grow with the years. You had distinction once—there's some in your diary —and the only way to increase it is to *cultivate your own garden*. And the only thing that will help you is poetry, which is the most concentrated form of style. . . .

Example: You read *Melanctha,* which is practically poetry, and sold a *New Yorker* story—you read ordinary novels and sink back to a Kitty-Foyle-Diary level of average performance. The only sensible course for you at this moment is the one on *English Poetry—Blake to Keats* (English 241). I don't care how clever the other professor is, one can't raise a discussion of modern prose to anything above tea-table level. I'll tell you everything she knows about it in three hours and guarantee that what *each* of us tells you will be largely wrong, for it will be almost entirely conditioned by our responses to the subject matter. It is a course for Clubwomen who want to continue on from Rebecca and Scarlett O'Hara. . . .

Strange Interlude is good. It was good the first time, when Shaw wrote it and called it *Candida.* On the other hand you don't pass an hour of your present life that isn't directly influenced by the devastating blast of light and air that came with Ibsen's *Doll's House.* Nora wasn't the only one who walked out of the Doll's House—all the women in Gene O'Neill walked out too. Only they wore fancier clothes. . . .

Well, the old master wearies—the above is really good advice, Pie, in a line where I know my stuff. Unless you can break down your prose a little, it'll stay on the ill-paid journalistic level. And you can do better.

August 3, 1940

It isn't something easy to get started on by yourself. You need, at the beginning, some enthusiast who also knows his way around—John Peale Bishop performed that office for me at Princeton. I had always dabbled in "verse," but he made me see, in the course of a couple of months, the difference between poetry and non-poetry. After that, one of my first discoveries was that some of the professors who were teaching poetry really hated it and didn't know what it was about. I got in a series of endless scraps with them, so that finally I dropped English altogether....

Poetry is either something that lives like fire inside you—like music to the musician or Marxism to the Communist—or else it is nothing, an empty, formalized bore, around which pedants can endlessly drone their notes and explanations. *The Grecian Urn* is unbearably beautiful, with every syllable as inevitable as the notes in Beethoven's *Ninth Symphony*, or it's just something you don't understand. It is what it is because an extraordinary genius paused at that point in history and touched it. I suppose I've read it a hundred times. About the tenth time I began to know what it was about, and caught the chime in it and the exquisite inner mechanics. Likewise with the *Nightingale*, which I can never read through without tears in my eyes; likewise the *Pot of Basil* with its great stanzas about the two brothers: "Why were they proud, etc."; and *The Eve of Saint Agnes*, which has the richest, most sensuous imagery in English, not excepting Shakespeare. And finally his three or four great sonnets: *Bright Star* and the others....

Knowing those things very young and granted an ear, one could scarcely ever afterwards be unable to distinguish between gold and dross in what one read. In themselves those eight poems are a scale of workmanship for anybody who wants to know truly about words, their most utter value for evocation, persuasion or charm. For awhile after you quit Keats all other poetry seems to be only whistling or humming.

August 12, 1940

Working among the poor has differing effects on people. If you're poor yourself, you get their psychology and it's

[298]

broadening—for example, when a boy of the bourgeoisie ships before the mast on a tramp schooner where he has to endure the same privations as the seamen, undoubtedly he achieves something of their point of view forever. On the contrary, a Bennington girl spending a month in slum work and passing the weekend at her father's mansion in Long Island gets nothing at all except a smug feeling that she is Lady Bountiful.

August 24, 1940

I can imagine the dinner party. I remember taking Zelda to the young * * * *'s when we were first married and it was a pretty frozen dish, though in general the places we went to even from the beginning were many flights up from the average business man's ménage. Business is a dull game, and they pay a big price in human values for their money. They are "all right when you get to know them." I liked some of the young Princeton men in business, but I couldn't stand the Yale and Harvard equivalents because we didn't even have the common ground of the past. The women are empty twirps mostly, easy to seduce and not good for much else. I am not talking about natural society women like * * * * and * * * * and some others, who made their lives into pageants, almost like actresses.

However, you seem wise enough to see that there is something in * * * *'s angle. College gives you a head start, especially a girl, and people are not in any hurry to live and think your way. It's all a question of proportion: if you married an army officer you would live half a lifetime of kowtowing to your inferiors until your husband made his way to the top. If, as the chances are, you marry a business man—because for the present business absorbs most of the energetic and attractive boys—you will have to play your cards properly in the business hierarchy. That was why I have always hoped that life would throw you among lawyers or men who were going into politics or big time journalism. They lead rather larger lives.

Advertising is a racket, like the movies and the brokerage business. You cannot be honest without admitting that its constructive contribution to humanity is exactly minus zero. It is simply a means of making dubious promises to a credulous public. (But if you showed this letter to * * * *, it would be the end of everything in short order, for a man must have his pride, and the *more* he realizes such a situation, the *less* he can afford to admit it.) If I had been promoted when I was an advertising man, given enough money to marry your mother in 1920, my life might have been altogether different. I'm not sure, though. People often struggle through to what they are in spite of any detours—and possibly I might have been a writer sooner or later anyhow.

October 5, 1940

Glad you liked *Death in Venice*. I don't see any connection between that and *Dorian Gray*, except that they both have an implied homosexuality. *Dorian Gray* is little more than a somewhat highly charged fairy tale which stimulates adolescents to intellectual activity at about seventeen (it did the same for you as it did for me). Sometime you will re-read it and see that it is essentially naïve. It is in the lower ragged edge of "literature" just as *Gone With the Wind* is in the higher brackets of crowd entertainment. *Death in Venice*, on the other hand, is a work of art, of the school of Flaubert —yet not derivative at all. Wilde had two models for *Dorian Gray:* Balzac's *Le Peau de Chagrin* and Huysmans' *A Rebours*.

December, 1940

My novel is something of a mystery, I hope. I think it's a pretty good rule not to tell what a thing is about until it's finished. If you do, you always seem to lose some of it. It never quite belongs to you so much again.

A great social success is a pretty girl who plays her cards as carefully as if she were plain.

I felt all my life the absence of hobbies, except such for me abstract and academic ones as military tactics and football. Botany is such a definite thing. It has its feet on the ground. And after reading Thoreau I felt how much I have lost by leaving nature out of my life.

So many writers, Conrad for instance, have been aided by being brought up in a métier utterly unrelated to literature. It gives an abundance of material and, more important, an attitude from which to view the world. So much writing nowadays suffers both from lack of an attitude and from sheer lack of any material, save what is accumulated in a purely social life. The world, as a rule, does not live on beaches and in country clubs.

One time in sophomore year at Princeton, Dean West got up and rolled out the great lines of Horace:

> *"Integer vitae, scelerisque purus*
> *Non eget Mauris iaculis neque arcu"*—

—And I knew in my heart that I had missed something by being a poor Latin scholar, like a blessed evening with a lovely girl. It was a great human experience I had rejected through laziness, through having sown no painful seed.

It has been so ironic to me in after life to buy books to master subjects in which I took courses at college and which made no impression on me whatsoever. I once flunked a course on the Napoleonic era, and I now have over 300 books in my library on the subject and the other A scholars wouldn't even remember it now. That was because I had made the mental tie-up that work equals something unpleasant, something to be avoided, something to be postponed. These scholars you speak of as being bright are no brighter than you, the great majority not nearly as quick, nor, probably, as well endowed with memory and perception, but they have made that tie-up, so that something does not stiffen in their minds at the mention that it is a set task. I am so sure that this is your trouble because you are so much like me and because, after a long time milling over the matter, I have concluded that it was mine. What an idiot I was to be disqualified for play by poor work when men of infinitely inferior capacity got high marks without any great effort.

I never blame failure—there are too many complicated situations in life—but I am absolutely merciless toward lack of effort.

The first thing I ever sold was a piece of verse to *Poet Lore* when I was twenty.

While my picture *is* going to be done, the producer is going to *first* do one that has been made for the brave * * * *, who will defend his country in Hollywood (though summoned back by the British Government). This affects the patriotic and unselfish Scott Fitzgerald to the extent that I receive no more money from that source until the company gets around to it; so will return to my old standby *Esquire*.

How you could possibly have missed the answer to my first question I don't know, unless you skipped pages 160 to 170 in *Farewell To Arms*. There's nothing vague in these questions of mine but they require attention. I hope you've sent me the answer to the second question. The third question is based on the Book *Ecclesiastes* in the Bible. It is fifteen pages long and since you have it in your room you ought to get through it carefully in four or five days. As far as I am concerned, you can skip the wise-cracks in italics on pages 766, 767 and 768. They were written by somebody else and just stuck in there. But read carefully the little introduction on 754 and note also that I do not mean *Ecclesiasticus*, which is something entirely different. Remember when you're reading it that it is one of the top pieces of writing in the world. Notice that Ernest Hemingway got a title from the third paragraph. As a matter of fact the thing is full of titles. The paragraph on page 756 sounds like the confession of a movie producer, even to the swimming pools.

Am glad you were reading about Twentieth Century Sophists. You meet them every day. They see their world falling to pieces and know all the answers, and are not going to do anything about it.

We have reached a censorship barrier in *Infidelity*, to our infinite disappointment. It *won't* be Joan's next picture and we are setting it aside awhile till we can think of a way of halfwitting halfwit Hayes and his legion of decency. Pictures needed cleaning up in 1932-33 (remember I didn't like you to see them?), but because they were suggestive and salacious. Of course the moralists now want to apply that to *all* strong themes—so the crop of the last two years is feeble and false, unless it deals with children. Anyhow we're starting a new story and a safe one.

About *adjectives:* all fine prose is based on the verbs carrying the sentences. They make sentences move. Probably the finest technical poem in English is Keats' *Eve of Saint Agnes.* A line like:

> The hare limped trembling through the frozen grass,

is so alive that you race through it, scarcely noticing it, yet it has colored the whole poem with its movement—the limping, trembling, and freezing is going on before your own eyes. Would you read that poem for me, and report? ·

Don't be a bit discouraged about your story not being tops. At the same time, I am not going to encourage you about it, because, after all, if you want to get into the big time, you have to have your own fences to jump, and learn from experience. Nobody ever became a writer just by wanting to be one. If you have anything to say, anything you feel nobody has ever said before, you have got to feel it so desperately that you will find some way to say it that nobody has ever found before, so that the thing you have to say and the way of saying it blend as one matter—as indissolubly as if they were conceived together. . . .

Let me preach again for a moment: I mean that what you have felt and thought will by itself invent a new style, so that when people talk about style they are always a little astonished at the newness of it, because they think that it is only *style* that they are talking about, when what they are talking about is the attempt to express a new idea with such force that it will have the originality of the thought. It is an awfully lonesome business, and, as you know, I never wanted you to go into it, but if you are going into it at all, I want you to go into it knowing the sort of things that took me years to learn.

All good writing is *swimming under water* and holding your breath.

The conclusion is: it will not win you financial independence or immortality. But you will be wise to publish it, if you can—if for no gain and only in a college magazine. It will give you a sense of your own literary existence, and put you in touch with others trying the same thing. In a literary way I cannot help you beyond a point. I might say that I don't think anyone can write succinct prose unless they have at least tried and failed to write a good iambic pentameter sonnet, and read Browning's short dramatic poems, etc.— but that was my personal approach to prose. Yours may be different, as Ernest Hemingway's was. But I wouldn't have written this long letter unless I distinguished, underneath the sing-song lilt of your narrative, some traces of a true rhythm that is ear-marked Scottina. There is as yet no honesty—the reader will say "So what?" But when in a freak moment you will want to give the low-down, not the scandal, not the merely *reported* but the *profound* essence of what happened at a prom or after it, perhaps that honesty will come to you—and then you will understand how it is possible to make even a forlorn Laplander *feel* the importance of a trip to Cartier's!

Most of my contemporaries did not get started at twenty-two, but usually at about twenty-seven to thirty or even later, filling in the interval with anything from journalism [or] teaching [to] sailing a tramp-schooner and going to wars. The talent that matures early is usually of the poetic [type], which mine was in large part. The prose talent depends on other factors—assimilation of material and careful selection of it, or, more bluntly: having something to say and an interesting, highly developed way of saying it.

I'm going into a huddle on this script and probably won't be able to write you again at length before Vassar starts. I read the story in *College Bazaar* and was very pleased with it. You've put in some excellent new touches and its only fault is the jerkiness that goes with a story that has often been revised. Stories are best written in either one jump or three, according to the length. The three-jump story should be done on three successive days, then a day or so for revise and off she goes. This of course is the ideal—in many stories one strikes a snag that must be hacked at, but, on the whole, stories that drag along or are terribly difficult (I mean a difficulty that comes from a poor conception and consequent faulty construction) never flow quite as well in the reading.

Again let me repeat that if you start any kind of a career following the footsteps of Cole Porter and Rogers and Hart, it might be an excellent try. Sometimes I wish I had gone along with that gang, but I guess I am too much a moralist at heart, and really want to preach at people in some acceptable form, rather than to entertain them.

I started Tom Wolfe's book on your recommendation. It seems better than *Time and the River*. He has a fine inclusive mind, can write like a streak, has a great deal of emotion, though a lot of it is maudlin and inaccurate but his awful secret transpires at every crevice—he did not have anything particular to say! The stuff about the GREAT VITAL HEART OF AMERICA is just simply corny.

He recapitulates beautifully a great deal of what Walt Whitman said and Dostoevsky said and Nietzsche said and

Milton said, but he himself, unlike Joyce and T. S. Eliot and Ernest Hemingway, has nothing really new to add. All right—it's all a mess and it's too bad about the individual—so what? Most writers line themselves up along a solid gold bar like Ernest's courage or Joseph Conrad's art or D. H. Lawrence's intense cohabitations, but Wolfe is too "smart" for this, and I mean smart in its most belittling and modern sense. Smart like Fadiman in the *New Yorker*, smart like the critics whom he so pretends to despise. However, the book doesn't commit the cardinal sin: it doesn't fail to live. But I'd like you to think sometime, how and in what way you think it is superior to such a piece of Zolaesque naturalism as Maugham's "Of Human Bondage" or if it is superior at all. . . .

I'm taking a day off from my novel to go to the dentist, the doctor and my agent, to the latter in order to discuss picture business when and if I go back to it in February.

Once one is caught up into the material world, not one person in ten thousand finds the time to form literary taste, to examine the validity of philosophic concepts for himself or to form what, for lack of a better phrase, I might call the wise and tragic sense of life.

By this I mean the thing that lies behind all great careers, from Shakespeare's to Abraham Lincoln's, and as far back as there are books to read—the sense that life is essentially a cheat and its conditions are those of defeat, and that the redeeming things are not "happiness and pleasure" but the deeper satisfactions that come out of struggle. Having learned this in theory from the lives and conclusions of great men, you can get a hell of a lot more enjoyment out of whatever bright things come your way.

You speak of how good your generation is, but I think they share with every generation since the Civil War in America the sense of being somehow about to inherit the earth. You've heard me say before that I think the faces of most American women over thirty are relief maps of petulant and bewildered unhappiness.

"Those debutante parties in New York are the rendezvous of a gang of professional idlers—parasites, pansies, failures, the silliest type of sophomores, young customers' men from Wall Street and hangers-on. The very riff-raff of social New York who would exploit a child like Scottie with flattery and squeeze her out until she is a limp colorless rag. In one more year she can cope with them. In three more years it will be behind her. This year she is still puppy enough to be dazzled. She will be infinitely better off here with me than mixed up with that sort of people. I'd rather have an angry little girl on my hands for a few months than a broken neurotic for the rest of my life." But I don't have to tell you this —you probably read the *Life* article on the dim-witted * * * * girl and the razz on her in the *New Yorker*.

Three Letters about "The Great Gatsby"

FROM GERTRUDE STEIN

Hotel Pernollet
Belley
(Ain)

Belley, le 22 May, 192-[1925]

My dear Fitzgerald:

Here we are and have read your book and it is a good book. I like the melody of your dedication and it shows that you have a background of beauty and tenderness and that is a comfort. The next good thing is that you write naturally in sentences and that too is a comfort. You write naturally in sentences and one can read all of them and that among other things is a comfort. You are creating the contemporary world much as Thackeray did his in *Pendennis* and *Vanity Fair* and this isn't a bad compliment. You make a modern world and a modern orgy strangely enough it was never done until you did it in *This Side of Paradise*. My belief in *This Side of Paradise* was alright. This is as good a book and different and older and that is what one does, one does not get better but different and older and that is always a pleasure. Best of good luck to you always, and thanks so much for the very genuine pleasure you have given me. We are looking forward to seeing you and Mrs. Fitzgerald when we get back in the Fall. Do please remember me to her and to you always

Gtde Stein

Pavillon Colombe
St. Brice-Sous-Forêt (S&O)
Gare: Sarcelles

June 8, 1925

Dear Mr. Fitzgerald,

I have been wandering for the last weeks and found your novel—with its friendly dedication—awaiting me here on my arrival, a few days ago.

I am touched at your sending me a copy, for I feel that to your generation, which has taken such a flying leap into the future, I must represent the literary equivalent of tufted furniture & gas chandeliers. So you will understand that it is in a spirit of sincere deprecation that I shall venture, in a few days, to offer you in return the last product of my manufactory.

Meanwhile, let me say at once how much I like Gatsby, or rather His Book, & how great a leap I think you have taken this time—in advance upon your previous work. My present quarrel with you is only this: that to make Gatsby really Great, you ought to have given us his early career (not from the cradle—but from his visit to the yacht, if not before) instead of a short résumé of it. That would have situated him, & made his final tragedy a tragedy instead of a "fait divers" for the morning papers.

But you'll tell me that's the old way, & consequently not *your* way; & meanwhile, it's enough to make this reader happy to have met your *perfect* Jew, & the limp Wilson, & assisted at that seedy orgy in the Buchanan flat, with the dazed puppy looking on. Every bit of that is masterly—but the lunch with Hildesheim,* and his every appearance afterward, make me augur still greater things!—Thank you again.

Yrs. Sincerely,
Edith Wharton

* The name should be Wolfsheim. Hildesheim was misspelled Hilde-shiem in the first edition of *The Great Gatsby*.

I have left hardly space to ask if you & Mrs. Fitzgerald won't come to lunch or tea some day this week. Do call me up.

FROM T. S. ELIOT

FABER AND GWYER LTD.
Publishers

24 Russell Square,
London, W.C.1.
31st December, 1925

F. Scott Fitzgerald, Esqre.,
% Charles Scribners & Sons,
New York City.

Dear Mr. Scott Fitzgerald,

The Great Gatsby with your charming and overpowering inscription arrived the very morning that I was leaving in some haste for a sea voyage advised by my doctor. I therefore left it behind and only read it on my return a few days ago. I have, however, now read it three times. I am not in the least influenced by your remark about myself when I say that it has interested and excited me more than any new novel I have seen, either English or American, for a number of years.

When I have time I should like to write to you more fully and tell you exactly why it seems to me such a remarkable book. In fact it seems to me to be the first step that American fiction has taken since Henry James....

By the way, if you ever have any short stories which you think would be suitable for the *Criterion* I wish you would let me see them.

With many thanks, I am,

Yours very truly,
T. S. Eliot

P.S. By a coincidence Gilbert Seldes in his New York Chronicle in the *Criterion* for January 14th has chosen your book for particular mention.

[310]

A Letter from John Dos Passos

[October?, 1936]*
Truro, Mass.

W HY Scott—you poor miserable bastard, it was damn handsome of you to write me. Had just heard about your shoulder and was on the edge of writing when I got your letter. Must be damned painful and annoying. Let us know how you are. Katy sends love and condolences. We often talk about you and wish we could get to see you.

I've been wanting to see you, naturally, to argue about your *Esquire* articles†—Christ, man, how do you find time in the middle of the general conflagration to worry about all that stuff? If you don't want to do stuff on your own, why not get a reporting job somewhere. After all not many people write as well as you do. Here you've gone and spent forty years in perfecting an elegant and complicated piece of machinery (tool I was going to say) and the next forty years is the time to use it—or as long as the murderous forces of history will let you. God damn it, I feel frightful myself—I have that false Etruscan feeling of sitting on my tail at home while etcetera etcetera is on the march to Rome —but I have two things laid out I want to finish up and I'm trying to take a course in American history and most of the time the course of world events seems so frightful that I feel absolutely paralysed—and the feeling that I've got to hurry to get stuff out before the big boys close down on us. We're living in one of the damnedest tragic moments in history—if you want to go to pieces I think it's absolutely O. K. but I think you ought to write a first rate novel about it (and you probably will) instead of spilling it in little pieces for Arnold Gingrich—and anyway, in pieces or not, I wish I could get an hour's talk with you now and then, Scott, and damn sorry about the shoulder. Forgive the locker room peptalk.

Yrs, Dos.

---

* Fitzgerald was forty years old September 24, 1936, and had broken his collarbone the summer before. There are references in the letter to these two events.

† *The Crack-Up.*

A Letter from Thomas Wolfe

July 26, 1937

Mr. F. Scott Fitzgerald
c/o Charles Scribners' Sons
597 Fifth Avenue, N.Y.C.

Dear Scott:

I don't know where you are living and I'll be damned if I'll believe anyone lives in a place called "The Garden of Allah,"* which was what the address on your envelope said. I am sending this on to the old address we both know so well.

The unexpected loquaciousness of your letter struck me all of a heap. I was surprised to hear from you but I don't know that I can truthfully say I was delighted. Your bouquet arrived smelling sweetly of roses but cunningly concealing several large-sized brick-bats. Not that I resented them. My resenter got pretty tough years ago; like everybody else I have at times been accused of "resenting criti[ci]sm" and although I have never been one of those boys who break out in a hearty and delighted laugh when someone tells them everything they write is lousy and agree enthusiastically, I think I have taken as many plain and fancy varieties as any American citizen of my age now living. I have not always smiled and murmured pleasantly "How true," but I have listened to it all, tried to profit from it where and when I could and perhaps been helped by it a little. Certainly I don't think I have been pig-headed about it. I have not been arrogantly contemptuous of it either, because one of my besetting sins, whether you know it or not, is a lack of confidence in what I do.

So I'm not sore at you or sore about anything you said in your letter. And if there is any truth in what you say— any truth for me—you can depend upon it I shall probably get it out. It just seems to me that there is not much in what you say. You speak of your "case" against me, and frankly I don't believe you have much case. You say you write these things because you admire me so much and because you

* This was Fitzgerald's real address, an apartment hotel, in Hollywood.

[312]

think my talent unmatchable in this or any other country and because you are ever my friend. Well Scott I should not only be proud and happy to think that all these things are true but my respect and admiration for your own talent and intelligence are such that I should try earnestly to live up to them and to deserve them and to pay the most serious and respectful attention to anything you say about my work.

I have tried to do so. I have read your letter several times and I've got to admit it doesn't seem to mean much. I don't know what you are driving at or understand what you expect or hope me to do about it. Now this may be pig-headed but it isn't sore. I may be wrong but all I can get out of it is that you think I'd be a good writer if I were an altogether different writer from the writer that I am.

This may be true but I don't see what I'm going to do about it. And I don't think you can show me and I don't see what Flaubert and Zola have to do with it, or what I have to do with them. I wonder if you really think they have anything to do with it, or if this is just something you heard in college or read in a book somewhere. This either-or kind of criticism seems to me to be so meaningless. It looks so knowing and imposing but there is nothing in it. Why does it follow that if a man writes a book that is not like *Madame Bovary* it is inevitably like Zola. I may be dumb but I can't see this. You say that *Madame Bovary* becomes eternal while Zola already rocks with age. Well this may be true—but if it is true isn't it true because *Madame Bovary* may be a great book and those that Zola wrote may not be great ones? Wouldn't it also be true to say that *Don Quixote* or *Pickwick* or *Tristram Shandy* "become eternal" while already Mr. Galsworthy "rocks with age." I think it is true to say this and it doesn't leave much of your argument, does it? For your argument is based simply upon one *way*, upon one method instead of another. And have you ever noticed how often it turns out that what a man is really doing is simply rationalizing his own way of doing something, the way he has to do it, the way given him by his talent and his nature, into the only inevitable and right way

[313]

of doing everything—a sort of classic and eternal art form handed down by Apollo from Olympus without which and beyond which there is nothing. Now you have your way of doing something and I have mine, there are a lot of ways, but you are honestly mistaken in thinking that there is a "way." I suppose I would agree with you in what you say about "the novel of selected incident" so far as it means anything. I say so far as it means anything because every novel, of course, is a novel of selected incident. There are no novels of unselected incident. You couldn't write about the inside of a telephone booth without selecting. You could fill a novel of a thousand pages with a description of a single room and yet your incidents would be selected. And I have mentioned *Don Quixote* and *Pickwick* and *The Brothers Karamazov* and *Tristram Shandy* to you in contrast to *The Silver Spoon* or *The White Monkey* as examples of books that have become "immortal" and that *boil* and *pour*. Just remember that although *Madame Bovary* in your opinion may be a great book, *Tristram Shandy is* indubitably a great book, and that it is great for quite different reasons. It is great because it *boils* and *pours*—for the *unselected* quality of its selection. You say that the great writer like Flaubert has consciously left out the stuff that Bill or Joe will come along presently and put in. Well, don't forget, Scott, that a great writer is not only a leaver-outer but also a putter-inner, and that Shakespeare and Cervantes and Dostoevsky were great putter-inners—greater putter-inners, in fact, than taker-outers and will be remembered for what they put in—remembered, I venture to say, as long as Monsieur Flaubert will be remembered for what he left out.

As to the rest of it in your letter about cultivating an alter ego, becoming a more conscious artist, my pleasantness or grief, exuberance or cynicism, and how nothing stands out in relief because everything is keyed at the same emotional pitch—this stuff is worthy of the great minds that review books nowadays—the Fadimans and De Votos—but not of you. For you are an artist and the artist has the only true critical intelligence. You have had to work and sweat blood yourself and you know what it is like to try to write a living word or create a living thing. So don't talk this foolish stuff to me about exuberance or being a conscious artist or not bringing things into emotional relief, or any of the rest of it. Let the Fadimans and De Votos do that kind of talking but not Scott Fitzgerald. You've got too much sense and you know too much. The little fellows who don't know may picture a man as a great "exuberant" six-foot-six clod-hopper straight out of nature who bites off half a plug of apple tobacco, tilts the corn liquor jug and lets half of it gurgle down his throat, wipes off his mouth with the back of one hairy paw, jumps three feet in the air and clacks his heels together four times before he hits the floor again and yells "Whoopee, boys I'm a rootin, tootin, shootin son of a gun from Buncombe County—out of my way now, here I come!"—and then wads up three-hundred thousand words or so, hurls it back at a blank page, puts covers on it and says "Here's my book!" Now Scott, the boys who write book reviews in New York may think it's done that way; but the man who wrote *Tender Is the Night* knows better. You know you never did it that way, you know I never did, you know no one else who ever wrote a line worth reading ever did. So don't give me any of your guff, young fellow. And don't think I'm sore. But I get tired of guff—I'll take it from a fool or from a book reviewer but I won't take it from a friend who knows a lot better. I want to be a better artist. I want to be a more selective artist. I want to be a more restrained artist. I want to use such talent as I have, control such forces as I may own, direct such energy as I may use more cleanly, more surely and to better purpose. But Flaubert me no Flauberts, Bovary me no Bovarys. Zola me no Zolas. And exuberance me no exuberances. Leave this stuff for those who huckster in it and give me, I pray you, the benefits of your fine intelligence and your high creative faculties, all of which I so genuinely and profoundly admire. I am going into the woods for another two or three years. I am going to try to do the best, the most important piece of work I have ever done. I am going to have to do it alone. I am going to lose what little bit of reputation I may have gained, to have to hear and know and endure in silence again all of the doubt, the disparagement and ridicule, the post-mortems that they are so eager to read over you even before you are dead. I know what it means and so do you. We have both been through it before. We know it is the plain damn simple truth. Well, I've been through it once and I believe I can get through it again. I think I know a little more now than I did before, I certainly know what to expect and I'm going to try not to let it get me down. That is the reason why this time I shall look for intelligent understanding among some of my friends. I'm not ashamed to say that I shall need it. You say in your letter that you are ever my friend. I assure you that it is very good to hear this. Go for me with the gloves off if you think I need it. But don't De Voto me. If you do I'll call your bluff.

I'm down here for the summer living in a cabin in the country and I am enjoying it. Also I'm working. I don't know how long you are going to be in Hollywood or whether you have a job out there but I hope I shall see you before long and that all is going well with you. I still think as I always thought that *Tender Is the Night* had in it the best work you have ever done. And I believe you will surpass it in the future. Anyway, I send you my best wishes as always for health and work and success. Let me hear from you sometime. The address is Oteen, North Carolina, just a few miles from Asheville, Ham Basso, as you know, is not far away at Pisgah Forest and he is coming over to see me soon and perhaps we shall make a trip together to see Sherwood Anderson. And now this is all for the present—unselective, you see, as usual. Good bye Scott and good luck.

Ever yours,
Tom Wolfe

F. SCOTT FITZGERALD*

by PAUL ROSENFELD

THE utmost that can be charged against F. Scott Fitzgerald is that too oftentimes his good material eludes him. Of the ultimate values of said material there is no dispute. Certain racehorses run for the pure joy of running, and the author of *The Beautiful and Damned* and *Tales of the Jazz Age* is such an animal. He is a born writer, amusing himself with tales and pictures; and eventually nothing is interesting except the natural bent. Salty and insipid, exaggeratedly poetical and bitterly parodistic, his writing pours exuberantly out of him. Flat paragraphs are redeemed by brilliant metaphors, and conventional descriptions by witty, penetrating turns. Ideas of diamond are somewhat indiscriminately mixed with ideas of rhinestone and ideas of window glass; yet purest rays serene are present in veritable abundance. They must come to this bannerman of the slickers and flappers in a sort of dream, unexpectedly out of some arcana where they have been concealing themselves, and surprise him by smiling up at him from underneath his pen. For so they startle the reader, unprepared to encounter, in writing as carelessly undertaken, ideas so mature and poignant and worthy of fine settings.

Not a contemporary American senses as thoroughly in

* This essay appeared in Paul Rosenfeld's *Men Seen: Twenty-Four Modern Authors*, the preface to which is dated February 14, 1925—before *The Great Gatsby* was published.

every fiber the tempo of privileged post-adolescent America. Of that life, in all its hardness and equally curious softness, its external clatter, movement and boldness, he is a part; and what he writes reflects the environment not so much in its superficial aspects as in its pitch and beat. He knows how talk sounds, how the dances feel, how the crap-games look. Unimportant detail shows how perfect the unconscious attunement: the vignette of a boy drawing gasolene out of an automobile tank during a dance so that a girl can clean her satin shoe; the vignette of a young fellow sitting in his B.V.D.'s after a bath running his hand down his naked skin in indolent satisfaction; the vignette of two bucks from a pump-and-slipper dance throwing hash by the handful around Childs' at six A.M. Not another has gotten flashes from the psyches of the golden young intimate as those which amaze throughout *The Beautiful and Damned*. And not another has fixed as mercilessly the quality of brutishness, of dull indirection and degraded sensibility running through American life of the hour.

Taken as things, nevertheless, both the novels of Fitzgerald, and the majority of his tales as well, lie on a plane inferior to the one upon which his best material extends. He has the stuff for pathos, and this fact he fairly consistently ignores. Certain preoccupations seem to intrude between him and his material, spoiling his power to correctly appreciate it. Hence, instead of the veritable stories he has to tell, there appear smart social romanzas and unhappy happy endings. Of Fitzgerald's preconceptions, the chief sinner appears to be the illusion that the field of his vision is essentially the field of "youth." Now, it would be insanity to deny the author's almost constant preoccupation with exquisite creatures in chiffon and their slender snappy companions, or to deny the jolly subjects of his observations vivacity and frankness of spirit, and perfect elegance of texture. There is a place where an eternal dance proceeds, and this place for the while they occupy, filling it with their proper motions and gestures. And whatever the quality of these, who can for even an instant maintain that it is inferior to that of the dreadful motions and gestures which filled it a generation, or two or three generations ago? What one does affirm, however, and affirm with passion, is that the author of *This Side of Paradise* and of the jazzy stories does not sustainedly perceive his girls and men for what they are, and tends to invest them with precisely the glamour with which they in pathetic assurance rather childishly invest themselves. At the time of the appearance of Fitzgerald's first book, it was evident that to an extent he was indebted to Compton Mackenzie for the feeling with which he regarded the "dreaming spires" of Princeton; and since then it has become apparent that he tends a trifle overmuch to view everything which he sees in the light of Europe's past experiences. His protagonists he observes through the enchanted eyes of a perpetual Maytime, perceiving among the motors and crap-games a wave of cool spring flowers, a flutter of white and yellow ephemeridae. Even when he marks the cruel and shabby side, the decay and ignobility of his objective, he tends to overplay the general attractiveness more than the detail warrants. The couple in *The Beautiful and Damned*, charming and comely enough and yet portrayed at length in the horrible effort to perpetuate a state of narcissistic irresponsibility, we are begged to perceive as iridescently wonderful bodies and souls.

And it is fresh, juicy and spontaneous that the American juveniles of the class described by Fitzgerald exactly are not. Superficially, perhaps. But was not the forest green which Europe called by the name of youth somewhat more a thing of courage? And the number of us willing to face the world without the panoply of elaborate material protections is not overwhelming. It is claimed that in the American South virgins are carefully trained to inquire out the income and prospects of suitors, and nip in the bud any passion which threatens to direct itself upon an unworthy object. But it does not seem probable there is any truth in the report. For such maneuvers can scarcely be necessary. It is undoubtedly physically impossible for any really nice American girl South or North to respond to the desires of a male who does not make the spiritual gesture paralleling the Woolworth Building's. Through either external persua-

[319]

sion or inherent idealism, and which it is we know not, and undoubtedly it is both, the self-respecting damsels early acquire the conviction that splendidly complete orientation onto the business of material increase is the primary characteristic of maleness, and that any offer of love unaccompanied by the tautness for money is the profoundest of insults to the pysche seated in the tender depths of them. And the strapping, college-bred, Brooks-clad youths no less than they share this beautiful innate belief. They too seem unable to face life without having at the back of them the immense upholstery of wealth. Nothing which they might be or do, were they relieved of the necessity of being a worldly success, appears to them capable of making good to the lady the absence of the fur garment and the foreign roadster, and the presence of inevitable suffering. Thus the spirit of the business world is established well before the advent of puberty; and the spirit of business is compromise, which is not exactly it would seem the spirit of youth.

And even the lightest, least satirical of Fitzgerald's pages bear testimonial to the prevalence of the condition. A moralist could gather evidence for a most terrible condemnation of bourgeois America from the books of this protagonist of youth. And yet, *Lieb Vaterland, magst ruhig sein.* It is not a state of immorality in the general sense of the word that might be uncovered. If by morality we mean obedience to the *mores* of the tribal, then Fitzgerald's diverting flappers and slickers are in no sense licentious. By means of necking parties and booze fights of the sort he describes the republic is maintained. Business rests on them. But immorality may be taken to signify a falling away from the ideal spirit of life, and in that sense America is proven the breeding ground of a kind of decay. In all unconsciousness Fitzgerald shows us types of poor golden young too shallow to feel, vainly attitudinizing in the effort to achieve sensation: girls who know they cannot live without riches and men perpetually sucking the bottle for solace. The people aren't young: they are merely narcissistic. Knowledge of life is gotten from books, and the naïveté is not quite lovely. That is all very well; one has no fault to find with it; it is quite sanitary and not at all messy as passion usually is; but why call it spring? And occasionally Fitzgerald drops the light guitar and with cool ferocity speaks the veritable name. *May Day*, perhaps the most mature of all his tales, brings the bitter brackish dry taste of decay fully to the mouth. With an air of almost glacial impersonality Fitzgerald gives a curious atmosphere of mixed luxury and rottenness of the heart. Through the entire story there seems to run the brutishness of the two soldiers hiding among pails and mops in the dust closet waiting for some stolen liquor to be handed in to them. And in the fantasia *The Diamond Big as the Ritz*, Fitzgerald strikes perhaps quite undeliberately further notes of satire: Mr. Braddock Washington, the richest and most profoundly unsympathetic man in the world, looks dangerously like a jazz-age portrait of the father of the country.

But the world of his subject-matter is still too much within Fitzgerald himself for him to see it sustainedly against the universe. Its values obtain too strongly over him, and for that reason he cannot set them against those of high civilization, and calmly judge them so. Hence, wanting philosophy, and a little overeager like the rest of America to arrive without having really sweated, he falls victim to the favorite delusions of the society of which he is a part, tends to indulge it in its dreams of grandeur, and misses the fine flower of pathos. He seems to set out writing under the compulsion of vague feelings, and when his wonderfully revelatory passages appear, they come rather like volcanic islands thrown to the surface of a sea of fantasy. By every law *The Beautiful and Damned* should have been a tragedy, the victims damned indeed; yet at the conclusion Fitzgerald welched, and permitted his pitiful pair to have the alleviations of some thirty millions of dollars, and his hero tell the readers he had won out. To be sure, a steady growth has been going on within this interesting author. The amusing insolence of his earlier manner of writing has persistently given way before a bolder, sharper stroke less personal in reference. The descriptions in *May Day:* the sight of the avenue, the drinking scene in Delmonico's, the adventures of Mr. In and Out, are done with quiet virtuosity. A very genuine gift of fantasy arrives in *Benjamin Button*. There are even Lawrence-like strong moments in *The Beautiful and Damned*. And still, in spite of *May Day*, Fitzgerald has not yet crossed the line that bounds the field of art. He has seen his material from its own point of view, and he has seen it completely from without. But he has never done what the artist does: seen it simultaneously from within and without; and loved it and judged it, too. For *May Day* lacks a focal point, and merely juxtaposes a number of small pieces. Should Fitzgerald finally break his mold, and free himself of the compulsions of the civilization in which he grew, it might go badly with his popularity. It will be a pathetic story he will have to tell, the legend of a moon which never rose; and that is precisely the story a certain America does not wish to hear. Nevertheless, we would like hugely to hear him tell it. And Fitzgerald might scarcely miss his following.

THE MORAL OF
SCOTT FITZGERALD[*]

by GLENWAY WESCOTT

F. SCOTT FITZGERALD is dead, aged forty-four. *Requiescat in pace; ora pro nobis.* In the twenties, his heyday, he was a kind of king of our American youth; and as the news of his end appeared in the papers there were strange coincidences along with it. A number of others—a younger writer who was somewhat of his school and, like him, had committed his talent unfortunately to Hollywood, and that writer's pretty, whimsical wife, and another young woman who was a famous horse-trainer, and the young leader of a popular jazz-band—also met sudden deaths that week. I was reminded of the holocausts by which primitive rulers were provided with an escort, servants and pretty women and boon companions, for eternity. The twenties were heaven, so to speak, often enough; might not heaven be like the twenties? If it were, in one or two particulars, Scott Fitzgerald would be sorry; sorry once more.

His health failed, and with a peculiar darkness and deadweight in mind and heart, some five years ago. Then in a wonderful essay entitled *The Crack-Up* he took stock of himself, looking twenty years back for what flaws were in him or in the day and age, what early damage had been done, and how. Thanks to that, one can speak of his weaknesses without benefit of gossip, without impertinence.

* This essay appeared in *The New Republic* of February 17, 1941, just after Fitzgerald's death.

And so I do, asking for charity toward him and clarity about him; and a little on my own mortal account; and for certain innocent immature American writers' benefit.

My theme is as usual personality rather than esthetics; but my sentiment on this occasion is not personal. Aside from our Midwestern birth and years of foreign residence, you could scarcely find two men of the same generation less alike than we two. Neither our virtues nor our vices appeared to overlap at all. I did not have the honor of his particular friendship. I have only one vivid memory of conversation with him, which was on a Mediterranean beach. Across the Bay of Angels and over the big good-for-nothing city of Nice, some of the Alps hung in the air as pearly as onions; and that air and that sea, which has only delicate tides, quivered with warm weather. It was before the publication of *The Sun Also Rises*, the summer of 1925 or 1926, and Hemingway was what he wanted to talk to me about. He came abruptly and drew me a little apart from our friends and relations, into the shade of a rock.

Hemingway had published some short stories in the dinky de-luxe way in Paris; and I along with all the literary set had discovered him, which was fun; and when we returned to New York we preached the new style and peculiar feeling of his fiction as if it were evangel. Still, that was too slow a start of a great career to suit Fitzgerald. Obviously Ernest was the one true genius of our decade, he said; and yet he was neglected and misunderstood and, above all, insufficiently remunerated. He thought I would agree that *The Apple of the Eye* and *The Great Gatsby* were rather inflated market values just then. What could I do to help launch Hemingway? Why didn't I write a laudatory essay on him? With this questioning, Fitzgerald now and then impatiently grasped and shook my elbow.

There was something more than ordinary art-admiration about it, but on the other hand it was no mere matter of affection for Hemingway; it was so bold, unabashed, lacking in sense of humor. I have a sharp tongue and my acquaintances often underestimate my good nature; so I was touched and flattered by Fitzgerald's taking so much for granted. It simply had not occurred to him that unfriend-liness or pettiness on my part might inhibit my enthusiasm about the art of a new colleague and rival. As a matter of fact, my enthusiasm was not on a par with his; and looking back now, I am glad for my sake that it was not. He not only said but, I believe, honestly felt that Hemingway was inimitably, essentially superior. From the moment Heming-way began to appear in print, perhaps it did not matter what he himself produced or failed to produce. He felt free to write just for profit, and to live for fun, if possible. Heming-way could be entrusted with the graver responsibilities and higher rewards such as glory, immortality. This extreme of admiration—this excuse for a morbid belittlement and abandonment of himself—was bad for Fitzgerald, I imagine. At all events he soon began to waste his energy in various hack-writing.

I was told last year that another talented contemporary of ours had grown so modest in the wage-earning way, fallen so far from his youthful triumph, that he would sign a friend's stories and split the payment. Under the friend's name it would have been hundreds of dollars, and under his, a thousand or thousands. Perhaps this was not true gossip, but it is a good little exemplary tale, and of general application. It gives me goose-flesh. A signature which has been so humiliated is apt never to be the same again, in the signer's own estimation. As a rule the delicate literary brain, the aching creative heart, cannot stand that sort of thing. It is better for a writer even to fancy himself a Messiah, against the day when writing or life goes badly. And there is more to this than the matter of esthetic integrity. For if his opinion of himself is divided by disrespect—sheepish, shameful, cynical—he usually finds his earning capacity as well as his satisfaction falling off. The vast public, which appears to have no taste, somehow senses when it is being scornfully talked down to. The great hacks are innocent, and serenely class themselves with Tolstoy and Dickens. Their getting good enough to compare with P. G. Wodehouse or Zane Grey may depend upon that benign misapprehension.

Probably Fitzgerald never fell into any abuse of his reputation as unwise and unwholesome as the above-mentioned confrères. His standard of living did seem to the rest of us high. Publishers in the twenties made immense advances to novelists who had and could lend prestige; and when in the thirties Fitzgerald's popularity lapsed, movies had begun to be talkies, which opened up a new lucrative field of literary operation. Certainly he did write too much in recent years with his tongue in his cheek; his heart in his boots if not in his pocket. And it was his opinion in 1936 that the competition and popular appeal of the films—"a more glittering, a grosser power," as he put it—had made the God-given form of the novel archaic; a wrong thought indeed for a novelist.

This is not the ideal moment to reread and appraise his collectable works. With the mind at a loss, muffled like a drum—the ego a little inflamed as it always is by present-ness of death—we may exaggerate their merit or their shortcomings. I remember thinking, when the early best sellers were published, that his style was a little too free and easy; but I was a fussy stylist in those days. His phrasing was almost always animated and charming; his diction excellent. He wrote very little in slang or what I call baby-talk: the pitfall of many who specialized in American contemporaneity after him. But for other reasons—obscurity of sentiment, facetiousness—a large part of his work may not endure, as readable reading matter for art's sake. It will be precious as documentary evidence, instructive example. That is not, in the way of immortality, what the writer hopes; but it is much more than most writers of fiction achieve.

This Side of Paradise haunted the decade like a song, popular but perfect. It hung over an entire youth-movement like a banner, somewhat discolored and wind-worn now; the wind has lapsed out of it. But a book which college boys really read is a rare thing, not to be dismissed idly or in a moment of severe sophistication. Then there were dozens of stories, some delicate and some slap-dash; one very odd, entitled *Head and Shoulders*. I love *The Great Gatsby*. Its very timeliness, as of 1925, gave it a touch of the old-fashioned a few years later; but I have reread it this week and found it all right; pleasure and compassion on every page. A masterpiece often seems a period-piece for a while; then comes down out of the attic, to function anew and to last. There is a great deal to be said for and against his final novel, *Tender Is the Night*. On the whole I am warmly for it. To be sane or insane is a noble issue, and very few novels take what might be called an intelligent interest in it; this does, and gives a fair picture of the entertaining expatriate habit of life besides.

In 1936, in three issues of *Esquire*, he published the autobiographical essay, *The Crack-Up*, as it were swan-song. I first read it at my barber's, which, I suppose, is according to the editorial devices of that magazine, a medium of advertising for men's ready-made clothing. There is very little in world literature like this piece: Max Jacob's *Defense de Tartuffe*; the confidential chapter of *The Seven Pillars of Wisdom*, perhaps; Sir Walter Raleigh's verse-epistle before his beheading, in a way. Fitzgerald's theme seems more dreadful, plain petty stroke by stroke; and of course his treatment lacks the good grace and firmness of the old and old-style authors. Indeed it is cheap here and there, but in embarrassment rather than in crudity or lack of courage. Or perhaps Fitzgerald as he wrote was too sensitive to what was to appear along with it in the magazine: the jokes, the Petty girls, the haberdashery. He always suffered from an extreme environmental sense. Still it is fine prose and naturally his timeliest piece today: self-autopsy and funeral sermon. It also, with an innocent air, gravely indicts our native idealism in some respects, our common code, our college education. And in general—for ailing civilization as well as one dead Fitzgerald—this is a day of wrath.

He had made a great recovery from a seemingly mortal physical illness; then found everything dead or deadish in his psyche, his thought all broken, and no appetite for anything on earth. It was not from alcohol, he said, evidently proud of the fact that he had not had any for six months, not even beer. We may be a little doubtful of this protestation; for protestation indeed is a kind of sub-habit of the alcoholic. Six months is no time at all, in terms of the things that kill us. Alcohol in fact never exclusively causes anything. Only, just as it will heighten a happy experience, it will deepen a rut or a pit, in the way of fatigue chiefly. Who cares, when a dear one is dying of a chest-cold or an embolism, whether he is a drunkard or a reformed ex-drunkard?—Yes, I know, the dying one himself cares! But when Fitzgerald wrote his essay he still had five years to live, quite a long time. It was not about ill health, and of course he was as sane as an angel. His trouble just then and his subject was only his lassitude of imagination; his nauseated spirit; that self-hypnotic state of not having any will-power; and nothing left of the intellect but inward observation and dislike. Why, he cried, why was I "identified with the objects of my horror and compassion"? He said it was the result of "too much anger and too many tears." That was his snap-judgment; blunt sentimentality of a boy or ex-boy. But since he was a story-teller above all, he did not stop at that; he proceeded to tell things about the past in which the mystery showed extraordinarily.

The Crack-Up has never been issued in book form; and perhaps because the pretty pictures in *Esquire* are so exciting to thumb-tack up on the wall, back numbers of it are not easy to come by. So I am tempted to try to summarize it all; but no, it must be published. Especially the first half is written without a fault: brief easy fiery phrases— the thinking that he compared to a "moving about of great secret trunks," and "the heady villainous feeling"—one quick and thorough paragraph after another, with so little shame and so little emphasis that I have wondered if he himself knew how much he was confessing.

He still regretted his bad luck in not getting abroad into the trenches as an army officer in 1918, and even his failure at football in 1913 or 1914. On certain of those unlucky days of his youth he felt as badly as in 1936, and badly in the same way; he makes a point of the similarity. Perhaps the worst of the early crises came in his junior year, when he lost the presidency of one of the Princeton clubs. Immediately afterward, as an act of desperation and consolation, he made love for the first time; and also that year, not until then, he turned to literary art, as the best of a bad bargain. Ominous! Fantastic, too, that a man who is dying or at least done with living—one who has had practically all that the world affords, fame and prosperity, work and play, love and friendship, and lost practically all—should still think seriously of so much fiddledeedee of boyhood! Very noble convictions underlay Fitzgerald's entire life, and he explains them nobly. But when he comes to the disillusionment, that too is couched in alumnal imagery; it is along with "the shoulder-pads worn for one day on the Princeton freshman football field and the overseas cap never worn overseas" that his ideals are relegated to the junk-heap, he says. It is strange and baroque; like those large bunches of battle-trappings which appear decoratively in seventeenth-century architecture, empty helmets and empty cuirasses and firearms laid crossways, sculptured up on the lintels of barracks and on the lids of tombs. Those condemned old European societies which have been too much militarized, too concerned with glory and glorious death, scarcely seem more bizarre than this: a kind of national consciousness revolving to the bitter end around college; and the latter also seems a precarious basis for a nation.

Aside from his literary talent—literary genius, self-taught —I think Fitzgerald must have been the worst educated man in the world. He never knew his own strength; therefore nothing inspired him very definitely to conserve or budget it. When he was a freshman, did the seniors teach him a manly technique of drinking, with the price and penalty of the several degrees of excess of it? If they had, it might never have excited him as a vague, fatal moral issue. The rest of us, his writing friends and rivals, thought that he had the best narrative gift of the century. Did the English department at Princeton try to develop his admiration of that fact about himself, and make him feel the burden and the pleasure of it? Apparently they taught him rather to appreciate this or that other writer, to his own disfavor. Did any worldly-wise critic ever remind him that beyond a certain point, writing for profit becomes unprofitable; bad business as well as bad art? Another thing: my impression is that only as he wrote, or just before writing, *Tender Is the Night*, did he discover certain causes and gradations of mental illness which, nowadays, every boy ought to be taught as soon as he has mastered the other facts of life.

Even the army failed to inculcate upon Lieutenant Fitzgerald one principle that a good army man must accept: heroism is a secondary virtue in an army. Lieutenant Fitzgerald had no business pining for the front-line trenches in advance of his superior officers' decision that it was the place for him. The point of soldiering is to kill; not a mere willingness to be killed. This seems important today, as we prepare again for perhaps necessary war, and again too much is made of the spirit of self-sacrifice and embattlement of ideals; and not enough of the mere means of victory. And with reference to literature, too, as Fitzgerald drops out of our insufficient little regiment, we writers particularly blame him for that all-out idealism of his. No matter what he died for—if he died *for* anything—it was in too great a hurry; it was not worth it at his age.

In several of the obituary notices of Fitzgerald I detect one little line of mistaken moralizing, which I think is not uncommon; and his example and his fiction may have done something to propagate it. They seem to associate all rebellious morality somehow with a state of poor health. This is an unfair attack, and on the other hand a too easy alibi. Bad behavior is not always a feeble, pitiful, fateful thing. Malice of mind, strange style, offensive subject matter, do not always derive from morbid psyche or delicate physique. Wickedness is not necessarily weakness; and *vice versa*. For there is will-power in humanity. Its genuine manifestation is only in the long run; but, with knowledge, it can have the last word. Modern psychology does not deny it. Whether one is a moralist or an immoralist—a vengeful daily preacher like Mr. Westbrook Pegler, or an occasional devil's advocate like myself, or the quietest citizen—these little distinctions ought to be kept clear.

Fitzgerald was weak; we have the proof of it now in his demise. Fitzgerald, the outstanding aggressor in the little

warfare which divided our middle classes in the twenties—
warfare of moral emancipation against moral conceit, flaming youth against old guard—definitely has let his side
down. The champion is as dead as a doornail. Self-con-
gratulatory moral persons may crow over him if they wish.

There is bound to be a slight anger at his graveside;
curse-words amid our written or spoken obsequies. The
whole school of writers who went to France has been a bit
maligned while the proletarian novelists and the politico-
critics have enjoyed the general applause. Some of us are
reckless talkers, and no doubt we have maligned each other
and each himself as well. It was the beautiful, talented Miss
Stein in her Paris salon who first called us "the lost generation." It was Hemingway who took up the theme and made
it a popular refrain. The twenties were in fact a time of
great prosperity and liberty, a spendthrift and footloose
time; and especially in France you got your American
money's worth of everything if you were clever. Still I
doubt whether, in dissipation and unruly emotion, we
strayed much farther out of the way than young Americans
ordinarily do, at home as abroad. I think we were somewhat
extraordinarily inclined to make youthful rebelliousness,
imprudent pursuit of pleasure or ambition, a little easier for
our young brothers. Heaven knows how it will be for our
sons.

In any case, time is the real moralist; and a great many
of the so-called lost are still at hand, active and indeed con-
spicuous: Bishop and Hemingway and Bromfield and Cummings and V. Thomson and Tate, Gordon and Porter and
Flanner and others, the U. S. A.'s odd foreign legion. We
were a band of toughs in fact, indestructible, which perhaps
is the best thing to be said for us at this point. For the next
step is to age well. Relatively speaking, I think we are aging
well; giving evidence of toughness in the favorable sense as
well: tenacity and hardiness, and a kind of worldly wisdom
that does not have to change its platform very often, and
skepticism mixed in with our courage to temper it and make
it last. Sometimes we are still spoken of as the young or
youngish or "younger" writers, but there can be no sense

in that, except by lack of competition; every last one of us is forty. That is the right age to give advice to the immature and potential literary generation. For their sake, lest they feel unable to take our word for things, it seems worth while to protest against the strange bad name we have had.

In any case we are the ones who know about Fitzgerald. He was our darling, our genius, our fool. Let the young people consider his untypical case with admiration but great caution; with qualms and a respect for fate, without fatalism. He was young to the bitter end. He lived and he wrote at last like a scapegoat, and now has departed like one. As you might say, he was Gatsby, a greater Gatsby. Why not? Flaubert said, *"Madame Bovary, c'est moi!"* On the day before Christmas, in a sensible bitter obituary, *The New York Times* quoted a paragraph from *The Crack-Up* in which the deceased likened himself to a plate. "Sometimes, though, the cracked plate has to be kept in service as a household necessity. It can never be warmed up on the stove nor shuffled with the other plates in the dishpan; it will not be brought out for company but it will do to hold crackers late at night or to go into the ice-box with the left-overs." A deadly little prose-poem! No doubt the ideals Fitzgerald acquired in college and in the army—and put to the test on Long Island and in the Alpes-Maritimes and in Hollywood —always were a bit second-hand, fissured, cracked, if you like. But how faithfully he reported both idealization and ordeal; and how his light smooth earthenware style dignifies it!

The style in which others have written of him is different. On the day after Christmas, in his popular column in *The New York World-Telegram*, Mr. Westbrook Pegler remarked that his death "recalls memories of a queer bunch of undisciplined and self-indulgent brats who were determined not to pull their weight in the boat and wanted the world to drop everything and sit down and bawl with them. A kick in the pants and a clout over the scalp were more like their needing. . . ." With a kind of expert politeness throughout this *in memoriam*, Mr. Pegler avoids commenting upon the dead man himself exactly. His complaint is of anonymous persons: the company Fitzgerald kept, readers who let themselves be influenced by him, and his heroes and heroines: "Sensitive young things about whom he wrote and with whom he ran to fires not only because he could exploit them for profit in print but because he found them congenial. . . ." I suppose Mr. Pegler's column is profitable too; and if I were doing it I should feel easier in my mind, surer of my aim, if I knew and liked my exploitees. Joking aside, certainly this opinion of his does not correspond in the least to my memory of the gay twenties. Certainly if sensitive young men and women of the thirties believe Pegler, they will not admire Fitzgerald or like the rest of us much.

Too bad; there should be peace between the generations now, at least among the literary. Popularity or no popularity, we have none too many helpful friends; and in a time of world war there may be panic and conservatism and absent-mindedness and neglect of literature in general, and those slight acts of obscure vengeance so easy to commit when fellow citizens have begun to fear and imagine and act as a mass. There should not be any quarrel between literature and journalism either. Modernly conceived and well done—literary men sticking to the truth and newspapermen using imagination—they relate to each other very closely, and may sustain and inspire each other back and forth. In a time of solemn subject matter it is more and more needful that they should.

In any case Mr. Pegler's decade is out as well as ours; the rude hard-working thirties as well as the wild twenties. The forties have come. Those of us who have been youthful too long—which, I suppose, is the real point of his criticism—now certainly realize our middle age; no more time to make ready or dawdle, nor energy to waste. That is one universal effect of war on the imagination: time, as a moral factor, instantly changes expression and changes pace. Everyman suddenly has a vision of sudden death.

What is the difference, from the universal angle? Everyone has to die once; no one has to die twice. But now that mortality has become the world's worst worry once more,

[333]

there is less sophistication of it. Plain as day we see that the bull in the arena is no more fated than the steer in the slaughterhouse. The glamorous gangster's cadaver with bellyful of bullets is no deader than the commonplace little chap overcome by pernicious anemia. Napoleon III at the battle of Sedan, the other battle of Sedan, rouged his cheeks in order not to communicate his illness and fright to his desperate army. An unemployed young actor, a friend of a friend of mine, lately earned a living for a while by rouging cheeks of well-off corpses at a smart mortician's. All this equally—and infinitude of other things under the sun—is jurisdiction of death. The difference between a beautiful death and an ugly death is in the eye of the beholder, the heart of the mourner, the brain of the survivor.

The fact of Scott Fitzgerald's end is as bad and deplorable as could be; but the moral of it is good enough, and warlike. It is to enliven the rest of the regiment. Mere tightening the belt, stiffening the upper lip, is not all I mean; nor the simple delight of being alive still, the dance on the grave, the dance between holocausts. As we have it—documented and prophesied by his best work, commented upon in the newspaper with other news of the day—it is a deep breath of knowledge, fresh air, and an incitement to particular literary virtues.

For the private life and the public life, literary life and real life, if you view them in this light of death—and now we have it also boding on all the horizon, like fire—are one and the same. Which brings up another point of literary criticism; then I have done. The great thing about Fitzgerald was his candor; verbal courage; simplicity. One little man with eyes really witnessing; objective in all he uttered, even about himself in a subjective slump; arrogant in just one connection, for one purpose only, to make his meaning clear. The thing, I think, that a number of recent critics have most disliked about him is his confessional way, the personal tone, the *tête-à-tête* or man-to-man style, first person singular. He remarked it himself in *The Crack-Up:* "There are always those to whom all self-revelation is contemptible."

I on the other hand feel a real approval and emulation

of just that; and I recommend that all our writers give it serious consideration. It might be the next esthetic issue and new mode of American letters. It is American enough; our greatest fellows, such as Franklin and Audubon and Thoreau and Whitman, were self-expressers in so far as they knew themselves. This is a time of greater knowledge, otherwise worse; an era which has as many evil earmarks as, for example, the Renaissance: awful political genius running amok and clashing, migrations, races whipped together as it were by a titanic egg-beater, impatient sexuality and love of stimulants and cruelty, sacks, burnings and plagues. Fine things eventually may be achieved amid all this, as in that other century. I suggest revelation of man as he appears to himself in his mirror—not as he poses or wishes or idealizes—as one thing to try a revival of, this time. Naked truth about man's nature in unmistakable English.

In the Renaissance they had anatomy: Vesalius in Paris at midnight under the gallows-tree, bitten by the dogs as he disputed with them the hanged cadavers which they wanted to eat and he wanted to cut up. They had anatomy and we have psychology. The throws of dice in our world—at least the several dead-weights with which the dice appear to be loaded against us—are moral matters; and no one ever learns much about all that except in his own person, at any rate in private. In public, in the nation and the inter-nation and the anti-nation, one just suffers the weight of the morality of others like a dumb brute. This has been a dishonest century above all: literature lagging as far behind modern habits as behind modern history; democratic statesmanship all vitiated by good form, understatement, optimism; and the nations which could not afford democracy, finally developing their supremacy all on a basis of the deliberate lie. And now is the end, or another beginning.

Writers in this country still can give their little examples of truth-telling; little exercises for their fellow citizens, to develop their ability to distinguish truth from untruth in other connections when it really is important. The importance arises as desperately in the public interest as in private life. Even light fiction can help a society get together and agree upon its vocabulary; little strokes of the tuning-fork, for harmony's sake. And for clarity's sake, let us often use, and sanction the use of, words of one syllable. The shortest and most potent is the personal pronoun: I. The sanctified priest knows that, he says *credo;* and the trustworthy physician only gives his opinion, not a panacea. The witness in the courtroom does not indulge in the editorial we; the judge and the lawyers will not allow it; and indeed, if the case is important, if there is life or liberty or even a large amount of money at stake, not even supposition or hearsay is admitted as evidence. Our worldwide case is important.

Not only is Anglo-Saxondom all at war with the rest of the world in defense of its accustomed power and prosperity, and of the luxuries of the spirit such as free speech, free publication, free faith—for the time being, the United States is the likeliest place for the preservation of the Mediterranean and French ideal of fine art and writing: which puts a new, peculiar obligation upon us ex-expatriates. The land of the free should become and is becoming a city of refuge; but there is cultural peril even in that. France has merely committed her tradition to our keeping, by default; whereas Germany has exiled to us her most important professors and brilliant writers. Perhaps the latter are bound to introduce into our current literature a little of that mystically philosophic, obscurely scientific mode which somewhat misled or betrayed them as a nation. Therefore we must keep up more strictly and energetically than ever, our native specific skeptical habit of mind; our plainer and therefore safer style.

In any consideration of the gravity of the work of art and letters—and upon any solemn occasion such as the death of a good writer like Scott Fitzgerald—I think of Faust, and that labor he dreamed of when he was blind and dying, keeping the devil waiting. It was the drainage of a stinking sea-marsh and the construction of a strong dyke. Fresh fields amid the eternally besieging sea: room for a million men to live, not in security—Goethe expressly ruled out that hope of which we moderns have been too fond—

but free to do the best they could for themselves. Does it seem absurd to compare a deceased best seller with that mythic man: former wholesome Germany's demigod? There must always be some pretentiousness about literature, or else no one would take its pains or endure its disappointments. Throughout this article I have mixed bathos with pathos, joking with tenderness, in order to venture here and there a higher claim for literary art than is customary now. I am in dead earnest. Bad writing is in fact a rank feverish unnecessary slough. Good writing is a dyke, in which there is a leak for every one of our weary hands. And honestly I do see the very devil standing worldwide in the decade to come, bound to get some of us. I realize that I have given an exaggerated impression of Fitzgerald's tragedy in recent years: all the above is based on his confession of 1936, and he was not so nearly finished as he thought. But fear of death is one prophecy that never fails; and now his strength is only in print, and his weakness of no account, except for our instruction.

A NOTE ON FITZGERALD

by John Dos Passos

T HE notices in the press referring to Scott Fitzgerald's untimely death produced in the reader the same strange feeling that you have when, after talking about some topic for an hour with a man, it suddenly comes over you that neither you nor he has understood a word of what the other was saying. The gentlemen who wrote these pieces obviously knew something about writing the English language, and it should follow that they knew how to read it. But shouldn't the fact that they had set themselves up to make their livings as critics of the work of other men furnish some assurance that they recognized the existence of certain standards in the art of writing? If there are no permanent standards, there is no criticism possible.

It seems hardly necessary to point out that a well written book is a well written book whether it's written under Louis XIII or Joe Stalin or on the wall of a tomb of an Egyptian Pharaoh. It's the quality of detaching itself from its period while embodying its period that marks a piece of work as good. I would have no quarrel with any critic who examined Scott Fitzgerald's work and declared that in his opinion it did not detach itself from its period. My answer would be that my opinion was different. The strange thing about the articles that came out about Fitzgerald's death was that the writers seemed to feel that they didn't need to read his books; all they needed for a license to shovel them into the ashcan was to label them as having been written in such and such a period now past. This leads us to the inescapable conclusion that these gentlemen had no other standards than the styles of window-dressing on Fifth Avenue. It means that when they wrote about literature all they were thinking of was the present rating of a book on the exchange, a matter which has almost nothing to do with its eventual value. For a man who was making his living as a critic to write about Scott Fitzgerald without mentioning *The Great Gatsby* just meant that he didn't know his business. To write about the life of a man as important to American letters as the author of *The Great Gatsby* in terms of last summer's styles in ladies' hats, showed an incomprehension of what it was all about, that, to anyone who cared for the art of writing, was absolutely appalling. Fortunately there was enough of his last novel already written to still these silly yappings. The celebrity was dead. The novelist remained.

It is tragic that Scott Fitzgerald did not live to finish *The Last Tycoon*. Even as it stands I have an idea that it will turn out to be one of those literary fragments that from time to time appear in the stream of a culture and profoundly influence the course of future events. His unique achievement, in these beginnings of a great novel, is that here for the first time he has managed to establish that unshakable moral attitude towards the world we live in and towards its temporary standards that is the basic essential of any powerful work of the imagination. A firmly anchored ethical standard is something that American writing has been struggling towards for half a century.

During most of our history our writers have been distracted by various forms of the double standard of morals. Most of our great writers of the early nineteenth century were caught on the tarbaby of the decency complex of the period, so much more painful in provincial America than on Queen Grundy's own isle. Since the successful revolt of the realists under Dreiser, the dilemma has been different, but just as acute. A young American proposing to write a book is faced by the world, the flesh and the devil on the one hand and on the other by the cramped schoolroom of

the highbrows with its flyblown busts of the European great
and its priggish sectarian attitudes. There's popular fiction
and fortune's bright roulette wheel, and there are the erratic
aspirations of the longhaired men and shorthaired women
who, according to the folklore of the time, live on isms and
Russian tea, and absinthe and small magazines of verse.
Everybody who has put pen to paper during the last twenty
years has been daily plagued by the difficulty of deciding
whether he's to do "good" writing that will satisfy his conscience or "cheap" writing that will satisfy his pocketbook.
Since the standards of value have never been strongly established, it's often been hard to tell which was which. As a
result all but the most fervid disciples of the cloistered muse
have tended to try to ride both horses at once, or at least
alternately. That effort and the subsequent failure to make
good either aim, has produced hideous paroxysms of moral
and intellectual obfuscation. A great deal of Fitzgerald's
own life was made a hell by this sort of schizophrenia, that
ends in paralysis of the will and of all the functions of body
and mind. No durable piece of work, either addressed to the
pulps or to the ages, has ever been accomplished by a double-
minded man. To attain the invention of any sound thing, no
matter how trivial, demands the integrated effort of somebody's whole heart and whole intelligence. The agonized
efforts of split personalities to assert themselves in writing
has resulted, on the money side, in a limp pandering to every
conceivable low popular taste and prejudice, and, on the
angels' side, in a sterile connoisseur viewpoint that has made
"good" writing, like vintage wines and old colonial chairs,
a coefficient of the leisure of the literate rich.

One reason for the persistence of this strange dualism and
the resulting inefficiency of the men and women who have
tried to create literature in this country is that few of us
have really faced the problem of who was going to read what
we wrote. Most of us started out with a dim notion of a
parliament of our peers and our betters through the ages
that would eventually screen out the vital grain. To this the
Marxists added the heady picture of the onmarching aveng-
ing armies of the proletariat who would read your books

round their campfires. But as the years ground on both the aristocratic republic of letters of the eighteenth century and the dreams of a universal first of May have receded further and further from the realities we have had to live among. Only the simple requirements of the editors of mass circulation magazines with income based on advertising have remained fairly stable, as have the demands of the public brothels of Hollywood, where retired writers, after relieving their consciences by a few sanctimonious remarks expressing what is known in those haunts as "integrity," have earned huge incomes by setting their wits to work to play up to whatever tastes of the average man seemed easiest to cash in on at any given moment.

This state of things is based, not, as they try to make us believe, on the natural depravity of men with brains, but on the fact that for peace as well as for war industrial techniques have turned the old world upside down. Writers are up today against a new problem of illiteracy. Fifty years ago you either learned to read and write or you didn't learn. The constant reading of the bible in hundreds of thousands of humble families kept a basic floor of literacy under literature as a whole, and under the English language. The variety of styles of writing so admirably represented, the relative complexity of many of the ideas involved and the range of ethical levels to be found in that great compendium of ancient Hebrew culture demanded, in its reading and in its exposition to the children, a certain mental activity, and provided for the poorer classes the same sort of cultural groundwork that the study of Greek and Latin provided for the sons of the rich. A mind accustomed to the Old and New Testaments could easily admit Shakespeare and the entire range of Victorian writing: poetry, novels, historic and scientific essays, up to the saturation point of that particular intelligence. Today the English-speaking peoples have no such common basic classical education. The bottom level is the visual and aural culture of the movies, not a literary level at all. Above that appear all sorts of gradations of illiteracy, from those who, though they may have learned to read in school, are now barely able to spell out the cap-

[341]

tions in the pictures, to those who can take in, with the help of the photographs, a few simple sentences out of the daily tabloids, right through to the several millions of actively literate people who can read right through *The Saturday Evening Post* or *The Reader's Digest* and understand every word of it. This is the literal truth. Every statistical survey that has recently been made of literacy in this country has produced the most staggering results. We have to face the fact that the number of Americans capable of reading a page of anything not aimed at the mentality of a child of twelve is not only on the decrease but probably rapidly on the decrease. A confused intimation of this situation has, it seems to me, done a great deal to take the ground from under the feet of intelligent men who in the enthusiasm of youth decided to set themselves up to be writers. The old standards just don't ring true to the quicker minds of this unstable century. Literature, who for? they ask themselves. It is natural that they should turn to the easy demands of the popular market, and to that fame which if it is admittedly not deathless is at least ladled out publicly and with a trowel.

Scott Fitzgerald was one of the inventors of that kind of fame. As a man he was tragically destroyed by his own invention. As a writer his triumph was that he managed in *The Great Gatsby* and to a greater degree in *The Last Tycoon* to weld together again the two divergent halves, to fuse the conscientious worker that no creative man can ever really kill with the moneyed celebrity who aimed his stories at the twelve-year-olds. In *The Last Tycoon* he was even able to invest with some human dignity the pimp and pander aspects of Hollywood. There he was writing, not for highbrows or for lowbrows, but for whoever had enough elementary knowledge of the English language to read through a page of a novel.

Stahr, the prime mover of a Hollywood picture studio who is the central figure, is described with a combination of intimacy and detachment that constitutes a real advance over the treatment of such characters in all the stories that have followed Dreiser and Frank Norris. There is no trace of envy or adulation in the picture. Fitzgerald writes about

Stahr, not as a poor man writing about someone rich and powerful, nor as the impotent last upthrust of some established American stock sneering at a parvenu Jew; but coolly, as a man writing about an equal he knows and understands. Immediately a frame of reference is established that takes into the warm reasonable light of all-around comprehension the Hollywood magnate and the workers on the lot and the people in the dusty sunscorched bungalows of Los Angeles. In that frame of reference acts and gestures can be described on a broad and to a certain degree passionlessly impersonal terrain of common humanity.

This establishment of a frame of reference for common humanity has been the main achievement and the main utility of writing which in other times and places has come to be called great. It requires, as well as the necessary skill with the tools of the trade, secure standards of judgment that can only be called ethical. Hollywood, the subject of *The Last Tycoon*, is probably the most important and the most difficult subject for our time to deal with. Whether we like it or not it is in that great bargain sale of five and ten cent lusts and dreams that the new bottom level of our culture is being created. The fact that at the end of a life of brilliant worldly successes and crushing disasters Scott Fitzgerald was engaged so ably in a work of such importance proves him to have been the first-rate novelist his friends believed him to be. In *The Last Tycoon* he was managing to invent a set of people seen really in the round instead of lit by an envious spotlight from above or below. *The Great Gatsby* remains a perfect example of this sort of treatment at an earlier, more anecdotic, more bas relief stage, but in the fragments of *The Last Tycoon*, you can see the beginning of a real grand style. Even in their unfinished state these fragments, I believe, are of sufficient dimensions to raise the level of American fiction to follow in some such way as Marlowe's blank verse line raised the whole level of Elizabethan verse.

THE HOURS

by John Peale Bishop

*In the real dark night of the soul it is
always three o'clock in the morning.*

—F. Scott Fitzgerald

I

All day, knowing you dead,
I have sat in this long-windowed room,
Looking upon the sea and, dismayed
By mortal sadness, thought without thought to resume
Those hours which you and I have known—
Hours when youth like an insurgent sun
Showered ambition on an aimless air,
Hours foreboding disillusion,
Hours which now there is none to share.
Since you are dead, I live them all alone.

II

A day like any day. Though any day now
We expect death. The sky is overcast,
And shuddering cold as snow the shoreward blast.
And in the marsh, like a sea astray, now
Waters brim. This is the moment when the sea
Being most full of motion seems motionless.
Land and sea are merged. The marsh is gone. And my
    distress

Is at the flood. All but the dunes are drowned.
And brimming with memory I have found
All hours we ever knew, but have not found
The key. I cannot find the lost key
To the silver closet you as a wild child hid.

III

I think of all you did
And all you might have done, before undone
By death, but for the undoing of despair.
No promise such as yours when like the spring
You came, colors of jonquils in your hair,
Inspired as the wind, when woods are bare
And every silence is about to sing.

None had such promise then, and none
Your scapegrace wit or your disarming grace;
For you were bold as was Danaë's son,
Conceived like Perseus in a dream of gold.
And there was none when you were young, not one,
So prompt in the reflecting shield to trace
The glittering aspect of a Gorgon age.

Despair no love, no fortune could assuage . . .
Was it a fault in your disastrous blood
That beat from no fortunate god,
The failure of all passion in mid-course?
You shrank from nothing as from solitude,
Lacking the still assurance, and pursued
Beyond the sad excitement by remorse.

Was it that having shaped your stare upon
The severed head of time, upheld and blind,
Upheld by the stained hair,
And seen the blood upon that sightless stare,
You looked and were made one
With the strained horror of those sightless eyes?
You looked, and were not turned to stone.

IV

You have outlasted the nocturnal terror,
The head hanging in the hanging mirror,
The hour haunted by a harrowing face.

Now you are drunk at last. And that disgrace
You sought in oblivious dives you have
At last, in the dissolution of the grave.

V

I have lived with you the hour of your humiliation.
I have seen you turn upon the others in the night
And of sad self-loathing
Concealing nothing
Heard you cry: *I am lost. But you are lower!*
And you had that right.
The damned do not so own to their damnation.

I have lived with you some hours of the night,
The late hour
When the lights lower,
The later hour
When the lights go out,

When the dissipation of the night is past,

Hour of the outcast and the outworn whore,
That is past three and not yet four—

When the old blackmailer waits beyond the door
And from the gutter with unpitying hands
Demands the same sad guiltiness as before,

The hour of utter destitution
When the soul knows the horror of its loss
And knows the world too poor
For restitution,

Past three o'clock
And not yet four—
        When not pity, pride,
Or being brave,
Fortune, friendship, forgetfulness of drudgery
Or of drug avails, for all has been tried,
And nothing avails to save
The soul from recognition of its night.

The hour of death is always four o'clock.
It is always four o'clock in the grave.

VI

Having heard the bare word that you had died,
All day I have lingered in this lofty room,
Locked in the light of sea and cloud,
And thought, at cost of sea-hours, to illume
The hours that you and I have known,
Hours death does not condemn, nor love condone.

And I have seen the sea-light set the tide
In salt succession toward the sullen shore
And while the waves lost on the losing sand
Seen shores receding and the sands succumb.

The waste retreats; glimmering shores retrieve
Unproportioned plunges; the dunes restore
Drowned confines to the disputed kingdom—
Desolate mastery, since the dark has come.

The dark has come. I cannot pluck you bays,
Though here the bay grows wild. For fugitive
As surpassed fame, the leaves this sea-wind frays.
Why should I promise what I cannot give?

I cannot animate with breath
Syllables in the open mouth of death.
Dark, dark. The shore here has a habit of light.
O dark! I leave you to oblivious night!

New Directions Paperbooks